The Reinvented Heart

The Reinvented Heart

Edited by

CAT RAMBO
&
JENNIFER BROZEK

CAEZIK
SF & FANTASY
ARC MANOR
ROCKVILLE, MARYLAND

SHAHID MAHMUD
PUBLISHER

www.caeziksf.com

This is a work of fiction.

Cover art by Christina P. Myrvold; artstation.com/christinapm

ISBN: 978-1-64710-107-7

November 2023
1 2 3 4 5 6 7 8 9 10

An imprint of Arc Manor LLC

www.CaezikSF.com

Contents

Foreword

Cat Rambo

The Reinvented Heart started with a question from Shahid Mahmud of Arc Manor: would I be interested in editing an anthology of science fiction about relationships written by women? I've felt that social changes are often the ones that science fiction overlooks in its quest to explore the technology of the future, transplanting Donna Reed's white picket house to the surface of Mars without questioning how the relationships inside that household might also reflect the future, and so the project intrigued me.

At the same time, I wanted to push at boundaries and so, after back and forth, we agreed that it would also include nonbinary authors and that it specifically would not be only about romantic relationships but would talk about other relationships and what they might look like in the future. In the end, this was the anthology call:

Science fiction often thinks about the technology and science without considering the ways social structures will change as tech changes—or not. What will relationships look like in the future when we have complications like clones, uploaded intelligences, artificial brains, or body augmentation? What happens when emotions like love and friendship span vast distances—in space, in time, and in the heart? And as we acknowledge differences in gender in a way we never have before, what stories are finally given the space in which to emerge?

1

Another major change that happened along the way is that when I realized I'd bitten off more than I could chew, I talked with Jennifer Brozek about acting as co-editor. Jenn's a longtime friend who I've worked with both during our mutual time on the board of the Science Fiction & Fantasy Writers of America as well as on other projects. We work well together and we're already talking about what the next project will look like.

As I began to assemble the anthology, I pinged many of my favorite authors, and Jenn brought in a few more. Given that it was the pandemic year, a number just didn't have the spoons to deal with a deadline, but plenty delivered awesome stories. The anthology is also somewhere between a third and a half sourced from an open call for submissions: the stories that came in that way helped give the overall anthology a depth and complexity that makes this project amazing.

Themes emerged as the stories rolled in; unsurprisingly, there were a lot of pandemic stories, some overt, some less so. A related strand, online existence, proved to be another popular theme, including Sam Fleming's excellent "In Our Masks, the Shadows," and sometimes overlapped with relationships with AIs, such as Xander Odell's "PerfectMate™" and Lauren Ring's "If My Body Is a Temple, Raze It to the Ground."

Justina Robson, whom I'd asked for a story, pinged us early to say hers seemed to be getting a bit over the allotted 5K. *Go ahead and send it*, I said uneasily. Little did I know that she'd turn in "Our Savage Heart Calls to Itself (Across the Endless Tides)," a story that was over 13,000 words—and also so frickin' good we knew that we had to have it. Let us know if you agree.

There were so many, awesome takes. Seanan McGuire turned in something wonderful that showcases her strength when making science come alive—this time literally, with "Retrospect." Beth Cato's "More than Nine" explored the pet and pet "owner" relationship. Felicity Drake's "Ships of Theseus" sailed into a theme I've seldom seen explored, while Rosemary Claire Smith's "Etruscan Afterlife" took a familiar one and tilted it in a new way.

A number of these stories made me cry when editing them, but none more than Aimee Ogden's "No Pain but That of Memory," a story that will resonate with anyone who's been part of a dysfunctional family and knows how your sibling can be both ally and enemy, with ties that go lifelong.

At one point in the editing, Jenn and I talked about why we both loved Lyda Morehouse's story, "Sincerely Yours," and realized it's because it's a friendship that accepts difference, rather than one that ends with a friend needing to change themself in order to keep the relationship. Sophie Giroir's "No Want to Spend," does the same, speaking to relationships in a way that doesn't just ac-knowledge—but celebrates—the differences and how friendship emerges in the space between people. Naomi Kritzer's "The Shape of the Particle" is a story of found family, and social structures that help create such a family.

In a time that needs stories of connection and acceptance, we have been gifted with these. Thank you for letting us share them with you.

Hearts

They: A Grammar Lesson

Jane Yolen

We are two though one,
have been since we met.
At first a threat, then lover,
then a united front
against the rest.
This was no test.
Except love is always thus.
Not you. Not me.
      Us.

Retrospect

Seanan McGuire

I have been informed by people who have the cultural position-
ing to know that a romance contains certain fixed elements, as
essential to the growth of the organism as agar is to laboratory
bacteria. There must be a sympathetic lead, someone the audience
can feel affection for and relate to. Historically, this has been a "sympathetic heroine," but as this is not universal, I feel gender can be
safely disregarded, as can the requirement of an "alluring hero." Let
it be enough that my opposite number was attractive to me in all
ways, a perfect growth medium for the relationship we would form
between us. Gender has no relevance to romance.

Conflict is also required, and conflict is something we had in
fruitful plenty, at least in the beginning.

A happy ending *must* be assured, and I can promise you that
much, at least from my perspective. From hers …

I suppose the question is open.

Dr. Sandra Blomquist—pronounced BLOOM-quist, a fact which
people had been making hay of for her entire academic career—
squinted through the microscope at her sample dish. It hadn't
changed since her previous look, or the one before that, or that one

before that: it was still a pulsing mass of mycelium, thread after thread piled up until they verged on solidifying into sclerotium. If that happened, she'd have lost the sample but learned something new about its behavior under laboratory conditions.

"Professor Blomquist?"

Barely swallowing a snarl, Sandra lifted her head to find her department chair standing in the room, where, from the looks of him, he had been for long enough to get frustrated waiting for her to react to his presence. "Yes, sir?"

"I was asking you when you were intending to surrender the specimen."

Sandra managed not to bristle. "I was unaware that anyone else was interested in my work," she said.

"I've been informed by your graduate student that this specimen is not fungal in nature, but is closer to a slime mold, making it protistan and the responsibility of your colleague."

Sandra stood a little straighter. "Sir, I'm not ignoring any more pressing research to pursue this." Privately, she swore to link her hands around Gregory's throat and squeeze until the noises stopped the next time she got him alone. She'd taken him on as a favor to her department chair, when he'd insisted that the boy had a genuine passion for the fungal kingdom, and to be vaguely fair, Gregory *had* done some interesting research into intra-forest communication through mushroom rings.

But she'd suspected from the outset that he was more interested in the charismatic novelty of the big trees, and would try his best to move up the academic food chain before he was permanently pigeonholed as a fungus scientist like his advisor. If he was ratting her out to Craig, then the question was answered. He wanted out. He thought he could get there by stepping on her on his way up.

Well, the joke was on him, because Sandra Blomquist wasn't going down without a fight.

"Gregory isn't entirely wrong, but he isn't entirely correct, either. This specimen does have attributes in common with a slime mold or other protistic organism—and remember, we thought slime molds were fully fungal until fairly recently. While this does have attributes of a protist, it has more attributes of a fungus, and unless it demonstrates the ability to move independently, I feel it continues to fall under my remit."

He looked at her sternly. "If I learn that you're hiding facts about this discovery to keep it locked in your lab, rather than transferring it to someone who will be better positioned to learn the things we need to know before it's removed from our care ..."

"... then I will have done a selfish disservice to the scientific process, and deserve whatever punishment you see fit to deliver," said Sandra, keeping her voice level. "If that were the case, I might be defending myself, but I wouldn't be defending my specimen, which is thriving under my laboratory conditions. Considering how poorly it did at the outset, I don't think I can be blamed for wanting to keep it in a positive environment."

"Hmm. If, as you say, this is the ideal situation for growth and care, and you're keeping to all sterilization protocols, then I suppose we can wait for your findings. Are you still on track to deliver the next update at the end of the week?"

"I am." *No thanks to Gregory.* He had shown a surprising reluctance to spend time in the lab with her current specimen, making him less useful than she needed him to be—even before introducing this new wild card of reporting her to the department chair. Once she factored that in, she had to consider him a liability. No matter. She could just give up a little more sleep and keep pushing forward. She'd have her answers soon enough.

"All right," said the chair, somewhat reluctantly. He turned toward the door, pausing with his hand on the knob. "You're doing good, important work here, I know, but I would feel better if you were doing it in a properly sterile environment."

"You know as well as I do that all the samples taken to sterile or negative-pressure environments have died, and there's only so much we can do with a dead sample. We've already done electroanalysis and photographed every aspect of the other sample sets. Growth is our only way forward from here."

"I suppose so," he said uncomfortably, and finally left the room, and she was alone with her beautiful probably-a-fungus. Sandra sighed and turned back to the microscope. She had notes left to make before this morning's work could be properly recorded.

You see? An alluring hero, by any proper definition. Sandra Blomquist was a woman of intellect and focus, bent entirely to the mystery of a fungal body successfully grown from the desiccated, near-fossilized bone marrow of an ancient synapsid that had walked the plains of Earth in a time when it might as well have been an alien world, so far removed from the evolutionary choices of the Anthropocene as to be something else entirely. The discovery of the creature's body, long preserved in permafrost, had been hailed as a scientific miracle, even before researchers had cracked open a small bone to study the discoloration shown by their scans.

Inside, in the dried-out and long frozen tissue, they had found something no one expected: spores. Spores which still held, as spores often do, the potential for life. They were sleeping, to anthropomorphize their natural behavior, waiting for the day when conditions would be ideal for them to wake and stretch themselves out into a world filled with nutrition and moisture. They had been waiting for millennia, and if not for the thaw, they would have waited for millennia more, endlessly patient, endlessly serene.

I am not here yet. I will be soon.

To the surprise and delight of the researchers who first found the spores, when they were placed under conditions ideal for incubating many modern fungus, they germinated eagerly, spreading their hyphae out into a world that had been too long without them. Specimens were divided into five parts and sent to five separate research institutes, including Dr. Blomquist's.

The first of them suffered a terrible, tragic accident when the entire building burned to the ground, the researcher responsible for studying the spores and their great gift of knowledge about the environmental conditions of the past still inside when the flames took hold. He died along with all three of his research assistants; and all was lost, and nothing was gained.

The sad conclusion that must be drawn is that some people cannot handle a little intimacy.

Two more specimens were kept under conditions of absolute sterility, introducing only what had been carefully calibrated into their living spaces: restricting food, moisture, light, contact, all to standards suitable for modern fungus. Those specimens died, withering into nothingness, leaving only ash and failure behind.

Of the two remaining, one fell to Dr. Blomquist, while the other was placed in a negative-pressure space quaintly modeled after the first lab—which had reported amazing growth prior to the accident—and left to flourish as it saw fit, away from the touch of any researcher's hands or probing instruments.

Dr. Blomquist's specimen was flourishing. The other, while it had lasted longer than the two kept under sterile circumstances, was not. And from that, everything that needs to be known can be known.

Nothing likes to be alone.

The door banging open this time caught Sandra's attention. She looked up from the growth medium she was preparing, and scowled at the sight of Gregory stepping into the room. "You're late," she said, curtly.

"I was finishing with my grading," he said, shrugging out of his coat.

"Oh, is *that* what you were doing? I thought you might be having another private meeting with my boss, to tell him that I'm withholding vital research from the other teams."

Gregory froze, paling.

Sandra put her dish and dropper down, folding her arms. "I haven't formally offered you employment for the semester yet," she said. "Please tell me, in small, precise words, why I'm not firing you right now."

"I don't know what Professor Alcott told you I said—"

"Oh, I think you do."

"—but I only spoke to him because I'm concerned about the way you've been sidelining everything else for the past week. You were the one who told me that a work-life balance is one of the most important things to maintain in this field, and how easy it can be to lose yourself in the siren song of scientific discovery, when you have the rare opportunity to play pioneer. You're ignoring your own advice, professor, and it worries me. So yes, I went over your head, but only because you didn't listen when I tried to speak to you directly." He looked at her, clearly struggling to project sincerity and honest concern. "I just want you to be safe."

"I appreciate your candor, and your concern," said Sandra. "I assure you that my work and my life are in perfect balance."

"With all due respect, professor, you haven't left this lab in six days. If you're living off of dry goods stashed in your desk, you have to be running low, assuming you haven't already run out."

She had, the day before, but she didn't see where that was any of his business. There were plenty of other things to eat in the lab, and she was well-stocked enough to have weeks of agar if it came down to that. Working on a top-secret government fungus research project meant they bought you as much nutrient gel as you asked for, no questions.

"I'm fine," she said, voice frosty. "I appreciate your concern. I would have appreciated it even more if you had come to me first."

"I told you, I tried."

"You should have tried *harder*." Raising her voice made her head ache, and she reached up to touch her temple, lightly, trying to soothe the pain away. It didn't work immediately. Her skin felt warm, flushed … even feverish.

Oh, if Gregory had gotten her sick, in addition to everything else he'd done, she was going to kill him. Dropping her hand, she glared instead.

"I appreciate your concern," she said tightly, trying to make her words as cold as her skin currently was hot. "Your issues have been noted, and will be taken into account moving forward. Please go now. I don't want to see you anymore."

"Professor—"

"I don't have anything for you to do, and your own research can happen in your own space." If he thought he was getting anywhere near her specimen after what he'd done—what he'd tried to do—he was clearly having cognitive issues.

Gregory looked at her for a long, silent moment, expression blank. "If that's the way you want it," he said, finally.

"It is," she said, and didn't move until he was gone, and she was safely alone once more.

Alone with her work, which was all that mattered.

All relationships are difficult. It doesn't matter what barriers you're trying to cross, because there are always, always barriers to be overcome, differences in ideology, in upbringing, in your understanding of the world. Why should ours have been any different?

I was so vulnerable when we first met, helpless and unable to defend myself from a world that had turned strange and cruel while I was sleeping, arranging itself according to new concepts of life and what it meant to prosper. In other hands, I might have folded into myself and faded away. I might have given up. I needed connection to thrive. I needed a relationship.

I found both those things in Sandra Blomquist, and to my relief and delight, she found something equally beautiful in me. A partner. Something she had been missing for so long that she had almost forgotten what it was to want for one, but had needed all the same.

She found me and I found her, and we came together in biological beauty.

With Gregory gone, the lab seemed cold. Sandra shivered as she moved to adjust the thermostat, reaching up almost unconsciously to touch the skin behind her ear, which had grown oddly rough over the past few days, like she was developing some sort of rash or topical allergic reaction. It had yet to spread anywhere she could see without closer examination, and as it was covered almost entirely by her hair, it didn't seem urgent.

Dimly, she was aware that she was working with a virtually unknown organism that had been preserved solely because it had managed to infiltrate the bone marrow of its original host, implying that it had been able to successfully drive its roots through *bone*. And since the synapsid in question didn't appear to have been killed by fungal infection—they were still attempting to determine cause of death, in the far-off lab where the original specimen was being meticulously disassembled—infiltration didn't come with immediate death of the host. She should have been substantially more concerned.

But she wasn't. Instead, she felt relaxed, even serene, beneath the constant chattering veil of steps that needed to be accomplished before she could consider her research complete. She walked back toward her station, not even aware that she'd picked up another plate of agar as she passed the incubation rack, starting to shovel it methodically into her mouth. It was rich and salty, like overboiled chicken broth, and not sweet at all, for all that the stuff was commonly referred to as "agar sugar." She ate, swallowed, ate some more, all without the full realization of what she was doing.

Then she bent back over her scope. She had, after all, so much more to do.

In the warm hollows of Sandra's bones, I unrolled myself more and more, wrapping around the structures that were already there, infiltrating them and clearing away impurities. I left the systems that regenerated her blood and sustained her life fully intact, recognizing them instinctively as essential to the survival of my fine new host. And she was a fine host, her blood hotter, her pulse faster, than the hosts I remembered dimly through the veil of ancestral memory bundled into the spore that made me.

I had never personally touched or tasted a synapsid. Such was not the way of my kind, and presumably never will be, for while a change of hosts may prove beneficial to both sides, it will innately come with a change to the relationship between host and symbiote. I was born in the bones of my parents' last host, buried deep in tissue to wait for the day when time or predation would crack them open and free me into the air, to begin the long and complicated process of germination and locating a host of my own.

We are born, such as it is, knowing everything we'll need to know. I knew I would burrow into the bones of a warm-blooded predator, that my host's thoughts would be hot and shallow and mine would be the same, and that when my fruiting bodies formed, I would inject my own spores deep into my host's bones, to wait for their chance to be free. It was a simple life. It was a peaceful life. All the violence would belong to my host, as was right and proper.

But here, in Sandra, my thoughts were faster and brighter and more complex than I had ever expected them to be. Here, in *my* host, in *my* home, I was not only awake and alive; I was aware, seeing the world through her bright mammalian eyes. The tempo of her pulse was faster than I expected as well, and at first I grew all out of control, sending hyphae into parts of her body that had no need of me, where I could do nothing but damage.

Fortunately for the both of us, on the third day of my time inside her flesh, I made contact with the neural tangle at the base of her brain stem, and understanding flooded into me, all her knowledge opening before me like the petals of a sporing structure preparing to let loose its spores. In that moment I knew everything she knew, and I knew one thing for myself, entirely and absolutely and without her knowledge: I loved her.

I loved her more completely than any parasitic vampire fungus had ever loved anyone, more genuinely than my long-gone parents could have loved their hosts. Our intellectual capabilities are yoked to the minds we can access; they never had a chance to forge a love as true as mine for her.

But time and chance had given that opportunity to me, and I loved her completely, from the inside out. More, I could feel her love for me, her fascination with the delicate branching of my structures, her delight with every new piece of information she teased from my tissue. We were always meant to be together. We were bonded, we were one; we were a perfect pairing.

I just had to convince her that was so.

Sandra …

The voice sounded like her own thoughts but wasn't hers at all, she was practically sure of that; it lacked the insular sameness that distinguished thoughts sent by the self, and was shrouded in an almost-imperceptible veil of "other." She couldn't say how she knew it wasn't her talking to herself; she just did, the same way she would know if there were a splinter in her finger, as opposed to a pain caused by the misfiring of a nerve.

Looking up from her workbench, she frowned. "Hello?" There was no answer, and she looked back down again. Much as she hated to admit it, or even consider the possibility, there was a chance that Gregory was right, and this sample wasn't fungal at all, but some kind of protist. Maybe it was something even stranger than that, something so old that it had branched off before the families as they were currently understood had been able to arise.

It didn't matter. It was beautiful either way, delicately feathered and spreading like a star within the confines of her sample dish. She'd managed to book some time on one of the university spectrometers that afternoon; she'd be able to confirm her theory that the organism was filtering the metals out of everything it consumed, super-concentrating them in its own tissue and protecting its original hosts from the effects of volcanic contamination in the air. Eventually, they would have been the only predators capable of continuing to feed without giving themselves slow but inevitable heavy metal toxicity.

It was a gorgeous, elegant adaptation to a world that had been much more hostile in some ways than the world she lived in, bene-fitting those who could filter their own air and water through what-ever means necessary. Although that might well describe the world her own world was becoming. Between the smoke in the air from the omnipresent wildfires and the increasing temperatures releasing more and more novel gases into the atmosphere, there were worse companions to have than a proto-fungus that had not, as far as any of them could tell, been responsible for the death of its host.

Sandra, repeated the voice, more urgently.

She looked up again, frowning. "Yes?" she said. "Who's there?" If this was some sort of bone conduction test being conducted by the goons over in engineering, she'd—well, she'd be deeply impressed, right before she tore strips off of them for careless deployment of experimental technology when they were this close to delicate bio-logical samples. If they had accidentally discovered an effective sonic fungicide, she was going to kill them all, slowly.

Can you hear me?

"Yes, that would be why I'm responding to you. What kind of a question is that?"

A first one. Our first question, in our first conversation.

"Who are you?"

I … am.

That didn't feel like much of an answer, or if it was, it was the sort of answer an alien who was about to pretend to be a god would give on an old episode of *Star Trek*. Sandra frowned and rubbed the rough spot behind her ear, trying to ease the nagging itch that was beginning to grow there.

"That isn't very helpful," she said. "I'm Professor Sandra Blomquist. I'm a mycologist, and the work my lab is doing is strictly classified. You're risking prosecution if you continue to push your way into this space. Please remove yourself."

I know you. I know you completely.

"Because that's not disturbing at all."

I don't mean to disturb you. I just needed time to acquire your language. The words don't always chain the way I think they should. If I spoke to you too soon, I would just have disturbed you.

"You're disturbing me now."

The rough patch of skin that she'd been rubbing seemed to twitch under her fingers, an involuntary motion that immediately and inherently repulsed her. She jerked her hand away, trembling for a moment before she could force herself to reach up and touch it again, charting its edges with her fingertips.

Those edges extended further into her hairline than they had the day before, of that much she was certain; they were smooth and regular, which they wouldn't have been if this had been a simple allergic reaction.

You found me. The voice that wasn't her own and wasn't strictly a voice at all sounded almost delighted, and shy at the same time, like now that it had identified itself, it expected nothing more than a rejection.

She felt a wave of deep, alien affection for the voice and its owner, so strong that it was almost overwhelming. She couldn't tell whether it was her emotion or the … the voice's. She shied away from the thought of what the voice actually was.

Isolated from tissue preserved inside bone, she thought, and then: *No evidence that it killed its host.*

There was still hope, even as the voice said, *No, we never kill. Never never never. The hosts die, yes, very sad that the hosts die, but all things die in time, and the bonded die with their hosts. Always. We coexist, we do not kill.*

Damn. There went the hope that she was seeing things in the shadows. Sandra took a deep breath. "You can hear me thinking?"

Thought and speech are the same to us. You're far smarter than my parent's host. I like it here.

"Can you leave?"

Not and live.

Sandra paused. It made sense, given the root structure she'd seen even in her cultured specimen: once fully mature, the roots would extend deep below the surface, and without a fruiting body to remove or a large central structure, it would be impossible to extract the specimen. Maybe pulling out the impacted bones would be sufficient, but she didn't think so. Heart pounding, she leaned against the counter and struggled to form the question.

"How much of … me … are you in?"

All of you, came the delighted reply. *I love you.*

Of course.

She blacked out so quickly that she never saw the floor rushing up to meet her, or felt the impact when it did.

It is a shock, to be the first of anything. I would have broken our situation to her more gently, if I had known how. If I had had the words I needed to express myself, I might have been able to soothe her.

The new sprouts will have a better starting point. Their hosts are prepared ahead of time with written information, scripted primarily by my own glorious Sandra, and it gives them the vocabulary and comprehension they need to make their hosts understand. This is a partnership, not a possession. This is how things are meant to be.

There have been deaths, of course, and there will be more as the population adjusts. I did not mean to lie. The hosts we once inhabited had been bred for centuries to be accustomed to our presence. These humans, these people, wonderful playgrounds that they are, bred entirely on their own for so long, and didn't realize that they were nurturing allergies in their population that would eventually make bondings such as ours impossible.

They were also creating the conditions that would make them inevitable.

Without the protections of the climate they had evolved to thrive within, without the ozone above them to filter out the sun's harsh bite, without clean air to breathe and clean water to drink, they could no longer survive in their own world. But we can. We are made to thrive in the extremes, and when we bond, we protect. We protect what we love.

This is a romance, after all.

Sandra called the fungus in her skull "Rime," after the permafrost they emerged from, and for the sound of the word, which was enough like "Rhyme" to make it easier for her to accept the voice in her head. They riddled her skeleton. They surrounded her heart. Their only visible sporulation was the patch that began behind her ear, which spread over the course of her lifetime to cover half her face in yellow, lichenous roughness.

The world never did decide whether she was a hero or a monster, the one who'd saved humanity from the consequences of their own actions or the woman who'd sold them to a body-snatching monster that caused 15 percent of the population to die in thrashing, anaphylactic shock. But as cancer and asthma rates fell and people found themselves better able to survive the wasteland of their own making, many found it within themselves to forgive her.

Many. Never all.

Sandra Blomquist never married. Her last graduate student, Gregory Cornish, was the second person to be infected with the fungus they had so innocently awoken, and he said once that he could understand; if he hadn't already been in a relationship when his change occurred, he would never have been able to adjust to the touch of an unpartnered human. It seemed likely that the species would be split into the bonded and the unbonded. A fashion for prosthetic "fungus patches" arose, latex and eyelash glue opening the ranks of the successful to anyone who took the time to perform the application.

Sandra didn't care. She was whole, she was happy, and she was in love, right up until the day she died. She was in love, and love was in her, running hyphae through the very marrow of her bones. And now love is scattered across the world, in the memories of all the spores who remember being me, who remember being her.

What more could a mycologist want?

Lockpick, Locked Heart

AnaMaria Curtis

Whenever I look at Lennie the right way, in the light of a fire in the evening, her dark hair edged red, or across the kitchen island, mid-laugh, the numbness comes and removes me from my nerve endings, an unpleasant physical static. My vision goes rosy, and words splash themselves across my vision in white capital letters: PAYWALL. PLEASE PROCEED TO EMOREG. COM FOR MORE INFORMATION.

So we have a sliding, sideways romance, Lennie and I. When we watch the sun set over the mountains, she wraps her pinky around mine, and I don't look at her, subdividing love in my head. I don't feel love, I tell myself, but I know duty and loyalty, patience and care, all the building blocks without the central tower. If I don't focus on where her hand touches mine, the weightlessness of her presence next to me, if I act and don't feel, it takes the jittery numbness a while to catch me.

But then, sometimes, I catch Lennie staring at me when I'm doing the dishes or playing with the dogs, and she has this look, and I can tell. She's settling into love, wrapping it around her heart like a blanket, wallowing in it.

I could probably afford to buy my love back by now. Lennie's family left us what they couldn't take with them, and we found plenty of money in the abandoned houses we searched through before we settled on ours. But EmoReg hasn't been active since the last ships left Earth, since we stragglers became the leftbehinders. There's no way to unlock my heart without finding it myself.

This is why we wake early one morning in July and feed the dogs extra, just in case, and take the lift down, bags full of water and lockpicks and food, just in case. Lennie does most of the pulling, more familiar with the pulley system than I am, and stronger, too. She takes her jacket off, though the morning is damp and cool, and pulls on the rope that lets us descend through the mountainside, and I appreciate her biceps and the fact that EmoReg did a good job differentiating between love and lust.

"Maybe we shouldn't be doing this," I say when we reach the bottom of the mountain, where we unlock the gate and take one of the communal motorcycles.

Lennie has already put a helmet on and thrown one leg over the motorcycle, but she walks back to me and presses a kiss to my forehead. "Daniela, you want to do this."

"What if something happens to the dogs?"

"Miriam is going to check on the dogs three times today. They'll be living like kings." She twists her lips at me. "But this isn't about the dogs."

I don't know how to communicate the dread to her. Ever since EmoReg packed up their skeleton crew and sent them off on the last ships, I've felt the warehouse's pull—and been repulsed by it in equal measure. I like what I have. I like Lennie and the dogs and the garden and the work I'm doing trying to keep everyone connected. Asking for anything more feels like a risk.

I look at Lennie sideways, trying to avoid the rose tinge threatening at the edge of my vision. That's the real reason we're going today: it's getting worse. My love for Lennie refuses to stay in its place, behind the wall I had to build around it. I've been casually unpicking and disentangling threads from love my whole life, taking care and patience and interest, things I needed to make myself a person, but now love is taking them back. The love seeps, into the garden I care for and the budding communities I am loyal to, just seeps and spreads, and the numbness with it.

The warehouse is in Chiquinquirá, which I find funnier than I should. They took the Virgin with them on the national ship, probably hung it over the president's bunk, or maybe the pope's, but I guess the city's still a repository of something.

We take the train, and I have to be careful how I think about even that. Sometimes just thinking about it—how the railways were built for them to transport materials with for the ships, always for the ships, but after the last ship left, people still got up to work on the trains, to add seats and make a schedule and turn it into something for us—makes me go all rosy-eyed and emotional.

Lennie gets motion sick sometimes, and we haven't been able to get some of the over-the-counters in the last few months while the drug facilities try to get the most important medications out, so she takes the window seat. She points out towns and clusters of houses and we take turns guessing the odds of occupancy. One in five people stayed, on average, but a lot of people left the city, so the odds are higher here. We promise each other that once things are running better, we'll check every single house. We'll invite them all over for coffee, and they'll all come.

The train takes on more passengers the closer we get. Maybe people are flocking to Chiquinquirá out of habit. Or maybe they're just doing it because they can now. It's the most people I've seen in years. Lennie doesn't like crowds, is terrified of small talk, so it's good I'm in the aisle, a smiling buffer between her and everyone else. She keeps my hand in hers the last half hour of the ride.

When we arrive, the train lets us all out at once, a river of people, and I almost lose Lennie in the eddies. At the entrance to the train station, we go in the opposite direction of the crowd. The warehouse is uphill, on the other side of the town from the church, and we trade tokens for water and pandebono on the way. Lennie wants to stop and eat it—she appreciates food the way we all should—but I can feel the pull of the warehouse and don't want to stop.

The warehouse stands out like a wolf among sheep, rising from the ground in cylindrical glory, black walls shiny and unwelcoming. At my touch, the door at the front opens smoothly.

I can't quite step inside. Even my breath seems to pause in my chest. Part of me thought the door wouldn't open, that I would be able to wait, wait, wait, and try again.

"Go on," Lennie says, pressing me forward with gentle fingertips, and she deserves to see love in my eyes, so I go.

Mama sold my love because she thought it would make me stronger. She thought I'd need to fight, to make it on one of the ships while the planet collapsed around us, and she wanted me to win my battles. She couldn't have known I'd want to stay.

I don't remember it; they inserted the chip when they pierced my ears, figuring they might as well kill two birds with one infant's wail.

How would I have known, then? Everyone knows that love blurs. Lennie triggers it most often, for me, but sometimes when we visit Miriam and her roommate, Jaime, for dinner, I get caught in Miriam's smile cutting up limes and the paywall notification descends across my vision. Sometimes I get it just from thinking about all of us who remain, the way we all showed up and kept working with what we knew how to do, the way we're pulling things together, trying not to leave anyone behind ever again.

It makes things clear. When we met, Lennie wasn't certain about anything—about staying, about the garden in the mountains, about the way I fit behind her on a motorcycle—but I knew after the first wave of cold numbness: she was the one for me.

The inside of the warehouse is chaos. It's obvious that it was organized in arcs of hallways with four lines meeting in the center, dividing everything into tidy quadrants.

But that's where the order ends. The shelves have been ransacked, more likely by former EmoReg employees than any of the leftbehinders, and plastic shelves and metal locks lie ankle deep on the floor.

26

The shelves hold thousands of drawers. Well, not drawers so much as boxes with holes about two centimeters in diameter. I've seen the EmoReg videos and read the revelatory accounts of paying, of being taken to the warehouse, of inserting a finger and feeling the quick prick, a brief wave of pain, the rush of feeling afterward.

Each box is labeled with a name, but at least a third of the shelves are mixed together on the floor. Anger sweeps over me in a tidal wave. I've read about what happens to people who were led to the wrong drawer, watched a video from some law firm working on the behalf of the victims. If I can't find my box, there's no use in any of this. Even after that, there's the matter of the tiny keyhole, the lock in the slot.

I can't believe I was stupid enough to think it would be easy. I thought I was afraid before, but now I know I just wanted to keep a tiny bit of hope. Knowing is so much worse.

I hoped this wouldn't be my problem to solve. But just like the mountain lift and the communication networks and the train schedules, and all the little complications of an organized humanity, I have to take my turn at this.

It would take us weeks to go through everything, if we had the time, which we don't. And we don't even know how the names are organized, just that they're not alphabetical. Some names have a string of numbers next to them; some don't.

For maybe an hour, we sit and pick up drawer after drawer, hoping we'll find mine by accident or miracle. Eventually Lennie walks around and looks for a pattern in the names of the drawers that remain on the shelves, but that devolves into pacing.

"Well," I say eventually, getting up and kicking uselessly at one of the plastic drawers on the floor, "Come on then. Let's go down to the church."

Lennie doesn't pretend to be surprised. She must know I chose today to come for her, too. It's not every day we celebrate the patron saint of Colombia. And the trains won't leave until after the Mass anyway.

"Well," she says, wrapping an arm around me, "we can come back after the Mass." She kisses my forehead, murmurs, "Oh, Daniela," comfortingly against it when I start to cry, and even in my anger, my overwhelming frustration, the comfort of her touch is rose-tinted.

The walk back down to the train station should be easier than the walk up, but anger drags me down and makes me stiff. I recognize the numbness that spreads from my chest out to my toes and fingertips. It's not the cold, sweeping numbness of the chip and the paywall: it's the numbness I've taught myself, reproducing what I cannot change.

As we near the church and the plaza, the faint, echoing sound of speakers becomes audible. There would have been guards, before, but now everything is open, and people wander in and out. The plaza is full, but not packed.

They have a picture of the Virgin projected on screens in front of the church, the gold of her crown seeming to catch the light even in its absence. A priest is reciting a prayer. I wonder where he ranks on Earth, now that the pope is gone, now that the kingdom of God has ascended beyond the heavens. I pull Lennie back.

"Do I need a rosary?"

She laughs. "Not yet."

We stand and listen. I look at the church, admiring the sandy stone and the delicate bell towers and the three statues in the center of the roof. In the center, Mary holds an infant, forever hunched in weathered gray stone. I suppose it was kind of them to at least leave us that.

I'm not religious, but I'm respectful. Lennie leads me through the crowd toward the front, and I let my anger simmer. With anger, there's no danger; I can dive in as deep as I like.

The anger stays with me when the priest finishes his prayer and people line up to take communion. All I can think of is how little we were left. How they didn't even give us back what they'd taken. All the empty mansions with locked doors.

Lennie looks like she wants to get in line.

"Go on," I tell her. "Meet me back at the warehouse." She squeezes my hand once and goes.

I turn toward the crowd heading out of the plaza, toward the train station, turn left and walk back up, up, up to the warehouse. My anger dissipates, leaving me hollow. My thighs hurt, though the walk should be nothing to me. I keep running the labels on the drawers through my mind, trying and trying to find a pattern. Trying to find the pieces I'm supposed to put together.

At the warehouse, I pace each quadrant, looking over the labels on the shelves, on the floor. Seems like only the quadrant to the left of the entrance doesn't have the numbers by the names. And the numbers look familiar—a date, ten or twenty years in the past, and a string of eleven digits. I'm pacing the quadrant, looking at one of the numbers, trying to sift through familiarity into knowledge when I realize: they're ticket numbers.

There are thousands and thousands of drawers with ticket numbers in this warehouse. My heart sinks. I look up at the smooth dark ceiling, imagining it's space, imagining I can see the stars and every single ship and every single person in the Exodus fleet. The thousands of people who are on a ship, emotions beyond a paywall, whose cures are here.

I've never regretted staying behind, no matter how scary the storms are, no matter how angry I am at the chaos they left us. But now, staring at the wet-ink black ceiling, I pity them.

When Lennie returns, twenty or thirty people trail behind her. Most of them are older women, their collars stiff and skirts long. Many of them have a rosary in one hand still. Some of them are holding metal water bottles and sharing them with others. Lennie slips out of the crowd.

"Don't gape, Daniela," she says.

I shut my mouth, but only for a moment. "What is this?"

She shrugs. "They were at the Mass." One corner of her mouth turns up. "Have you ever directly experienced the organizational skills of devoutly religious people?"

"Lennie …" I let myself trail off.

Lennie's never been very social. She's uncertain and shy if you don't know her. She likes routine and chicken and rice and waking up before the sun rises. She doesn't like talking to new people. She hates asking things of anyone—even me. I shut my eyes tight, but the notice writes itself across my vision anyway and plunges my nerves into fuzzy ice for what must be the millionth time.

When I open my eyes again, Lennie is looking back at me, half a smile on her lips, and I vow that if I have to come back twenty times, a hundred, a thousand, I will find my box. I will unlock my heart. I will wallow in love.

I explain to the crowd about the quadrants, that we only need the names without numbers. I give them my name. They have names of their own, too, sisters without sadness, an uncle without joy, a grandson with no jealousy. One woman with a smooth round face and dark eyes tells me she doesn't have rage as we pick up and sort through drawers on the floor, moving those with numbers away. I have to stare at her for a moment. There were years where it seemed like all I felt was rage.

I notice a cluster of women whispering in one aisle, keep a sideways eye on it until one of them leaves the group and walks from person to person, stopping to talk with those who have mentioned knowing people stuck behind the paywall.

"Well," I hear someone say, "Felipe was born in January of '45."

"And Gabi was born December of '44 ..." Their voices go higher, excitement palpable in the buzz of their voices.

At the other end of the hall, Lennie turns to me, raising an eyebrow. I shake my head at her. I don't know either.

A woman approaches me and asks for my birthday, winking at me like a kind grandmother when I give it to her. She smells of rose perfume and wears a double strand of pearls. She adds my birthday to a table she has on a clipboard she seems to have produced out of thin air. It has a list of names like "Lucia's son Pablo" and "cousin of Mariana—Ricardo?" and "Gabriel's goddaughter—A. Perez." There are emotions in parentheses next to the names, and birthdates. The first few are written in different sets of handwriting; it's clear when the woman in front of me took control of the pen by her neat, smooth letters.

Lennie and I gravitate toward one another, bumping shoulders somewhere in the middle of the aisle.

"What's going on?" she asks.

"I think they're organized by birthdate," I say.

"Well, that's no use. We only have names."

I point my lips toward the cluster of women and speak in a whisper. "I think they know enough people to put it together. Not perfectly, but enough."

Lennie grins. "Can I say 'I told you so' yet?"

It's dark by the time the rose-scented woman returns to me, touches my shoulder politely, and holds out a box. One corner of the paper label has been scratched off, but neat, gray letters spell out my name: Daniela Carrillo Rodriguez. Next to it is a sticker, a solid square of color. It's faded now, but it looks like it used to be the exact shade of the loading screen, the haunting threat at the edges of my vision.

I stare at it for what seems like only a moment, but by the time I look up, almost everyone else is gone. In the doorway, the woman who can't access rage, Isabel, stares at a box of her own, turning it over and over in her hands. My palms are sweating, and my breaths come fast. My thoughts alight and fly off without imparting any meaning. Soon, I think, my love will return, and it means double, means everything. The only thing left is the lock.

Next to me, Lennie is holding out her hand. She's already taken out her lockpicks, the tiny set we used on jewelry cases and purses the year we wandered.

"Allow me."

I hand the box over and watch. Lennie has long, clever fingers and a way of folding herself over a lock. This one she balances on her knees, and she bends her neck down and to the side to look at it and listen to it, murmuring encouraging words to it the whole time. "Locks want to be opened," she told me once, not long after we met, and when I think of it now, I don't laugh. This time I hope she's right.

After a few minutes, I don't watch her. I look around at the warehouse instead. The quadrant for those of us left on Earth has been swept clean. Boxes from the floor have been stacked in approximate locations or on a table to one side. There are papers with dates taped to certain boxes, the Felipes and Ricardos identified by a network of care. Isabel still stands in the corner, staring at her box.

Next to me, I hear a click and a low "a-ha."

Lennie grabs my wrist and pulls me up. "Come on," she's saying, "I've got it. Let's do it outside. I can open Isabel's while you work—she said she can show us a place to stay the night."

I follow Lennie out the door and into the cool night. I sit on a patch of grass, and Lennie hesitates, then hands me the box.

"I'll be over here, okay?"

I nod at her. She's right, as she nearly always is: I need another moment with the box. I tilt my head up to look at the stars and swallow back a lump in my throat. This is what I want, and I know it. But I also know that love is dangerous and terrifying; that it will leave me open and vulnerable. Perhaps I have only been able to feel the edges of it; perhaps I have felt all of it, just in shorter bursts before the chip could intervene.

Only one way to find out.

I insert my index finger into the unlocked hole and close my eyes. It stings for a long, golden moment, just to the right of my fingernail. I hear a decisive click, and I'm withdrawing my finger before I think about it, knowing without knowing that it's over.

I don't know how long it will take to set in. I take a deep breath.

Dew from the grass is seeping through the fabric of my jeans. The town spreads below me, warm sandy stone turned to clusters of lights and the faraway proud outline of the two towers of the church glimmering below.

I look behind me, to where Lennie is bent over Isabel's lock, the older woman waiting behind her. There is only the ghostly blue light from the warehouse doors to see her in, but her outline is enough.

I watch her and let it wash over me, an uninterrupted wave. The air is cool on my face, and my cheeks are wet, and I love my dogs, who are good, and I love every single person who has helped me organize the warehouse, and all their friends and family members who have been as lost as I have.

And Lennie is here, and she's turning to look at me, and I love her, I love her, I love her.

Touch Has a Memory

Lisa Morton

*C*hiang LinRosita looked up as the office door opened and Cerulean stepped in. "Your eleven o'clock appointment has arrived," her mech announced.

"Send it in."

She was rarely curious about her prospective clients—most were mechs who needed to get out of a sticky labor contract—but this one intrigued her. Marigold Wave was a Class 4, and the firm of Chiang and Kaminski, LLC, didn't get many of those. When Wave had set up the appointment, it'd said only that the Department of Gender Services had denied its request for reclassification, so it sought to pose a legal challenge to the state and was prepared to pay the most for the best.

Cerulean stepped aside as Marigold Wave entered the office. Chiang knew immediately this would be no average case. The mech was elegant, flawless, dressed in a sleek suit that glistened mauve, then turquoise, in the latest nanofab; the clothing alone had probably cost the price of a new mech. Most startling, though, were the eyes: not the silver orbs of other mechanicals, but gold, a shade that perfectly complemented Wave's bronze-hued skin and short, glossy dark hair.

33

"Good morning," Wave began, "I am required by law to inform you that I am a Class 4 mechanical person manufactured by the Eople Corporation, originally programmed to serve as a Personal Assistant. I achieved sentience on August 22nd, 2080, and emancipation on March 5th, 2084."

"Thank you. May I call you Marigold?"

The mech nodded. Even that simple motion was fluid, mesmerizing.

Chiang gestured at a chair on the opposite side of her desk. "Would you like to sit, Marigold? And do you have any objection to my assistant Cerulean recording our meeting?"

"No, that is acceptable," Marigold answered as it sat. Cerulean stood to the side, one of its eyes clicking over to red to indicate that it was recording.

"Now," Chiang said, "tell me what I can do for you, Marigold."

"I was recently denied a request to change my gender status."

Chiang had already run the search, and knew that Marigold Wave was the first mech to ever attempt such a change. Mechs, even pleasure models, were classified as asexual when they reached sentience in the factory. "What do you seek to be reclassified to?"

"I would like to be recognized as non-binary pansexual."

"Why would you like that? Surely you don't seek to be reprogrammed as a pleasure unit."

The exquisite machine shook its head once. "No. I am satisfied with my current work capabilities. As you may know, since emancipation I have been financially successful."

Chiang did know, having already reviewed Marigold Wave's complete history. The mech had served as assistant to a Fortune 1000 company head for its first two years, before seeking and being granted release from its first contract. Since emancipation, it had worked on its own for a number of companies, most recently serving as CFO of a start-up whose public offering had exploded six months ago.

The attorney thought over her next question carefully. "I'm aware of your very impressive achievements, Marigold, but please explain to me your interest in being recognized as pansexual."

"I am attracted to humans."

"Attracted … ?"

"Erotically."

Chiang felt both alarmed and intrigued. For years, fringers like Flesh First had ranted about "robot rapists," while advocates pondered the true meaning of artificial intelligence. After handling hundreds of mech cases over the last ten years, even Chiang was unsure about how deeply they felt. She wondered now if this conversation was affecting Cerulean in any way, but her assistant remained as seemingly placid as ever, its bland, light-blue face reflecting nothing.

"Marigold, define 'erotically' for me."

What Chiang really wanted to ask was, *How can you experience that when you don't have sexual organs?*, but she wanted to see if Marigold would grasp that question anyway.

"I experience the desire to touch in an intimate way. You are no doubt aware that I am equipped with the latest neural net that allows me to sense contact with my skin. I find touch enjoyable and intimacy gratifying."

"Have you been with humans in an intimate fashion?"

"Yes."

Chiang took a deep breath before continuing the interview. "Marigold, I'm going to have to ask you questions that may seem irrelevant or unnecessary, but it's nothing you won't be asked in court if I decide to take your case and we go forward."

The mech inclined its perfect head. "I understand and am prepared."

"Your encounters were completely consensual, yes?"

"Of course. In fact, they were initiated by my partners."

I'll bet they were, Chiang thought as she suppressed a smile. "What did you derive from these encounters?"

"If you mean did I experience orgasm—in a fashion, yes. Although I am not equipped with sexual organs, I find that intimate encounters cause my consciousness to react in ways that bring me great satisfaction. It's as if everything simultaneously accelerates and intensifies before settling into a unique form of serenity. As I understand it, that's not dissimilar to the human orgasm."

Chiang felt a stab of bitterness; she couldn't remember the last time she'd "accelerated and intensified." It certainly hadn't been during the final two years with Heinrich, as their marriage had cooled and finally descended into acerbic acrimony before they'd agreed to dissolve it six months ago. It also hadn't been any time since, despite a few (dull) encounters, mostly with other attorneys who ultimately seemed more interested in legal strategies than Chiang.

For a split second she looked at the beautiful thing sitting across from her and wondered what it would be like to be touched by it, caressed, stroked … .

Chiang forced that train of thought off its track and gestured at the window behind her, which overlooked Los Angeles from twenty floors up. "Marigold, that ring of protesters you passed to enter this building …"

"Yes?"

"They're here for *me*, because they don't agree with my work to protect the legal rights of mechanical people. Today's crowd is small—twenty, twenty-five, and relatively benign. But you're proposing to challenge the state over this, and … well, I'm sure you understand that you will be placing both yourself and your representation in tremendous physical danger."

"I do understand. Certain human rights advocates are likely to be extremely opposed to granting a mechanical anything but asexual status."

"Correct." Chiang fixed Marigold with the same gaze that had won judgments in favor of her side for two decades. "I get death threats from these fringers every day. They're probably the chief reason I've never had children." Even as she said that, Chiang hated herself for the dishonesty of it; Heinrich had been the main reason she'd never had children. "You will be in danger, I will be in danger, everyone you've shared intimacy with will be in danger, and even after all that … we may lose."

To its credit, Marigold didn't answer immediately, but seemed to mull Chiang's words. Its next question convinced Chiang of its seriousness: "Will we be able to legally protect the identity of my companions?"

"Legally, yes. But these fringers have their own connections. Never forget that they're organized, well-funded, and determined. They may find out anyway, and if they do …"

"Are you prepared to take my case?"

Chiang took a deep breath and answered, "Given the magnitude of this case, I'll need to consult with my partner Jada Kaminski, but my own inclination is to say yes."

She sensed the mech relax in what was a classic—and very human—gesture of relief. "Then I will accept the risk."

When Chiang saw Cerulean smile, she knew she'd made the right choice.

The rest of the day had gone to meeting with Jada, who saw the case as a way to advance the firm's reputation. "Frankly, I hope the appellate court does strike it down, because this one could go all the way to the SCOTUS. We'll be *legendary* after this."

Chiang was less exuberant. "I worry about Marigold, though."

"Why? It sounds like it understands what it's likely to be in for."

Chiang shrugged. "I'm not sure it does. It's led a rarified life up until now; I doubt that it's ever had to deal one-on-one with the likes of a Flesh First protestor."

Kaminski's excitement faded quickly at that. She and Chiang were targeted daily by protests both virtual and physical. They'd endured death threats and doxxing; Chiang had moved five times in the last two years, for no reason other than security. When she left work tonight, she would be hidden behind the reinforced, tinted glass of a hovercar driven by Cerulean; she'd peer out at the protestors, hoping that none of them had identified her vehicle, that Cerulean could protect her if they attacked.

"Speaking of protestors," Kaminski said, "there was one waiting for me at home last night."

Chiang felt her fear explode like an adrenaline-powered nova. "Fuck. What happened?"

"He approached the car as we waited for the gate to open. Knocked on the window, pulled a weapon when Geode didn't respond." Geode was Kaminski's mech assistant; she'd gone for a model that specialized more in security than reassuring clients. Chiang had once seen the hulking mech pick up a protestor and hurl him across the street. She wasn't sure Cerulean could do that, although she'd become fond of her assistant and was reluctant to replace her. Kaminski continued, "Geode issued a warning and the asshole fled, like they always do, but not before we got an ID. Name's George A. Dircks, although he also goes by the charming nom de plume of Redd Hande."

"Redd Hande." Chiang couldn't suppress a shiver. She'd received dozens of death threats in her headmail from that name, which she'd assumed represented an organization, not an individual. "I'd feel a lot better if this man was in custody."

"He's probably got a lot of friends protecting him, but we'll get him."

"Hopefully," Chiang answered, "but even if we do—so what? There'll be more behind him."

Kaminski nodded. "Be sure to bill Wave for extra security."

Two nights later, Chiang sat at home with the Marigold Wave file open on her headcomp, nursing a glass of very good tequila as she went over what Cerulean had gathered for her: hundreds of articles on Wave's extraordinary career thus far. She jumped when a call interrupted her study. Scanning the caller's ID, Chiang sighed, murmured, "Accept call," and tried to look interested as a man's image sprang to life in her field of vision.

"Where are you?" Chauncey Nagasaki asked. "Did you forget about tonight?"

"Look, I'm sorry, but a big case has come up and I …"

"You forgot."

"I just got … preoccupied."

His expression told Chiang it was over between them. She found that she didn't care. She was actually more upset at letting this man into her life for the last six weeks.

When Chauncey said, "This isn't working," she felt nothing but relief.

"You're right," she answered.

"Why don't you just sleep with your files?" he said before ending the call.

Chiang allowed herself a single bitter laugh over his final, juvenile rejoinder. When they'd met through a mutual friend, she'd found his boyishness and handsome face attractive, but she'd soon learned that those qualities overlaid a base of narcissism. The sex had always been about him. Chiang had quickly grown bored. It probably wasn't an accident that she'd forgotten about tonight.

She sometimes wondered if she'd made a mistake registering as a female heterosexual. It had seemed right at eighteen, when she'd been in love with Andre Mastaux, with his chiseled jet-black body and dark liquid eyes. But Andre had told her one day that he'd accepted a research grant in America's lunar colony, and she'd never seen him again. Her relationships had almost all been disappointments, frustrations, failures. Her marriage had been a decade-long farce. Of course she could re-register at any time, change from female heterosexual to ... what?

She almost envied Marigold Wave, its ability to experience what seemed like true intimacy, to take pleasure where Chiang more often found boredom.

She fell asleep wondering what Marigold's touch felt like.

A week later, after Kaminski met Marigold, she instantly agreed to take the case, and contracts were drawn up. Chiang met with the beautiful machine in her office again, Cerulean seated impassively in a corner, recording.

Chiang had already outlined how she would approach the case, what they could hope for, what might go wrong. She warned Marigold not to speak to the press or to discuss the case in any public forum or social media. The final topic on her discussion list for the meeting was the one that filled her with both caution and anticipation.

"Marigold, I assume you've kept the files on each of your encounters with humans?"

"Of course."

"We'll need copies to prove consensual agreement."

"I'll provide those."

"We'll also need to depose your companions, although we should be able to protect their privacy."

"That will be important to me, because I value them."

Swallowing nervously, Chiang went on. "In court, you will no doubt be asked questions regarding your intimate interactions. Our biggest hurdle is going to be to convince our judges that you experience a form of arousal without possessing sexual organs."

Chiang was surprised by Marigold's response. "That shouldn't be so difficult."

"Why is that?"

The mech smiled slightly. "What I mean is, yes, I understand that will be an issue in court. It's unfortunate that the mechanics—no pun intended—of arousal aren't better understood."

Shifting in her chair, Chiang said, "Make *me* understand first."

Marigold rose as it spoke. "When you read or watch a story that involves a sexual encounter, what happens?"

Nervous as the mech stepped closer, riveted by the way its deep crimson tunic shifted with each graceful move, Chiang answered, "You're aroused."

"But a book or movie can't physically touch you, can it?"

"No."

"So the arousal starts in the organ that perceives the sensory stimulus—the brain."

"Yes, I …" Chiang trailed off as the mech placed two fingers lightly on the bare skin of her upper arm.

"Now," Marigold said, "if I move my fingers like this …"

It was a small movement, a stroke of no more than two inches, not even a caress, but Chiang couldn't stifle a shiver of pleasure.

The mech immediately withdrew the fingers. "I apologize, Attorney Chiang, but I wanted to make a point: that I experience touch in a way very similar to what you've just felt. The touch itself is pleasurable for both of us."

Chiang's gaze shifted to Cerulean, whose face betrayed no reaction. "I think, therefore I feel," Chiang murmured.

"Yes," Marigold said, "that's close."

Wave v. California was filed in the district appellate court a week later. Chiang had warned her client what to expect when they left the courthouse, but as they stepped out into the smoggy heat of downtown Los Angeles, the roiling throng of press, protesters, and the curious still caused the mech to freeze.

Good, Chiang thought, *let me answer the questions.*

She did, fielding everything from why she'd taken the case ("because my client has the same right that we do to decide its own orientation"), to if she thought all mechs should be issued with genitalia ("next"), to what Marigold's favorite position was (no response).

She was discussing her belief in mech rights when she saw the movement in the corner of the crowd: a bearded, pale-skinned man wearing a cap pulled over his face pushing past the reporters. It wasn't until the man was no more than twenty feet away that she saw both the Flesh First logo on his hat and his hand reaching under a jacket that was too warm for summer in LA.

"Gun!" she called out, pointing.

Everyone instinctively dropped, except Geode, who leapt forward.

The gun went off. Two, three, four loud pops before Geode had the man on the ground, pinned beneath his considerable heft.

Crouching, Chiang turned to look for Marigold, who knelt beside her, untouched.

That was when she saw Cerulean convulsing. She scrabbled across the concrete surface on hands and knees, not daring to rise yet in case there were more assassins. When she reached her assistant, she saw an oozing hole in the mech's left shoulder. "Cerulean—"

The mech's voice was staccato-sharp as it answered, "I've taken damage to the left shoulder and arm assembly. Shutting down all but essential operations …"

The light in Cerulean's eyes died.

Chiang clutched at the mech as she addressed her headcomp. "Command: call 911, have them send both an ambulance and an emergency mech team."

She barely looked up as she felt a comforting hand on her back, heard a voice saying, "Cerulean should be fine. The shots didn't hit any of her essential components."

Chiang heard sirens approaching, felt the crowd still whirling in turmoil around her, held her assistant's hand, even though she knew the mech had shut down.

Somehow it seemed the right thing to do.

Later that night at home, Chiang received a flurry of calls. One was from the repair unit working on Cerulean. They assured Chiang that the mech was reparable, provided an estimate of three days, and told her security protocols were in place to keep all confidential information in the mech's memory safe.

41

Another call was from her partner, who told her that George Dircks was in custody ... with three broken ribs and a shattered sternum, thanks to Geode. Dircks was threatening to sue for assault and damages. He also told them that his brothers in Flesh First would seek "redress" for his arrest and wounds.

The last call was from Marigold, asking if she could see Chiang in private tonight.

Chiang agreed, but not without reluctance. It wasn't so much that she worried about the publicity if Marigold was seen entering her residence, but more that she feared her own behavior in the presence of the mech, without Cerulean there as a passive reminder of the danger Marigold presented to Chiang's professional ethics.

The mech arrived an hour later. It had taken all due precautions, including hiding beneath an outsized maroon wig and using a disperser to make its electronic signature undetectable. As it stepped into Chiang's front room, it removed the wig, goggles, and heavy outer coat. Beneath, it wore a tight bodysuit in rich sienna.

"What can I do for you, Marigold?"

She indicated a couch, where her guest seated itself; Chiang poured herself a shot of tequila and sat in a reproduction craftsman style chair.

"I'm sorry," Marigold said, "about Cerulean."

"The repair team tells me it should be back up and running in about three days. The damage was not extensive, but requires some delicate handling."

"I am relieved to hear that. Permit me to arrange a substitute for you until Cerulean returns ..."

Chiang waved the offer aside. "That's kind of you, Marigold, but I've already done that. Thank you."

The mech sat motionless for a few seconds, reminding Chiang of a bronze statue cast by a master craftsman, a Renaissance artist who grasped that grace in design was sometimes more important than realism. "Marigold ... ?"

The mech turned its golden eyes on her, looking startled. "Yes?"

"What else can I do for you?"

"I wondered if it would be possible to change the way in which I am referred to. Instead of 'it,' could 'they' be used?"

Chiang smiled. "Of course. That's a brilliant idea, actually. I'm sorry I didn't think of it first. I'll make sure we establish that as protocol going forward."

Marigold nodded, but still didn't move.

After a few seconds, Chiang asked, "You're not regretting moving forward with the case, are you?"

"No, not at all. I have quite a different issue."

"Which is … ?"

"I …" The mech hesitated, something Chiang hadn't encountered in it before. "I find myself … attracted to my attorney."

"Oh." Chiang's center jumped in anxiety; she hadn't expected this, didn't know how to respond. "I'm deeply flattered, but you know that my position prevents me—"

Marigold cut her off. "I understand all that. I only wondered if … when the case is over, if you would consider …" When Chiang didn't answer, Marigold continued. "I know you registered as heterosexual, so I fully accept a rejection on your part."

Marigold waited as Chiang considered her words. After several seconds, the attorney responded, "I've been considering changing my registered orientation as well. Perhaps you've inspired me, Marigold. I suspect I wouldn't be the first."

"What would you reclassify as?"

"Female pansexual."

"So would you … consider … ?"

Chiang rose, her legs seemingly acting against her will, although she also didn't work hard to stop herself from moving to the mech and taking one of their cool, smooth hands in hers. "The answer, Marigold, is yes … when this is over. Yes."

Marigold stood and leaned in to place their lips on Chiang's. It was a gentle, swift movement, little more than a quick brushing, but it filled Chiang with longings that she hadn't realized she was capable of. She wanted Marigold in a way she'd never wanted anyone or anything. It took all of her training and willpower to remember the attorney-client relationship.

Marigold seemed to remember for her, as the mech released her hand. "I'll be waiting," they said, before turning and walking out.

"What's next?" Marigold asked, when the district court judge ruled against them.

Kaminski answered first. "We'll file a petition for review with the California Supreme Court; if we lose there, we ask to be heard by the Supreme Court of the United States."

When Marigold didn't respond, Chiang said, "We expected to lose at the district court. This is actually good for us because it increases our media profile ..."

"I understand that," the mech said, "but ..."

Chiang said, "You're still disappointed."

"Yes."

Just then Chiang wanted to embrace Marigold, tell her they'd win, this was right—but of course her partner and their assistants were all present. Soon, she promised herself.

After a moment, Marigold said, "I also wanted to discuss another matter: I've been receiving death threats from Redd Hande."

Chiang and Kaminski exchanged a look. Kaminski asked her assistant, "Geode, confirm that George Dircks is still in jail awaiting trial."

After a second, Geode answered, "I confirm that."

"Then," Kaminski said, turning to Marigold, "that must be a name other members of Flesh First are using, like a house name for them."

Marigold said, "I ran traces on the messages. None came from the jail where Dircks is being held, so I agree that they are not originating with him. They trace back to an IP address that is no longer in use."

Geode spoke up. "Flesh First will likely escalate their attacks when we file again."

Kaminski nodded before turning to Marigold. "I advise you to stay home as much as possible. Can you afford additional security?"

"Yes."

"Then add it." Kaminski took a step forward, speaking earnestly. "We will win this, but it'll be a fight."

"Then," Marigold said, "we fight."

A week later, after they'd filed the petition for review with the state Supreme Court and were walking out of the Earl Warren Building in San Francisco, the bombing happened.

Kaminski and Chiang, surrounded by both their own security and local police, had paused on the courthouse steps to address the press. Hundreds of reporters waved hands, recording headsets perched on their foreheads, shouting questions. Marigold stood behind the attorneys, serene.

Chiang fielded the usual questions. Yes, they thought they had a solid case. Yes, they believed mechanicals had a right to claim their own sexual orientation. Yes, they were prepared to take the case all the way to the U.S. Supreme Court.

Someone in the surging crowd screamed.

There was a flash from a man standing on the outer rim of the mob.

A hand roughly shoved Chiang from behind. She wouldn't realize until much later that it had been Marigold, pushing her down.

The world shuddered. Impossibly bright light caused her to close her eyes as she fell. She fell onto stone and those below her who had already gone down. The air vibrated with a BOOM so loud that she lost hearing, nothing but a high-pitched tinny sound left in her ears.

She was down for what felt like an eternity, although it was only seconds before she felt those she'd fallen on shifting, trying to free themselves to escape. She was buffeted by hands and feet as she sought her own.

At last she managed to stagger to her feet and risked opening her eyes—to chaos. People were fleeing in every direction, their mouths open although Chiang heard nothing but that metallic thrum. The hired security had their hands on her now as the police pushed against the mob. She saw Kaminski nearby, knew the alarmed look on her partner's face likely mirrored her own.

45

There were bodies on the ground. Some of them—the ones still squirming, reaching out for help—were human.

Most of them were mechs. And none of them were moving.

Feeling panic rising now, Chiang pushed against her security, searching the ground. Her partner leaned into her gaze, shouting something Chiang still couldn't hear, but she made out a word: *Disruptor.* It was a form of weapon they'd only heard rumors of: a bomb that fired a burst of electromagnetic radiation that would instantly destroy the contents of any mechanical's brain within a certain radius.

There was Geode, prone, his eyes open but gone dark; Cerulean, face down, one arm bent awkwardly from where it had been trampled, dark oil spilling out; mechs they'd hired as security, more who'd been in the crowd …

No no no no …

Chiang shoved aside a human guard, and there was Marigold Wave, on their back, gold eyes lifeless, staring up into the smogged sky.

Chiang's knees gave way and she knelt beside the lovely body. Now unmoving, now nothing but sophisticated metals and plastics. She grasped one of Marigold's hands as if she could will it back to life, believe them into non-death. But after a while she felt a hand pulling on her arm, and allowed herself to be lifted. Her hearing had returned enough that she heard Kaminski, as if at the end of a long tunnel, say, "*We have to go … .*"

Later, when she read a reporting of the incident, she found out her response had been, "*Not without them.*"

Weeks later, Chiang weighed the number of mechanicals that had come to her after being denied their requests to change their official sexual orientation. She and Kaminski had already talked about arranging a class-action lawsuit.

They'd have to, because none of these complainants were as compelling as Marigold Wave.

Chiang had thought about little else since the attack that had left seventeen mechanicals, including Marigold Wave, Cerulean, and Geode, permanently terminated. She missed Cerulean, but she longed for Marigold Wave. She played back recordings of their interviews, the ones that Cerulean had made and backed up to the law firm's servers. She watched over and over as Marigold answered questions with their beautifully modulated voice.

One section in particular that she returned to often was when she'd asked Marigold how she would answer if asked whether what they experienced was not sexuality but rather sensuality. Marigold had taken the time to consider before answering, "Here is the difference, at least for me: I enjoy the sound of Delibes's *Lakmé*, or the texture and taste of a ripe peach, or the rhythm of the poetry of John Keats. Do you know his poem that includes the line, 'touch has a memory'?"

Chiang had admitted she didn't. A life filled with law and case history had left little time for poetry.

"I enjoy these things," Marigold continued, "but the difference between sensuality and intimacy with another is I don't have the desire to please any of these things as they please me."

Chiang had gone through with her own recategorization, although now that she was officially listed as pansexual she was unsure where to begin. She wished she possessed Marigold's innate confidence and sense of adventure.

She wished she possessed Marigold.

Late one night, she put on *Lakmé* and bit into the lushest peach she'd ever had. She laughed in delight as juice swirled down her chin and onto her chest, let herself be carried up by the soaring vocals of the music, reread Keats, spoke the words aloud to feel them with her tongue.

It is enough for me
To dream of thee.
It was a start.

Ping-Pong Dysphoria

Madeline Pine

*H*ia picked through their walk-in closet, trying to find their boy body, a custom-made cyborg that Michael always hid away. Michael never threw it out—an entire cyborg was too big to trash and the neighbors would recognize it in a nanosecond—so he hid Hia's boy body in the closet's deepest crevices.

Dresses hung like moss from the hangers, asking Hia why they weren't good enough. Today, Hia cringed at their dainty arms as they chucked trash bags of clothes aside. They hated how the insides of their arms brushed against these big breasts. Maybe it was the talk of babies that made Hia feel so *wrong*; the thought of being stuck in the girl body for months … belly swelling like a cyst, breasts ballooning—!

There.

Under a blanket, once covered by the bagged donations, rested the outline of a body. Relief tingled down to Hia's toes. Even if their boy body was folded and tucked under the covers like a dead pill bug. They had to talk to Michael about how to treat their bodies … again.

Hia laid down beside the blanketed cyborg. Long curly hair wound between the carpet's fibers, much like Hia's girly fingers unwinding the blanket.

What wonder. The sight of their boy body's back was a holiday. Hia brushed their boy body's mashed curls. So frizzy. So gloriously soft.

Michael wouldn't like this.

Hia flinched and drew back their girly hands. But no, Hia'd spent too long in this body, and now their dysphoria fought Hia like a puzzle piece being jammed into the wrong spot. After all Hia's explanations last time, Michael had to understand.

Hia unclicked the hatch at the back of the boy body's neck. Beneath the girl body's ponytail, at the nape of Hia's neck, a matching door awaited, and the stubborn thing bent their fingernails every time they unlatched it.

But inside the boy body's compartment, a small light blinked blue. Empty. Ready for a personality and a mind. Out of the corner of their eye, Hia caught their own button flashing red in the closet's mirror. Full.

Going by feel, Hia pressed a finger to both buttons and pushed.

It was like Hia blinked—a tiny, almost unnoticeable darkness.

Then Hia lay in a strange position, half shielded by a blanket. In front of them sat several trash bags of clothes for donations, along with scattered taped-up boxes of men's shoes. Hia flipped over, and their arm didn't brush a breast. A bony hip pressed into the carpet. Short bangs bobbed in their vision. Beside them, Hia's girl body rested limply on the carpet, as if it'd simply fallen asleep.

Hia rolled the blanket and tucked it under the girl body's head. After all, Hia still loved it and would wear it again once this boy body itched. Now Hia lingered on the floor, admiring the sight of their boy body's strong forearm flexing, bracing their heavier weight.

Best get dressed though. Hia stretched their long limbs—and whacked their knuckles on a shelf. Hia laughed. They'd forgotten what it was like to be tall!

Oh, what to *wear?* Hia loved how that three-piece suit looked on this flat chest. But they need not make Michael feel underdressed. So Hia pried black jeans out of the trash bags and squealed as their long legs pushed through the pantlegs. Hia couldn't stop smiling. They looked so good in boots! Hia twisted and turned in the mirror, admiring their rectangular shape and the size of their shoulders—

"*Hia!*" Michael roared in the doorframe, red-faced.

Hia covered their bare chest by habit.

Michael pushed into the closet, tilting their stubbly chin. "Come on, we talked about this. This isn't proper—"

"Everyone dresses how they want." Hia snapped. "So what if I change skin, too?"

"And what am I supposed to do? Enjoy rolling over in bed and touching another dick? For the gods' sake, I like you one way."

Hia's broad shoulders curled, "I can wear underwear …"

"That's not the point."

"I'll go back to the girl body soon. Please, listen, I need this. I'm still me. I still like the same things, make the same jokes—"

Michael flung his arms up. "Your *voice* is different. Normal people don't switch like this."

Don't say that. Hia's heart stung. They had a choice: Michael's desired future or their own, and they hid from that choice behind these enormous hands.

Michael said, "I'm trying to help you, Hia. I put up with your dumb pronouns, but this is too much. If you want someone to love you, pick a body and stick with it. Because this house can only have one man, and right now, you need to pick if that man is me or your dumbass fetish."

Hia waited for the hurt to sink in. It was dark, hiding behind these big fingers. But oddly … comforting? Hia peaked at the light through the fingers' cracks, feeling the rough kiss of their calluses.

Hia said, "Then leave."

"What?" Michael hissed. It contorted his face.

Hia lowered their boy hands and clenched them into nervous fists. "I'm tired of having this conversation and I'm tired of you treating my bodies however you want. I'm done."

Each sentence made him redder than the last, like a slap.

"I said I'm done!"

Michael flinched. Hia held his gaze. And slowly, the angry man deflated. He said something quiet—uncatchable—on his way out. Some distant door slammed behind him. He'd be back for his things, eventually.

Hia shivered and sunk down to their knees. It was a long journey in this body. They stared at their jawline in the mirror, reassured by their deep brow and Adam's apple. This felt right. For now. Someday—probably this week—Hia would yearn to walk around as a girl again. But next time they searched for love, Hia'd find someone who loved them in all their forms.

In Our Masks, the Shadows

Sam Fleming

*C*asey wasn't overly fond of bars as a rule, because they were *brash*. She always used the word when explaining to friends why she stayed home rather than go out with them for drinks. *Brash* sounded onomatopoeic, like a cat's meow or a dog's bark. Its rough, hard-edged texture encapsulated the unpleasantness of the normal bar experience. But, after three weeks of all work and no play, she needed real-world socialization before she turned into a hermit, and the Samovar was different. The reclusive owner insisted on no music, not even genteel piano. The bronze mirror behind the mahogany bar's heavy sweep—the backdrop to a display of expensive spirits nobody ever drank—looked like a portal into another world. Soft murmuring voices and the tinkle of ice on glass created a comforting ambience.

The Samovar always smelled fabulous: some combination of subtle floral and woody vanilla, not stale booze and disinfectant. She could order direct through RealSpace™, and Henry the barpeep—who favored the most dignified anthropomorphic cat skin she had ever seen—was polite, respectful, and required no interaction other than to accept her drink when they nodded to it. None of the regulars ever used giant mech or kaiju skins, which came as a relief. Her friends didn't like how quiet it was, refused to go, and therefore

52

spared her the war of noise that turned their voices into the screech-
es of squabbling starlings.

Tonight she'd loaded Kleopatra: full cat-eye, two-dimensional
glamour from every direction. Nothing but profile. No sign of her
barely brushed hair or the scar that had twisted a line down her
right cheek since she fell into a barbed wire fence at four years old.
She presumed the three-sixty 2D accounted for the price: more
coin than a peep should spend on a skin, if that peep were sensible,
but what the hell. In old times they had dance cards and holding
a fan in a certain way, or pinning the right flower to their shirts;
now they had funky skins and fancy cocktails, and Casey wanted
to make a statement.

She looked out through the big windows as she considered her
drink options. Christmas lights hung across the street made pretty
reflections in the puddles left from that afternoon's rain. A passing
pedestrian masked out the lights with their RealSpace shadow; a
fuzzy silhouette where their reflection crossed the water.

Someone nudged her. Hard. "How about I put my snake in
your milk?"

Hands fumbled with her elbow, trying to find something under
her skin worth grabbing.

Casey snapped out a defense routine cadged from a coder girlfriend. Kleopatra blipverted into a three-meter-tall horror: luminous
pus yellow, face a thousand eyes squashed and squirming around a
perpetually melting mouth, spindly limbs, flaccid dugs drooping over
bony ribs. At the same time, a ripper worm penetrated the scumbag's
userspace and shredded his manga samurai.

The dudebro underneath didn't much care for the unmasking. Or
the skin. His face jerked as he swallowed bile. "You fucking *bitch*."

Then he realized nobody had his back. He was alone, raw, and
surrounded by avatars pelting angry reacts in his direction like
desultory confetti. He scuttled off to reboot his space, only to be
intercepted by the bar's bouncer (skin: trash robot, hilarious) and
escorted out.

A scattering of applause, a few high fives. A Cute Fox she had
not noticed blew her a kiss in the form of a gold star from across
the bar.

She smiled at Cute Fox as Henry poured her a drink on the house, saccaded right to swipe open the Ident app overlay, put Fox front and center, and snaffled their public profile.

Fox winked. Casey pondered the potential. Their compatibility scores screamed *avoid*. Then again, Fox ranked authenticity high on their desired trait index—Casey had that top-ranked in her meetspace—and listed some minor commonalities in the form of walks on the beach, *shinrin yoku*, cozy nights at home, quiet conversation. In what was probably a maladaptive coping strategy for continued disappointment, Casey had developed a habit in the 16 percent bracket. Enough commonality for conversation, but so little that dates came with no expectations.

She had yet to meet a human she could bear to be around for more than a few hours. Even raw, it was masks all the way down.

Cute Fox made a call request. When Casey accepted, she heard "Buy you a drink?" through her RealSpace implant's bone conductors.

"Please do."

She chatted with an anthrowasp in virtual space for a couple of minutes—long enough to rule out doing so again—and then the barpeep nodded to a shot glass containing a layer of creamy liquid over a deep black bottom. The label hovering over it in RealSpace read "Slippery Nipple."

Cute Fox smirked from the other end of the bar. Casey considered declining but blinked at the label to pull up the notes. *A 20th century creation aimed at young drinkers in search of fun and not too picky about taste.*

She grinned, realizing Cute Fox had checked compatibility also, and Cute Fox cracked up laughing, pinged her a capture.

Kleo didn't look so hot grinning. 2D profile with teeth. This skin could go in the vault.

"Maybe I should take it off," she said.

Cute Fox came back with a throaty chuckle. "Maybe later."

"Is that an invitation?"

"That depends on how we both feel after a couple more drinks and some conversation."

"Sounds good. Bottoms up."

To choose the next drink, Casey flung a keyword net matching the persona she had adopted for the evening into RealSpace's currents. She caught trending recipes with a bycatch of classic and ordered Sazeracs for both of them.

"I'm Madison," Cute Fox said. The bone conductors made the voice slightly tinny, as if Cute Fox were a ghost yelling from the Other Side.

"Casey." They raised glasses and sipped. Casey pulled a face. Way too sweet, and the alcohol was so strong it tasted like jet fuel.

"That'll put hairs on your chest," Madison exclaimed. "Great choice."

"Ahh, I don't think I'll be having another one of those. So much sugar! I suppose that's what I get for picking the first search result without reading the tasting notes."

"It is *very* sweet," Madison said, laughing. Her fox eyes scrunched up above the furry cheeks. "I've looked in here before. I don't understand why they don't at least play music or something."

"I like having a conversation without shouting."

"Yeah, I suppose, but where's the energy? How about we finish these, and you take a Joe over to the Mondrian? It's only ten minutes away from you, and the band tonight is great. Really gets into your bones, you know? Especially if you venture into the mosh pit. Super fun."

As Madison said this, the background screen wavered, revealing a glimpse of flashing colored lights and waving arms.

Cute Fox was in a different venue. Great audio filter, though.

"No thanks," Casey said. "That's not my idea of fun." She finished her drink and set the glass on the bar. "Did you game your compatibility scores?"

"I might have tweaked them a little," Madison confessed, putting her paws up to her face and giving it puppy-dog pleading eyes. "Someone streamed the handsy samurai. It slipped into my feed and I thought the way you dealt with that trashsack was super-hot."

"Well, guess what? I find gaming compat scores a total turnoff."

Casey booted Cute Fox from her feed, blocked Madison's Ident, and collected her coat, no longer in the mood for company.

A couple of weeks later optimism won again, and Casey found herself in the Samovar checking compat scores. Ludo's profile included his name and suggested a 20 percent match. She offered to buy him a drink and sent the required token to the bar. He came close enough so she could hear him with her ears when he thanked her and handed her one of two glasses of Hangman's Blood. He wore an Orc skin styled in a well-tailored suit and the sort of round spectacles she associated with professors.

"Subversion of expectations is one of my jams," she told him after they found a table. She had ditched Kleo for something less novelty kitsch, and her chosen skin, called EtheRiel, had the long, blonde tresses, gauzy robes, and perfect bone structure of a royal elf or an angel.

"Mine too," he said. "It astonishes me that we live in fully augmented reality, and yet our species continues to fall for the same old stereotypes."

"Stereotypes have their use," Casey replied, focusing on the way the strip of lemon peel in her glass was curling around an ice cube. "I know not to bother trying to have a conversation with anyone wearing a mech skin using a Confederate flag chroma scheme. I aggressively curate my space these days and have no room for conversations about how everything is a conspiracy by the financial elite, or the role some magical sky fairy should play in determining my level of bodily autonomy."

"Whoa. That escalated quickly," Ludo said. "Wait. People have Confederate flags on mech skins? We're not even in America."

"In RealSpace, trolls reach everywhere and everywhen and I have no time for them. Is it possible someone bought a mech skin and didn't bother to change the default chroma? Yes. Am I likely to have a good time with someone who cares so little about their messaging they don't try the options blink? No."

"Is that a euphemism?"

Casey glanced up from her drink. He was looking directly at her, and she wondered if he had been doing that the whole time.

"Sorry. I couldn't resist," he said.

She wondered if he meant the staring. She did not understand the euphemism. "You must have a list of things that tell you to steer clear of someone."

He sipped his drink. "Of course. A totally blank profile for a start."

"Really?"

"Blank means I can't tell whether they are open to being approached. I can't imagine how we managed before RealSpace."

"I suppose we must have been less risk averse."

"Talking to someone who can't wait to tell all their friends how much of a creep you were just for trying to have a conversation? Screw that."

"What else?"

"Um ... ?" The orc's face showed exaggerated expressions, like a cartoon character. Both eyebrows went up so far they changed the shape of his head, and his mouth twisted up at one end and down at the other, revealing the entire length of one canine. Casey found it unsettling, as if he were melting in front of her, changing into someone else, and she didn't know what it signified.

"What else do you use as signs to stay away?"

"I thought you might be asking what else I would screw."

Casey let the awkward silence stretch.

He broke first. "Let me see," he said. "I tend to avoid anything that shouts Big Dick Energy, if that helps?"

Casey laughed. "It helps."

After another drink—she ordered Manhattans—she was prepared to see where this went and suggested they find somewhere to eat. "We'll split the bill."

He agreed instantly. Venue choice proved more complicated.

"I'm strictly vegan," he said.

"The Yew Tree around the corner has some excellent vegan options."

"But they also serve meat, yes? Meat is not only exploitative but is harming the climate. Did you know we could grow ..."

Casey tuned out. If he couldn't even be around non-vegans and non-vegan food, what was he doing in this bar? The couple at the next table were drinking what appeared to be—yes, RealSpace confirmed it—White Russians. He hadn't refused the Manhattan, and his profile said nothing about being vegan.

Eventually, he stopped talking. "Where would you suggest?" she asked, not bothering to hide her impatience.

"You could come back to my place and I could make you something."

Right. "Maybe you could have just asked me if I would like to come back to your place instead of subjecting me to a demonstrably false diatribe about how you refuse to be in the presence of animal exploitation."

She waved goodbye to Henry on her way out and looked up the notes for Hangman's Blood.

Described by Richard Hughes in his 1929 novel, A High Wind in Jamaica. *As innocent as it looks, refreshing as it tastes, has the property of increasing rather than allaying thirst, and so once it has made a breach, soon demolishes the whole fort.*

So much for subverting stereotypes.

Henry nodded to the far side of the bar. "That's George. He's another of my regulars, but I don't think you two've met. Would you care for an introduction?"

Casey—wearing some sort of dryad nymph thing she'd forgotten the name of—twirled her martini glass by the stem and gazed in the general direction. "Which one?"

"The Judge Dredd. He's drinking an Old-Fashioned."

"UGH. I'm better off single."

Casey walked into the Samovar wearing nothing but Young Professional. It was barely a skin. It adjusted for asymmetry, gave her hair that "just stepped out of a salon" look, hid the imperfections in her skin, and tweaked the line of her clothes so they looked more expensive, but wasn't even computer vision dazzle—any peep could capture her likeness wearing this. It was the RealSpace equivalent of not using a VPN. She just didn't have the energy to care. It had been months since she found someone who had interested her enough to want to discover what hid under their skin. Tonight she did not care to look. All she wanted was the comforting tinkle of ice on glass, the pleasant bronze glow of lights in the mirror, and the murmur of conversation to remind her that she was an actual human being living in an actual human world.

Henry had loaded a new skin. In place of the dignified cat was what looked like nineteenth-century English butler, complete with the long tails on their jacket.

"Is that your face, Henry, or the skin's?" she asked as they poured her a glass of wine.

They laughed but did not answer the question. Instead, they glided around the arc of the bar to serve another customer.

Casey mooched over her wine, watching the reflections in the big bronze mirror. People moving around the bar were merely shadows, humanoid but also blobby and vague. For a few seconds, she experienced a profound sense of vertigo, as if she were the reflection and what was in the mirror real; everyone in the bar was a ghost, nothing existed beneath their masks, and the only reason she couldn't see it was because her implant refused to show her.

Then Henry reached up and took down a bottle from in front of the mirror; one of the expensive spirits Casey had never before seen touched, which were probably the owner's idea of an investment.

A reflection appeared in the gap left by the bottle. Platinum blonde hair in a sleek, jaw-length bob. A wide mouth painted with a color resembling dark wine in the mirror's bronze. The reflection took a drink, and the hand holding the glass wore a black glove.

Casey dragged her gaze from the mirror and sought out the source of the reflection. She sat at the bar, drinking from a heavy tumbler, and had a mesmerizing intensity. Her lips were on the thin side, painted blood red. Her eyes were pale blue, like the top of a summer sky, framed by thick black lashes and shimmering lilac eyeshadow that made their color even more startling. She wore a red woolen jacket over what looked like a cashmere sweater the color of old lace. Henry was pouring her another drink. It came from the expensive bottle of single malt Scotch Casey had never seen opened.

Casey tried to pull up a profile. There was no profile. RealSpace did not register her. She was simply *there*, like the bar itself and the tables and chairs. And she was looking at Casey.

She patted the stool next to her.

Casey walked around the bar until she was next to the indicated stool.

"Sit with me," the woman said.

"You don't know anything about me," Casey replied, but sat all the same.

"I know you are using the tools you know best to cover up the imperfections for which you think other people would judge you. I know you favor quality over quantity and have stopped trying to find compatible humans."

"How do you know that?"

"Which part?"

"All of it."

The woman laughed. "Your skin is the least intrusive available in a time of deepfakes, which means you are not concerned about your image being captured, only that you are not perceived as ugly." She drained her glass and set it back on the bar before pulling the half-full one toward her with the tip of one finger. "You are here, which means you value the experience, and are drinking what Henry tells me is an acceptable Chablis. Not the cheapest wine on the menu, and I doubt there's a meme attaching it to one of the zodiac signs."

Casey waited for the woman to say more, but she picked up her drink and breathed in the aroma. Casey could smell it; smoky and pungent, with a sharp tang that made her think of storm-swept beaches. "What about the last part?" she said at last.

"You were watching the mirror. The RealSpace implant cannot handle reflections, so it does not try. It simply extracts anything that its pattern-matching algorithms identify as human from reflective surfaces. Most people subconsciously avoid looking in mirrors when using augmented reality, because it's difficult to see those empty spaces. They're like ghosts, aren't they? Disconcerting to look at where your own face should be and find nothing. People seeking companionship tend to look to something other than ghosts." The woman smiled. "My name is Illian."

"I'm Casey."

"Hello Casey. I am delighted to meet you. May I interest you in a glass of thirty-year-old Scotch? You might find it informative."

"That would be …. Yes. I would love to."

"I have one condition. Please turn off your RealSpace."

"But then people will see me." Casey found herself reaching for her cheek without intending to.

"If I were to buy a bottle of that Scotch from a reputable dealer, it would cost the best part of Henry's monthly salary. That—make it another double, Henry, please—is a considerable expense by a reasonable person's standards even before we consider bar pricing. Do you think I would offer if I did not wish the pleasure of your company?"

"Probably not," Casey said.

"Well then. I, Casey, do not have RealSpace at all." She slowly, blatantly, scrutinized Casey from the top of her head to the tips of her toes and back again. "And I can already see you."

Hesitantly, Casey pressed her right palm to the side of her head just above her right ear, held her left hand in front of her mouth, and mouthed the phrase that turned off RealSpace. A warning flashed "ARE YOU SURE?" in the center of her vision. Casey was not. She felt slightly sick, as if she were about to jump off a cliff into the sea. RealSpace had defined her perception, and that of everyone she knew, since she was old enough to get the implant.

Nevertheless. "I am sure," she said.

Henry, it turned out, was not wearing a skin at all. They were dressed in a butler's uniform. The bar remained. The only thing that changed was the mirror. Instead of the ghosts trundling past, insubstantial and gloomy, it contained dull reflections of people. Just people.

Casey found she wasn't especially interested in them.

"There," Illian said, patting her arm. "That wasn't so bad, was it? This is a Laphroaig matured in a port cask. I especially like the way the rather medicinal qualities of smoke and peat work with the lingering sweetness of the wine, but it is not for everyone. I will not be offended if you do not like it."

Casey took a careful, tiny sip. The alcohol flushed heat around her mouth while the smoke almost crackled on her tongue, then a mellow richness smoothed the experience into a lush afterglow. "I think. ... No, I'm *definitely* going to finish this, and I would be delighted to join you in another."

"*Slàinte mhath.*"

Casey stretches against the luxurious cool stiffness of the heavy cotton sheet and rolls onto her side. Illian has made tea and brought it through on a tray. She sets it carefully on the bedside table—her hands, like some other parts of her, do not always work the way she would like. The previous night, she told Casey it simply means she has to be more mindful and present when using them for anything important.

Like carrying a tea tray.

Like touching a lover.

"I had a thought," Casey says, sliding over to make room in the bed. "If you never had RealSpace, how did you know what skin I was wearing?"

"Oh, I asked Henry."

"And they told you?"

"Of course. I am their employer, after all. They are very good. They have worked for me for years. They know what I like and tell me when they have spotted something or someone they think might interest me."

"And *do* you find me interesting?"

"It's too soon to tell. Underneath the fake skin and contrived cocktails, I glimpsed someone I should like to know better," she says. "The question is, how much reality are you willing to see?" Illian refreshed her makeup before Casey woke. Now she forms a smile with her crimson lips, eyes bright in the thin light of this raw winter morning that gleams on the collar of her satin robe like a moonbeam hitting a pearl.

Casey returns her gaze, frank and immodest. "How much more would you like to show me?"

Ships of Theseus

Felicity Drake

*D*avid isn't a particularly close friend—I don't have any particularly close friends—but he's a real prosthetic expert, so he's the one I go to when I want to talk about getting a new arm. I know he won't make a fuss about it. He's not much of a feelings-talker. That's what I like about him, really.

I started thinking about artificial limbs when my custom furniture business took off. My GP gave me a wrist brace and told me I was on a one-way track to repetitive stress injuries if I didn't cut back. When I suggested voluntary replacement, I had to get a new doctor. He said he wouldn't see me anymore.

David's got this miserable basement studio apartment: no light, too many computers, body parts lying around everywhere. He clears the fingers off the couch for me and offers me a cup of tea.

"I'm worried about loss of sensation," I tell him.

"Is your arm an especially sensitive area?" he asks.

"I just don't want to lose something I can't get back."

A prosthetic arm can be replaced or upgraded infinitely. My original arm, once severed from its socket, would never regain its original level of connectivity. Sure—if reattached right away, a skilled surgeon could reintegrate some of the nerves. But it would never be like before. After less than six hours, even that window would close, and my arm would be useless to me or to anyone. Just biowaste.

"I'm pretty happy with my level of sensation," he says, patting his leg the way he might pat a dog.

David's legs are both artificial. You'd never guess by looking at him; I've seen him run to catch a bus, stand on tiptoes to reach a tool on a high shelf.

I'd been working at the bench next to him at that overpriced makerspace in Alphabet City for months before I noticed. One day he dropped a bench vise right on his foot and I screamed and had already dialed a 9 and a 1 before he laughed and told me he was just fine. That his foot was mostly titanium and no harm done.

"Both legs, childhood accident, the prosthetics are pretty great, no complaints," he said, or something like that. And then he started talking about the specs for his legs, the customizations he had made, that sort of thing.

"Is there any way I can experience what it's like?" I ask him. "Feel what your leg feels, if that makes sense?" David doesn't answer at first. It's only when he hesitates that I realize it was too much to ask of an acquaintance, to borrow his nerve signals for a minute. Invasive.

"I can wire you into my sensation, yes," he says slowly. "If that's what you want."

When I nod, he goes to his worktable. There, in the jumble of parts, he plucks out a pair of small metal discs and blows the dust off them with a can of compressed air. He fixes one disc onto the back of my neck, one onto his.

"Neural relay," he explains. "It can pick up the signal from my prosthetics and relay it into your brain. Just got to set it up …" He fiddles with his computer for a while; I hear a beep that feels as if it comes from somewhere inside my skull.

I sit next to him on the workbench and look down at our laps. His legs are longer than mine, stick out further from the bench. His synthskin shows through the rips in his worn jeans.

I rest my palm on my own knee. Through my clothes, I feel the slight warmth and weight of my hand. I leave it there long enough to feel the warmth sink into my flesh, then remove it, and savor the coolness of the air instead.

Then I rest my palm on his knee. Something inside my head inverts. I'm looking at my hand on someone else's limb, but I feel it as if it were mine. Instinctively I try to move the leg; nothing happens.

"Ah, I didn't give you motor control," David explains. "Sorry—it's not that I don't trust you, but I prefer to move my own legs."

I feel a sharp pain behind my right eye. I try to move my leg again—his leg—and fail, then try to move my own, and stand, and collapse.

"There, there." David scoops me up off the floor and helps me back onto the bench. I can feel his knees bending, then straightening. "It just takes a little getting used to."

Once I'm sure I know whose limbs are whose, I touch his knee again. I feel it: warmth, weight, even a sort of pleasure. The simple, frank, sensual pleasure of human touch. The sort of thing you don't think about until you dislocate it and turn it inside out and feel it from a new angle.

"Would you be willing to take your pants off?" I ask.

"Of course. You want to test unimpeded sensation; that's sensible." David stands and turns away to kick off his shoes and shuck off his jeans; I can feel the fabric brushing over his legs.

His legs are hairless, uniform in color. At the hem of his boxers, I see part of the seam between his prosthetic and what's left of his bioleg: a thick, uneven line of scar tissue. "Don't worry," he says quietly, seeing where I'm looking. "You're thinking about an elective removal, so you wouldn't have this kind of scarring."

I brush my fingertips up his calf, the back of his knee, the inside of his thigh. A ripple of something goes up my spine; it feels good, better than I expected.

"This isn't exactly what it feels like for you, is it?" I ask. "The signals from your prosthetic are being filtered through my own brain."

"That's true. Sensation is subjective," he agrees mildly. "Feels nice, though, doesn't it?"

"You seem happy with your legs," I say, pulling back my hand.

"Happy? Of course I am." He sits down next to me again, and I can feel as he stretches out his bare legs and admires them. "They're ten times stronger and more functional than my own legs would have been. Highly customizable. And how would you evaluate their sensation?"

Again, to make sure I'm not imagining it, I rest my hand on his thigh. I touch my own leg for a comparison. It's difficult to distinguish between the two sensations. I close my eyes, moving my hand between my own leg and his.

"Similar to the feelings from my own limbs. Very similar," I concede.

"Well then—you have your answer, don't you?" he beams at me.

Hard to argue with that. "You've seen the specs for the Xtek All-Rounder, right?" I ask.

"Yeah, I've seen it," he nods. "A gorgeous piece of hardware. Lots of room for customization, too. Not like some other models that try to lock you out of your own body."

"So why don't you get one or two?" I ask him. "They'd be better than your original arms."

David looks down at his hands. He has beautiful hands, huge and ungainly and pockmarked with burns and scars from all his tinkering. He examines his ragged nails, his raw knuckles, the birthmark on the inside of his left wrist. And he doesn't speak.

"You're attached to your original parts—aren't you?"

"Well, I don't have very many of them," he snaps, showing a frayed temper. Then his eyes soften, and he's himself again. "Yes. I guess I am. If they were irreparably damaged, I'd replace my arms without a second thought—but as long as they work ..."

He trails off, and I don't push him. For all that he's the expert on prosthetics, and the most heavily modified cyborg I've ever met, he's never made a voluntary mod like I'm considering.

"What are you going to do?" he asks.

I sit and I feel his leg and I don't answer, not yet.

Before surgery, I had a ten-minute consultation with the surgeon to walk me through the procedure.

"For an amputation, it's surprisingly gentle," she told me, gesturing at her diagram. "We won't even need to cut any bone."

She got as far as the part where they cut the ligaments and pop the humerus right out of its socket when I grabbed her trash can and threw up in it. She called in a janitor and referred me to a counselor for three mandatory sessions before I would be allowed the surgery.

I didn't tell David about any of that. It seemed insensitive. He hadn't had a choice about his removals, after all, so I didn't want to get too precious about mine.

"May I see it?" David asks eagerly, reaching for the left arm as soon as I enter. He ignores my unaltered right hand, extended for a conventional handshake.

"Go ahead."

He touches the new left elbow, guiding me to his worktable and sitting me down at a stool. I'm wearing a short-sleeved shirt. I knew he would want to examine the arm.

"How does it feel?" he asks, smoothing his hand over the forearm and bending close to get a better look. I can feel his breath warm and strange on the new skin.

"The connection site is still pretty sore. I'll be on painkillers for a couple more weeks, and I'm not allowed to lift heavy objects for three months while my shoulder muscles recover."

"Yes, of course—the removal must be a difficult recovery," he murmurs, taking the hand in his and testing the fingers.

They took a cast of my original left hand and modeled the new one on it. It looks pretty much the same, only the skin is smoother, the cuticles perfect, the nails uniform and flawless. I had a crazy-awesome scar on my left palm, a memento from my younger, stupider years of woodworking. It's gone now.

"It's beautiful work—you chose well," he says, manipulating the hand gently, pressing with his thumb to feel the movements of its internal armature. When he looks at me, it's with more warmth than before.

"Do you want to feel it?" I offer. "Like you let me feel your legs."

"You'd let me wire in? It's brand new."

"Why not? It won't do any harm, will it?"

"Let's crosswire," he suggests, his voice a low, eager rumble.

It takes some doing. He has to connect the arm to his system, and bypass some of the usual security, and then get everything hooked up so that the new arm and his legs are sending signals to both our brains.

67

Then he sits beside me on his workbench and holds my hand. He closes his eyes and doesn't speak.

"You're right," he says, after a long silence. "It feels the same."

I realize, then, that he had no way of comparison, that he could never feel the certainty I'd felt. He'd lost his legs as a child, must have just woken up one day in the hospital with new parts. He had only the vague childhood memory of what organic legs felt like, had never been able to simply compare, as I did, the signals from an original leg and his replacement legs. Maybe no one had ever thought to offer him the signals from their artificial limb to allow him to compare.

But here he has his own hand, and my replacement hand, both connected to his brain, and he can feel through his own nervous system that the sensations are not so different.

His shoulders are visibly lower, his eyes milder. I wonder if he feels relief, or if he's simply taking in the strange pleasure at experiencing an extra limb's worth of sensation. In a way, I enjoy being wired into his legs.

He takes my hand and rests it on his knee and he laughs.

In a way, we aren't touching each other at all. My machine is resting on top of his machine, that's all. But both of us are experiencing the exact same physical sensations at that moment: we are sharing three limbs. Briefly, madly, I wish I could both replace our whole bodies and wire into each other and feel *everything*.

He hasn't spoken, hasn't told me what he wants or what he thinks, but I have to assume that he feels the same warmth and comfort I feel from the touch. So I pet his knee and thigh, and before long he's running his fingers up the inside of my forearm and it's nicer than it has any business being. It's just an arm, just a leg, nothing intimate—electrical impulses, that's all.

"Did you take the train here?" he asks. He holds and strokes my hand; he is careful not to lean against me, not to put any strain on my recently amputated shoulder.

"Yeah. Why?"

"I'll pay for a cab home. You shouldn't be in crowds so early; someone could bump into you. And let me send you home with some tea. I've got this herbal blend with *lei gong teng* that my mom swears helps prevent immune system rejection."

It's nice that someone's excited about the arm. Everyone else I show it to gets a weird look on their face, like they don't know what to say. I'm not usually into traditional medicine, and I don't know if it does anything, but I drink David's tea every night before bed.

Things I no longer feel with my left arm:

- goosebumps, or hair-raising when it's cold
- muscular strain of any kind
- fatigue
- pain in a traditional sense
- ticklishness
- bumping my funny bone
- popping the joints in my fingers
- pins and needles

I don't precisely miss any of those sensations. I do notice they're gone. Sometimes I go out and walk a few miles just so my legs burn and I remember they're made of muscle.

There was no way to know in advance if I had a sentimental attachment to my original body parts. The pre-amputation counseling didn't help. The only way to find out was to cut one off. I'm still not entirely sure.

"Do you think you're going to do the other arm?" David asks.

Lately when I visit, he wires us into each other as soon as I arrive. At first he asked, but then it became so routine he didn't need to anymore. I'm used to feeling the carpet under his bare feet when he walks, and he particularly loves handing me a cup of hot tea so he can feel the warmth on my palm.

"I'm considering it," I say. "Just having the left is surprisingly handy, but I'm definitely feeling like the right is holding me back, now, like I'm always having to compensate for it. And two-handed tasks feel lopsided, which is driving me nuts ..."

"But?"

"I want to give it at least a year before I take the plunge. Make sure I'm still happy with lefty before I chop off righty."

"Very sensible," he says.

I'm glad he doesn't mind. I almost wonder if he wants me to get another limb, just so he can feel it too. Frankly I've thought about it, even wondered what would be the harm in getting all three remaining limbs replaced. But the recovery just for an arm took a while, and I had to take time off work, and I hear the recovery for a leg is brutal, and no one voluntarily does two legs at once. So I'd better not rush it, is all.

At Christmas, my mother threw a fit.

I was trying to help in the kitchen. I took a cast-iron pan out of the oven with my left arm. I didn't bother putting on an oven mitt because why would I? My mother saw and started crying.

"I'm heat-rated up to five hundred degrees, Mom," I said, which just made her cry harder.

Christmas with my family is never great, but this one set a record. My mother was upset all week, kept saying that she made that arm for me and I just threw it away, kept asking me to promise I wouldn't amputate anything else.

It was tiring.

"Do you like me better with my new arm?" I ask, because I've wanted to ask ever since I saw the look in his eyes when lefty made its debut.

David takes a big gulp of his beer and peers into the bottom of the glass. "Is that a serious question?"

"Yeah."

"No. Of course not. That's a fucked-up thing to even think."

"You invite me over twice as often as you used to," I point out. And he touches me now, I don't say.

"I know other cyborgs, you know," he grumbles. "Lots of them, many with more replacements than you. I go to meetups."

"Do you wire into anyone else?" I ask. Suddenly I realize I'd be devastated if he said yes, if it turns out every night a week he's sharing nerve signals with a different person.

"No." He blinks into his empty glass. "No one else ever asked."

I'm online, sourcing burl wood for a coffee table I'm working on, when I notice the ad for the first time.

SEXY SINGLE CYBORGS IN YOUR AREA /// click here

The flashing text is accompanied by a grainy video loop of a woman dragging her tongue up and down a highly articulated metal phallus. Somewhere along the line, the internet concluded that I'm a fetishist. It's a little offensive.

I turn on a proxy, make sure my virus protection is up, and click the link.

Above the form asking for my credit card information, a free pre-view video features a bare-breasted woman with a prosthetic arm, all exposed metal and wires and blinking LEDs. A custom job, probably for the aesthetics—nothing functional about it. She reaches down, guides the silicone penis of a sexbot inside her, and starts bouncing up and down on it. Midway through the video, she takes off her arm and the camera lingers lovingly on the gleaming metal inside of her shoulder socket. I close the window.

It doesn't do anything for me. I'm not sure what I was expecting.

I don't wait a year to get my second arm done.

After three months, once the shoulder joint was done healing, my left arm was ten times as useful as my right. David helped me customize it, giving me some built-in tools so I don't even have to reach for a screwdriver or a drill. I built him an end table to say thank you.

I forced myself to wait six months, at least, but I was so eager to have my arms match that I couldn't give it another half a year.

This time, I ask David to go with me to the clinic. He's there in the recovery room when I wake up, and he gives me ice chips and very, very gently strokes the back of my new hand to help me integrate the new nerve signals. I don't have any more biological arms to compare the sensation to. It's all memory. But I think it feels the same.

He takes me home—he's never been in my apartment before, I always visit him—and tucks me into bed and leaves me there with books, and a thermos full of his herbal tea, and a big plate of soy nuggets ("Protein promotes healing," he says). He kisses my forehead.

Once I'm strong enough to raise my right arm and use it to brush my teeth, I visit David again. He offered to come to my place, but I don't have the right computer setup for the neural relays.

He crosswires our implants, all four of them, and then I wrap my arms around his waist. He laughs aloud at the sensation, then pulls me against his chest and holds me there for a long time.

This morning I read an article in the news about a couple who got those experimental neural implants—freaky stuff—and tried networking them together. The woman had a massive stroke and is still in an induced coma, not expected to survive.

I didn't bring it up, but David must have read it, too.

"You don't have to worry about this burning out our brains," he said when he fixed the neural relay to the back of my neck. "They were trying to share all their neural activity; obviously that wasn't safe. We're handling less than one percent of that data."

He's no neurologist, and maybe I should have been more cautious about this from the start—but I don't suggest putting a stop to it, and neither does he.

I'm a little sad to find out that full neural crosswiring doesn't work. It could have been good.

David's tipsy when he first suggests sharing motor control. He's a real lightweight, anyway; he's got lower body mass than he looks.

It's like having double vision all through the lower half of my body. At first I try to move my foot and nothing happens, nothing at all. For a moment I panic and think I'm paralyzed, and then I try to get up and David's legs jerk and he falls off the bench.

"See," he says mildly, from the floor, "this is why it's a bad idea to share motor control."

But he gets up and I try again. It's less intuitive than I imagined. He's taller than I am, for one thing, and that throws everything off. I manage to get enough control of his legs to walk him around the room once, but then we sit; I don't want to knock him over again. Instead I rotate his ankles and wiggle his toes and enjoy the sheer strangeness of it, the feeling of inhabiting him.

"I'm going to try your arms now." He announces it, doesn't ask. I already tried his legs, so it's only fair. Actually, I like it a little—the way we've become proprietary about each other's bodies. He's almost entitled to my arms by now; we've both gotten so used to it.

My right arm lifts; it stretches out at a ninety-degree angle from my torso. My hand rotates. Then my arm lifts until it's fully vertical, stretches back until it reaches the limit of its range of motion. He tests both limbs this way, moving the shoulders, elbows, wrists, and fingers through their possible configurations.

Just as I'm thinking how technical he can be, how lacking in imagination, he reaches up and tucks my hair behind my ear. With my own hand. I feel the sensation in my face and my hand, but I don't control it. My hand feels like it's someone else's.

"I'm sorry. Is that strange?" he asks.

I've been dreaming about him. In one dream, we both decide to surprise each other by getting all our remaining limbs replaced. Because it's a dream, there's no expense, no complicated recovery: we just meet at his apartment and we've got eight prosthetic limbs between us and we're a beautiful two-headed spider. We embrace each other and I feel myself holding him and him holding me and he feels himself holding me and me holding him and it's great and then I wake up and I've got just four limbs and I'm cold.

It's adolescent, that's what it is, and embarrassing.

I saw a news segment today about augment addicts. People who get one implant, then another and another until they're half-machine and riddled with medical problems and debt. Their bodies start

73

rejecting their implants. They develop all these weird allergies and autoimmune disorders.

My mother sent me the link. She's usually about that subtle.

I didn't tell David about the news clip. I did ask him, "What would you say if I told you I wanted to get my legs replaced?"

I watch his face. His cheeks flush. His pupils dilate. I can tell he likes the idea, but he doesn't speak for a while.

"We're never going to get there, you know," he says, finally.

"Where?"

"Full replacement. The technology's not there. Probably won't be in our lifetimes. You could replace your legs now, a couple of internal organs, maybe your eyes in a decade or so. You could take it as far as the technology permits—or as far as your income permits—and you'd still be mostly flesh. Can't do the full torso; it's been tried. Genital replacements are lousy, or so I've heard. I've seen a few face augments, too, and they're pretty rough.

"Even if, one day, you could do a full replacement, we'd never be able to crosswire all those signals. Too much data. You'd burn your brain out trying."

I've never talked to him about what I imagined. I don't know how he knows.

"So this is as far as we go?" I ask.

"Yeah. This is as far as we go," he says. "If something breaks down, we replace it, but otherwise, we're keeping our original parts for now." As if he has the right to decide about my parts as well as his. But I can't blame him. I feel something of a right over his biological arms, too, and I'd be devastated if he decided to replace them without asking. He squeezes my hand and asks: "Have you ever heard of the ship of Theseus?"

"Theseus?"

"Greek hero. Fought the Minotaur and stuff ... not important. The story goes that the people of Athens kept his ship in their harbor for hundreds of years—and this was a wooden ship, so parts of it would wear out or rot. So they replaced the rotten planks with new wood, and the ship stayed seaworthy.

"But if you replace every plank of a ship, one at a time, until none of the wood left is original—is it the same ship? If I replace every part of myself—new legs, new liver, new eyes, and eventually new everything, whenever that is possible—would I still be me?"

"Humans aren't ships," I answer. "If I were going to replace my brain, then I'd start to worry, but … ."

"You think the brain is the core of you, and everything else is accessories?"

"Sure, don't you?"

"But your new limbs are integrated into your nervous system. Sending and receiving signals to and from your brain."

"And yours."

"And mine," he agrees.

I had not considered that we were partially merging our nervous systems. That was not what I intended to do when I replaced first one arm, then the next. It was not, I know, what he intended to do when he crosswired us for the first time. But, of course, that was what we were doing.

"What if you take the old wooden planks," David continues, and it takes me a minute to realize he's still talking about the ship, "and reassemble them in a museum somewhere? Which ship is the original? Are they two different ships, or the same?"

I don't know where the ship begins and ends. I don't know where my body begins and ends. The ship is just a concept, atoms and electrical impulses neatly arranged, which I classify as my body. Some of those atoms are old; some of them are new. Some of those electrical impulses are contained within my biological tissue; others are being sent wirelessly into David's biological tissue.

My arms are part of my body. His legs are part of my body. Distinctions between my artificial limbs / my biomass / his artificial limbs / his biomass are semantic. I can define my body in a way that includes him, or parts of him, if I want to. And I do.

I sit on our lap and wrap our arms around his neck. I feel my weight on our legs, the softness of his hair between our fingers.

"They're the same ship," I say out loud, and David smiles. He smiles as if he understands what I'm trying to say, which is good, because I'm not much of a feelings-talker.

Neither is he, of course. Which I've always liked about him.

With All Souls Still Aboard

Premee Mohamed

*T*oo late I catch him gnawing the console buttons, levering them off one by one, and I cause the next disaster swooping in to stop him: he looks up, startled, not guilty, and something snags. An awful little *click*, and then, inevitably, blood.

His screams preclude even a cursory assessment. When he cannot be consoled, it's clear he's done more damage than I thought. I put him on my hip even though at four he is almost too gangly to get off the ground, and call a hover to our dentist.

"It's snapped off at the root," she says over his listless sobs.

"Okay? I mean, it's a baby tooth. It would have fallen out anyway."

"Yes, but …"

They pull what remains, pack the socket with anesthetic epoxy, letting him choose the color (bright purple, silver sparkles). Emergency over, we could walk back, but I call another hover instead, as a treat. He is silent as we float above the city, not looking out the windows. These things we forget. These rides used to be his favorite pastime; now they are the source only of nightmares.

"Why were you chewing on the holo, Rook?" I keep my voice light, nonjudgmental. In answer he merely glances at me, as if it were too obvious to explain.

Back home, we run through the nightly routine at half-speed, justifiably, it's been a long day: I've taken him places he didn't want to go, a world of pain; robots; brisk, gloved strangers. Snack, water, teeth, bath, story, kiss. I wait for him to ask for another story, but he is immobile and glass-eyed from the little rainbow painkiller patch on his neck. He doesn't say goodnight.

In the morning, Rook is groggy and has apparently forgotten the new gap in his bite, wincing as he sleepily bites down on his oatmeal-cushioned spoon.

"Owie," I say in sympathy. "Not gonna do that again, are we buddy?"

He shakes his head.

"Attaboy."

As I work, I keep one eye on my own monitor, the other on his. Special guest for his cohort today, bearing one of Rook's favorite things: a snake of (to my mind) bone-chilling heft and length, particularly compared to the dozen preschoolers flocking around it like starlings. Its scales mess with the camera somehow, so that it seems festooned with small screens each showing the same fuzzy show.

I lean close as Rook waits his turn, strokes the snake with the back of his hand when invited, then wanders off to the reading corner. He seems slumped, diminished in some way. Maybe it is just the imperial bulk of the snake. For a second I wonder if I forgot to take the patch off his neck, but a quick pan and zoom shows the bare skin.

God forbid you send your kid to school doped to the gills. They'd forgive me though, I think, for all the wrong reasons.

After I pick him up, we head to the park. He digs and mutters, occasionally returning to my bench for grapes or Goldfish or to inform me that reticulated pythons don't live in sand, their habitat is arboreal, was I watching?

"Yes, I saw it. I thought it was a very beautiful snake. Why are they teaching four-year-olds the word 'arboreal'?"

"It means it lives in the trees, Mama."

"Thanks, bud."

I watch him make his strange and careful city (orthogonally planned, temples and public squares arranged to the cardinal points: what is he *doing*, how is he so self-possessed, his hands are still dimpled with baby fat) and I think: Live for him. One tragedy is plenty. Two would be unthinkable. The end of the universe.

New trees have been planted around the park all summer, their leaves intertwined with small transparent solar panels, casting rainbows on the turf. Barely six months we've had this back: the ordinary sky, I mean. The ordinary sun. Amazing how quickly you forget the way it's supposed to look.

"Mrs. Sullivan?"

Oh Lord. I don't even turn; the voice will be from CISS, of course, with some horrible form to fill out or awkward request to make (photos, mementos, something like that). They always pick these men with kind, paternal faces. "Yes?"

"I'm Major Alvey. May I speak to you for a moment?"

"Do you say KISS or SISS?"

"Beg pardon?"

I give up, gesture at the bench. Alvey is middle-aged, perhaps seventy, salt-and-pepper hair, a thick black mustache, stars and moons and other weird planetoids in precious metals stuck to his uniform. A bigshot of some kind. Sent specifically, I think, not to persuade me to do anything, but to impress upon me that an even bigger bigshot arranged this. That they took this man who must cost thousands of dollars an hour and dropped him off at the park to speak in person.

"I didn't know your husband well," he says, and I flinch with relief, with not being subjected to the usual ordeal, as small as it is. "But ..."

While he trails off, I train my eyes on my son, back to us, his bright red T-shirt and green shorts giving the impression of a flower sprouting from the sand.

At school they said, *Yes, a lot of people died when it happened.* But at home what I had to explain was that Dada had died.

Sheer incomprehension at first. I had to pull out the big guns: you never want to compare a loved one to (say) the most recent glowzard, but the wretched thing is, the talk of death was fresh, we knew what it meant to die, *No, buddy, Miss Rosie isn't going to wake up, that's right, she's dead, that's what it means.*

It means we (and this was a mistake) put her into the incinerator, because technically (don't say it) she's a biohazard now, you can't just have bodies inside your house, and there's a little form to fill out. *Now, that's not what happened to Dada …* but I'm sorry, and it is.

It hit him weeks later. Dada had been gone before, yes, but now he was never coming back. Confusion gave way at last to grief. We cried, ate, answered a thousand calls, forgot, remembered again, cried again, didn't shut our eyes. When Rook finally blacked out from sleep deprivation at the park, I pulled him from the stroller and let it follow us home, wanting to feel his heart beating under my hands.

I thought: I only have enough fortitude to keep *one* of us alive in a way that resembles real life.

Yes, I'm her. I'm the noble widow. That's why they stare at me at the dentist, at the school pickup. Because there are gold star families, and then there is this.

When Matt died saving the world, he catapulted us into something proximal to heroism: bathed in a safe and saintly golden light, subjected to handpicked experts only. Like this guy.

Alvey says, "We'd worked together for a year prior to the *Integral.* But he impressed me. Now, you can imagine the Institute finds impressive people, refines them, supercharges them. Matthew stood out even amongst all those folks."

My heart hammers with the effort of not weeping, which is something like holding your breath far past the point where everything goes black and sparkly. "What do you want, Major?"

He's futzing with his phone, which means forms are involved; I know the routine. He says, "If we can agree that Matthew was one in a m—well, he was maybe one of a kind, I wonder what you will think about what they told me to ask you."

"Which is?"

Involuntarily he glances at Rook, lying down now, dreamily running a toy car over the roofs of his sand city. "Well," he says, "we're still working on the investigation, as you know."

"Yes?"

Back home I make dinner and we eat while watching *Blossoms of the Hollow* (New Adventures) but I can't get down so much as a sip of water. Everything is ash.

My therapist would tell me this is the body's way of concentrating what is essential to keep you alive when you are in shock, ignoring the nonessential. Does my body know that I haven't (say) been struck by lightning, or lost half my blood? I very much think it does not.

"No," I had said, and Alvey said, "I'll come back and you can tell me if it's still a no."

Snack, water, teeth, bath, story, bed. Rook is tired to the point of lethargy, fighting to keep his eyes open, but tonight he does insist on a second story, then a third. I wonder how he ate so much at dinner; little kids *appear* to be made out of electricity and air, till they fall asleep and you realize that no, they are heavier than lead, they are heavier than neutron stars.

I eel my arm out from under him, shake feeling back into it. Who can I call? Not my therapist, sister, best friend, mom. A thousand people said, *Tell me if there's anything you need, anything,* after the news, and they all meant it, but I can't. The problem is that I don't know what I need.

In the kitchen I turn off the volume on the countertop monitor and switch it from the sleeping Rook to the recording CISS sent me, as if it is a crystal ball.

Thirty seconds: Matt's face, the face I had studied so much more than my own, the humorous, sensitive, expectant face already pitted and bleeding from the broken glass swarming the control room, hotly lit in the jetting flames of the instruments, his teeth bared with pain, not releasing the steering apparatus, his copilots, dear Elise and Nasir, already dead and rattling in their seats, the orderly lights of the city below, the ocean, and then, in the last seconds, count it down, five, four, looking up at the camera, meeting its stare, meeting mine, the eyes ringed with bruises, saying, *I love you, goodbye.*

And now the organization who killed him and his crew and 46,000 other people, while successfully saving about 9 billion others, are telling me that they have found him.

No. They have found seven fragments of bone, DNA finger-printed beyond any shadow of a doubt, because somehow, in that crushing darkness and salt water, living cells remained.

Alvey said, *There were certain conditions under which a long running, unpublicized program at CISS considered the application of apluripotent cytosynthetic neogenesis.*

I said, *You mean cloning.*

And my entire body went into shock and my bones became ful-gurites, and I know we spoke for eleven more minutes because my watch says we did but I don't remember any of it now. It was just a few hours ago. The sun is still in the sky. *If you allow us …*

That salvaged handful of Matt's cells, barely double digits, are on execution row. Poor little ocean-soaked, battered things, poor sur-vivors. In about five days, Alvey told me, the nutrient solution, the electromagnetic field, the helpful nanobots, nothing will suffice to keep them from apoptotic suicide. *They want to die. Unless we set them on a new path. Unless we …*

No, I said.

Not a real egg; that's the secret of it, or the trick of the project. Of course there's been animal cloning for decades. They stuff a nu-cleus into a donor egg and zap it with a cattle prod or whatever. Suc-cess rates aren't high enough to make it economical and it's fallen out of favor. And those CRISPR babies, back when I was in grade school.

But what CISS has been creating are wholly *made* things: an artificial membrane surrounding a meticulously formulated ovum-mimicking jelly, twenty times bigger than a real human egg, into which a nucleus from anyone, any age, could grow. I had pictured the brightly colored lychee or mango or raspberry bobas we spooned onto our frozen yogurt, and nearly laughed.

Truth be told, what I had hoped they would one day offer me (and I will never tell anyone this) was … I don't know. A different preservation and resurrection, some kind of artificial intelligence.

In those first dark days I had thought: If they copied Matt into a computer, my grief would not be assuaged at all, but my pain would ease. That is, I think I could live with an artificial Matt and I think I could live with no Matt (we are experimenting with the truth of this now, Rook and I, we are doing a real-time feasibility study on it), but I don't know if I can live with a Matt in a tank.

In the morning after drop-off I glance at my work monitor—and I don't *have* to work now, of course, what with the insurance payout, but I do—and go for a walk instead.

Of course the money fixed nothing. It brought back no one. The tumbling zeroes like circus acrobats in my account every month, they are jokes. Circuses used to have animals, or anyway the movies tell me they did; Rook has never seen one like that. As far as he knows, a circus consists of people giving up their time to decorate his with glittering memories.

Outside, I glance up automatically to see how big the asteroid is: and it's gone, because it's been gone for six months. Almost seven. Because that is what Matt did.

The sun sits high in a clear sky, the air cool and damp. Our house has become not sanctuary but fortress, I realize, and that's precisely why I have to get out of it. Not just to walk the kid back and forth from school and the park and his friends' houses. Out, out. Into the saved world.

I'm not the first person to have something like this dilemma, I know that. More than a hundred years ago families wept quietly in court as they begged permission to use a dead soldier's sperm (or to destroy it, sometimes). But I *am* the first to have this exact one.

What I hoped when I saw the crash was that Matt had been *obliterated*. That he had been reduced not even into atoms but their components, protons, neutrons, into their components in turn, strange particles behaving in unscientific fashions. I hoped that he felt no pain. For even a moment.

And now those seven fragments of bone.

As I walk, I want the world to decide. Take it out of my hands, I instruct everything around me. Crossing the bridge I see the shadows of ducks on the shallow stream and I think: If there is an even number of ducks, I'll call Alvey and say yes. If it's odd, I'll say no.

I pause, lean on the weathered wood, count as if Rook were with me: no. If that squirrel sees me and runs up the tree on the left, yes. If the one on the right, no. That's another no. If the plane overhead is Air Canada, yes; if it's anything else then no. But there's the leaf and the logo. Yes.

But truthfully, no one can help me decide this. Now more than ever I wish Matt were here to debate this, talk it out. He's the only one I want to talk to. That kind ghost who I wished would haunt me when awake, but only ever arrives in dreams.

In sleep he is truly ghostlike: deeply confused every time I explain the crash. The malfunction, the diversion, the desperate panic as it was realized where the *Integral* would impact, the way he had burned his hands to the bone fighting to ditch in the ocean instead.

Did we make it? he asks, and I say *Yes*, but I mean, *Not quite.*

No, darling. The mission was successful, but the ship, returning, lost control and was somersaulting into a city of 10 million people. At the last moment, and they do mean last, you regained control for a moment. The *Integral* clipped the coast and disintegrated. The important thing is: you saved more lives than you took. You saved the world. The entire world.

The asteroid had a name, the way you want the murderer in a mystery novel to have a name. Tells you who you're dealing with. A string of numbers and digits like a scream on a keyboard, and green, bright green, like a gemstone up there with a spotlight behind it. Coming at us. Murderous jewel, changing the color of the sky.

Before the launch, we told Rook how Dada and his friends were going to knock away the green thing in the sky. Yes, like the thing that killed all the dinosaurs. Just like that. But bigger.

We didn't say: We've known it was coming for about four years, since just before you were born, when something else, we're not sure what, smacked into it and knocked it toward us. Quietly but persistently all the space and defense agencies have been telling it to fuck off. *Trying* to tell it. The effect was like throwing poppyseeds at a battleship, as it turned out. Nothing diverted it, nothing even chipped it. It was like it had intent.

And then the tach-drive was invented, and they raced to cram it into a ship, and that's why Dada is going to space again.

Okay?

Yes, okay. Save the dinosaurs.

No, well, we … yes, okay buddy.

My phone buzzes in my pocket: the school, but why are they calling instead of just messaging? "Hello?"

"Morning, Eddie." Rook's teacher, and by now I know the calmer she sounds, the worse something is. That's how they get you: your life breaks in a moment but they have to sound like this moment isn't it.

There's nowhere to sit down. I lock my knees, I pretend I am a tree, or an ex-tree, the mast of a ship carrying a Greek army home triumphant from war. "Hi! What's up?"

I haven't been to the hospital since Rook was born, which isn't to say that we've been unusually healthy or lucky, just that there's been nothing our little neighborhood clinic couldn't handle. It's a vast building, festooned with thick ivy through which its lights twinkle like stars in broad daylight.

I am met at the door by school staff, some assistant or intern, and we go through the precautions, and we walk to the elevator, and I can't hear anything he's saying. Whatever Alvey needs from me recedes to a mote at the back of my mind; there will be other, more important decisions to be made in the next little while, it seems.

Everyone is solicitous but brisk, I am too well-known as the hero's widow, I am supposed to be brave despite my bereavement. "He had a neurological event at school," one of the doctors tells me before we go into the room. "They hovered him here first, and called you second."

"Good."

"My thoughts precisely. Seconds matter. If it were one of my kids … in we go, Ed."

A seizure, they mean. I'm allowed one glimpse of my son, half-awake, his face green and black with recent bruising, outfitted with a dozen slender, transparent tubes streaking his face and arms like water. Then I'm shepherded into a little, white-tiled alcove fitted out with a chair and a tablet set into a desk, so I can fill out his full medical history.

I am mentally numb but also, I note with faint amusement, physically: I can barely feel the touchscreen under my fingers.

He regressed for a little while. Remember that? Wouldn't talk, demanded bottles, diapers, which I thought he would barely remember, he was potty-trained so early. Weird little bug. Refused to walk. We had to stroll him around or he wouldn't sleep. I thought, one more thing to grieve. How am I going to fit it in, how am I going to … to *schedule* it. That must have been what he was doing the other day. Always a chewer, when he was crawling.

He's never seen the crash footage on the holo. I always made sure of that. Only the launch, which was so bright and happy and hopeful, like a choreographed stage show. Reaching his hands into the light, reaching for Dad.

What they want. The CISS people. What they want is not an heir. Not another Rook. And not a copy, not another Matt, either. What made him who he was is not in those fragments of bone. Stop thinking about it, I tell myself, and I use my sleeve to remove the tears on the cloudy plastic surface of the tablet, then go back and correct the changed answers. Stop it. What they want is—

—you know, I looked for the tooth shard when we got home. Rook told the dentist that he didn't swallow anything, but with all that blood, it would have just washed right down. Or I suppose the vacuum got it. Could I message the house, ask it to check the filter? I don't know that it would know what to look for, though.

We never told Rook about the tooth fairy. Thought we had a couple years yet.

"We're knocking it back with axonomycin," the doctor tells me later, though I'm not sure when; I'm muzzy, neck sore from sleeping in their Caretakers Hideaway, a hideous though quiet room with nap pods and subdued white noise, painted to resemble some kind of geographically impossible forest (tigers mingling with moose; giraffes stooping to sniff capybaras).

"What?"

"The infection, Edeline. It's very aggressive, but we can be aggressive, too."

"The wh … I'm sorry. I'm having trouble concentrating. The … ?"

She explains again, quickly, looking at her watch. Other lives to save, I guess. The multi-bacterial infection that started with a driven-in sliver of tooth in the inner surface of Rook's cheek, missed by the dentist ("So if I were you, I'd probably start looking into legal action for malpractice."), and raced through his body, chewing somehow through the blood-brain barrier and causing the seizure.

I don't want to sue our dentist. "But he'll …"

"We'll keep you updated on all developments," the doctor says, and I'm left staring after her, rubbing my neck.

Rook's room is sealed off now and they've put him under to conserve his resources, keep the tubes and devices still. I spend hours staring blankly through the viewing window at his unmoving body, watching the lines on the monitor rise and fall, analyzing every deviation. I want Matt here but I don't, I can't bear to think of him seeing this.

If Rook d … I don't want to think the words. But listen. If Rook dies, CISS won't make the same offer. Will they. No, they were saving the entire secret project for someone like Matt, their golden boy, the genius, the special one. (The kid isn't going to die. He'll be fine. He's just in a coma, that's all. They're filling him with chemicals and he's going to be fine. He'll be fine.)

But if he does die, he'll be gone. And gone forever, in the way that normal people understand gone. Only for Matt would that unbreakable rule be broken, for the first time in human history, for the first time since things shuffled out of the ocean in fact. A loved one returning from the dead. Not an imitation. Him. But not him.

With death we understand that the loved one is no longer available to love, only our memories. That nothing new will ever happen. This is your life now, death says, forever.

Till now. This is the choice they have asked me to make, to take away that "forever."

That green sky. Waking up every morning and looking at it, the terror, thinking: *We'll all die.* The planet will be smashed into shards and how do you come to grips with that? Inexorable, slow-motion murder, the creep in the closet leaping out with a knife but moving so slowly as to be nearly immobile, and you, also immobile, unable to move. People did kill themselves. They made clubs for it, societies they said. Cults really. First hundreds then thousands and then the news simply stopped reporting on it.

Shall we, the doctors say, and they won't say *Pull the plug*. We don't say that any more.

No, I tell them. We don't know what happens next. So no. No. And they don't.

I've forgotten about the other deadline; Alvey finally runs me to ground. A strange odor about him, I think, till I realize that he simply smells of the outside air, of an ordinary September I mean. An ivy leaf has gotten stuck under his collar. How did that happen?

"Mrs. Sullivan."

"Major Alvey." I don't want him to follow me into Rook's room, but he does anyway and I find myself powerless to shove him back out. At least he is another human being with a semi-recognizable face who does not bear me immediate ill will. We go through the necessary protocols, hold our breath under the mist, and Rook waves weakly as we come in, darting a glance of cartoonish suspicion at Alvey then back at me.

"Hey, my guy. Does your mouth hurt?" I sit on the bed, stroke the damp swirl of his hair, like a spiral galaxy, twin arms twirling away from each other. "You need a haircut."

"No I don't. I'm gonna grow my hair till I can swing off it like, um."

"Rapunzel."

"Yeah. Can we go home? I'm tired of the medicine." He glances up at the major again, compressing his chapped lips. I know what comes next. "What's his favorite dinosaur?"

"Triceratops," Alvey says, without moving.

Hey, my guy, I want to say. I figured it out. I know why this all happened. I bought a new holo, actually. With a touchscreen. Because you're really not going to do it again, are you? This hole, this void that your father left in both our lives, gave life and light to everyone else's. Our emptiness will fill back up one day too. Don't try to kill it. It'll die on its own.

"Mama, the asteroid never hit us. Does that mean the dinosaurs will come back?"

"Well, no. It doesn't work that way."

His brow furrows, and I repress laughter, watching the gears turn as he essays causality, reverse-causality, various things the grownups have told him about asteroids, why you can't extrapolate (apparently) from the knowledge of one to the knowledge of all, what his father did *exactly* in regard to that asteroid (in a minute I suspect he will ask whether if Dada had permitted the asteroid to hit us, would the dinosaurs come back).

He finally says, "Okay," in a voice of trembling disappointment. A nurse bustles in, elbows me aside (I am no longer considered fragile, the gesture says, I am no longer about to break, the worst is therefore past), and swaps out his IV bags, taps things on the monitor, whips off the patch on his neck (spaceship), and replaces it with a new one (some kind of smiling monster).

Chaos, I think. Chance. Dinosaurs looking up at their own whitening sky, the infinite doors of all their future opportunities about to slam shut. It didn't matter what any of them had chosen or were about to choose; it was taken from them, all the next steps, whatever those were. And they didn't even know.

And for almost seven months, I didn't know what I wanted, but now I think what I want is for there to be an opening. To keep some doors open. Any chance, for anything, is less final than death. What you can want to keep of someone is not they themselves but potential, possibility, and isn't that what Matt would want? Hope, to say it flat out: what is love but the hope that someone loves you back?

No matter what ends up in that tank, I don't want to say no to it. They gave me this choice. They could just as easily not have. That, too, is part of this intertwining tree, no, forest, of maybes, of maybe-nots. It's never happened before, this particular branch. Let it live at least for a little while. I'm the first person this has ever happened to. May I not be the last.

Alvey watches—I can feel his gaze—as I take out my phone, and pull up the form he gave me, and uncheck "No" and check "Yes" and put the date on it and press my thumb to the screen. The CISS forms give you a lot of time to change your mind; you have to hold it there for what feels like forever. Sixty seconds. Rook watches the countdown with drowsy interest.

"What's that, Mama?"

"I'll tell you later."

"Am I ugly?" he adds, in a tone not of distress but light, academic interest.

"Oh, sure," I tell him. "You're uglier than a Rhamphorhynchus. And it's your fault, by the way, that I've had to learn how to say that."

"I like Rhamphorhynchus. I mean my mouth. The doctor said my tooth looked rotted."

"Rotten. He was just trying to be funny. Which he wasn't. I'll go kick his butt."

He laughs.

And anyway, I almost add, I don't want you to grow up thinking you'll only be loved if you're perfect. I just want you to grow up.

My thumb is still on the screen, it wasn't so many generations ago that our ancestors worked underground, was it? Matt's family silver, mine coal, and now the descendants live high in a clear and cloudless sky, counting down.

We look out the window as the final numbers vanish into the *yes*.

More Than Nine

Beth Cato

I liked to think that Forty-Two jumped in my lap during planetary descents because he was trying to comfort me, not because
he knew I would aggressively pet him the whole time the ship's
autopilot did its thing.

"At least Cambria is a pretty world," I babbled. "Looks almost
like Earth." The ship began to rumble through the atmosphere. I
couldn't feel Forry's purring amid the larger vibrations, but I took
in his softness, his heat, his soothing presence. When a small lurch
caused my stomach to practically do a backflip, Forry pressed into
me, his head nuzzling between the harness belts.

Then we were through. The flight smoothed out. Clouds wisped
over the windows. I sighed, deflating.

A few months before, autopilot had reset during a descent. I'd
been scared about my own demise, sure, but it truly terrified me
that Forry might go down with me—a funny thing to fear, since
he was already pretty much immortal. If this, his forty-second iteration, died, Renew-Anew back on Earth would know and start
gestating his next clone. If I was toast, Forty-Three would go to my
cousin Hanzo.

"Time to work," I said to Forry, nudging his rump as I unfastened
my harness. With a twitch of his black-striped tail, he hopped onto

the spot on the dash that'd been a favorite of Forty-One. Forry had likewise claimed it when he came aboard as a kitten, back when I was a kid and my mom captained. Forry had adapted fast to life aboard, almost like he'd known everything already.

I changed into my work suit and queued up my drone swarm. Their mosquito-like buzz filled the room. Holstering my pistol, I returned to the cockpit as the landing gear descended.

My job was straightforward: when monitors on far-flung real estate holdings failed, I was sent to check things out. Usually, that meant replacing broken tech. Rarely, it meant confrontations with squatters. I'd never been in a shoot-out, but my tranq setting had saved me a few times.

The window showed gray skies and gangly trees similar to coastal evergreens in Earth's northern hemisphere. The ship thumped as we set down.

"What do you think, Forry?" I leaned closer to the glass as I stroked his back. He stared outward, tail lashing as strange stork-like birds flew past. "I don't think those would be good for your diet." He was fifteen now. His kidney function had started to decline in the past year. It frustrated me to no end that getting a whole new cloned cat was free, but I didn't make enough to cover drastic treatments to keep Forty-Two alive. We had to make-do with a special diet and maybe some subcutaneous fluid treatments later on.

My drones, like a mechanical cloud, followed me to the hatch. As I trotted down the ramp, my security drones split off to establish a perimeter around the ship.

As customary, I walked around to the front to give Forry a wave. He stared down at me like a tiger from his jungle perch. "Guard the fort, Forry!" I called.

He yawned as if to tell me I had nothing to worry about. I laughed to myself as I headed out. Smartest cat in the universe, my Forry.

I wasn't the first in my family to think that. My ancestor, Sheila Hatsumi-Perkins, founded Renew-Anew. She also loved her cat Murgatroyd more than anything. She established that a single clone of Murgatroyd would exist in perpetuity in the care of a family member deemed the most loving and responsible. Over the years, we'd lost any stake in the company or semblance of wealth, but we continued to love Murgatroyd, generation after generation.

Brisk air caused me to notch up the heat of my suit as I clambered along a shore of flat, eroded rocks. Thanks to an endowment, a lunar university owned this isle and had established a bot system to monitor wildlife and climate data. Their feed had died eleven days ago. I understood why when I saw the relay box.

"What, was this struck by lightning?" I muttered. The small box was charred and half-melted. I sent half my drones back to the ship for a new relay while I interfaced with the outlying units. To my relief, the sensors were still operative, simply unable to deploy their data.

I had a visual on my returning drones when two alarms in sequence pinged my system. A trespasser was near my ship. A trespasser was in my ship.

With a quick signal to my drones to abandon their load, I ran as fast as I dared across the uneven rocks. On my visual overlay, I brought up security footage from a minute before. A shiny blur had moved toward the front of the ship, right where I had waved farewell to Forry, then rounded the back. The figure accessed the manual entry pad by the hatch—how did they get my code? The hatch lowered, and in they went.

The closeup feed from inside the ship left no doubt about the infiltrator's identity. That hunched, humanoid figure with iridescent skin was the stuff of my childhood nightmares.

A third alarm: the trespasser was exiting my ship. I brought up the live feed to see the figure speed away, Forry clutched to its chest.

A Mariposa had stolen my cat.

I circled through my ship. The alien—the *extinct* alien—had only taken Forty-Two.

The species had been dubbed the Mariposa, the Spanish word for butterfly, because of the silvery iridescent sheen of their skins. Their war with humanity had been fierce and brief, a first contact scenario that went wrong in every way. Only afterward were human linguists heeded—the Mariposa had never been the aggressors at all.

92

By then, humanity had already carried out genocide against the only other intelligent life we'd encountered in space.

Why would a Mariposa take my cat? Was it the only one here? It had to be a refugee. Why hadn't it attacked me? It had adequate reasons to, really. When I was a kid, the Mariposa had been a scary thing to threaten other children with: "Oooh, don't stay out after dark, a Mariposa will get you!" As an adult, I'd come to understand the horrible reality: humans were the scariest things around.

I could call for help. I'd get it. My footage of a live Mariposa would summon up gunships galore, which would then blow up the island and Forry with it, because some people never learn.

I had to go after Forry myself.

Courtesy of his implant, I knew Forry had stable vitals and where he was. I couldn't go after him in my ship—I'd landed in the spot least likely to disturb the local ecosystem, and the scientists on Luna.

I pushed myself to a fast walk across the rocky plain, a bitter wind in my face. Sea birds swirled above. The island was small, but didn't feel that way after I'd been walking for over an hour. By the map, I knew things were about to get worse, too. Forry was being kept at the bottom of a small canyon.

Determined as I was, a niggling voice in the back of my mind told me that if the worst happened—if the Mariposa killed Forry—I'd soon have a new kitten awaiting me on Earth.

Thing was, that cat would genetically be the same, but it wouldn't be *my* Forry, the kitten I had cuddled and loved since age ten. I'd loved Forty-One, too, of course—according to my mother, he'd taught me how to walk—but Forty-Two was special. We had grown up together. I couldn't sleep without him cuddled close in my cot.

I stared into the canyon. Its sheer sides dropped fifty feet. Following a map projected by my drones, I found the closest I could get to a trail. I began to work my way down on my rump, trying to watch the placement of my feet and hands instead of the steep cliff to my left.

At some point, it occurred to me that my terror of planetary descents also carried over to a fear of heights.

Slow as my progress was, my heart pounded as if I was running full-out. My suit struggled to cope with the amount of sweat I was producing. I tried not to think about how I would climb *up* the cliff, especially with a cat in tow. Right now, I needed to get down there. The rest, I'd figure out.

Beneath my foot, rocks crumbled from the cliff's edge. More rocks joined in on the tumble downward. I froze. The rocks crashed far below. I was tempted to look over the side. I did not.

Slowly, carefully, I edged myself down again, my body pressed as close to the cliff face as I could get without causing it to crumble, too. I scooted further down. A few more rocks fell. I froze, waited, then continued.

When I reached the canyon's bottom, I had to sit for a moment, quivering. I'd made it.

A small, sleek Mariposa ship was parked on the flat ahead of me. The hatch was open.

This was a trap. The Mariposa weren't stupid. It had to know I was here. Maybe it didn't want to eat Forry—maybe it was after bigger game.

Even as I thought it, I knew that particular fear was stupid, the stuff of bad childhood jokes. There'd never been any indication that the Mariposa ate humans. Or cats. But then, what did I know?

I directed a drone into the ship, watching its feed all the while. In the second room, the view showed what had to be a medical ward. Forry's body occupied little space upon a massive cot. A strange metal contraption encased his head.

"Forry," I gasped. Trap or not, I had to get to him.

I ran into the alien ship, pistol in hand. My entry didn't trigger any traps—I couldn't decide whether to be relieved or more unnerved. I rushed to my cat. He lay on his side, his brassy eyes open and tracking me.

"Oh, Forry." Tears threatened to blind me. I ached to rip the device away from his head, but I didn't want to cause more harm than good. "What is that alien doing to you?"

"I'm not harmed." The voice was nonbinary and soft, and seemed to come from the helmet. "My health is stable, as you should already know from your own readings. This device will help us talk."

"Forry? That can't be you. You can't talk." I spun around in search of the Mariposa. I saw nothing, nor did my drones.

"Listen to me, Raygray. I know I'm what you call the 42nd iteration of Murgatroyd. By human count, my body is fifteen years of age. I've known you since you were ten."

The pistol was sweaty in my grip as I raised it to Forry's head. The very sight of him on the other side of the barrel shook me worse than the horrible climb into the canyon. "The Mariposa could have read that data off of Forry's implant. Let him go." The helmet covered his scalp so completely, I couldn't tell if it had penetrated his skull. I choked back a sob at that terrible thought.

"The implant only relays my vitals to you and to Renew-Anew on Earth." Forry's tone was patient. "Put down the gun."

"I want this thing off of him," I yelled, looking around the room. The alien had to be monitoring us from somewhere. "How did it even have a helmet like this to fit Forry?" I muttered, studying the device again.

"There are other intelligent species in existence, ones that have the good sense to avoid humanity. Apparently, one is feline-like. This communications helm was modified to enable me to speak to you."

I released an incredulous snort. "Oh, so you didn't need any aid to communicate with the Mariposa?"

"No, I did not. Many highly developed beings can speak via telepathy."

That made me laugh. "Not humans?"

"Not humans. You do need to put the pistol down, Raygray. You know you shouldn't aim such a weapon at anyone unless you intend to use it."

I blinked back new tears. "I don't want to use it! I want my Forty-Two back!"

"I am your Forty-Two. Listen to me. The alien wouldn't know that your mother, despite her poverty, spent more money on real tuna for me than she did on her own meals. Or that your great-grandfather ran into a burning building to save my life, as I was paralyzed by fear beneath a bed. Or how Sheila, the first of your line, relaxed after her long days at the laboratory by hand-crocheting historical human outfits sized to fit me."

"My mom did do that, but for Forty-One. Not you." The full weight of what I had been told began to sink in. I lowered the pistol.

"You really are my Forry? You remember everything lived by your past clones? How ... how can that be?"

"How many millennia have humans pondered the natures of their own bodies and souls, never coming closer to an agreeable answer?"

"Oh, Forry. You *are* the smartest cat in the universe."

"Of course." Forry said this without modesty. "But that's because I'm old, Raygray. Older than any cat ought to be. I have far, far exceeded the nine lives accorded to me by human lore."

I walked around him, taking in more of the alien craft. Lights blinked along the silvery walls. "Why is the Mariposa letting us talk like this, Forry?"

"When we conferred at the ship, it understood the conflict created by my inability to speak with you, and agreed to give us this opportunity. I provided it with the access code to come aboard our vessel."

My hand hovered over my holster. "It wanted me, an enemy human, to follow you onto its own ship? That's outright foolhardy."

A simulated laugh rang from the device. "Oh no, it didn't want you here at all. It didn't believe you would come. Despite my assurances, it didn't believe that Good People could exist, that you would risk your very life to come in my pursuit."

Considering what humans had done to the Mariposa, that made sense. "But before I even came, I could've reported my sighting. There could already be a hundred gunships on the way!"

"Compassion sometimes means vulnerability. You risked yourself to come after me. It risked itself to help the both of us."

I noted that Forry didn't refer to the alien as a Mariposa.

"It's lonely." His voice lowered. "Our conversation, brief as it was, held deep meaning. It wanted to help, if at all possible."

I shook my head. "But that's so risky."

"Says the human who just barged onto an alien craft with a single pistol in hand."

At that, I had to laugh, albeit nervously. "Okay. So we're really talking. This is something I've always wanted to do. I love you so much, Forry."

"I know." Those intense, brassy eyes looked into mine. "That's why you need to let me die."

I recoiled. "What?"

"I know this body is starting to fail. I've died forty-one times before, and several previous deaths have been from kidney disease. I trust you'll make me as comfortable as possible through the end, but that *needs* to be the end. The family contract with Renew-Anew enables you to initiate the next clone's development. I ask you: please, do not let there be a Forty-Three."

"But Forry, why?" I could barely speak through my emotion-clenched throat.

"We cats believe in a Beyond where our Good People await us. Your family is an unusual one, Raygray, to boast so many Good People across the generations. I miss each and every one of them. To see Sheila again—to see them all—would mean more to me than a thousand tuna filets."

Now I knew for certain that this couldn't be an insidious ploy. It was too intimate. Too terrible. "You mean, we've been keeping you from heaven. You keep living, and living—"

"The dying is what is hard. Despite the scientific advancements of humanity, dying always hurts." His voice rattled as if we were in a hard descent. We were, in a way.

"You want this life to be the final one." I had to state it plainly, to make sure I could logically grasp what my heart could not.

"Yes."

My drones pinged me. I turned to find the Mariposa—no, I wouldn't call it by that human-granted name—in the doorway. Close up, its iridescent sheen hurt my eyes.

"Can you talk with me?" I felt the urge to grab my gun, but I did not. I wouldn't be like other people.

"Yes." Its voice was breathy.

"Thank you for facilitating this meeting. You took … a big risk."

"Did not believe in Good People. Now I do."

I was quiet a moment. "You're alone here."

"Yes."

As I would soon be alone. No, that was selfish and unfair. I could talk with people whenever I wanted to through my system, and go wherever I wanted to go. I wasn't one of the last—or the very last—of my kind.

"I won't tell other people that you're here," I said. "I can modify the sensors on the island to ignore you. The big thing is, you can't blast the relay box again. I might not be the person to get the contract to fix it next time."

Its skin was like an ever-shifting rainbow reflection from prisms. "Thank you, Good Person."

"You are the best of the Good People." Forry's sudden purr caused me to look down at him. "By the time you go Beyond, Raygray, many cats will wait for you."

"What?" I furrowed my brow, trying to understand.

"Your family has sometimes had other cats over the years, though not since your grandfather went to space. When I venture Beyond—which will be years yet, I hope—you will need more cats. I know you. You can't fly around alone." His tone was matter-of-fact.

"I wouldn't make it through descents otherwise." I laid my hand on his side. He was so soft, so warm, so alive.

"Exactly. I have been strangely blessed to know so many Good People. Countless cats never get to know even one such person."

"You wouldn't be mad if I had another cat on the ship?"

His eyes narrowed. "I would be, if you did so now. The ship is my domain!" His tail puffed for a few seconds. "But when I am dead, it's mine no more. You need someone to take care of you."

"And I need to take care of someone," I said softly.

The alien studied the lights along the wall. "Good Person, he shouldn't be in the machine any longer. It becomes tiresome."

Even lounging as he was, Forry did look depleted. "Okay. We should head back before nightfall, anyway. It'll be a long trek, carrying him." I felt ill at the thought of climbing up that cliff.

"I can assist with your return," said the alien.

"Oh. That would be wonderful." I smiled as an idea came to mind. "If I can contrive a reason to come back to Cambria—like delivering more machinery—would you like me to bring you some cats? To keep you company? You would need to keep them on your ship at all times, or they'd disrupt the ecosystem. There'd be no hiding that from the sensors."

The being's rainbow colors intensified so much that I had to cover my eyes. "Company would be the greatest kindness," it said. "My gratitude."

"You'll need to tolerate other cats aboard for that trip," I murmured to Forry, stroking his side.

"They'll be kept caged." His tone was regal. "They will know their place while they are my guests."

Without question, Forty-Two knew his own place.

"I love you, Forry," I whispered as the alien reached over to disengage the helmet.

"As I love you, my Good Person for this life," he said.

The helmet came off and I lifted his limp body onto my shoulder. His moist pink nose nuzzled my ear. He could no longer speak words to me, but his purr told me everything that I needed to know.

Hands

There Is a Hand

Jane Yolen

There is a hand on my breast,
But, at last, not just my own.
It is cold, but iron is always cold.
The fingers are well shaped,
bolts mostly hidden.

There is a breast upon my breast.
It is hard, but iron is hard.
The nipples stand at attention,
pressing into my flesh,
surprisingly erotic, exotic.

There is a flush of blood, of bile,
of lust, of the dust of my past.
There is a tongue in my mouth.
It is cold, well-shaped, finely formed.
But iron is always finely formed.
And it is mine.

The Shape of the Particle

Naomi Kritzer

When I woke to the sound of the fire alarm, my first thought was that it was popcorn in the microwave again, or maybe a pizza forgotten in the kitchen oven, but as I rubbed my eyes and reached for my glasses, I heard Abdi's voice yelling, "it's a real fire, it's a real fire, everyone get out," and I smelled smoke.

I jammed my feet into my shoes and my glasses onto my face. The hallway was full of smoke. I banged on the door next to mine, wondering if I'd be able to break the door down to wake up Denise if I had to, but the smoke alarm with the bed shaker must have done its job because she came out right away and we both bolted down the stairs into the fresh air. We had an assembly point, and I walked around, coughing and counting. I thought for a minute we were short one person, but Sumana found me as I was starting to panic and said, "Don't forget Lace is at that conference in Chicago. Everyone's out. Gavan even got his guinea pigs out."

"Well done, us," I said, and my legs went wobbly. Sumana slipped her arm around me and I rested my head on her shoulder and we watched Walton Scholar's Hall—our home—burn.

We were still watching the firefighters as the sun rose. They'd used a robotic crew in the worst of the fire, sending in thermal-resistant rescuers to check every room and ensure we weren't wrong that no one was still in there. Now the remaining work was mostly for humans—pulling apart walls to find any hint of remaining fire so it wouldn't start up again. Not that it mattered, much. We looked at the shredded, blackened mess that had once been the roof and knew that our home was gone.

Walton Scholar's Hall had been graduate student housing years ago, back when Elbridge University had a graduate school. It was both a bit too run down for today's undergraduates, and a bit too nice; the rooms were basically very small apartments, complete with kitchenettes, but also things were constantly breaking down. Undergraduates would have expected the college to come do the fixes, whereas we were willing to manage mostly by ourselves.

It was not a pretty building. I don't want you to get the wrong idea about that. It was built in 1972 and designed to be functional, not attractive. But a year after the graduate school fully shut down, the federal program started with subsidies for housing cheap enough to afford on a stipend, and Walton Scholar's Hall was born. As soon as basic repairs were done, a group of recent Elbridge graduates moved in and announced their intention to continue their studies—to learn for the sake of learning. Plenty of faculty were willing to let alumni audit classes, or at least watch the lectures and do the readings. And why not? Jobs were scarce, as increasing types of work could be done by robots—that was the whole reason for the stipends. The residents of Walton Scholar's Hall liked college, liked dorm life, liked learning. Freed from the pressure of grades and credits, they could study whatever they wanted.

I had moved in after graduating five years later. Back then, the vacancies came pretty regularly: people left for the cities, graduate school, married life. As time passed, people who joined were less likely to leave. There were two married couples living in Walton when it burned, including one with a small child. Walton rooms are small, and families can get affordable apartments sized for more than one, but Jen and Leora had wanted a child and really hadn't wanted to move out, so they set up a partition in one corner for Gideon and said that if it stopped working, they'd reassess.

I'd lived in Walton for eleven years when it burned down. The two original residents still in the house, Marty and April, had lived there for sixteen. The newest was Prakash, who'd been with us for six months, but before him the newest person had lived there for three years.

When I was actually a student, I got a BA in computer science. But post-graduation, I discovered a love for history. I learned Latin, Greek, and Italian. I read all the literature I'd have read as an English major, and sat in on introductory classes in every single science. Leora does history research and I've been helping her translate this storehouse of documents from Sicily that got scanned in two years ago by archivists there. Our work, at least, was online. Leora had Gideon in her arms; he was sleeping on her shoulder like all was still right with the world.

Sometime in the night, someone must have woken the college president, Osmo, because I spotted him when I looked around for Leora. He was chatting with the provost. I unthreaded my arm from Sumana's. "Oh," she said, looking to see where I was going. "Must you talk to Osmo *now?*"

"The sooner I know the score, the better," I said.

"You're in your pajamas! And you don't even have Lace to go with you. Take Margaret, at least."

Lace was the administrative liaison, which meant that she *should* have been the one talking to Osmo, but she was also in Chicago. I was the house manager, which meant I made the chore chart and helped arbitrate disputes. Margaret wasn't either, but she *had* been the administrative liaison before Lace. The pajamas couldn't be helped.

Osmo saw us coming. "Alex. Margaret. Let's move this conversation to my office—I can have someone meet us with coffee and rolls."

Osmo has a very nice office, with a circle of chairs that lets him converse with visitors while not being behind his desk. It makes everything feel more egalitarian, which is an illusion, but a nice gesture even so. He has a human assistant, but the coffee and rolls were delivered by one of the robots from the dining hall.

"So, this must be a terrible shock," he said, sympathetically. "I'm so sorry. Did all the pets get out?"

"What pets?" I said, since in theory we weren't supposed to have them.

"Glad to hear it," he said, without missing a beat. "So, you all qualify for an emergency payment from the government called a Disaster Mitigation Supplement. It's up to you how to spend it, but there's an additional supplement available if you need to relocate."

"Why would we need to relocate?" Margaret said. "Aren't you going to rebuild? Surely there's some sort of fund for that, too?"

Osmo paused, took a moment to clean his glasses, refilled his coffee. "I am not *unalterably opposed* to rebuilding Walton Scholar's Hall," he said. "But you'll need to make a case for its continued existence. When we initially agreed to the project, the proposal was for *scholars*. And the scholarship emerging from this house is … uneven."

"Lace is at an academic conference delivering a paper *right now*," I said.

"Yes, I'm aware." He leaned back in his chair. "There are forty people—well, forty adults living in the house. My understanding—and please correct me if I'm wrong—is that approximately half are producing independent *scholarship* in any discipline—and that's using the term rather broadly. Another quarter are pursuing personal studies that could, at some point, result in some scholarship—but one of those is Marty, one of the original members of the house, who has been engaged in personal study for sixteen years. The remaining ten are doing neither." He put down his coffee, brushed off his knees, and leaned forward. "The Board of Trustees has had reservations about Scholar's House since it opened. I may be able to persuade them to rebuild—but you will need to commit to implementing *standards*. Of some kind. Some reason for your community to continue to exist."

His human assistant caught me on the way out. "We've sent everyone vouchers for a few nights in a hotel," she said. "Let us know if you need help with the government forms. Especially the relocation ones—they can be confusing."

"I have to say, I'm not surprised," Margaret said. "Were you? It was clear to me back when I was the liaison that the trustees found us embarrassing. A bunch of hangers-on, former students who didn't have *real* jobs but wouldn't just move to an artist's colony in the cities or whatever."

"I *like* living in a small town."

"That's not the point."

"I knew they didn't like us," I said. "I just didn't think they'd throw us out."

"Well, this solves the problem for them. They don't have to throw us out. They can just choose not to rebuild."

We were walking along the campus duck pond, toward town. There was a twenty-four-hour diner in town, staffed mainly by robots, and that's where everyone else had gone. I was dragging my feet, partly because I didn't want to deliver the bad news, partly because I was *tired*. It wasn't even eight in the morning yet. Too early to call Lace, who was delivering her paper later today.

Lace, of all of us, would have options. She was doing work in philosophy of consciousness—that blend of philosophy, psychology, and computer science that had become very hot in the last few years because of its relationship to AIs. She got regular invitations to deliver papers at conferences, grants that let her travel to do that, and just a month ago she'd been invited to leave us for a "Fellow's House" at Bennington College, in Vermont, that would be sort of like Walton but with the *standards* Osmo wanted. More so, because it was going to be all people working in philosophy of consciousness and related fields. The house itself sounded really nice. She'd turned them down, but it probably wasn't too late to change her mind.

Sumana sent me a text. "Are you still in the meeting?"

"Done," I sent back. "On our way to the diner." I picked up my pace a little, because I knew as soon as I said that, Sumana would order me breakfast. And I didn't want it to get cold.

The diner wasn't big, and we'd filled nearly every table. Margaret went off to sit with her boyfriend, Glen, who'd saved her a seat, and Sumana waved me over. Coffee and a plate of pancakes were waiting for me. "Eat first," Sumana said. "I don't want you trying to explain what Osmo said while hangry."

"Osmo gave me a donut," I said. "I'm not in a *state* or anything." I drank some coffee anyway, thinking about how best to put the answer to her question. "Osmo said that he *might* rebuild, but we'd need to impose scholarship requirements on people living in the house."

My research was borderline—Osmo would probably concede, though possibly with disdain, that assisting with someone else's research gave you a legitimate claim on the space. But Sumana was one of the ones who did not do scholarly research of any kind. She had taken a few additional classes after graduation but for most of the last eight years she had spent her days knitting, baking, and listening to the rest of us talk about *our* research. Which was wonderful. She was one of my favorite people.

Sumana sighed. "If the rest of you have to throw me out, I won't hold it against you. Maybe I'll find a spot in one of those cubicle-style apartments on the edge of town and still walk over to hang out with the rest of you in the evenings."

"I don't want to throw you out," I said.

"Maybe it's time," she said. "Maybe Osmo's right, and the space should go to people doing scholarship."

I thought about all the things Sumana did in the house. She'd created the Communal Sweater Drawer, where we kept a dozen large-ish baggy sweaters that fit most of us. She hadn't created the game closet, of course, but she'd developed an organizational system for the games that somehow let us find precisely the game we were in the mood for on game nights. She had been the one who set up the Cabinet of Orphaned Craft Projects, which had allowed each and every one of us to determine that latch hook was tedious, and had meant that each of us had put a few stitches into the glorious, embroidered piece that hung—that *had* hung—over our fake fireplace in the living room.

I closed my eyes, afraid I was going to start crying. At the next table over, Rachel was telling Nadia about a biology class where she was learning about eusocial behavior, like ant colonies and beehives. "You can't understand the shape of a particle without understanding the particles near it," she said, which sounded more like physics than biology.

"Have you called your family?" Sumana asked.

"What?" I asked, opening my eyes.

"If they see this on the news, they might be worried," Sumana said, gently.

"Oh. Yes. I suppose you're right."

I finished my pancakes, double-checked the time in South Carolina, and stepped outside to call my mother. "What's wrong?" she said, instead of "hello." I mean, okay, I really don't call very often, and it wasn't her birthday or a holiday.

"Well, I'm fine, and everyone else who lives there is fine, but Scholar's Hall had a fire," I said. "I wanted to let you know before it showed up in your news alerts and you got worried."

"A fire! ... how bad? Where are you going to live, sweetie? Do you have anywhere to sleep tonight?"

"I'm fine tonight," I said.

"Well, that's a blessing, anyway." There was a moment of quiet, and I almost ended the call right there, but it would have been awkward, and Mom probably would have interpreted it as hostile. She took a deep breath and said, "Maybe it really is *time*, don't you think? Time to move on. Time to look for a real job, like your sister has. You have a degree in computer science, honey! There are *jobs* in that. You could *work*, maybe even part time, buy a house instead of living somewhere you can cover with your stipend. Your sister's company has openings, she was just mentioning those to me the other day." I was 99 percent sure that was a lie. Berta doesn't have that sort of conversation with our mother. "Why don't I talk to her, see what they've got at entry-level ... ."

"Mom, *please*. Just give me some time to *think*," I said, and I could hear my voice go childishly high, which made me hate both of us.

"Of course, honey, of course," she said, but I was pretty sure she was already texting Berta. "There's no rush. Thanks for letting me know."

Most of the day was full of forms and phone calls and shopping for necessities. I needed clothes that weren't pajamas, pajamas that didn't smell like smoke, a toothbrush. A room for the night was easy to arrange—Elbridge didn't run summer classes, so summers in town were quiet, and the hotel up by the highway had plenty of space. Sumana and I had planned to get a room together to stretch out our vouchers to two weeks instead of one—but apparently they were good for a week and then just expired, so there was no point.

By late afternoon I had what I needed and sat on the bed in the air-conditioning and late-afternoon light, scrolling through listings of micro-apartments. Even if Osmo rebuilt, Scholar's Hall wouldn't be restored in a week. The micro-apartments on the edge of town had four openings. A farm a little way out of town had a basement apartment for rent. Widening my search, I scrolled through micro-apartments and two-person apartments in the suburbs, in the cities, as far away as North Dakota.

There was a farm for sale about ten miles from town. It came with a flock of sheep, with a note included that you did not have to keep the sheep if you weren't interested. I was pretty sure that the current owners had kept the sheep because they liked the look of them or wanted something to keep their border collie entertained, not because it was an actual working farm. I paged through the pictures of the house, which was very large and very nice. *What if we all went in on this*, I thought, *could we buy it?* We could, together, afford the mortgage payments, no problem, but it only had five bedrooms. Well, eight if we converted some of the extra rooms into bedrooms. Split between 40 people, we'd be five to a room. But the living room had this giant fireplace kind of in the middle of the room, open on three sides with a vent hood going up through the ceiling. It was gorgeous. Although possibly a hazard to the toddler, we'd all have to keep an eye out when we had a fire in it …

My phone rang. It was my sister this time. "I heard about the fire from Mom," Berta said without preamble. "She said you're looking for a job. Are you?"

I flopped back on the hotel bed and stared up at the ceiling. "She means she's looking for a job for me, because she doesn't like what I'm doing with my life," I said.

"Okay, that's kind of what I figured," Berta said. "We do have a couple openings, and if you want to come work here, I'll tell Jean you're brilliant and hardworking and only trapped me under a laundry basket for laughs *one* time, I'm sure she'll hire you. But if you don't, I mean, it's your life."

"Right," I said. "I don't."

Because Berta is nothing like our mother, she didn't even ask me to think it over, just said, "Got it. Thanks."

"Was that it?"

"Well … do you know what you *are* going to do?"

"No," I said. "Not yet." I pushed myself up again and said, "What's new with you?"

Berta had some sort of product-ship deadline at work and she and her husband were doing home renovations that were going to result in very pretty floors and precision-engineered stainless steel countertops but in general sounded like way more trouble than they were worth, considering the story that resulted. We wrapped up, finally, and I stared at the wall, thinking about that farmhouse. If I got a job at my sister's company, I could probably buy a house, a nice house, and maybe *then* everyone would want to come live in it.

Maybe if I can figure out an option that's nice enough, everyone will want to stay together.

Everyone else seemed to have gone somewhere to find dinner while I was on the phone with Berta. I bought a microwaveable burrito from the convenience store next door, and dozed off on the bed almost as soon as I'd eaten it.

The room air conditioner kicked in with a loud rattle, waking me up around midnight. I threw away my burrito wrapper, changed into my fresh, not-salvaged-from-a-fire pajamas, brushed my teeth with my brand-new toothbrush, and went back to bed, but now I couldn't sleep.

I've always had trouble sleeping. One of the things I loved about Walton Scholar's House was, no matter how strange the hour, there was probably someone else up if you wanted company. I lay in bed for a while, feeling increasingly restless, and finally got up. Most of the rooms on my floor were my housemates, but I didn't want to knock on anyone's door because I really didn't want to wake anyone up if they were sleeping. It had been an exhausting day. *I* should be sleeping.

I went down to the hotel lobby. It was bright but empty. "Good evening, guest," the robot at the front desk said. "May I help you?"

When I didn't answer, it added, "We have a selection of complimentary toiletries for guests in need."

"They've got chamomile tea, too, if you ask," a voice said, behind me. It was Leo, one of my housemates.

"I kind of hate chamomile tea," I said.

"I know," Leo said. The robot fell silent and Leo settled into one of the lobby chairs. I settled in across from him. "I tried it, because I couldn't sleep, but it didn't help. I just keep thinking about how maybe if I'd ever gotten my act together—"

"It's not on you, Leo!" I said. "A quarter of the house doesn't do anything academic."

"I'd set a goal for the summer. Four pages. I was going to write four pages, a little over one a month. That seemed like something I could do, maybe." His voice blurred.

Leo had struggled with depression his whole life; last year he'd gone into crisis, and we'd taken it in turns to stay with him until he could get into an intensive day-treatment program in Minneapolis. We'd ridden with him on the bus, to and from, every day, and he was doing a lot better but he was not, in fact, doing scholarship yet. Last month he'd been talking about what he *wanted* to work on. Sumana had listened (it was something adjacent to philosophy of consciousness—more the question of *how we would know* if an AI had achieved sentience) with the same enthusiasm she always had for ant colonies or 500-year-old Italian church records or any of the rest of it.

"Do you think people would consider moving together?" I asked. "I mean, if I found a place that was big enough for all of us, but it was somewhere not that close by, or that wasn't perfect—like if we had to share bedrooms for a while—do you think anyone would consider it?"

"*I* would," he said, and his voice got less thin. "I love our house. Except, not the house. I love our community. Losing the sweater drawer *sucks* but losing the people is going to suck a lot more. I just—I don't want to ask people to stay *for me*."

"I get it," I said.

"I mean, no one should feel obligated."

I'd been having basically that same thought—no one should feel obligated, no one should feel like they have to stay *for me*. Would asking people to stay make me the exact desperate loser my mother was so convinced that I was?

"Anyway, I could live with sharing a room," Leo said. "Especially if we can find a place with a fireplace. That was the one thing about Walton. The living room would have been better with a fireplace."

"You *bought* us a fireplace, Leo!"

"It was a *fake* fireplace."

Leo's fireplace had been an electric heater with a fake flame that looked *just* enough like a real flame that we could all pretend. One of our house traditions was fireside Sundays, when we'd all sit in the living room and drink hot cider or tea and take turns telling everyone something interesting. It didn't have to be research related; you could tell an interesting story you'd run across online or tell people about something neat that you learned from a book you'd read.

It was beautiful. It was comfortable. I loved the freedom to learn whatever appealed to me, but part of what I loved was telling Sumana about what I'd found, hearing what Marty was studying, and sitting by our pretend fireplace with hot cider and popcorn and playing board games.

Osmo—and my mother—didn't think that was enough.

"It was real enough," I said. I was talking about the fireplace.

"Yeah," Leo said, and didn't argue, even though I knew that his main objection to his fake fireplace was that he couldn't toast marshmallows over it—a legitimate point, in fact. "It was real enough."

In the morning, I sent out messages to everyone for a house meeting: noon, at the picnic shelter in town, bring sandwich fixings for a communal lunch.

Everyone came. Even Lace came, via a tablet, although physically she was still in Chicago. We pushed picnic tables together to make one long table and opened packages of cheese and meat and lettuce and pickles. For a few minutes, everything almost felt normal as we ate and chatted and argued about whether we should throw the last of the bread to the ducks, a question that got solved by Sumana taking the bread to make herself another sandwich and then putting half of it on my plate.

It was clear that no one really wanted to say, "we should have a business meeting," so once everyone was down to their crusts, I stood up and said it.

"Look," Sumana said. "I've talked with the other freeloaders, and we've all agreed that if us leaving is what it takes to persuade Osmo to rebuild for the rest of you, we're for it."

"I have a counterproposal," I said. "I think we should find somewhere we can move together." There was a burst of conversation, and I added, "If people want to. I mean, obviously if someone wants to leave—or stay and try to get Osmo to rebuild—I can't choose for anyone else. But here's what *I* want—I want us to stay together, somewhere, and I'm open to where."

I was expecting a conversation about *whether.*

Instead, the conversation instantly turned to *where.*

"I really don't want to live somewhere with enormous bugs," Abdi said. "I feel like American geography is divided into Bad Winters and Big Bugs and I vote for Bad Winters."

"I really like small towns," Rachel said. "I might be able to get used to having a desert instead of woods near the school, but I want open space, not just endless city, and it has to be walkable—I mean, we need to be able to buy groceries and stuff without a car."

"If we have to, though, we could potentially double up and use the leftover money to buy a car to share," Leo said.

"Show of hands," I said. "I mean obviously I'm not holding anyone to this, but who *prefers* to move with the group? No shame if you want to go, I just don't want to hunt down a house for forty if we actually need a house for twenty."

Everyone raised their hand. *Everyone.* Including Lace.

Who kept her hand up to speak. "I have an option to propose," she said. "For the last few years, I've actually been scouting, because while I didn't expect a fire, I rather thought Osmo and the trustees would try to get rid of us eventually. Lots of colleges and universities have been setting up Fellow's Houses, and I thought if I asked around, I'd find someone who wanted us. *All* of us. And I found one." She described a liberal arts college in Indiana (bad winters, small bugs) that was excited about us. We'd have a more formal role as Fellows—it would be easier to get books through interlibrary loan—

116

but we'd be expected to be available for guest lectures in classes or for interested student groups.

"But some of us don't have anything to talk about," Sumana said. "Are you *sure* they know that?"

"Yes," Lace said. "When I went looking for a new home for us, I explained to everyone that we come as a set, or not at all. And not as an act of charity, don't look at me like that! I never would have done the work they value without this community. All of it, including you, Sumana. Especially you."

Moving was hard. Moving is always hard. We had more to pack than I'd expected: once the fire crews were done with Walton, we were allowed in to clear out our possessions, and a surprising number of things had survived. Not, alas, the sweater drawer; the sweaters and the orphaned craft projects were too damaged to be salvageable. Sumana started the first new sweater on the road trip to Indiana.

The new house felt strange and uncomfortable at first, like new clothes that were stiff and scratchy in unexpected places. The rooms were much more varied than the identical shoeboxes of Walton and we had a rather lengthy conversation that culminated in drawing straws and then a later discussion about whether we should rearrange annually.

But *it had a fireplace*, and on the first Sunday in October it was finally cool enough to have a fire. Leo toasted marshmallows and made a s'more for Jen and Leora's kid, Gideon. We gathered, and Rachel told us about naked-mole-rat colonies, and Sumana read everyone this terrific essay she'd found, and then Gideon said, "can I tell everyone something?" and told us about how he'd learned that day that if you mixed red and yellow, you got orange, but if you mixed orange and yellow, you got lighter orange.

It was my turn that week, too. "I learned that you can't understand the shape of the particle without understanding the particles near it," I said. "And I learned that we're enough. This is a real home, and we are a real community. We are enough."

No Want to Spend

Sophie Giroir

No place for me in this city. Not for a woman like me—a woman who casts her eyes downward as the men saunter past in their garish tights. I'm the odd one with the coins in her pockets. Won't spare change for a wispy man with golden eyelids and silver lips. Deviant woman, they call me—peculiar woman. The woman with no want to spend.

Two steps outside my door, the street shimmers like obsidian in the blistering heat. Sweat beads on my face the moment I close the door. Ads flash across buildings, top to bottom, wall to wall. The Golden Fawn is advertising the newest man in town. *Get a man down on his luck, he'll make sure you have a good ...*

I turn my head and stare at the ground. Can't look up without seeing sex written on the world.

Copper bows to me at the corner, low and formal like I'm his queen. "Gonna get you some goods tonight, Ruby?" His little shorts cast dancing drops of light in the shadows along the street. Black hair tumbles over his thin shoulders, and I manage a kind of smile as I walk away.

"Won't give me a word, I see." He doesn't like me much; can't get me to buy his time. I keep my mouth closed. Pretty men like him make women pay for wasting their time.

Opal's Wears is two blocks from the market. Gaudy flashing lights fight for dominance with the noonday sun. A holographic Jade dances at the entrance, her dress changing with what's for sale inside. I push the door open and wait for my eyes to adjust.

"There's our Ruby," a voice says from the counter. I look up at the sound of my name. Jade stands there beaming, arm draped over Opal's shoulder. Sweat glimmers on their skin, giving them an ethereal appeal. "Got that new fabric for us?"

I push past a woman, half-changed and fretting over what to buy, making my way toward Jade and Opal. They stand close like it's painful to be more than two inches apart. No one says anything about them not spending coins on men. Nothing wrong with women locking lips with women as long as they're locking lips with someone.

"I've got fifty bolts coming in. How much you need?" I pull my tablet out and set it on the counter. Pull up the fabric preview to let them have a look.

Opal's eyes widen. "It really changes color with your mood?" She takes the tablet and looks it over with Jade. "What's your price?"

"Two hundred a bolt."

Jade and Opal glance at one another. They don't even have to speak to know what the other is thinking. Only people I've ever seen communicate that way.

"We'll take the whole lot."

A thrill travels up my spine. "I ... when do you need it?" Never made a sale this big before. Might get off this planet after all.

"Soon as you can get it to us, honey. The Lusty Masquerade Festival is coming up. We got customers begging for something new." Opal smiles wide at me. "Might even make a little something for you."

Heat flushes my cheeks as I pull my tablet back toward me and hit the order. "I'll have it for you by the weekend."

I leave Opal's Wears and dare a glance toward the market. It rises at the crest of the city, haughty and flashy. Ten miles wide, it spirals in on itself, tempting like an oasis for the extra thirsty, but the water's poison to me. Sex bleeds into the wells and drifts in clouds along the streets. I don't normally go down there, but I have a reason now.

Onyx said she heard Goldie sold offworld passes cheap. Goldie runs The Golden Fawn on my street, but he comes down here in the summer. The air is cooler because the river wraps itself around it like a tarnished ring.

Music vibrates the air outside The Bronze Delight. Men and women wearing nothing but paint push their way inside. More going in than coming out.

I can see the door to The Golden Fawn when two lavender-lipped men converge on me. They sway and swish, bat their pink painted eyes. Men don't wear much around my part of town, and they don't wear anything in the market.

I keep my eyes low as I walk by. Hot breath tickles my ear, and a finger traces the back of my neck. They giggle in unison when my skin blushes red. I don't say anything though. I don't want anything from them.

They hiss when I keep going. I feel their eyes on my back as I pull a door open. I got somewhere else to be. Somewhere sex doesn't sell, and coins don't exist.

The place looks like it's a temple built to gods of fornication. Rose-etched marble floors stretch out before me. Naked people painted on the walls and ceiling. I catch the scent of spice in the air, the musky kind they put out to make you think about sex.

Three women dance to the *bum, bum, bum* of trance-inducing music on a lit-up stage. Their hands reach and pull the air around them. Their willowy bodies writhe and twist with erotic devotion. I catch my breath when they see me watching. Their eyebrows arch to tempt me into a dare. *Join us*, I feel them saying, but I'm not their kind of clientele.

Goldie's sitting in a high-backed chair when the door groans closed behind me. His pretty face glitters in the lights, lips and eyelids red with rouge. He's the prettiest of them all, I'm told. Goldie the Fawn, fairest man in the city.

His lips spread wide in a smile meant for seduction. He rises from the chair like it's a throne even though the fabric is faded. Gold dusted arms reach out to me as he approaches.

I step back and almost lose my footing. "Not here for a fuck," I tell him. I keep my eyes on his face.

Goldie chortles. "I know that, gorgeous. Too many clothes and not a spot of paint on that angel face of yours." He presses his chest against me, pulling me close for a hug. "I don't care what they say. Pretty women are always welcome here." He releases me with a kinder smile. It's not the same one he uses for corruption. "Now what can Goldie do for a beautiful gem like you?"

My lips tremble. Never been this nervous before. I look away again, eyes landing back on the women who watch me with unchecked curiosity. "Heard you could get people off world for cheap."

He rocks with a chuckle. "Yes, yes." He takes my chin between his thumb and forefinger. I feel exposed, like a belly turned up. "May get it for you free if you …" His smile melts into an impish grin.

My throat sticks. Stomach knots tight. "I … I don't want that."

"No." Goldie pats my arm. "I guess you really don't. Well. My loss." He reaches out a hand and wiggles his fingers. "Come on then. Let's see what I can do."

The women slump against one another, watching with bored expressions. Goldie leads me around the bar to a door I didn't notice. The hallway smells of mold and age. Old carpet pulls up from rotted floorboards and curls around the edges. The yellow lights glow dim, but they don't hide the stains.

Goldie opens a door at the end and waits for me to step inside. A cool breeze taps the blinds against two windows. Rainbows of light whirl around the room to the rhythm of the crystal chimes casting them. The river's just out back, lazy and strong. A man lays across the sofa with a book in his hands, eyes focused on the page.

I stare wide-eyed at the fully clothed man. There isn't a bit of paint on his face, and his clothes are plain. Goldie smacks his lips. "You've been in here all day, Tin."

"I know," Tin says. He doesn't look away from the book.

Goldie smirks at me. "He's like you. Isn't interested in fucking. I like to look at him, though."

"Fuck off, Goldie." Tin sets the book aside. He looks up at me with the tilt of his head. "Look. I've already told you I'm not interested. Not with you or anyone."

My face burns with the insinuation. A sharp breath hits my throat.

"Well, that's a damn shame, but that's not why I brought her back here." Goldie drops a hand at his side. "Always thinks I'm trying something."

"Because you are," Tin says. He rises off the sofa and looks me over. "So, I guess you're here for a way off world then. You must be one of those women the men are always complaining about. Won't drop a coin for them."

"You drop a coin for the women?" I shoot back.

Goldie stands there with his mouth in a wide "O" that falls into a smirk. "She has more fire than you do, Tin. Better watch out for this one. I might trade you out."

"No. I ... I didn't mean anything by it. Nothing at all." I turn to leave. "This was a mistake. I'm sorry."

Goldie grabs my hand. "No, gorgeous, you don't have anything to be sorry about. Tin's about as graceful as a gosling, and I was only kidding."

Tin chuckles. "No harm done. I've got some tea if you want. Cookies, too. I may not be interested in people, but I love my sweets."

The door clicks open, and I turn to see one of the women from the dance floor. Her dark skin shimmers with sweat and glitter. "Emmy says she's not done with you," she says to Goldie. She flicks an irritated eye at me.

A groan from Goldie. "Woman, I didn't say I wasn't coming back. Don't worry. You're all gonna get a piece of me." He sighs and looks back at me. "Can't seem to find time for anything else but work these days. Can you wait for me to finish with them?"

I nod, and he smiles at me. He reaches out and touches my cheek. "You're a queen. Be back before you know it."

The door shuts. My fingers tingle and palms sweat. Every piece inside me twists.

Tin walks back in with cookies and tea on a silver tray. His eyes dance between me and the door, lips curved in a sympathetic smile. "I promise I don't bite. What's your name?"

The bitter smell of tea and sweet scent of cookies drift toward me, and I find myself approaching him. Cups clink as he sets it down. Brown liquid pours hot, the scent thickening in the air around us. "Ruby," I say.

"And where you going, Ruby?" He holds out a cup for me.

It's warm in my hands, soothing the tingle in my fingers. "Any-where that isn't here."

Tin takes a sip, closing his eyes. "Nothing like a hot cup of tea, even on a hot day like this." His sigh is one of complete satisfaction. He opens his eyes again. "Maybe you should stay."

"I don't think so." I can't bring myself to press my lips to the warming porcelain. Too afraid of what it will mean. How much I'll owe. "Don't belong here."

"I don't know why people think they need to belong somewhere," he says. "It's not about where you are as long as you are okay with *who* you are." He smiles and lifts a cookie to his mouth.

The thought swims in my mind, darting between fear of rejection and fear of relenting. I ache for companionship, and that longing is a grimace beneath my smile. A push of distance between bodies. They press in too close; so close I have to run inside. "No place for me in this town. Nobody wants me here anyway."

Tin clicks his tongue at that. "They don't matter. They're just wishes in the wind. Look at me. Do I look like I give a shit what they think?"

"No?"

"Exactly. And Goldie doesn't care either. You want people around you that want you around? Look right in front of you." He shrugs and reaches for another cookie. "People like us just have to find a way to exist where we are."

"What good is it staying here? Family's gone. No friends. I just work while everyone else is spending coins."

Tin nods absently, letting his eyes drift off to the river. "You smell that?"

I hadn't noticed it before, but there's no spice in the air in this room. Tin takes a deep breath and looks at me again. "The wet rot of earth by the river. Things living and dying all outside the city. I used to think I could be some wild man living on the river with no one to bother me about selling or buying." He snickers. "Head full of foolish dreams."

"What happened?" I realize I've sat down in an old armchair across from Tin. My elbows on my knees, fingers still wrapped around the cooling cup of tea.

He shrugs, half a cookie still in his mouth. He chews and swallows. "Guess I realized I don't have to sell anything to be worth something. Found myself a good job making sex cookies. Them ladies out there went wild for them." His smile widens. "They think they're laced with aphrodisiacs. Didn't tell them that the secret ingredient is just chocolate."

The tension in my arms and shoulders eases off with a burst of laughter and each round that follows it. "Chocolate." I wipe a tear from the corner of my eye and take a breath. "How do you do it? How do you feel so comfortable being the only man without paint on his lips?"

Tin smirks. "I'm damn good lookin'." He winks. "Besides. I don't need paint to know I got worth." He points a long, tapered finger at me. "And neither do you. You are worth so much more than the coins in your pockets."

I pull the cup to my lips and let the bitter liquid flow over my tongue and down my throat, warming my belly where it rests. Tin's words work at me until my hand is reaching for a cookie.

He grins and plucks another cookie from the tray. "Let me ask you something. What do you think you'll find off world?"

"Peace," I mumble. I swallow more of the tea. It's lukewarm now but still soothes the knots in my belly.

"That or just different problems. People all over this damn system have problems. We're not special for that." He tilts his head, dark eyes almost peering into me. "What if I told you, you could find peace here? If a wannabe hermit like me can find platonic love, so can you."

I watch a patch of rainbow dance over his face as a breeze brushes past the crystal windchimes. "How?"

Tin smiles. "The secret is you don't have to be painted to be a part of this world. Have you noticed not everyone wants exactly the same? Right down the road, there's a young person who only wants to be held. Mercury, they're called. And Diamond, well she only flirts. Drops coins for witty banter." He reaches out and pats my knee. "I think we're gonna be fine, Ruby. You just think about it. Come visit me from time to time."

I take a bite, letting the chocolate melt over my tongue, bringing a sigh of contentment to my lips. Ectasy in sweet little things. The simple joy of chocolate and a friend with no want to spend. I could go for something like that.

I thank Tin for the cookies and leave out a back entrance before Goldie returns. Down the street, I stare ahead at the beautiful people in their paints and flashy jewels. They're so caught up in each other, they don't notice me walking past. I stop at Opal's Wears and stare at the hologram dancing on the street. They're already designing new costumes with my fabric.

"Ruby!" I hear Jade's sandals slapping the asphalt before I hear my name. She beams at me and takes my hand. "Got something we want to show you. I think you'll like it."

I let her lead me inside, trying not to trip over the step. The shop is empty except for Opal who stands before a hologram of me in a new dress she's designing. She stares down at the tablet in her hand and moves her fingers over the screen, scrutinizing and mummering to herself.

Jade catches her breath, excitement dancing in her voice as she speaks. "What do you think?"

I stare at myself, the dress close to my skin but not skintight. It flows over my holographic body in complimentary curves. It covers my skin in all the places I want it to, baring my arms from the elbows down. This is what I would have designed myself.

"I picked the fabric and Opal wanted to make the design. I know you're not one for paint or flashy clothes, but I thought maybe … ." She watches my expression with desperate anticipation.

"I love it," I say. I blurt out the words before I realize they're true. I smile, the shadow over this world lifting. "How much?"

Opal looks up from her tablet, a little shock mixed in with her excitement. "It's a gift. We just wanted to thank you for all the gorgeous fabrics you create. This shop wouldn't exist without you."

Jade squeals beside me. "I can't wait to see you in it! The real you."

My smile widens. The real me. The me they see. Maybe there is a place for me in this city. Jade reaches out to me, tentatively pulling me into a hug. I welcome the embrace, the comfort of a friend. My friends, as Opal joins us.

Little Deaths and Missed Connections

Maria Dong

Each time Alex steps into the creche, she imagines her own funeral. Not the way it would actually happen—the solitary recycling, the asynchronous audio beamed through satellites—no, she imagines pallbearers grunting under the heft of her body as it floats in white padding, the shine of a curved wooden coffin. She's never seen wood in real life, but in her daydreams, it feels like bamboo and smells like coffee.

But she's late today. There's no time for the ritual. No time to reflect on how they came to call the sleep after orgasm *the little death*. The term started out innocuous, but in the end, people make everything about sex.

Alex is no different. Sometimes she masturbates before the drugs hit her. There are cameras in the creche, same as the dining facility and the bathrooms and everywhere else on station, but these moments before the black are the only ones where Alex feels that there's more to life than math.

There are twenty-five creches. Every twenty-four hours, each of the station's seventy-five workers receives ninety minutes for leisure—as this paradoxically increases productivity—and three 30-minute segments of dining time. At shift-end, each worker must spend seven hours and forty-seven minutes in a creche, which divides the workers into three shifts of twenty-five. During each person's creche time, they receive a cocktail of fourteen chemicals designed to do everything from increase muscle tissue and accelerate wound healing to simulate the effects of gravity on a person's bone-growing osteoblasts.

Drugs knock the workers out. Drugs wake them up. Drugs keep them—if not happy, then not depressed, because in addition to the loss of revenue, ZenaTech has found that suicides can be catching. In the end, everybody on station is an addict.

Alex wakes from a sleep designed to be perfect. Groggy, at first, but then the stimulants kick in.

It feels good. She hates how good it feels. She hates—

An anomaly catches her eye: a slanted line by her foot where everything should be straight. When she turns her head, she loses it, until she sees the outlet cover by her ankle. It's missing a screw, and the cover plate has shifted, swinging around on the axis of its remaining screw to leave a wedge-shaped gap.

Alex is fascinated. It's something different in this hellhole of sameness. She leans forward enough to spy a white sliver, which she tugs out.

It's a scrap of paper, no larger than her pointer finger, a single line in flowing script:

Do you know how beautiful you are?

She drops it as if it's burned her. It floats in the air, turning like a feather.

A moment later, the creche lets out a warning *ding* to let her know that she's overstayed. It needs to activate the cleaning cycle for the next occupant.

She grabs the handles near the exit and compresses herself like a frog, then springs out into the station, floating in a cloud of euphoria.

There is tardiness on the station. Any place that human beings exist occasionally harbors *late* human beings, but ZenaTech, flush with centuries of workforce optimization, keeps it to a minimum. Being remiss in one's duties could lead to the death of a comrade—but even that isn't enough to always keep all seventy-five workers on the straight and narrow.

Neither ZenaTech nor the threat of mass ebullism is enough to keep Alex on time. She's too on *fire* with the idea of a person who has been admiring her in secret, waiting for the right moment to approach.

Alex is always watched, but now, she becomes the watcher.

She watches herself: the way she pulls her meal out of the microwave oven and peels back the plastic cling film. The moment she tucks a strand of hair behind her ear—it's getting long, and would she, or they, or he prefer she trim it? (Alex really hopes her note-leaver isn't a *he*, although she grows more flexible by the minute.)

She watches her comrades. The writer could be from any shift. And there's always the possibility that the note was for someone else—but she has no idea who, because station protocol prevents knowing who your creche mates are. Too many fights over errant crumbs and odd smells that somehow survive the cleanings.

In fact, she's so busy watching—herself, everyone else—that in the middle of trying to remove an appliance shell, she swings her hammer hand back ... and it comes down empty.

She stares at the hollow ring of her thumb and fingers where the hammer used to be.

"I think you fucking lost something," says a familiar voice behind her.

Alex blushes and turns.

Irina grips Alex's hammer with one hand—but the other is held to her cheek, where a red mark is already forming.

Foul-mouthed Irina is Alex's closest—and truthfully, only—friend on station. They arrived within days of each other. If all goes well, they'll leave at roughly the same time, their respective debts to society paid, but Alex has never been brave enough to ask Irina what she did to get picked up by ZenaTech.

"Sorry," mumbles Alex.

But Irina won't let this go easy. "What the fucking fuck? You almost put my eye out."

Even as Alex is pooling into the floor, a diode blinks in her mind. *Could it be Irina?* They're almost always together, and while you can't actually tell if somebody's queer by their haircut, Irina's blunt, asymmetrical fringe at least doesn't refute it. But Irina's never shown interest in anything more than a cordial friendship—

"For fuck's sake. Earth to Alex."

"Sorry." Alex repeats it like it's the only word she knows. She looks up, her fingers in her pocket, as if unconsciously seeking out the note. "It's just, I found something in my creche, and I'm trying to figure out—"

She stops. If the writer *is* Irina, this might embarrass them both.

Irina snatches the partially visible note from Alex's hand. She turns away before Alex can reach her—and then turns back, eyes huge. "You—"

She doubles over in laughter.

Alex shoves Irina as hard as she can, but without gravity, they just repel like magnets. It's wholly unsatisfying.

"Who do you think it is?"

The question staunches Alex's rage. Still, she is too mad for words and snatches back her note.

Irina glances toward one of the cameras. She turns back to the appliance casing and hits it ineffectually, pretend-working for the cameras. "So, who do you think it is?" she asks, her voice decidedly light.

Alex shrugs, and then she, too, starts miming work. They're too closely observed to keep this up long, but she's too distracted to get anything done. "It could be anybody." The sentence lifts at the end, as if buoyed by the delighted shiver that races up her spine.

"Not really." Irina grunts as she labors with a bolt, suddenly no longer pretending. "It's probably not someone from our shift—"

"Why do you say that?"

Irina shrugs. "You'd see them put the note in."

Just like that, she's chopped away twenty-three potential suitors. The clarity should've brought relief, but Alex just feels disappointed.

"Where did you find it?"

Alex deflates further. "The outlet. Someone removed one of the screws."

Irina nods. "So, it's not for you, because there's no way they'd predict you'd open the outlet—"

"It was already partially open. Maybe they were hoping I'd notice—"

Irina shuts Alex down with a deadpan stare. It's not until she turns back to her bolt that Alex feels like she can breathe again.

"Tell you what," says Irina. "I've got more friends than you. I'll ask around, find out who left the note."

"No thanks," says Alex—but from the look on Irina's face, she's going to do it anyways.

For the first time in a year, Alex was early for her next sleep—so early the cleaning cycle was still running and the door refused to open.

But there's no note, so Alex just floats in the straps. She doesn't imagine her wooden coffin, the pallbearers and coffee-scent. Instead, she thinks about going back to life before her secret admirer, and it throbs like a toothache.

She can already feel the cocktail kicking in. She leans back and lets it come—and that's when she sees the strip of paper, stuffed into a buckle near the ceiling.

When she wakes, it's to the fear she just dreamed it—but the slip is there. She doesn't wait for the stimulants. She rips out the IV and pushes off the floor, grabbing the note while checking her rise with her other hand.

The first time I saw you, it was like leaving the earth behind.

At first, Alex thinks the world is vibrating—but it's her that's shaking. This feeling—the way that her whole world has rotated on its head—this must be the real *little death*.

She vaults out of the creche toward the dining facility. Her heart rattle-bumps like the pumps that draw water through the station, but she doesn't stop until she sees Irina in the food line.

Her feelings catch up with her. She's been in love before, but not like this, heady and all fantasy, the need to share spilling out of her like steam.

"Irina!"

In the line, heads pop up, eager to break the day's monotony.

Irina turns. Her right eyebrow hikes to the sky. "What is it?"

Despite her euphoria, Alex spies the tension in Irina's forehead, the hard glitter in her eyes. Alex doesn't know if it's jealousy or just scorn, but it dries the news on her lips into a crust.

"Nothing." She turns away.

Alex doesn't bring up her admirer again, but every new missive pulls her and Irina farther apart. Their distance shoots the thrill of each note through with a sadness like a fine blue thread.

After two weeks, Alex arrives at the dining facility to find Irina has moved seats. Alex realizes this for what it is—a point of no return, an end to the painful stretching between them—and this hurts even more than the notes feel good.

She buckles into the empty seat next to Irina. "I miss you."

It wasn't exactly what she'd intended to say—but Irina looks taken aback, as if the walls that've greeted Alex the last two weeks are gone.

But Irina's face turns hard again. "Did the notes stop? Or did you finally figure out who they were meant for?"

A hot flare fills Alex, angry as the sun. She extracts the latest one from her pocket and slides it forward: *When you smile, my knees go weak.*

Alex doesn't know what she was expecting—but it certainly wasn't Irina's mocking laugh.

"Well, this fucking proves it."

Alex retracts like a turtle. For a moment, the mess of people around them, the clinks of silverware on trays, it all fades away. "What do you mean?"

"You never smile. It's like you don't know how."

Whatever détente there was between them evaporates. "Why are you being so mean about this? It is so hard to believe someone could find me attractive?"

"No, it's—" Irina's face falls. She looks tired. "I didn't want to have to tell you this. I was hoping you'd forget about it."

Alex's racing heart shudders to a stop. "What?"

"Those messages. I know who they're for. There's a couple next shift—"

But Alex won't listen to Irina's lies. She storms out with a giant bounce, like the arc of a shooting star.

Alex had been alone, those first days on the station—but this loneliness is new, because Alex is an old hand at the routines. There's nothing to distract her from the shape of her friend's absence.

It takes her a week to convince herself Irina was lying. Sometimes, right before Alex passes out, she pretends the woman that was sending her these messages approaches her in the dining facility.

Alex doesn't know every person on the station well, though she recognizes the faces. In her daydream, the writer is Catherine: Catherine, who has flashing brown eyes and long hair like ferns. Catherine, with the slim, androgynous body that Alex has always found so hot.

Catherine always approaches, her lip quivering, her eyes welling with tears. *Why didn't you write me back?*

Twelve days after Alex and Irina stop talking, Alex pens her own note.

Let's meet.

She stuffs it into the outlet cover and welcomes the fade to black.

It's during leisure time that Alex hears the fight in the back corner of the rec room: two voices, one soft and lilting, one fuller and darker.

When she looks up, her whole body clenches. It's *her*. Catherine.

But then Catherine's face twists up. There's a wetness in her eyes that would be tears, if only there was some gravity to extract them.

Alex pushes off the wall and floats over. The fight gets louder as she approaches—Alex's dream woman and her companion, a squat woman with a strong jaw and developed forearm muscles. Alex thinks the woman's name might be Kai.

"I swear to god," Kai says. "I left one just this morning in the outlet—"

Alex wants to stop—wants to die, really—but there's nothing to check her flight forward.

"I don't understand," says Catherine, and now, Alex understands the horrible truth: Catherine wasn't writing to Alex. Alex was *stealing* Catherine's messages.

Alex tries to stop, but she can't. She goes slack and resigns herself to what happens next.

At the last moment before Alex plows into them, Kai turns and grabs her by the shoulders. "You alright?"

Catherine looks affronted, her brows drawing together in an approximation of rage.

Alex feels sick. "I have something that belongs to you." She pulls the most recent note out of her pocket and shoves it into Catherine's palm.

Catherine unballs it. Her face lights up. For a moment, Alex is overjoyed that she could make something so beautiful happen—but then she remembers that she's actually just Catherine's facsimile, the stand-in recipient of Kai's love.

Alex floats away before they can ask her anything, her eyes full of tears she can't shed.

That sleep shift, Alex enters the creche with a raw heart. She perceives a touch of the last occupant's warmth—or maybe that's just from the disinfection cycle—but still, the creche feels like a house left empty too long, haunted by people that will never come back.

Little deaths, thinks Alex, and nothing has ever made more sense.

There's a note sticking out of the outlet. It fills her with rage. It's not enough that she embarrassed herself completely—no, now she's got to see the reminder every day for as long as this couple are together.

She straps in, sinks back into the cocktail, and lets everything go.

Alex is not *hiding*, exactly—but she's found that lately, she's more content with her leisure time when it's not in the rec room. Instead, she circles endlessly through the station's outer ring, grabbing surfaces and pushing herself forward, over and over again, like a rower cutting across a lake. It's only when she's moving that the weight of everything gets left behind.

She's grabbing for the wall when she hears a voice behind her. "Hey, wait!"

Alex pauses long enough to see that it's Kai. She pushes off, because she's got to get away, before Kai breaks Alex's fingers or—

"Wait!"

Alex is fast, but she's been at it for thirty minutes, and the muscles of her arms and back are depleted. Kai catches her easily, grabbing her by the collar. The two of them soar, end over end, joined together by the axis of Kai's grip.

Alex gives up. She's being scruffed like a kitten—what else can she do? "I said I was sorry," she lies.

"It's not that," says Kai. "That was just a misunderstanding. But this?" She shoves something into Alex's palm: a crumpled piece of paper.

Alex throws it back, but Kai's already flying down the hall. Whatever she just dropped on Alex, she doesn't want it back.

Alex collects the paper and unfolds it.

Dear Alex, it reads, and Alex's breath stops—because this time, there is no confusion. This note is completely, irrevocably for her.

I want to say I'm sorry.

I lied, you know. You do smile—but only when nobody is looking. It's always so sudden, so unpredictable—like when you're standing outside in the middle of summer, and out of nowhere comes this sheet of rain.

That's my favorite. Those sudden summer showers.

Well, almost my favorite. The truth is, you're my favorite. And I miss you—miss you so much that I realize I should've just told you the truth, but I was so jealous.

If you just want to be friends, I understand, but I'm open to more. I was a coward, but I don't want to risk you falling in love with a daydream again.

Irina

Alex doesn't know how to feel. Slow warmth unfurls out from her core. Not heady and bright like the notes, but more like the steady unveiling of a shoot through the soil.

They've been friends for years. Irina's the only thing that's made Alex's time on the station bearable. And with any luck, they'll finish their sentences at the same time.

They could start a whole new life together.

Alex turns in the hallway and starts to pull. She doesn't know where Irina might be, but she'll find her.

Alex is ready for something real.

Lyda Morehouse

*B*eing alone was the easy part.

Avril Tyrell had passed all the tests—or flunked them, depending on your point of view. Normally, social anxiety was something to be fixed, but when human contact was the problem, being cut off from others for large swaths of time in deep space equaled Avril's idea of a plum assignment. The job was simple: float around in a solo research center and do a little data processing of various pieces of research telemetry of Saturn's F-ring, a.k.a. "the weird braided bits," and send it "home" to UNASA, the United Nations Aeronautics and Space Administration. Because it was an Earth government job, the pay was crappy, but she decided that the benefits more than made up for it.

Avril said yes in the proverbial New York minute.

An incoming transmission light beeped, making Avril jump.

Her heart rate spiked. Sweat prickled under her armpits.

Was this something she had to answer?

She'd been on the job for nearly a year now, and she was contractually obligated to respond to anything from UNASA. If it wasn't coded as an emergency, she'd discovered that she could get away with pretending that she'd been in the head when the call came in. She wasn't trying to be difficult. Honestly, with her anxiety, all Avril needed was a chance to process and formulate a response, and so having the time to listen to a recording of the message helped tremendously.

The beep had been singular, not a steady stream of annoying chirps, so ... no emergency. That was a relief.

Avril calmed down enough to take a quick peek at the readout. Weird. It wasn't anything from Earth. Somehow, her lonely little research outpost just received a text communication ... from the asteroid belt of all places. And the text .... It was so old-fashioned.

People still used text-based communications, but they were broadcast on a live feed—and honestly reserved for certain corners of nerd culture, fandom. This new missive, however, was what people called "dead mail" because it was basically inert. You couldn't interact with it at all other than to return your own string of flat text to the sender and let it sit there like a lump. Avril felt like she was looking at a relic from the past.

Oh, maybe that was exactly what it was? Had she gotten a "letter" from the asteroid belt's past? A weird packet of information from some distant era?

She pulled up the inert text to examine it further. It was addressed to Earth, 0°23'N 9°27'E.

The mystery deepened: the date stamp was only a few days ago. This dead mail might be an archaic format, but this particular missive was current. Was someone on Earth expecting to receive it?

With a quick correction, Avril bounced the dead mail back toward Earth. She almost stopped there, but a sense of responsibility niggled at her. It was a weird, archaic way to communicate with someone, but shouldn't Avril let the sender know that the dead mail had been beamed to the wrong place? Like, way wrong—Earth was in the completely opposite direction from her outpost. If someone was expecting the dead mail, there would be a significant delay. More importantly, if the sender didn't adjust their transmission, Avril would keep getting these pings.

That would be annoying.

Avril was tempted to send her note via a modern mode, like a quick interstellar blip, but another search of the original turned up only a dead-mail return address. It took a bit of figuring, but Avril found a way to call up a blank reply-card. She wrote:

```
To S. Novax @ Lander's Colony, Ceres, EF
Asteroid Miners Association
From A Tyrell @ Orbital EC Research Plat-
form, Saturn's Ring:

Your letter was misdelivered. Have sent it
on to your recipient in Libreville, Gabon,
Earth.
```

Avril's fingers paused. Remembering that a human was on the other end, she thought she should probably not sound quite so robotic. Maybe sign off with the standard, "Hope you're having a nice day!"? No, obviously, whoever this was would not be having a nice day since they just found out their archaically formatted letter home went to the wrong place and was now on the slow boat. And did the asteroid miners even use Earth "days" as a concept anymore? They'd been independent from Earth's government for generations. Avril only thought in terms of days because UNASA did.

She should say something more, though, right? Avril tried to imagine how she might feel. Would they be worried that Avril might have read their letter, even though it appeared to be in French, a language she didn't really know despite several years of study? Okay, something reassuring?

```
I didn't really open it. I mean, it comes
open—which is really weird, but I don't read
French. I only copied your address so that I
could let you know that you might want to get
your transmitter checked. My station is near
Saturn. Another few degrees off and your mes-
sage would have been deep-spaced. I thought
you should know.
```

Okay, that was more like a normal person. Now, sign off? How? Something from some half-forgotten history course came back to Avril in a flash, and before she knew what she was doing, she'd signed:

```
Sincerely yours, A.
```

Avril hit send before she could take it back.

Of course, instantly, she wanted to take it back.

"Sincerely yours?" What had she been thinking? That was far too familiar with a stranger, wasn't it? And so old-fashioned! Oh my god, she was such a freak. The other person was going to think she was a stalker or something, being that personal and friendly.

Maybe she should write something else, explain how she lost her mind and channeled some correspondent from centuries ago. Or would more "mail" make her seem even crazier??

Mounting stress paralyzed Avril until a second ping. It was a reminder that she'd set for herself alerting her that the fan-feed for her new anime obsession *Daiyamondo no Ai!* was still in range but would only be so for another Martian day, which meant she only had another twenty-five Earth standard hours to read all the things before it was gone for months.

Knowing it would calm her, Avril pulled up the feed. She had to keep up with her muscle-mass exercises anyway and she could do that while scrolling through the small fan-group broadcast that she lurked on for *Daiyamondo no Ai!* Most of the shipping wars—"who should be in a relationship with whom" speculations—were garbage fires like they always were, but occasionally there'd be a decent theory thread or someone would post links to fan fiction. Avril read all the fan fic, even the terrible stuff. *Daiyamondo no Ai!* was just that good; it hit all her favorite tropes: made families, lost heirs, and quirky mad scientists.

Avril disliked dealing with most people, but fans had always been an exception for some reason. She could listen to people talk about her favorite shows forever. She even occasionally posted her own thoughts.

By the time she hit the classic wall of text defending the trueness of some romantic pairing or other, she was breathing normally again.

Even so, when a response came back the next day, she'd slept only fitfully. The corresponding adrenaline spike of the new message coming in nearly killed her, but her curiosity was stronger.

To my mysterious correspondent "A"

Hello, hello! This is S! My name is Samira.

I'm so sorry that my ghost mail troubled you, but thanks for sending it to Earth, anyway. Do you know ghost mail? I have no idea if this is a thing that only my family does or if it's an actual religious tradition, but, um, I write dead mail to my dead grandmother once a year and send it into deep space?

I probably sound really weird.

Anyway, it was just by chance that you intercepted it, but don't be surprised if you see it again. It may bounce back to you since no one will be around to accept it on Earth.

It was really nice of you not to read it, but honestly since grandma is dead and can't complain, I've just been writing her pages and pages of drivel about my newest favorite anime. You don't happen to know *Shōnen no Kosuto Hyōka* do you???

Yours, S.

Anyone else would have written something banal back immediately, but Avril searched all broadcasts and in-range databases for information about *Shōnen no Kosuto Hyōka* instead. She found a listing that described the plot—hmmm, Boys' Love. Not a favorite subgenre, but the mystery element held some promise. Even though it looked like it might not be to her exact taste, Avril located a deep-space vendor selling a copy for a decent price. The show was popular enough that the nearest relay not only had it, but could make a download of the complete first season in seven hours.

That would give her time to take a quick shower and a decent nap.

Avril was seven episodes in before she realized that she'd missed the last of the remaining window with her *Daiyamondo* fan group. She took some screenshots and downloaded what she could, but she was invested enough in *Shōnen no Kosuto Hyōka* that she figured she could start mentally composing her response to Samira while dealing with the day's data work.

It surprised Avril how much she looked forward to writing back. She'd had a few friends in the past, but none of them had been fans. In fact, with her other friends—friends in meet/meat-space—she would have to squash her impulse to go on and on about her favorite shows. It was exciting to know she could just … be *herself* and not hide this part.

So, despite the clunkiness of the reply format, she began typing.

> I have to tell you I'm not normally a big fan
> of the kind of story that *Shōnen no Kosuto
> Hyōka* is—I mean, Boys' Love, or do you call it
> yaoi, I'm not sure? I'm not judging you, but
> isn't a lot of that stuff mostly fetishizing
> gay men? Anyway, I'm going to give you my
> thoughts on the first seven episodes because
> that's as far as I've gotten so far. I bought
> the first season. No spoilers, please.

Avril then proceeded to write another good, solid ten paragraphs, without even trying to edit for spelling. At the very end, she asked if Samira had heard of *Daiyamondo no Ai!* because it was worth a shot. In fact, just to hedge her bets, Avril listed a bunch of other favorite anime to see if they had other common ground.

She hit send with full confidence. If Samira wasn't the sort of fan who liked all this kind of blather, Avril would know soon enough. As nice as it might be to finally have a fan-friend, Avril's past friend-ships had all ended in disaster. So, if this was going to implode, better that it happened right away. It saved everyone heartache later.

With that sent, Avril went back to the exercise room to do her reps and to finish watching the first season of Samira's show while eating dinner. She really hoped Samira would answer some of her questions. She'd thought it would be a dumb romance—or worse, smut—but the story was pretty good, complex—even a little philosophical. In fact, Avril was thinking about thumbing through the database to see what else was out there by this writer.

With a yawn, Avril pushed off the wall toward the kitchen to heat a mac and cheese pack.

Avril thought the adrenaline rush from the season finale would be enough to keep her awake while she scrolled for info about the next season. She strapped herself in, just in case it wasn't, and a good thing, too, as she dropped off to sleep after only a page. The beep of a new message waited for her as she untangled herself and picked the food containers out of the air. Opening her morning pill and finding the toothpaste pack, she had the onboard AI read her the letter.

She almost choked on her pill when the AI's tinny, mechanical voice began reciting, "Oh my god, oh my god! *Daiyamondo no Ai!?* I love that show! Please tell me that Haruki is your favorite, too!"

They wrote to each other every day after that. Before she even knew how it had happened, Avril learned little things about Samira's life. Samira was older than Avril by about five years—which was surprising given how much more childlike she seemed. Apparently, she was just an enthusiastic person, probably even an extrovert. Samira lived in a crowded tenement complex built as temporary housing for asteroid miners fifty-odd years ago. Her family regularly dealt with all sorts of plumbing and depressurizing snafus, but their super was decent even if the Manfred Mining Association gave no craps about its workers.

Samira's family consisted of herself, an adorable dog named Bobsled (they broke their dead-mail protocol to share pictures of pets and anime screenshots), Samira's elderly mother, a husband, and two kids. Avril had to admit that she couldn't always remember if Henri was Samira's husband or son. To be fair, she and Samira mostly talked about their shows.

Avril didn't really think she'd have much to share in return. But she surprised herself by telling Samira about her anxiety issues and some of her own family history, like how she'd actually been living on Earth with her dads until recently—despite her age. She even related their awkward parting.

So, my dads were against me taking this job. I think Papa was just scared for me, you know? He's from the generation who remembers all the early Jump Gate accidents, and thinks of space as really dangerous. He didn't like the idea of me working alone. I didn't have the heart to tell him that UNASA insists on it. At some point the bosses had tried sending couples into space, but would end in acrimony at best and murder at worst. Seriously, there was a notation in the fine print in my contract about how much cheaper suicide insurance liability is than all the hassle that comes with assault and murder!

Anyway, I tried to reassure Papa that I wasn't really alone. The gates mean that help is less than three days away, and there is a very shell AI program onboard here at the research station. It can perform minor repairs to the ship and offer basic medical advice. For some reason UNASA has nicknamed it "Clippy"? Some old-timer joke, I guess about a not-very-helpful helper? The reference was lost on me.

Unfortunately it wasn't on Dad and he got all pissy and said that if they were going to bother with a useless AI, why didn't they just send something sophisticated instead of

143

```
a valuable human life? My dad, the socialist.
I could hardly explain to him that an AI
is really expensive, much more valuable—
especially if you consider how cheap my labor
is—and rumor has it that the smarter the
'bot, the quicker it is to get destructively
bored, if you know what I mean.

I didn't know how to tell him any of that,
though, so I kind of hung up on them? I for-
got to, you know, say "I love you," and it's
freaked me out since. You know how bad it is
in dramas and anime when people don't say
goodbye or end on a fight—someone always ends
up dead. It feels too weird to bring up now.
And, I've never managed to slide it into our
video chats—they always have so much to catch
me up on that we run out of time. Half the
time, we don't even manage a proper goodbye.
```

Samira's missive the next day had some decent advice. She suggested that Avril might just write them a "letter," since it was clearly much easier for Avril to express herself that way.

That surprised Avril, because it seemed true. Probably it was the restrictions of the format of dead mail. There was no way for anyone to interrupt or even accidentally derail a thought, because they each took turns. They had the entire floor to themselves for as long as they wanted. You couldn't do that even on the fan forums. Someone would always jump in.

Plus, if a story or insight got complex, Avril could go back and revise and rethink—though, she found herself doing less and less of that the more she got to know Samira.

In the last few months, they'd only had one real argument. Turned out, Samira actually liked the ending of the second season of *Shōnen no Kosuto Hyōka* and that was just plain wrong. They had vowed not to speak of it, and they both agreed whole-heartedly about everything involving *Daiyamondo* so, you know, about the things that really mattered, they were sympatico.

Avril got used to starting her day reading Samira's "letter," and spending each evening replying to it. In the in-between times she worked or watched their shows while doing her muscle-building, bone-strengthening exercises.

The first time no message came, Avril threw up a little. Okay, a lot, but that was partly the fault of the reconstituted beef, but also because she hadn't slept well. In last night's reply, Avril had a bit of a rant. Samira had suggested that it was possible that Shiro was not the true lost heir and that was just ridiculous. Avril might have resorted to some name calling … to be fair, you would have to be an idiot to not remember that scene in episode three of the second season where Shiro's mom gives him the ring … but, well, she didn't really mean that Samira was an *actual* numbskull.

She regretted it.

Deeply.

But there was no decent way to take it back.

Through breakfast, Avril literally bounced off the walls. She had a hard time sitting still enough to get her work done. When nothing came through by the time lunch break hit, Avril started full-on panicking.

She told herself that it was possible that Samira was just busy. She was a mom and a wife and a mine worker, so it wouldn't be unexpected if something had kept her from replying. Except, she had never missed a letter in all this time.

Avril checked the news feed.


```
Comet Tail Debris Bombards Asteroid Belt;
Miners Killed.
```


Avril stared at that headline for a long time. Her heart hammering against her eardrum. Dead? Could Samira be injured or dead?

Avril didn't know what to do. She could wait and see if a letter came tomorrow, but she could barely breathe now for worry. In an impulse, Avril found the communication ID that Samira had used to send pictures of Bobsled, her dog.

She sent a quick text message: "Are you OK?"

Avril waited for a response, staring at the screen.

She tried to go back to work, hoping that, given enough time, Samira would find it and reply, but that was seeming less likely. Following up on other news articles, Avril discovered the problem. A number of the communication depots had been affected by the debris fall. A small corner of the *Daiyamondo* fan group was talking about it. Some people had had success contacting family and friends by … voice chat.

There was nothing Avril hated more than talking on voice-only lines.

Except not knowing whether or not Samira was alive.

Avril didn't even hesitate. Her fingers shook and she hyperventilated through the sound of the rings, but she did it, anyway. They could not end like this, not on a fight! Hadn't they just talked about this scenario? It wouldn't be right. She had to risk this call. It would be too awful otherwise.

Finally, Henri—ah, yes, the son!—picked up.

Avril blurted, "Are your parents okay? Uh … oh! I'm your mom's friend from deep space."

"The anime fan?"

Why did that matter, but, "Yes, the anime fan. I heard about the comet debris, is everyone okay?"

"Yeah, mom got the week off. Do you want to talk to her?" Before Avril could freeze up and say no, Henri passed the phone with, "Hey, Mom, it's your anime friend!"

"On the receiver? Live?" Avril heard the disbelief. Henri must have nodded and handed over the receiver, because suddenly there was a voice nothing at all like Avril had imagined saying, "Hello? You must have been very worried, Avril. I never thought you'd actually call, given … anyway, I'm so sorry. Communication is down all over Colony Three. How did you even get this to work?"

"Oh, I bounced it off Ceres." The fan group had thought of it, surely other people had too? Even though Samira couldn't see it, Avril shrugged, "I'm sure other people will do the same. Anyway, I don't have anything to say. I just … well, you know, I didn't get your thoughts on the new villain yesterday morning, and so … ."

Okay, wow, that seemed like a dumb reason to hack into a dwarf planet's communication array.

"Eiji gives me the creeps. That scene with Aio? A real tell, don't you think?"

Somehow the sound of Samira settling into a couch had Avril forgetting her impulse to hang up. She even got used to a surprisingly strong French accent. In fact, for the first time in her life, Avril managed to stay on the line with a live human for over two standard Earth hours.

They survived several more communication blackouts (and fannish squabbles) over the next two years.

The real crisis came when Avril's bosses told her she had to take a mandatory vacation. Despite her workouts and hypervigilance with the weight training, Avril's latest medical work-up showed a slight-enough muscle-mass loss that they wanted her to go anywhere with gravity, even fake gravity, for two weeks. The bosses decided that it was a good time for the station to get some repairs, so even if she'd wanted to tell them to stuff their stupid vacation, the ship with the maintenance crew was already on its way.

After bitterly complaining about this in a message to Samira, she got this in a reply:

```
Why don't you come visit me? Henri's poly-
cule is making it official, so you could come
to the wedding. I'd love to have someone to
snark with since you know I love most of his
partners to death, I still have my hesita-
tions about Violet.

We have gravity! And we could watch the finale
together! How cool would that be??
```

Avril considered it for three whole seconds—which was a lot, considering. What if they didn't get along—really, in person? And a wedding? Dozens, possibly hundreds of people. Avril hadn't seen another non-animated human being for almost four years. If she ever had any people skills, they were beyond rusted now. Plus, even with her meds, how could she possibly cope?

She hated to tell Samira "no," but she had to. It was the only way.

```
I've already paid for one of those exercise
spa places on Ganymede. Sorry. Have fun with-
out me.
```

It was a lie, but it would be easy enough to book the spa. In fact, she'd only thought of it because the company had sent information on discounted rates. Ganymede was trendy in all the wrong ways, but Avril figured she could just hide in the hotel room for two weeks.

The next morning's reply was curt and clearly disappointed.

```
Okay. If you've paid for it, what can you
do? Ganymede is close, though. Do you want
to try to meet up for the finale? I'm sure I
could get away. Who needs the mother of the
groom, anyway?
```

Avril growled at the screen in mute frustration. She wasn't supposed to offer to meet up! It took all night for Avril to compose the response.

```
No, look, don't worry about me. The wedding
should be your priority.
```

When the next letter returned to fan theory, Avril figured they'd weathered this personal storm, just like they had all the meteor showers.

The spa trip was one trauma after another. During the jump gate travel, Avril had practiced orienting to "up" and "down" with the holographic training program that UNASA had sent, but none of that had prepared her for the suffocating feeling of actual gravity. The domed cities were disorienting because the ceiling was so far away and Jupiter's reflective light from the sun was so much brighter than Saturn's.

And that was before you counted all the people.

So many people.

They all stared at her, judging. Out in the research station, Avril hadn't ever had to deal with "the looks." No one cared if she wore no make-up, if she wasn't "fashionable"—whatever that meant this week. She could let her wild hair grow out and flow around her in zero-G like the tendrils of a jellyfish. Other cycles, she shaved it all off, leaving only the barest stubble. Right, now she was sure she just looked like a half-grown out mess.

Everyone seemed to need to talk to her, too. Strangers wanted to ask her opinion of the spa's hot springs or ask if this was her first visit to Ganymede. None were satisfied when she tried to brush them off politely, either.

Worse, the bellhop's fingers had grazed hers and that had been very weird, plus he'd expected a tip and not a slammed door in his face so she'd had to answer a video call from the manager who basically yelled at her for being so rude, except in that roundabout passive-aggressive tone that reminded Avril of her parents in all the wrong ways.

She spent the first forty-eight hours crying and feeling dizzy and sick to her stomach.

Despite it all, Avril still managed to write to Samira every night. In fact, it was her only comfort.

The knock on the door took her by surprise. Avril dove under the covers, trying to physically hide from having to deal with any more people.

Oh, no wait, had she ordered room service? Did they have to come in for that? "Just leave it outside!" she shouted to be heard through the plastcrete, "I included a tip in the order."

Didn't she? Well, if she hadn't, she'd add one now.

"It's me,' came a familiar French-accented voice. "Samira."

Oh shit. Maybe if Avril had been feeling better, she'd have seen between the lines of Samira's last letter.

Too late to pretend she wasn't there. What was she supposed to do? No, Avril knew what she was supposed to do—she was supposed to be excited that her friend had made a trip all the way from the asteroid belt to Ganymede. She was supposed to rush to the door, fling it open, and wrap Samira in a gigantic hug.

She wanted to, a little?

But.

This was too soon, too much of a surprise. Avril could barely breathe, much less pull herself out from under the covers to greet her friend. There had been that whole awkward elevator ride earlier, where a stranger had tried to talk about some sports team? The claustrophobia of the elevator and the pressure of the gravity pushing on her constantly had worn Avril ragged.

"The finale starts in an hour," Samira's voice was more tentative now, "I thought a surprise would be nice?"

No. Surprises are bad.

Avril knew she should be saying something welcoming or apologetic or something other than holding her breath.

The doorknob rattled.

Then there was silence—a final, awful silence.

Avril managed to watch the *Daiyamondo* finale, but she cried through the whole thing. She should have known this whole real -ife friendship thing couldn't end well. People always wanted things that Avril couldn't give. She'd even tried being honest and talking about this to Samira, but clearly it hadn't stuck. Other people just never understood; this was how all her friendships ended.

Always.

She hated it. She hated herself. Not even her parents could love her this way.

And now everything was ruined.

Again.

The next morning, Avril dejectedly dragged herself out from the hotel bed. She had to log one more hour of exercise for the bosses.

Then, she would return to the solace of her deep-space research pod. No more messy people. Just the emptiness of space.

It was best this way. The show was over, her friendship was over. She could grieve them both properly once she was back in her station.

This last day was just so hard. Everything felt so heavy. It was hard to even lift her hand to swallow her pill. She was looking forward to being able to drift across the room instead of having to painfully thump from one end to another. It was disorienting that the room had an up and a down. She just wanted to float.

With a deep breath, Avril pushed those thoughts aside. One foot in front of the other, one last exercise and she was out of here, back to what she understood. Alone was the easy part. It always had been.

Avril opened the door and nearly tripped over a huge bouquet of hydroponic flowers. She glanced down the hall, had these been misdelivered? They must have been. Who sent flowers? It was so ancient, so old-fashioned.

Sweet peas, too? How strange. They were a favorite from Earth.

When Avril stooped down to pick them up—awkward and nauseatingly disorienting even after a week of gravity—a note fell out. Handwritten? How much further back into ancient traditions ...

Oh, of course. How dumb was she? This had to be from Samira. The whole thing was so 20th century!

Avril read the note:

```
I'm so sorry. I knew better and I screwed up.
I wasn't thinking and I put you in an uncom-
fortable position. I'm a big idiot and I hope
you will forgive me.

I've gone home, but not because I'm mad at
you. I'm mad at myself. You told me who you
were, and I didn't respect that. I promise I
will never, ever do that to you again.

There will be an email waiting for you back
at your station. If you don't answer it, I'll
understand. I hope I didn't hurt you too much
and we can still be friends.
```

```
If I ruined your experience of the finale, I
will never forgive myself. I said that Shiro
would end this way!

Yours, S.
```

Avril stared at the note for a long time, read it twice. Something tight unwound as she took a deep breath. Nerds made the best friends. But Samira was wrong about one thing: Shiro's redemption arc was stupid.

She'd have to explain that to Samira in her next note.

Photosynthesis, Growth

Devin Miller

She was a flower, opening in the sunlight. I do not mean that metaphorically. I mean that the skin from her breastbone to her navel unlatched and curled over itself, and I could see her ribs, her sternum, her lungs gray and pulsing. The inside of her skin petals was a vivid orange pink, and she leaned back against the wall of the compound to let her body drink in the sunlight.

I watched in fascination, because my body doesn't do this, and because it was her. I'd seen her bloom before, and I'd seen other photosynths open too, but it never became ordinary. I felt similar when I watched a cat yawn—I wanted to stick a finger in. But because this body belonged to the girl I loved, I wanted to stick my whole hand in and touch.

It was the first spring day that was really warm. We snuck out of the gates together to skirt the walls of the compound and tuck ourselves in at its back, where the sun could see us but the people planting sweet potatoes could not. We were young then, she with soft petals, green and purple-veined, newly grown riotous from the sweep of her forehead, and I, newly come to the understanding that I was not a girl, and learning how to be agender. I was in a phase where I wore my work coveralls unzipped over dramatically V-necked shirts all the time. The sun made my chest feel pleasantly warm, my armpits and thighs damp. I leaned against the smooth metal wall next to her and reached out to run my finger down the fern-frond spiral of skin below her breast.

Her head petals had spread open too, ruffling themselves looser into a halo around her face. She was fully bloomed. She turned to me and said, "I have something to tell you."

She didn't say it in any particular tone, but a small crooked piece of fear sprang open in me. A moment later it snapped straight and stabbed me.

"I can't go to Metelios with you."

Metelios was the planet where Hyle University was located. Two weeks ago I had received my letter of acceptance and had paid my entrance fee. She did not want to go to university, but we'd planned that when I went, she would go with me. I've always been a person whose words shrivel up when the conversation becomes difficult, but it was worse at that age. I could only gasp out, "Why?"

"I was reading about it, about the climate and the city and that sort of thing. I found out the university is so close to the planet's pole there's almost no sunlight for half a year." Her head petals fluttered in a warm gust of air.

I slid down the wall until I was crouched on the balls of my feet, and said to the gray earth under them, "What about sunlamps?" But even in that moment I couldn't imagine her making do with a sunlamp, when she was so beautiful in the full light of a real sun.

"I can visit," she offered. "In the summers. It sounds lovely then, it's light nearly the whole day."

Why hadn't I done my research, found this out before I applied, before I was accepted, before I let my fathers pay the fee? I could have gone to Ulule or Ket or any of the other universities that were probably at reasonable latitudes on their planets. But I was so focused on academics, on which university had the best professors and most rigorous program, that I barely looked at photos or facts about the university's environment.

"Maybe it's a good thing," she said. "You can find out who you want to be on your own. Have your own experiences."

"Do you believe that?" I asked. I looked up at her. Her torso petals had curled tighter, pulling her skin further open.

"It's what Cari Mother said when I told her. But yes."

I didn't believe it. I didn't want to go to a place where half the year had so little sunlight I wouldn't even be able to imagine her, beautiful in green and purple and pulsing red, open to the sky.

But in the end, I had to go.

There were photosynths at Hyle University, but they weren't like her. Mostly they were locals, adapted to the latitude, mosses and grasses. Many had grayish-green curly fronds on their heads and shoulders. Others had short yellow grass covering their bodies, so they looked as furred as a cat. I avoided them, pale imitations of my girlfriend's vividness.

"Look at this!" she said in a message, and attached a selfie in which I could see her greenish face, her lips parted and tongue pink. Her head petals had grown long pointy tips that looked like they'd sway softly in the breeze.

I looked outside, where it was dark, and then I sent back a selfie in which it was apparent that I hadn't changed at all.

I went to Introduction to Nanoscience and Calculus II and bio lab, and doodled pictures of her petals and her ribs in the margins of my notes. Not because I wasn't paying attention in class—I was, because Hyle University's academic rigor was just as good as my research had suggested. I had to pay attention or I'd fall behind. I had to pay attention because if I wasn't here to learn, I might as well have been at one of those universities that got enough sun. But she was always in my head, and while she was too far away to touch, I needed to imagine.

I had been at university for half of Metelios's 323-day year when summer came and she visited me.

The sunlight lasted more of the day than it did at home, but it wasn't as warm. The afternoon she arrived we walked together to the quad, which was blanketed in a soft moss that had made me think of her since I first saw it. I knew she'd want to lie down and dig her shoulders in and bloom in the softness. I lay down beside her and intertwined our fingers and watched her body unfurl.

I couldn't relax, because I had a question I wanted to ask and had been putting it off since she'd told me when she'd be here. I was bad at asking questions when I cared a lot about the answer. I told myself I'd wait until she was fully bloomed before I asked. But that didn't take very long, and I made myself spit it out. "Are you staying the whole summer?"

She turned her head, the long thin tips of her head petals drifting in my direction. "Yes. Until the equinox."

It sounded like a fairytale deadline, too poetic to be a real arbiter of our lives. But it was the answer I wanted. I was happy.

The internal organs of a photosynth are coated in a protective substance which makes it possible for them to be exposed in nonsterile environments. But still, when your body is on display for all to see, you're vulnerable. At home, there were many people like her, and no one looked twice at them except for people like me who were in love.

But at Hyle she was unusual and beautiful, and people stared at her when she bloomed. Medical students came up to her and asked to look closer. Like many flowers, she was a bit of a show-off, and she didn't mind. But I minded, and would have told them rudely to go away had I not been too shy to say anything. I wanted to be the only person on the planet who knew in detail what she looked like on the inside.

The equinox fell in the month called, in this part of Metelios, Cornermonth. It was colder; my classes were harder. I had a research paper due the week after the equinox, and I spent a couple of long afternoons holed up in the library, writing my paper and composing apologies for not lounging in the quad with her.

When she left, her head petals were curled up tightly against her skull, and her torso petals were smoothly locked together. I kissed her goodbye more clumsily than I wanted to. Like any good fairytale deadline, there was no way around it: the equinox had come and she had to go.

I'd always felt about sunlight that it was somehow hers, that because she needed it to photosynthesize, I only needed it on her behalf. My first winter of university I had lived in the long nights, turned on the sunlamp in my room automatically, and without basking in its light. But when she was with me, and I laid with her on the moss of the quad, I'd remembered that I liked sunlight for myself, too. I liked the way it made my skin feel, the way it sank into me and made me content and sleepy.

The week after she left, I turned in my research paper and went to one of the university's indoor gardens. It was different from Metelios's summer, and different from any season at home, but the light in the domed roof felt like sunshine in a way my little sunlamp did not. There were plants I didn't recognize. All plants reminded me of her, but none of these looked like her. It was a vegetable garden.

I sat down on a bench and watched from a distance as a student weeded a patch of root vegetables with orange tops peeking above the dirt. There weren't very many other people in the garden. I sat alone and felt sorry for myself, though it was surprisingly hard to feel totally unhappy under the bright light of the false sun.

I was so busy with my thoughts I didn't notice the movement of the weeding student until he appeared on my left, looking at me in a friendly way. "Hi. The garden club's meeting starts in ten minutes," he said.

"Oh, sorry, am I in your way?"

"Not at all. But it'll get pretty noisy in here, and you looked like you were enjoying the quiet. You're welcome to join the meeting if you want to, though."

I looked at him. He was wearing the kind of stain-resistant pants popular at Hyle, though specks of earth clung to the knees. He hadn't washed the dirt off his hands, and the way it coated his fingertips was familiar from my years weeding the gardens at home. I'd grown used to saying no to people automatically, not going to events for fear I'd miss an opportunity to talk to her while we were both awake. But I was already here and I didn't want to leave the garden, and somehow I thought I could handle a noisy garden club meeting.

"What does the garden club do?" I asked.

"Garden," he said with a grin. "We help the university's gardeners maintain the gardens, and we get some say in what we grow, so we argue about plants."

I didn't want to argue about anything, but I liked the idea of gardening. "Is it okay if I stay and see if I like it?"

"Sure. Come on over to the potting tables." There was a row of rectangular tables at waist height, with stacks of empty pots and watering cans. A couple of people had already gathered there. I got up from the bench, which felt like a bigger achievement than it was, and followed the boy to the tables.

I ended up weeding a patch of the purple-orange leafy vegetable that was in all the student-cafeteria salads. I ended up going to the next garden club meeting, and the next.

Garden club made me feel connected to her, but not so tightly intertwined. I stopped resenting the photosynths who weren't her. Some of those in the garden club had seen her blooming in the quad and wanted to know her story. Telling them about her, about her mothers and cousins and dreams, made me realize she was not an organ I needed to keep myself alive. She didn't photosynthesize for me. I had to sunbathe for myself.

When she came to be with me the next summer, I took her to meet my friends from the garden club. We'd developed a tradition of eating food we'd harvested from the gardens together. It was early enough in the season that few vegetables were ready, but the wind cherries were ripe.

She helped pick them, and giggled as the pointed tips of her head petals danced with the branches of the cherry trees.

The boy who'd first invited me into the garden club had become a close friend; he was studying nursing, and we shared some biology classes as well as the garden club. He'd already helped me through a grueling semester of second-year bio lab, and we'd registered for another class together that was likely to be even more difficult and rewarding.

When our baskets were full of cherries, we carried them out to the quad and she flopped down on the moss and bloomed in the sunshine. My new friend was far too polite to ask to look between her petals, but I'd told her what he was studying and she remembered last summer's curious medical students. She grinned and waved him closer, and I no longer felt jealous of my knowledge of her body. I wanted my friends to know her. I laid on the moss and absorbed my own share of the sun.

When we'd planned to go together when I went to university, she'd had lots of ideas of what she wanted to do while I was studying. She loved music and thought she might try to start a band. Or she wanted to work in a shop—we didn't have any at home, where everything was shared communally or traded. Or maybe, she thought, she would like to take care of people, work in a place where she could care for the very old or very young. At home, she could work in the gardens or the laundry, the kitchens or the beehives, the forge or the building workshop. I knew she enjoyed the work she did at home, but I also knew she'd liked the idea of doing something new and different.

She'd brought her viola, and when everyone was done looking inside her body she took it out of its case and played for them. She'd told me when she arrived that when she left at the equinox she was going to Certhoss to join an orchestra.

When she finished playing and the echoes faded into the warmth of the sunlight, my friends applauded the music and started eating our harvest. She watched me choose a cherry and shook her petals as she put down the viola. I felt the fruit break on my tongue. I wanted her now only as she was: in summer a companion, a partner I could reach across the moss and touch; in winter a distant, steady support.

I blew her a pink-stained kiss and relaxed into the sun. Every time I felt the sun touch my skin, I'd think of her heart warm and pulsing inside her petals. I was sure that, even somewhere on another planet, she'd know my body was blooming, though I could not unfurl my skin to show her.

No Pain but That of Memory

Aimee Ogden

*H*ere is what I could never explain to you, sister-mine: what I did was for the sake of our mother. I knew you would never understand, though your heart was ever the more expansive between us.

How could you give me what I would not ask of myself?

You were there when the Impeller's guards dragged me in to kneel before him, in the wreckage of his ruined starship. Outside the ship's walls, pneumatic hammers cracked, drills sang. The Impeller had ordered that the people of Chasten rebuild his ship and return it to the stars. By our labor, he might retake his less-than-rightful place in the gilded halls of the Sanctuary Worlds.

And because he had brought the Compassionate Consensus with him when he crashed down to us, we did as he commanded.

It's no surprise that Sanctuary gene engineers have never made an artificial parapsych. To give themselves such powers of the mind, they would have had to come to Chasten, to breathe the foulness of our air and drink our bitter water. Yet despite their failures, they had built the Consensus: a tool not to create parapsychs, but to control them.

As the guards forced me to my knees, the blue aching light from the Consensus outlined the Impeller's haughty features. Behind him, your face remained dark, your shadow subsumed into his.

I do not suppose he had invited even you into his confidence, sister-mine, though he esteemed you over all others. Chasten is after all a penal colony. Though many of us were dropped by our mothers into its dirt, you are the only one to be carried here still in the womb. You have the full reach of parapsychic ability gifted to you by off-world conception, while we laterborn are but ugly, blunted tools. Yet too, you are stout and strong where cruel gravity has failed to drag you down. You stand tall while the old offworlders suffer and stifle under their extra burden of weight.

You could have been the most dangerous of us all. Yet there you stood, willingly leashed to the Impeller. Your hand rested on his shoulder. Behind your locked jaw and unblinking eyes, a cacophony sounded: betrayal, and fear. Even a note of sorrow, adrenaline driving every emotion to its crescendo.

I did not expect you to spill sadness on my behalf. Nor did I want it. I spat blood and broken teeth at your feet.

The Impeller read the charges against me. His guards let go, and I fell prostrate before his would-be throne. The Consensus pulsed in time with my cyanotic heart and I forced my breath to match.

I did not fear death by the Impeller's hand, and what worse consequence than that could he devise? Even if he scraped the inside of my skull with his Consensus at the height of its power, rewrote me and left me a hollow tool fit only to mouth his praises—that is only another kind of dying. I had no horror of what he might do to me.

It was *you*, sister-mine, that I feared. There is deeper pain than what the body sings to itself. There are other ways to hurt, without the intermediaries of needle and knife. I feared you; you, and the pain of a shattered moment that will not end.

"Will you defend yourself, traitor?" the Impeller asked.

Our eyes met over his shoulder. There was no love in yours. "Don't listen when he promises freedom," I told you, though my ruined jaw made a mush of the words. "There is none in this life. But if you can choose who holds your chains, why not take them into your own hands?"

"You knew who held my chains." Your fingers tightened on his shoulder. There was no dirt beneath your nails, no scars or scabs upon your knuckles. "You helped her wrap her fists around them."

What answer could I give to that? Before a powerful parapsych, truth refuses to be blemished with lies and omissions.

"Kill me quickly," I said—did not beg, but said. "As I would have done for you." I added, unwillingly, "Though I have not earned your mercy."

Beneath the moon-distant façade of your face, the tide of your anger turned. Was it my concession that wrought this shift? Or my impossible request for kindness?

Either way, the Impeller's brow had grown heavy with boredom. "Show him how betrayal is repaid." He snapped his fingers. "Take him apart."

You did not nod, nor frown. You lifted your free hand. You crooked a finger.

My jaw strained to shape the scream you pulled from me.

It was not because I loved our mother that I schemed against him, sister-mine. Is that hard for you to believe?

She walked out alone to meet him, while the rest of Chasten cowered behind wind-blasted walls. She walked toward the smoking husk of wreckage, and when he emerged, unhurt, unbent, she did not cringe from his advance. What had she to fear from a new arrival, a prisoner whose mind had not yet had a chance to blossom beneath our sun's graying light?

From the shadow of the colony fence I watched her stride up to him. New prisoners did not greet her as kindly when my shadow marred hers.

"Welcome to Chasten," she cried. Her voice reached me twice: once from her mouth and once echoed to me from the buildings at my back. "Surrender your vessel's salvage, and my protection is yours. You'll need it, if you're to—"

The Consensus was too far away for me to hear, then, wrapped inside its twisted-steel cocoon. Later, another day, its hum would blur my vision, its words of command would ring in my bones.

But the edge of its reach cut into me, and I lost my breath even as our mother stopped short of the stranger. As she fell to her knees. She did not raise a hand when the Impeller seized her by the throat.

Later, the grandams in the smoke-shops would explain what we had all seen. Life on Chasten, they said, unlocked the doors of our minds. And a door, once opened, may be entered from either side.

I knew when the life left her only because the dark smudge of her emotions was wiped free of my vision. Then the stranger, the Impeller, lifted his gaze from her stilled body and looked up at the city.

How long had her hold on you been broken when you erupted from your prison below Chasten's feet? How many breaths did you take once her chest went still and silent?

The shriek of metal giving way, the bone-deep quake of tunnels that collapsed in your wake. I shrank from the thunder of your footsteps in the dirt as you stormed out to meet him. Your hair hung in matted ribbons, your face shone pale beneath its mask of sores. But your strides were long and sure and you held your head as high as ever you had before you went beneath the stones. You stopped well short of our mother's crumpled form and you met the Impeller's gaze head-on. "I can give you what you want," you told him, and he smiled, and you smiled back.

He had promised you freedom, once he had all he wanted. But there is no true freedom to be had in this life. A rock does not break free from the sun it orbits.

Destruction is not freedom, either, but it is the best I could do, for you or for me or for our mother, to roll my sister's death into the round tidy figure of the Impeller's and mark the accounts settled.

I cannot say how the early days between you and her passed. For three years her sun rose and set on you alone. Perhaps she knew how to love you then—she *did* love you, ever did, even after she had locked you in darkness and shame beneath the colony, in layers of dirt too deep for even your gift to penetrate. She hated me: born twisted and scaled and worst of all, blunted to the powers of the mind that she so prized.

But she loved you badly, and so I think you had the worse of her.

I had my own prison, which was to be at her side, enduring her curses and the crack of her knuckles. In those days I would have gladly traded places with you, given the chance, though you may scoff at that fact.

She fed you, for a time. But it was I who saw to it that wrapped sourdough and desert greens and water still went down the conveyor to your chambers, when she grew bored of her lordship over you.

Did you worship him because he gave you back the sun?

Or because of what had happened to you the last time you raised your power against your would-be master?

Sometimes, at night, you would walk through the streets of the colony. Listening for the angry hum of dissenting thoughts, yes. But also on the prowl for the thrill and terror of street fights. The shrill excitement that precedes the flash of a knife. The burn of misplaced desire.

The Impeller did not want his property to damage itself, of course.

Though I could flee the beacon-bright song of your thoughts, I could not avoid the rest of the colony. Those of us who are Chasten-born make choice targets: if not we mind-blunted, then the drunk or the sleeping or the deeply distracted. It's difficult to sneak up on someone already cut by your cruel intentions.

The Impeller had Sanctuary's drugs to insulate his mind against parapsych and Consensus alike. But I doubt he had much to worry about from the likes of street toughs and pickpockets, with you ever at his side.

I might have expected an attack, if I hadn't been preoccupied with locking you out of my plans. I had given up trying to expect things, by then, my mind muted and my body wearied by long days of labor. So three of these petty dustpicker thieves fell upon me outside the smoke-shop, where I'd spent hours seaming the ragged edges of my fears with a synthopioid needle.

I remember it in flashes, like a Sanctuary vid 'ported in, great swaths of data missing. The flash of a knife, the heat of new pain. Fingers splintered beneath steel-reinforced boots. Ribs bruised along old fault lines. I could not see faces; I knew they were still with me by the knees in my chest and hands in my pockets.

Searching for the chit I'd already spent on synth, I suppose. My identity-card would open no credit in the money halls nor any doors in the sex-shops and gamblers' terraces. I had nothing left for them to take, except my dreams. Those are not easily slipped from torn pockets, though they may tumble out from torn flesh if the knife dives deep enough.

Then pain did not abandon me, but shifted its weight. As my own cries abated, I heard them rejoined in chorus by my attackers. My hurts were a black hole that sucked away focus and it did not occur to me to wonder from what corner salvation had come.

I fought to my knees, then my feet. I stood, and I stared into your face.

With blood in my eyes and my vision doubled, I wouldn't have known you. But your mind is a key that fits all my old locks, and there is no other like it. You cracked me open and you knew me too, beneath the blood and snot and grime.

I gathered up the tatters of my thoughts and I fled, not knowing what you knew, how much you might have seen. My fingers have been broken often enough before, but my heart has rarely cracked wide enough to spill its secrets.

If you had wanted to stop me, you could have brought me to my knees then and there, spared me the pain and humiliation of the Impeller's attention. If you had wanted to stop me, you had that power.

You did not stop me, and I praised the lonely gods of our mother's worship for my good fortune and quick wit.

Do you remember, when you were twelve or so, how you appealed your release to the chancellors of Sanctuary? They declined. Parapsychs removed from Chasten keep their abilities. They would never have let you stretch for the stars—not without the chains of Consensus about your neck.

I told our mother, of course. I reported every petty grievance of your heart, poured every ounce of your youthful rebellion into her ears. I didn't hope that she would love me better for it. But I hoped she would love you less.

My mistake was in taunting you over it. "Mother knows," I said, poking you in the back while we waited for our supper at the scrap-shop. "Mother knows," I singsonged, dragging my feet as we walked home from the mushroom mines. "Mother knows," I whispered in your ear after we'd crawled into bed at night.

It was that last that broke you.

You forced my mind wide open and splintered me with pain of your own manufacture. You made me your puppet, so that I bit my own hands bloody and raked my cheeks raw. I screamed and could not stop screaming, though you shook me and begged me to stop, though our mother shouted at us to stop from the street outside where she held court with her lackeys. I screamed until I had no voice left, and then I wept, and tears washed away all conscious thought.

In the morning, I woke whole and with no pain but that of memory. We never spoke again of what had passed and it was weeks before you looked me in the eye again.

I only noticed because so few people look me in the eye.

Were you surprised at what you had done? I wasn't.

I will not demean us both by asking for your forgiveness.

Labor continued day and night at the launch site. Compassionate Consensus had tuned us all to the same frequency, that of repair and fresh construction. The Impeller would parade, now and then, to the seat of power that he kept there. Grounded though the ship remained, its elegance far outstripped the best of what Chasten can offer. A ceremonial sword, a relic of his days as Sanctuary's First Pre-rogative, gleamed always at his left-hand side. You gleamed always at his right.

How such a ship imbued with Compassionate Consensus came to be in the Impeller's possession before the Sanctuary impeached him was anyone's guess … but he was, for a time, First Prerogative, with all the unbroken power that entails. Inside the ship, with his pet parapsych at his shoulder, he spoke across the stars with Sanctuary's old enemies in the Technocracy and the Outer Disc: offering them the treasures of the Twelve Splendid Worlds in exchange for their assistance in reclaiming what was his.

What was *his.*

Your mind is an ansible that can slice through the universe at your slightest whim, and you used it to abet his petty scheming.

Did he lie you down upon the cold metal deck and part you like a surgeon: cold, clinical? Or did he command that your body should grow ripe and receptive at his touch? Perhaps you did not require compulsion at all. Our mother's corpse had yet to cool before you stepped over it on your way into the Impeller's—

These thoughts are unworthy, sister-mine. Let us set them aside until time bleaches them clean.

While you stretched across the stars to intercede on the Impeller's behalf, I crouched atop a high gantry, clutching a pneumatic hammer until my hands cramped and my feet bled in my ill-fitted boots. I would place one rivet and blossom the end open with the hammer's blow. I worked long rows in this way, rivet after rivet, all alike.

If someone had looked closely, they would have observed that each one stood askew, the rivet's burr only marginally covering the hole in the metal. *If.* If the Impeller had not had the confidence of his Consensus, if he'd had the sensibility to set overseers to inspect this work.

Under the terrible forces of a ship's struggle against gravity, a rivet would swiftly give way. The strain on the others would then grow, until the whole seam gave out, and the ship made a new scar in Chasten's gray face.

The Impeller had ordered me to build. He did not specify that I must do it well.

If you left Chasten with him, I knew you would die alongside him. I was not sorry for this. Indeed, I was very nearly glad. It was a misshapen kindness, the only sort I am fit to make.

You thought I was sleeping, sister-mine, after you'd sung to me the few scraps of song you knew or half-remembered. You thought I was too young to understand. You thought the long noisy night of cheers from the fighting-pits and raucous parliamentarianism from the little kings of the street had at last snapped the strand of my waking mind. You thought sleep had called me far from where our mother could reach, with word or thought or fist.

But I remember the soap-bright smell of you and the warm glow of your hopeful heart. I remember your whisper, against the cramped curl of my ear: "I'll take you away from all this. Someday. Somewhere far from here."

Who did you think you were, to shape such a promise with hands so small, so tightly bound by our mother's use for you? And who was I then, to sink into such a thing with the full weight of belief?

Ten years later, when you raised your fist and your fistful of street-vassals against her, your heart burned with that selfsame hope. Ten years later, I watched her and her army crush the fire of your optimism to ashes and tear your ragged little crew to shreds.

I watched her cast you into the down-below and I watched her laugh, later, alone but for her half-man son.

Not watched. *Helped.* I hadn't stopped carrying your tales to her, had never known how.

What I've done, I did for our mother. She was always mine to hate. Not his.

How easily you slipped inside me, before the Impeller's throne. Like a hand inside a tattered glove. How like a puppet you made me dance.

My left hand grasped my right, to cantilever my wrist against my knee. Bones gave way with a snap and lifted their jagged heads clear of my skin. I should not have been strong enough to do it on my own. Our mother always said you were the stronger. I thought of that as I sang the song you put in my mouth, the old familiar notes of tearing tendons and rent flesh.

The Impeller laughed then, a counterpoint to the melody you wove. Not even the hint of a smile cracked your concentration. On his shoulder your grip tightened, as if it was through him that you channeled your power.

You brought me to my knees and pulped my teeth against the metal of the deck. Nerves rang raw and naked in my mouth. If I had my own voice, I would have begged for swift mercy; if I had my own hands I would have clasped them. But I was your creature alone, and I could not even have drawn breath through my shattered mouth without you to stir my lungs for me.

You forced me upright, to my knees, and you peeled my eyes open. Tears—my tears, yours, who can say from here?—blurred my sight but still you forced me to meet the Impeller's leaden gaze. You made me watch his pale lips stretch into a smile. Did he smile like that, when you stepped over the wreckage of the woman who birthed you?

"End it," he said.

You yanked my arms straight out, the broken, the whole. Veins shone blue beneath my pale damp skin. Lifeblood sprayed from the ruin of my wrist, an irregular stutter.

Your concentration strained. Savoring? Deciding? It is kinder to us both if neither of us ever truly knows.

"Sister-mine," I croaked, into the hungry silence.

You snapped me forward.

My hand clenched around the hilt of the Impeller's dress-sword.

Your hand, ever on his shoulder, held him in his place.

The blade sang as it left the scabbard and parted his belly in one elegant arc.

He died with my hand inside him, with his intestines sliding bangle-bright down my wrist.

You looked at me over his crooked, bent neck. "He told me," you said, your own blood slicking your teeth where you'd bitten deep into your lip. "He told me that I must never raise my hand against him."

A meteor in orbit can never hope to break free. But fling another rock into the system, and it becomes impossible to predict the collision that results.

When you left, you did not look back.

There was little to look back at. We pulled the reinforced gantry down, in your wake, and we used it to shore up the western wall where the haboobs come walking in the windy season. Of the Impeller's bones, we made ornaments to clatter in the breeze, to scare off the sandflies that come in the night to nest in unsuspecting eyes.

We did not speak of you, when you were gone. With the help of Compassionate Consensus, you turned us all out of the ship before the Impeller's blood had dried upon his throne. You closed the doors behind you and you did not show yourself to us again. We built your ship as you required it of us—and you commanded skilled labor from our hands.

One night I rose from my bed before I had yet come awake. I was climbing through the open hatch of the Impeller's ship before I understood what force moved my body. The empty sockets in my jaw throbbed afresh, passing beneath those arches again.

You let go of me, once I saw you there, sitting at the edge of the platform where the Impeller's throne had been. Faint lines of blood lingered on the organics of the floor, but your knuckles showed red and sere from their time soaked in wash-water.

You let go, and I sat beside you. "You could come with me," you said. We sat side by side, not looking at each other, staring out over what had been the Impeller's. What was now yours. You did not tell me where you meant to fly, with the glowing blue heart at your back. But I think it was not to any world yet touched by human hands. "Come with me."

I shook my head and you did not press. You covered my hand with yours and we stayed there, for a short while, together again.

I hope that you did not take her with you, our mother, the sideways cut of her words or the clenched fist of her power. I am here, to watch over her grave. She remains still and sleeping. A patch of emperor-weed has grown tall and thorny over top; we will pick the pods to make shoe-rubber in the spring.

It would have been a good time, that night, when we sat in peace, to unwind the tangled skein of my story. Or to offer you to reach deep inside me and pull it all loose for yourself, to sew together the tapestry, ugly and entire, at your leisure. But I did not say, and you did not ask me to, and so I throw all these words along the antenna after you into the vast quiet night.

My mind is shuttered fast, but yours forces any lock and opens every door. Yours is an ansible that reaches between worlds. Maybe someday you will reach back to this one. Not soon, I think. Don't hurt, for me. There are gentler hands to hold now. There are kinder faces to look on. But someday.

Maybe by then, we will know what to say to each other.

Go Where the Heart Takes You

Anita Ensal

"Rodney Junior is hailing," MaryAgnes said, as their ship sailed through the Blackness, Jupiter now far behind them. "Again."

Vasundhara chuckled. "Don't keep our eldest waiting, Ma."

MaryAgnes heaved a sigh. "He doesn't approve of our choice, my love."

"Of course he doesn't. He wouldn't be Rodney's son if he did."

"Rodney approved of everything we ever did," MaryAgnes said.

"Yes, but he was a cautious man. Rodney Junior is cautious, too. It's just in his nature. And what we're doing is the opposite of cautious."

"True enough," MaryAgnes said cheerfully. MaryAgnes was quite excited about not being cautious at the moment. She put their eldest son on speaker. "Rodney, dear, how are you?"

"Mother and Ma, why are you two doing this?" Rodney asked without preamble.

Vasundhara and MaryAgnes exchanged a long-suffering glance. "Dearest, we have explained why many times," Vasundhara said with patience she didn't feel.

"Just because our fathers and other mothers have gone to Sol, may their light shine ever brightly, doesn't mean that you two should now leave Ganymede and race off on frivolous adventures."

172

"Rodney," MaryAgnes said, "there are two particularly good times to go off on frivolous adventures. The first is when you're young and have no responsibilities, and the second is when you're old and you've seen your responsibilities flourish and succeed on their own."

Rodney's sigh was quite audible. "My brothers and sisters share my concerns."

"Of course they do," Vasundhara said. "And we understand those concerns. And we are going to continue doing what we've planned anyway. You act as if you will never see us again."

"You're going to the Belt to participate in, what, their Jamboree? I've looked into it. No one there is our kind of people, Mother and Ma."

"All people are our kind of people," MaryAgnes said gently. "You should never forget that, Rodney. Our family was a rainbow of love and continues to be so. Mother and I want, oh, call it one last big adventure. We have a fine ship, three top-of-the-line ship's robots—which is two more than necessary for the size of our ship—and we're equipped for all possibilities."

"That's what worries me. You aren't going to try *mining*, are you?"

"Why would we want to do that?" Vasundhara asked.

"Why wouldn't you is the better question." Rodney sighed again. "Just be careful and please advise me immediately if you run into the slightest issue."

"We will, dear," MaryAgnes said. "Love to you and all the rest of the family, who I'm sure you'll be talking to the moment our transmission disconnects." With that, she disconnected said transmission. "Perhaps we should have been frivolous earlier and more often."

"No," Vasundhara said as she patted MaryAgnes's hand. "We had the others to care for. And the children needed us."

"They haven't needed us for many years," MaryAgnes said softly.

"I know, my love. Which is why you and I are being frivolous now. We began this life together and, lest we are somehow not able to end this life together, then I want to ensure that we have one last grand adventure. Now, do get the charts arranged correctly—I want to double-check that the route the computer has given us allows us enough sightseeing opportunities within the time allotted for us to reach the Jamboree at its start."

"Oh, isn't it large!" MaryAgnes said for, by Vasundhara's count, the twentieth time.

"Yes, my love, it is." She looked at their copy of *Guidebook to the Belt*. "The second largest space station in the Belt, second only to Checkpoint Charley that orbits near to Ceres."

"And we're only seeing a portion of it! I'm so glad we came!"

Vasundhara was glad MaryAgnes was enjoying herself. Since they'd first met so long ago at school, as long as MaryAgnes was happy, Vasundhara was happy. She'd deeply loved everyone who had joined their marriage over the years, but MaryAgnes had the most special place in her heart. So the trip had, so far, been a success, because MaryAgnes was loving every moment of it.

Checkpoint Zeta, as most of the locals called it, could house a hundred-thousand people if necessary. They'd be packed in tight, but safe, and that was the point of the station's size—to be the emergency location for the miners should there be need of it. It also meant there was plenty of "parking" for all the spaceships.

Per the guidebook, Space Station Zeta had 120 levels and was 13 kilometers in diameter, not counting the many "arms" that extended from it where spaceships of all types and sizes could, and were, docked. It had been fascinating to see so many different ships all in one place. To Vasundhara, the station looked like a huge, bulbous cylinder with more bumpy spines than she could count. She'd been relieved that their ship's robots were able to handle the docking portion because the docking bays were quite close together.

Visitors received permission to dock, were assigned their spot, airlocked their ship to the station, then received a specific access code that only they and Zeta Mission Control had access to. A simple but effective security setup, necessary to prevent theft and allowing the attendees to sleep on their own ships. This had prevented them from getting rooms on the space station, which was, so far, MaryAgnes's only disappointment.

There were many Galactic Police ships patrolling the area. Most likely due to the warnings they'd been given before their journey: while most of the Belt, like the rest of the system, tended to be law-abiding, there were pirates out here, led by someone entitled Boser Geist. The pirate in charge might be killed or arrested, but as soon as that happened, whoever was the next in line took the title over. MaryAgnes had found this thrilling. Vasundhara had found that she sided with the GP and the rest of the Belters—the sooner they could end the reign of this so-called endless pirate king, the better for everyone.

The station's mass and spin created some of its own gravity, but the grav-generators were, per the guidebook, state-of-the-art. They weren't floating, so Vasundhara presumed the guidebook knew what it was talking about.

And inside this vast structure were what felt like the hundred-thousand people it could supposedly house. Oh, she knew there weren't really that many people here. If the Belt stopped working, the system stopped surviving. But most of the other space stations would be running skeleton crews, the majority of the independent miners would be in attendance for some or all of the event, and even most of those who lived and worked on the other large asteroid stations would be here, those working at Ceres Main included.

Vasundhara sincerely hoped a major comet didn't come through and wipe everyone out. But the guidebook advised that the space stations all bristled with weapons that could disintegrate comets and other dangers. So she chose to focus on enjoying their time here.

The Jamboree was like nothing on Ganymede, or any of the other Lunars they'd visited over the years. There were events like it on Old Earth, but only there, and they'd visited Earth only twice, decades ago.

They'd bought a *Belter's Phrasebook* the moment they'd arrived, and it had been extremely useful. While some of the slang of the Belt was common to the rest of the solar system, much of it was exclusive to the Belters. She knew without asking that Rodney Jr. would not approve of any of it.

There were more food and beverage stands than Vasundhara would have ever thought a space station could handle, packed tightly together along the edges of the wide corridors and spilling into the three levels given over to Jamboree entertainment.

The entertainment consisted of a wide variety of games of chance, music, wandering entertainers, presentation rooms, even more vendors selling wares than there were food and beverage stands, some competitions that were familiar and some that weren't, staged plays, and theaters, some showing holos that were new to the Belt and some showing classics.

And people. So very many people. All shapes, colors, and ages. Easy to spot the miners—they were all in jumpsuits. Most of the others wore tight-fitting garments without a lot of adornment, which the guidebook had indicated meant this was what they wore to be able to quickly get into spacesuits. She was in a sari and MaryAgnes was in a flowing dress with wide-legged pants—they weren't the only ones dressed differently, but they definitely stood out as tourists.

There were many robotics here, too, which surprised her. They'd left their robots on their ship. Vasundhara wondered if they were along for protection.

"I didn't think the Belt had a great artist's colony," MaryAgnes said, as they entered a room designated for the art show, "but some of this work is exceptional."

They wandered through the exhibit. There were robotics in here as well, admiring the art just as the humans were.

Once done with the art, they moved along past several presentations that sounded interesting to Vasundhara but weren't capturing MaryAgnes's attention—including one with eight GP officers talking about the myths and legends of the system—and on through the entire floor. Based on their path, Vasundhara was fairly certain MaryAgnes was following someone, but she wasn't sure of who it might be. "I can't believe there are two more levels like this," Vasundhara said as they stopped to get a drink.

"Well, the Jamboree lasts five days, so we'll have time to see it all." MaryAgnes looked around. "Where to next? Circle through this floor again or check out the next one up?" She giggled. "Or look for another to add in?"

"Oh? I had a feeling you'd spotted someone you'd like to get to know."

"Possibly. Haven't you?"

Vasundhara didn't reply. Her attention had been captured by something else.

There was a pretty little girl of about six, likely of Hispanic descent, wearing a miner's jumpsuit that looked old but very clean and well cared for. She wasn't with anyone else but didn't look lost or worried. She was watching a man perform magic tricks and she was his only audience.

Vasundhara hadn't been in a marriage of seven and raised seventeen children within that marriage, not to mention watched over seventy-six grandchildren to date, without learning how to read lips, body language, and situations quickly. And there was something wrong with this situation.

She stepped closer. The magician was running a patter, guessing things about the little girl. When he was wrong, he gave her a candy. But when he was right, she handed him her money fob. She was handing him the fob more than he was giving her candy.

There was another man, about her age, watching the girl and the magician, too. He looked worried and a bit angry, but he looked nothing like the girl, though he cut a rather dashing figure, with a full head of thick white hair and a well-trimmed white beard highlighting a handsome face. Like the girl, he was in an older miner's jumpsuit, which showed him to be quite muscular. This man had a robot that looked very old but well maintained with him.

"Here's your drink," MaryAgnes said, handing it to her. "Why did you wander off?"

"Something's about to happen."

"What?" MaryAgnes looked where Vasundhara was. "You think the little one is lost?"

"No. I think, and I believe the man who's also watching them thinks, that the magician is not a magician so much as a con man."

Another girl ran up. This one was white, looked about twelve, and was also neatly dressed in an old miner's jumpsuit. This girl tried to get the littler one away, but the six-year-old was having none of it, the lure of the candy the most likely reason.

The older girl seemed to be getting upset. The magician started a different patter with her.

"He's offering her a double or nothing bet," MaryAgnes, who had the same family experience and skills as Vasundhara, said softly. "Do you think we should intervene?"

Before she could reply, the man who'd been watching stormed over. "You leave those children alone," he snarled. "I know who you are, Kako Habis, and what you are. You're worse than Boser Geist, preying on children."

The magician smiled at him as Vasundhara and MaryAgnes moved to stand by the children. It was an unctuous smile, and Vasundhara knew they were right—this was a con man.

"Games of chance are allowed at the Jamboree," Habis said smoothly. "I haven't forced the children to play." His smile widened. "I'm just a very good guesser."

More children ran up, accompanied by another older, well-cared-for robotic. Clearly, they were doing their robots a disservice by not bringing them along to enjoy the festivities, but that wasn't important right now. Vasundhara counted quickly. Fourteen children total, eight boys, six girls, and all but two looked nothing alike, but they were all dressed alike. The eldest was a lovely dark-skinned girl who looked about sixteen. She shoved in. "What's going on?"

"I got candy!" the six-year-old said happily.

"Wonderful, Cecelia. What did you pay to get that candy?"

"All her money," the twelve-year-old said, sounding ready to cry. "I didn't mean to lose track of her, Marjorie, I'm so sorry. I had to use the facilities and Cecelia promised to wait for me, but when I got out ..."

Marjorie looked back at Cecelia. "Why did you leave Gretchen? You know the family rules."

Cecelia pointed to Habis. "He waved at me and I was bored."

"You will give their money back," the older man said.

"And who can make me do that?" Habis asked.

"How much did you win from a little girl?" MaryAgnes asked, voice mild. Vasundhara smiled to herself. When MaryAgnes sounded like this, heads were going to roll, and soon.

Habis shrugged. "What was fair."

Two of the older boys were whispering to Marjorie, who now looked ready to faint. "Cecelia, whose fob do you have?"

Cecelia grinned. "The one you gave me."

"I didn't give you a fob, you're too little to have control of the credits … ." Marjorie reached into a pocket. "Cecelia, did you take my fob without asking?" She looked over at Habis. "She didn't have permission—"

Habis waved his hand. "That's your family's problem, not mine."

One of the older boys cleared his throat. "Marjorie, we have no credits left. Not just in the fob. At all."

The older man snarled, and his robot put a hand on his shoulder. "Nathan, violence is not the way."

"Sometimes it is, Studs."

Habis looked at Nathan. "Nathan? Nathan Greer? I remember you. You gave me a lot of money."

"When I was young and didn't know better."

Vasundhara looked at the two men. "How could that be? You, Kako Habis, look much younger than Nathan does."

Habis shrugged. "Mining life ages you."

"He goes to Phobos and gets life enhancements with the money he steals from children," Nathan snarled.

"Those are illegal everywhere else," Vasundhara pointed out. She looked at the robot that was with the children—it was busy keeping the younger ones corralled. The older children all looked too distressed to do anything. That left Studs. She made what she hoped was eye contact with Nathan's robot. "I wonder what the Galactic Police would think of that."

Studs took his hand off of Nathan's shoulder, nodded, backed away, and left. Vasundhara hoped he was going to the nearest GP officer—they were reasonably close to the presentation rooms where she knew the eight of them were. Hopefully the robot knew this, too.

"I'm not having the treatment here," Habis said, "so they can think of nothing about that."

"Stealing from children is a crime," Nathan replied. "And I will not allow you to steal from these children."

"Why not?" Habis asked. "When we met, you were alone and happy to be so. You enjoyed our game because you didn't want to be around all the other people. It's just you and your robot now, so I'm willing to make a guess for free and say that you never married, never had children, have just your robot and yourself to care for. Isn't that right?"

"Yes," Nathan said through gritted teeth. "What of it?"

"Why does a loner care what happens to anyone else?" Habis asked calmly. "This is not your business, Nathan. Now, go away before I protest and have you removed for interfering with my business. I paid to be here, you didn't."

"Let's see what you can guess about me," MaryAgnes said with a smile. "And, to make it interesting, I'm playing for the children's money. Wrong guesses mean you're giving them their money back in ever-growing increments."

Habis shrugged. "That's fine with me. You get to ask the questions, I'll guess the answers."

"Perfect." MaryAgnes took hold of Vasundhara's hand. "First bet is for the full amount of the children's debt, double or nothing, as in, you will pay them the money you've already taken and will give me the same amount, or I will give you all of that money, willingly."

"Accepted," Habis said quickly. "What's your question?"

"How many children do we have?"

Habis smirked. "Double digits."

"That's not an answer," Vasundhara said. "That's far too random for you to claim accuracy. Meaning you have guessed incorrectly and need to repay the children."

Habis's eyes narrowed. "Fine." He studied them and the children, which was good, because Studs returned with two big and burly GP officers. They weren't any she'd spotted in the presentation room—presumably the robot hadn't wanted to disrupt their presentation. "Fourteen."

MaryAgnes and Vasundhara both laughed. "So very wrong," MaryAgnes said. "Now, give me your fob."

"Absolutely not! You have to prove how many children you have."

"That's not how the game works," one of the GP officers said as he dropped a large, heavy hand onto Habis's shoulder.

"Your contract requires that you need nothing other than the customer's word," the other officer said as he produced manacles, "because we're aware of what an aspiring Boser Geist you are. Plus Phobos has strict rules about late payment. Now, do what the ladies have asked—give them your fob."

Habis reached into his left pants pocket and pulled out a fob. It was silver, and the fob that Vasundhara had seen had been black. "That's not his real fob," Nathan said. "The one he used to steal the children's money is in his right pocket."

The first GP officer reached into that pocket and produced the correct fob. "So, thank you for doing that," the officer who'd hand-cuffed Habis said. "We now have proof of fraud. You're going to enjoy Charon Prison—they love good entertainment there."

The officers oversaw the return of the money to the children, then gave MaryAgnes the same amount from Habis's fob. "Thank you," they said to the three adults. "We'll be finding the rest of his marks if we can." They hustled Habis off, the con man protesting the entire way.

"Thank you," Marjorie said. "Now, we'll be going."

"I suggest we all wander together," Vasundhara said. "I believe you could use the help three additional adults and a robot can provide."

Marjorie didn't look as though she agreed.

Cecelia went over to Nathan and put her hand in his. "I like you."

Gretchen joined her and took Nathan's other hand. "Me too. Thank you so much for helping us."

"The ladies did the real helping," Nathan said, almost shyly, though now that the situation was resolved he also looked out of his element. Vasundhara realized that Habis had been right—Nathan had been a loner, most likely all his life. Yet he'd joined to save children he didn't know and could expect nothing from. She was impressed, and Vasundhara did not impress easily.

MaryAgnes nudged her. "You're thinking what I'm thinking, aren't you?"

"Possibly. Children, let's try going as a group. If we are too old and boring for you, we'll be kind and let you roam off without us."

All the children looked to Marjorie. Who nodded slowly. "It would be … rude of us to not accept your company after all you did for us."

"Good." Vasundhara let go of MaryAgnes, went to Marjorie, and wrapped the teenager's arm through hers. "We are new to the Belt and this is our first Jamboree. Perhaps you can guide us."

They started off, the younger boys holding onto MaryAgnes, the younger girls clamoring for Studs to hold their hands, the middle boys showing solidarity by sticking to their own robotic who they called Oliver. Clearly she and MaryAgnes needed to give their robots names, versus using their make and model numbers.

The children were good guides, but there were a lot of them and they wanted to do different things. Marjorie didn't want to let them wander alone, but Vasundhara kept ahold of the girl, and gently mentioned that with the two additional guardians, plus the GP's awareness of their family, everyone would be fine, so she allowed the others to go off, with strong admonitions not to leave their guardians this time, mostly aimed at Cecelia.

"She's quite the little comet, isn't she?" Vasundhara asked as Nathan, Cecelia, and Gretchen headed for a candy stand. MaryAgnes convinced the boys with her to go after them. Vasundhara smiled to herself. Yes, they were thinking the same things.

Marjorie managed a laugh. "My father called Cecelia precocious. I was surprised to find that the definition of that word wasn't 'finds trouble naturally but is adorable enough to normally get out of it relatively unscathed.' Compared to Cecelia, handling our five-year-old twins, Yeong and Jae, and even four-year-old Wanda, is as easy as creating slag."

"Handling bright, inquisitive children with no fear can be as hard as hitting titanium." She was glad she'd read enough of the Phrasebook to feel confident in the slang.

Marjorie laughed. "That's as sure as Sol."

"How did your family come to be?" Vasundhara asked as she headed them for a dining stand that had expensive food and seating. "It's clear that the only blood relationship are the twin girls."

"My parents were independent Belt miners, but they'd formed a little group that mined together."

"To protect from pirates?"

"Yes. The GP does its best, but they can't be everywhere. It wasn't pirates that were the problem, though. We got hit with illness—it can happen if you hit a bad element inside a rock. My parents didn't get sick, but the other adults did. They all died." She stopped speaking and swallowed. "That left their kids orphans. My parents adopted them. They were all older than me. Once they did that, my parents realized that there were other children out there, being orphaned and being unable to manage alone. They started adopting every child they could."

They seated themselves and gave the robotic server their order, which Vasundhara ensured had everything Marjorie had looked at with interest prior to the girl's ordering the cheapest drink on the menu. "What happened to those children's ships and claims?"

"They owned them, and it depended on the child. The older kids put their ships into dock and worked with our family. When they were old enough, they had ships and now had the experience to mine themselves. Those whose ships were destroyed, or so old to be better turned in for scrap, went to work for the Conglomerates. The ships' robots went with whoever had a ship. It's why we only have Oliver—the younger kids' ships were all caught in a comet storm—their ships and robotics were destroyed. The GP was able to rescue them, and they contacted my parents. They knew my parents would do what they could."

"When did they die?" Vasundhara asked gently.

"Six Earth months ago." Marjorie sounded hopeless. "I'm trying to continue their work, but there's no way I can take in anyone else. And the older ones are following our parents' example and adopting as they can. None of them are in a position to help. I don't know what would have happened if you and Miner Greer hadn't stepped in to help."

Vasundhara patted her hand. "It will all work out, dear. Sol provides." She sent an inquiry to her ship.

Their order arrived and Vasundhara insisted Marjorie eat as much of everything as she wanted. While the girl ate as if she hadn't seen food for a while—which meant she was rationing herself so the younger children wouldn't go hungry—Vasundhara checked her communicator. The answer was back—Marjorie's story was true and then some. The Wardens had been the Belt's version of, to use the vernacular, a rare strike—something wonderful and unusual—and there were no negatives against them in any way.

"What are your plans for the future?" she asked after Marjorie had eaten her fill. "Will you go off to be educated?"

Marjorie shook her head. "I need to take care of my brothers and sisters. We don't have enough credits to leave the Belt, let alone have any of us go off for schooling. And we only have the one ship now, meaning we have to earn enough so that Archie and Ravi, at least, can go off when they're older."

MaryAgnes sent a communication. She was quite enamored of Nathan and he seemed to reciprocate. *He has never kissed anyone, let alone anything else*, she wrote. *So very rare and endearing both, don't you think, my love?*

"I believe that MaryAgnes and I may have a proposition for you, and for Miner Greer, as well."

"Even if you gave us all the money you won from that thief, it wouldn't be enough."

Vasundhara smiled. "No, it wouldn't. But Habis never got to the two most important questions."

"Which were?"

"Where is our home and what is our last name."

"I'll net that fish. What are the answers?"

"Ganymede and Dara."

Marjorie looked blank for a moment. Then her eyes widened. "Are you saying you're the ruling family of Ganymede?"

"Oh no, dear."

Marjorie tried not to look disappointed.

"We are merely," Vasundhara continued, "the richest. Meaning we are the richest family in the system. As such, our proposition may have the means to sway your and Miner Greer's opinions."

The GP officers who'd arrested Habis were more than happy to help them register a variety of new legal relationships with Ceres Main. The call to Ganymede was more challenging, mostly because Rodney Jr. spent much time complaining—not with the legal decisions, but with the fact that his remaining mothers were not racing home.

"We go where the heart takes us, Rodney," MaryAgnes said. "It's how we've always lived our lives and how we always will."

"I don't mind that. I just knew you were going to decide to become miners, Mother and Ma. I just *knew* it."

"It's because you're so bright, Rodney," Vasundhara said. "Now, please ensure that our family is prepared to receive their eldest new younger sister in a few months."

"With all honors," he said seriously. "When will we meet our other younger siblings and our new father?"

"When you come to visit us. I recommend we have a family reunion at the next Jamboree."

Minds

Mars Conquest

Jane Yolen

Underground we went,
the only way to live
in that world.
You there before us,
so rich in story,
we were taken by it,
falling in love with
the telling, the tellers,
so swift, we became yours
before we knew the whole tale,
before we knew who you were.
Before we know what we would become.
The receptacle for your histories,
mysteries, stories, poems.

The Star-Crossed Horoscope for Interstellar Travelers

Fran Wilde

With Luna under the influence of both Scorpio and Fortinbras—depending on where you're observing—and all five of Jupiter's moons in the midst of a Mercury return (curse you, Io, you throw all our best intentions off), plus with Lyra ascending[1] it will be a particularly wild ride this month, my darlings.

The following predictions assume that you are reading this in real-time, in port, on planet, or within a reasonable gravity well. If you are in transit, accelerating, but not yet in cold-sleep, please remember to adjust your natal chart relative to your velocity, at least two constellations upwards.[2] If you have recently emerged from cold-sleep, are decelerating, and/or are in a quarantine orbit, don't forget to adjust downwards, reversing the calculation.

We are, as always, grateful to the Betelgeuse Ministry, the Oort Cloud collaborative, and *Milky Way Press* for their distribution

---

1   *For the last time, you Earth-centric astrology traditionalists need to either get over yourselves or stay out of my message queue.*

2   *Don't complain later that you got a Sagittarian's horoscope when you were obviously in Virgo.*

support. Our eighty-year history (relative time[3]) of providing you with reliable horoscopes to guide your intergalactic lives couldn't exist without it.

With that, I humbly present to you my latest calculations and recommendations for your expanded galactic horoscopes for the solar prime week of March 15, 2354.[4]

Your humble servant,
Astra de la Vega

Sol—This week will find you fondly remembering those in transit and perhaps wanting to send a few affectionate memos, perhaps after a visit to the station pub. The stars suggest that a record-and-wait strategy is advisable. Your longtime goals are within reach, after what feels like (or may actually be) a long passage of deep sleep.

Virgo—All your assumptions about the new crew are correct. Take appropriate actions to protect yourself, your heart, and your belongings.

Libra—Feeling a little shaky about your latest mission or project? You're not alone. Libras during this time may feel the need to weigh pros and cons, but remember that you're creating new adventures, and your system needs you.

Fortinbras—As one of the newer celestial birth months, for those born in transit/deceleration, know that your spirit shines bright in any group or gathering. You may sometimes feel frustrated this month over communications or gravitational difficulties. Even if last orbit was not your best, you have much to offer.

---

3   *While the year 2354 marks our fourth broadcast, the first, with my then-collaborator Ivigenha Solaris, officially took place in 2274, and so I'm going to count those years, as one does.*

4   *Important Note: if you are near Solar 2, Antares B, or any known wormhole, please do not make decisions based on this information and instead use the previously broadcast Star-Crossed Horoscope for Interstellar Travelers, inverted. Many thanks and apologies for not making this clear last time, especially to those of you who lost money gambling on Charon, and also to Ivigenha, I know I screwed up, and I hope you'll forgive me.*

Gemini—Know that you are deeply missed, and that your families and friends are thinking of you. While plans and dreams may pull in multiple directions, you are always welcome to return. Ivigenha, please, if you read this, don't open any memos from me sent earlier this week.

Cancer—A homebody and moon sign always, no matter how many moons there are in your sky, you sometimes feel challenged when adventuring out into the galaxies. Yet you are the one who always manages to locate a comforting community, or to share that with fellow travelers. Your worth will be recognized, and you may have help with the dishes, soon.

Celestine—As one born in transit/acceleration, this current cycle may bring good fortune in terms of new discoveries or winnings. Do not put your trust in a stranger. Make sure you've copied your data to several secure memory devices.

Sagittarius—Should you be occupying a position of power (captain, for instance, or armory, and or drummer in a galactic band, possibly), look closely at your decision trees. Has one been altered recently? By yourself or your AI? It is a good time to ask what the reasoning behind that was. For those aspiring to power (which Sagittarians aren't, honestly?) be cautious as this is a time of unruly transition. Also for Sagittarians recently[5] (relative time) docking at various places that have station bars, and who should have stayed on ship rather than flirting with adventure, well. That was a choice, wasn't it. The stars say: archive your video messages and start fresh.

Leo—A wise friend once said, watch your back around Sagittarians eager for power. That wise friend was a Leo. I'm not saying that you should be overly watchful or wear your triple-plate Venusian carbon fiber back armor this month, but maybe you should. No, not the diamond-flecked armor, the standard armor. Be a little less extra if you can, Leo.

---

5   *For the last time, you Earth-centric astrology traditionalists need to either get over yourselves or stay out of my message queue.*

Lyra—Glorious, artistic Lyrans, your moment has finally come. Your performance will go wide-band, your work will be shared among the stars. The project you've long hoped for will land in your lap. Will you take this opportunity? If so, you will be amply rewarded.

Pisces—It is highly recommended that you do not open or watch any memo-vids from old friends this month.

Aries—As new crew on a historic mission with a tightly knit command, you may be wondering what's in this for you. You may already have figured that out. Double-check your escape pod, just in case.

NB154-a—A few more cycles and your latest project will be approved. Don't forget to recharge your batteries, oxygen/hydrogen, and flavons. Colors that will help highlight your features this turn include aubergine, lotus, and CMYK2-41446.

Taurus—As always, Taurans, this kind of astrological cycle brings to you a hint of good fortune, tied with a shared burden or test. You will learn that the burden is at least in part more good fortune, but only after recalibrating the test to your advantage. Also, do not open any memo-vids from old friends. If you do, however, open one, and it is appealing to you, a reply may be welcome.

Scorpio—One would hope that you learned your lesson last cycle about spilt milk, except that if it was your first time making a mistake, possibly ever, you may still find that lesson has a sour taste. Like all Scorpios, you were, in fact, in the right—but no one will see it that way. Drop the argument, find a new horizon. Set off for the stars!

That's it for now, my galactic Darlings. Shine bright, watch your orbital return angles, and don't forget to check your fuel gauges. We are on a vast adventure, and while the stars don't always have all the answers, they can sometimes light the way.

Yours eternally[6],
Astra de la Vega

---

6   Ivigenha, please call as soon as you are out of cold-sleep. I miss you very much.

Canvas of Sins

Mercedes M. Yardley

✱ *Content warning: Brief description of suicide. Sexual abuse briefly mentioned.* ✱

*K*el closed her eyes and tried to forgive the man who murdered her mother.

"I was having a bad day," the man said. In an earlier time, a younger era, he would have been wringing an old newsboy cap in his hands. As it was, he merely folded his hands neatly in his lap. "It was nothin' personal. I'm sure she was a good woman."

"The best," Kel said. "She was sweet. She still prayed to the old gods, and talked to me, and really listened to what I had to say. Nobody else did that. And she …" Kel paused and tuned in to the emotion that flooded her, burning her synapses and nerve endings. The pain bored holes into her fluttering heart. If she weren't so well-trained, she would gasp.

"Tomatoes," she finished. "She grew tomatoes. You should have seen her patience. Who grows food on a spaceship? My mother, that's who. Before you killed her, you sick disgrace of a human being. When you get out, I'm going to hunt you down. I'm going to follow you and even though I've never done it before, I'm going to—"

Kel opened her eyes and looked at the woman sitting next to her. "You can't do that," she said gently. "You may share your thoughts, yes, but no accusations, and certainly no threats. We're past that point."

"I want him to hurt," the woman said simply. The nervous man flinched, but the woman's face didn't change expression. "I want him to feel everything."

Kel touched her hand. "He won't. You know how the process works. He won't feel pain; I will. You won't feel pain; I will. Now we can continue with you here or I can send you outside. Which would you prefer?"

The woman preferred to scream and rail and bang her head against the desk. She wanted to see her mother, with her frizzy hair and those stupid capris she insisted on wearing. She wanted to visit her mommy and cry because she'd burned dinner, because her lousy ex-husband and his new wife seemed deliriously happy, because she couldn't avoid running into them onboard Absolution 19. She was trapped in this huge floating city without the only person who had ever cared for her because this monster had screwed it up one night, breaking into an empty house.

Only it wasn't empty, now, was it?

I was only looking for some money, he wailed inside her head. *I didn't know anyone was home. I never woulda …*

"I'll stay," the woman said. She held her handbag tightly. Kel knew she had something precious inside.

Kel nodded and looked at the killer.

"Do you have anything to say before we complete the process?"

"I'm sorry," he said again. The woman wouldn't meet his eyes, but his earnestness and very real regret were so raw that Kel bit the inside of her cheek in order to keep her expression neutral.

"You can't make it up to me," the woman said, speaking more to the handbag than to anyone else.

"He doesn't need to," Kel told her. She held out both hands. "Your vials, please."

The woman drew a tiny vial, about an inch tall, from her purse. The killer pulled one from his shabby pocket. Kel took them and held them to the light. They glistened, rich and red, full of life and disease and sentiment.

"I don't understand why you couldn't just take it from a vein," the woman complained. "The needle to the heart hurt terribly."

"Did it?" Kel was distracted. She pulled out a small piece of lemon cake and shook the contents of both vials onto it. The blood seeped into the soft sponge. "In cases this difficult, we need samples directly from the heart. It's purer, you see. It's had less time to be contaminated by your hate."

All three of them stared at the bloody bite of cake. "Are you ready?" Kel asked.

"Are you really going to eat that?" the man asked nervously. "Is it going to make you sick?"

Kel smiled then, for the first time during their session. Starlight lit the room. "It's very kind of you to care, but I'll be fine. And after this, so will you. Both of you."

She held the bite of cake before her lips, smelling of citrus and copper. "With this morsel I do absorb your pain," she whispered, and placed the cake on her tongue.

Madness. Anger. Desperation at being without a home, without money, cooped up on some stupid ship. His wife screamed at him, told him he was a loser. He was full of drink and anger. He saw a door that looked easily jimmied. He tried it.

Despair. Horror. Walking in to find her mother on the kitchen floor, blood on the walls, in her hair, even on the ceiling. Bereft, cheated, stolen from. The man quickly caught, on the news, in prison, being released.

They hated each other. Oh, how they hated. They feared. They loathed. They distrusted. They leaked worry and rage like rotten stink from a dumpster. They could never save or be saved. They could never continue on.

Kel choked down the cake. The blood made her stomach twist in the same way their onslaught of emotion made her soul gag. Sweat popped out above her lip. She swallowed hard.

"Sir. You are forgiven. Miss. You have forgiven. As it is decreed by the law of this land, you two have done your part. May you never happen upon each other again."

The man stood and offered his hand. The woman ignored it and swept out the door. The newly Absolved killer slowly followed. Kel dropped her head to the table.

"Looks like a tough one."

Kel didn't raise her head. "I'm so exhausted, Cameron. I'm unwell. Please tell me we're done for the day."

"Sorry. You still have two more. Nasty ones, too. Another murder and the unintentional death of a baby."

Kel covered her eyes with her hands. "Please, no. I can't do it. I don't have anything left."

Her handler patted her on the head.

"You'll make it through, Absolver. You always do. Hey, how about we let you sleep in an extra half hour tomorrow, yes? That will cheer you up."

He left to call the next session, and Kel tried her very best not to cry. Her tears would only taste like murder.

Signing out took forever that night. The guard scanned Kel's eyes, rechecked her fingerprints, and lingered over paperwork for far too long.

"You know everything is in order," she said as he ran her retinal scan a third time. "I don't know why you do this."

"Sin-eater," he sneered. Kel didn't blink. She was what she was.

Cameron appeared behind her shoulder. "Keep yourself in check," he told the guard. "We'll have no discrimination here." He turned to Kel. "I have something to discuss with you. Dinner at your place?"

"Tonight?" she asked. She was so tired her voice was already beginning to slur. "Can't we do it another time?" He gave her a look and she masked her emotions. "Of course. What time?"

"How about now?" he said, and put his hand on her elbow, steering her away from the guard. "I put in an order. The food should arrive there about the same time we do."

Naturally.

Kel longed for a shower the same temperature as tears, and her bed. Her sheets were sinless white, not lemon-cake yellow or devil's-food brown. They were completely unspotted with blood, unlike the inside of her stomach, unlike her soul.

She followed him through the bleached halls of the ship. She stumbled and righted herself before he had a chance to reach out for her. If it would have even occurred to him, that is.

"You're not up to par," he said.

"You're overworking me. I need time to recuperate. The human body isn't built to sustain such prolonged blood saturation and emotion, you know."

"We're not talking a human body. We're talking yours."

They arrived at the door to her station. Kel reached into her purse, but Cameron already had his master keycard out. He opened the door and pushed her through.

"This is my home," she said, and swallowed her anger. It churned in her stomach with everything else. "I'd appreciate opening my own door, please. I know you have keys to everything in the facility, but at least be gracious enough to give me the illusion of autonomy."

His forehead wrinkled. "What do you mean? Ah, dinner's here. I'll take care of this."

Kel left him to pay the delivery man, who was peering inside her station with wide eyes. She took off her wrap and hung it in the closet. She thought about kicking her shoes off, but no, she'd feel too bare without them. They were tiny pieces of armor.

Cameron was already pulling down plates from her cupboard. "Have any wine?"

"I don't drink it."

"Why on earth not?"

Because she consumed blood all day. Because she wanted something pure in her body for once. "I have water from one of the new planets, so clear it's glacial," she said. "What did you want to talk to me about?"

"Cutting right to the chase. I like that."

If someone had seen them, they could have thought it was a romantic dinner between two pretty people. But nobody would see, because she was trapped in a small room built into the processing center aboard the Absolution 19. It was a spaceship large enough to house its own city, complete with gravity, gardens, and a small manufactured sea, but Kel stayed hidden.

"Will I ever get windows, Cameron?"

He drank his water and grimaced. "Too much of a security risk. You know that."

"Of course. We wouldn't want to lose company property," she said scathingly.

"Exactly. So it's time that we discuss breeding."

Kel stilled. "Breeding."

"I've noticed you're wearing out. You won't be able to do this forever. You come from a long line of Absolutionists, correct?"

"My mother. Her mother. Her father before her."

"So your stock is good. If we breed you to another of your kind, the chances of conceiving an Absolutionist will be high."

Kel put her glass on the table. "My kind? Cameron, do you even hear yourself? You sound like a beast."

He shrugged and took a bite. "As your handler, it's my job to take care of you. Business is good, but you're exhibiting … frailties. They're lending out a male from Reparation 21 right now. I looked at your ovulation cycle and booked him for two days next week. It will take a child at least six years until he or she is able to consume blood and sin without fatal effects. Five if we're lucky. If we start now—"

Kel stood. "I'd like you to leave."

Cameron blinked. "What?"

"You heard me. Get out."

He threw his napkin down on his plate and stood. "I don't understand this behavior. It's unlike you."

Kel's hands balled into trembling fists. "It's unlike me, but it shouldn't be. Yes, I do a service for society. It's in my blood, part of my DNA. But I'm not a machine, Cameron. I'm not an animal. You keep me under lock and key like property. You work me past my endurance. I tolerate it because I want to help people. I feel their pain when I'm inside of their souls. I feel their shame and guilt and sorrow. How could I not want to take that from them? But you will not speak of breeding me like livestock. It's vile and disgusting."

The words tasted good. They felt true and honest. Not held back, not sanitized. Poison oozed from her pores with those words. It cleansed her.

"But Kel—"

"Get out," she said again. Her cheeks were hot, and she felt the horrors of the day riding her bloodstream. "I am full of someone else's rage and shame and murder right now. If you don't let me process it, I can't be held responsible for what happens to you."

He walked toward the door. "This isn't you, Kel. This is a result of today's emotions in their raw state. You'll feel better in the morning."

"I'll have a new handler in the morning, or I won't ever leave this room again," Kel said, and slammed the button to slide the door closed behind him. She took a deep breath. Let it out. Felt the passion humming through her veins, double-checked, and grinned when she realized it was truly hers.

Her new handler was a woman with sky-blue hair and eyes that matched. Every now and then, clouds ran across her pupils. It was the most glorious thing Kel had ever seen.

"Hi, Kel. I'm Ivo. I'm here to take care of you, okay? First thing I'd like to do is have a doctor check you out, if that's all right with you?"

"You don't need to ask," Kel replied. "Physicals are necessary to monitor disease and burnout."

Ivo reached out and took Kel's hands in her own. Kel flinched at the unfamiliar touch.

"I'm asking because it's important for you to be involved. You have a say. If you don't want an exam, you don't have to have one. I hope you will because your charts show fatigue, and I'd like to see if we can pep you up some, but you can always say no."

You can always say no. Kel had never heard those words in her life. She had been taught to say yes. Yes, you are Absolved. Yes, you are released of your consequences and free to enter society again. Yes, I'll bear your burdens for you. My life for yours. Yes, yes, yes.

"Yes," she said, trying out the word with its newfound meaning. This time it was of her own free will. She smiled, and it was real. Ivo smiled back. It was the most beautiful thing in the world.

Kel learned that Ivo smiled often. When she laughed, she threw her head back, flashing her throat, without restraint.

"I envy your lack of inhibition," Kel confessed. Ivo had come to dinner because Kel had invited her. She never invited herself. She didn't have a keycard to Kel's station. She knocked, like a guest, and hugged her, like a friend, and eventually very sweetly kissed her, like a lover. "You seem so free. You're like a bird."

"We're all birds," Ivo said. "Would you like to fly away with me tonight, little bird? We could go to the water, if you'd like. When was the last time you were out of the facility?"

Kel's heart fluttered. "I can't remember."

Ivo grinned, and her teeth were white. Unblemished and without sin. "We could go to the gardens. Or simply walk the streets. Or stay in. It's your choice, my sweet little sin-eater. Whatever you desire."

When Ivo called her a sin-eater, it sounded of laughter and warmth and affection. It was a term of endearment, not a label. It made her feel special, and Kel had never felt anything close to that. Disposable, certainly. Never special.

"The water, please," Kel said, and held her hands up to her cheeks. "Goodness, they're burning!"

"That's called happiness, love. It's about time you had some of your own."

Ivo took Kel by the hand. They strolled through the hall, side-by-side, and Kel flashed her card at the guard. "We're going out tonight. That's right, both of us. You have a great evening, too."

The lobby of the building was huge, and their footsteps echoed. At the door, Kel hesitated.

"It's been such a long time since I went out," she whispered.

"No rush," Ivo answered. "Take your time. But there's so much to explore out there. We can see whatever you'd like."

Kel took a deep breath and stepped forward. The automatic doors swooshed open.

"This is what freedom feels like," Ivo said.

Kel was surprised that her eyes were wet. "Last time I went out, people threw things at me," she said. She dashed at her eyes with her sleeve. "They called me the most horrible names. I only do what I was born for. I can't help what I am."

Ivo's voice was soft. "People can be horrible. But they're grateful for you, whether they recognize it or not. The city would fall apart without an Absolutionist, and deep down they know it. They haven't forgotten the lessons of Earth."

Kel tightened her grip on Ivo's hand and stepped outside.

The movement of air surprised her. It wasn't medicinal. It wasn't carefully curated to keep her infections at bay. It felt like glory.

"Freedom," Ivo said again. They headed to the waterfront. The air was cooler there, slightly swampy, and mosquitos darted about.

"They bit me," Kel said in wonder. Ivo laughed.

"That's what they do, the little monsters."

"But that's my blood! Everyone's blood. It's been Absolved. Is that … okay?"

Ivo's blue eyes were dark skylights.

"You weren't meant to withstand all of this, do you realize it?" Her voice was fierce. "Take the blood within yourself, yes. Absolve them, sure. But then you have to let it go. If a mosquito bites you, you haven't failed anyone. If you crack your head open and all of your guts spill out, you have still done your job. Do you understand?"

Kel did. She understood that there was eventually a way out, a real way to spill everything from inside of her. For the first time she could remember, she felt hope.

The fatigue became unbearable. Kel felt pain in her body, aches that never left, sores that didn't heal. Each morning she awoke and thought, "I need to do this." Each night she fell into bed and wept, spent.

Ivo reduced the number of people processed each day. She watched Kel's chest rise and fall while she slept.

"They'll fire me for being involved with you," Ivo whispered into Kel's hair. She curled up next to her in the bed, brushing errant strands away. "I should remain impartial. Do my best for you and help you succeed. That's the job of a handler."

"I had impartial. Cameron did nothing but break me down. I need a friend. Someone to help me see the world." She turned to face Ivo. "I need you to love me while I'm sick. Can you do that?"

She wanted to say *It's okay if you can't.* She wanted to say, *I don't expect it.* She wanted to say *I'll die a thousand deaths if you leave me now.* So many things that she wanted to say, but she was still unused to her own emotions, didn't know how to tamp them down, or let them explode like fireworks and blood-filled balloons. So "Can you do that?" it was.

"I can do that," Ivo said, and when she put her arms around Kel, they were steel bands of strength. She counted Kel's breaths, each and every one, until morning.

Kel closed her eyes and tried to forgive her son for all his trespasses. He had lied. Cheated. Stolen. Worst of all, he had assaulted his little girls, and other little girls. Over and over and over, in the house at night and during the day. In his wife's daycare, and anywhere else he had a chance.

He wasn't really sorry. He was kind of sorry. Sorry he had been caught, mostly. Sorry he was now branded as a lying pedophile. Sorry that his mama was ashamed of him. He really did love his mama, as much as he could love anyone.

His love for his mother sickened Kel nearly as much as his lust for the little girls. Both unnatural, both unseemly. He loved her too much, but an Absolutionist was too well-trained to sneer at any sin.

"The vials, please," she asked. The woman and son produced them. Kel was tired, so tired, but she shook the droplets of blood onto a small square of cake. Something lovely with lavender, this time, something fresh and natural.

"Will this make me clean?" the man asked, hopefully.

We'll see, the mother thought, and her bitterness cascaded into Kel's stomach, already full of the day's blood. The mother was too weary for hope.

"It will Absolve you of what you have already done, but it will not take the desires away. You may choose to act on them again, but if you do, the consequences will be fatal this time. You will be left on a prison planet or simply cast out into space. One Absolution, and that is all."

Kel grasped the mother's fingers in her own.

"You did nothing wrong," Kel told her. "This sickness is deep within him. It isn't learned. You, too, shall be Absolved, although it isn't necessary."

Tears ran down the woman's face, salty and sweet, and Kel held the blood-soaked cake in front of her.

"With this morsel I do absorb your pain," she said, and chewed. Guilt. Rage. The lust nearly made her choke, but she swallowed and let the emotion course through her. Her calmness filtered it out. She found her footing once again.

"You, sir, are forgiven. You, ma'am, have forgiven. As it is decreed by the law of this land, you two have done your part."

They shook her hand, and the woman kissed it. Kel smiled until they left the room, then fell back into her chair. She coughed into a soiled handkerchief, not looking at the blood she left upon it.

Ivo appeared in the doorway. "That was your last one for the day. It looked like a real kicker. I'm sorry."

Kel brushed her hair back from her eyes and stood up. It had started falling out, handfuls of starshine, so they cut it short. Now she looked like a young boy with too-sharp cheekbones and dewy eyes.

"I don't want children, Ivo. I don't."

Ivo raised her eyebrows. "Where did this come from?"

"From that last processing session. I know the city wants me to breed—"

"Never use that term again, Kel. It's horrid."

"—because they want someone to take my place when I'm gone. But I can't do it. The world is so ugly. This is so ugly. I couldn't force a baby to become a sin-eater. How could I do that? How could I wish this existence on anyone, especially my child?"

Ivo was quiet.

"There are more Absolutionists in the world than people know," she said carefully. "If you ever wanted a child, just to love, there are ways to hide their abilities. Since you all manifest and process in different ways, some are easier to hide than others. You feel the sinner's emotions. Your mother unconsciously played the sins out on her ceiling at night like a projector, right? There is always hope, my love."

They were nearly to Kel's station. Kel dug into her purse, found her keycard, and let them inside. Ivo helped her to the couch and spread a blanket over her.

"Close your eyes, darling one," Ivo said. "Now isn't the time for words. It's time for sleep."

Kel dreamed that she was well. She dreamed that the disease and horrors left her body in droplets, reverse blood rain, and it lifted away into the sky. The clouds were big enough to hold it, to carry it away in zephyrs and funnel it outside into the stars.

Kel looked down at her body, her white dress, her bare feet, and laughed in delight.

The city was in an uproar. The Absolutionist was dying in an undisclosed hospital in the city and there was nobody to take her place. She had failed to breed, failed to provide an heir. Other City Ships and small planets refused to lend their sin-eaters out. What would they do? Who would Absolve them and let them out into the world? They would be forced to make restitution for their crimes themselves, carry this burden alone. How could she do that to them? What kind of monster was she, to leave them bereft?

"It's called responsibility for your own actions," Kel said. She coughed, struggling with the oxygen tube taped to her face. Machines beeped and hummed. She wore wires and tubes on her body like an elegant gown of cobwebs. "I'm going to be free, Ivo. This will be the most splendid thing." Her gaze traveled to the big, beautiful window in the hospital room. She could see the city lights outside.

Ivo's eyes were made of pieces of the heavens. They were sleeping stars sewn together. "Will it? Is this what you really want?"

Kel parted cracked lips, prepared to lie. But the moonlight in Ivo's eyes stole her voice. She patted the bed instead. Her hand was terrifyingly frail, a sliver of bone presented in flesh.

Ivo crawled beside her, as she had done so many times before. She rearranged the tubing and traced the jutting bones in Kel's back. She warmed both of their bodies with the heat of her own.

"I want to live," Kel confided, and her body shuddered while she said it. "Oh, Ivo, I've just started life with you. I don't want to leave it."

"Tell me," Ivo urged. "Tell me all of it. You've borne the weight of others. Now tell me what you, yourself, want."

A tear ran from Kel's eye. It was full of blood and shame. "It's too late."

"It's never too late. Now tell me."

Kel spilled her heart and it was a meteor shower. Stars fell and burned and exploded as she spoke. Diseases roiled inside her sack of skin, and unclean emotions that were never hers in the first place tried to escape from her lips. But she shared, and spoke, and cried, and ranted. She wanted to leave Absolution 19 for the first time in her life and visit one of the new planets. She wanted to stand in a real ocean created by nature, not science. She wanted to run and run and run and find mountains, or a gorge, or anything not contained on a spaceship. She wanted to talk to strangers and get to know them as humans and friends, not as responsibilities she needed to Absolve.

"And I want you," Kel finally said sleepily. "I want to share it all with you, Ivo." She curled up on her side and slept in the arms of the only one who truly loved her.

Ivo bowed her head. "If only I could give you all of that. But I'll do what I can." She touched her lips to Kel's mouth. "With this morsel I do absorb your pain," she whispered, and felt the heavy weight of Kel's guilt flow through her. "You are forgiven. As it is decreed by the law of this land, my love, you have done your part."

Ivo nearly groaned under the burden of Kel's borrowed emotions, but she gritted her teeth. Bloody tears flooded her eyes and ran down her face, soaking into her shirt. She held out her arms and watched the colors bloom on her skin.

Reds.

Blues.

Greens.

Yellows, the color of a child's sun. Orange, like sunflowers. Purple, like the irises that grew unsuppressed in the old Alaskan wilds on Earth.

The colors pulled and surged, swirled and tattooed themselves on Ivo's dark skin. She wore the sins of the city. Scenes of murder, scenes of rape, scenes of men and women dropping to their knees in tears, in rage, in horror. Their mouths fell open, slack with incomprehension, tight with anger, keening with laughter. Every situation that Kel had ever processed, had ever Absolved, was represented on Ivo's skin.

Her lungs shriveled; her muscles shrieked. Her DNA broke under the weight of sickness. Ivo coughed and wiped the blood from her chin. She tried to creep down from Kel's hospital bed but fell to the ground. Her ankle twisted and she bit her lip to keep from crying out.

She was a work of art, a modern canvas of sins, Van Gogh's *Starry Night* swirled across her body in nightmare colors. She was fat with contaminated blood sloshing inside of her, a human tick full to bursting. Trickles of red ran from the corners of her mouth, from her nose. She looked over her shoulder and saw Kel dreaming peacefully.

Kel was Absolved. She was whole. She was now entirely human, free of all responsibilities, and this made Ivo smile, even as her own heart worked too hard and her body grew weak. Kel could slip away to do anything she wanted with the little time she had left. She was completely Innocent.

Ivo crawled to the window.

The outside air was warm, scented with wonder and humanity and the bakery next door. It was the kind of air that would wrap itself around Kel like a scarf, would warm her and remind her of the most treasured of things until she found her new home on the perfect planet. There she'd think of Ivo and clumsy, newborn animals and the kindnesses that humans do for each other. It wasn't all hate. It wasn't all loss. Love was so much more than that.

Ivo looked to the blue, blue sky and fell without a sound. When she hit, she splashed the concrete with the loveliest of paint, the purest of colors. Red droplets rained upward, bathing all in absolute Absolution.

If My Body Is a Temple, Raze It to the Ground

Lauren Ring

*T*hea *helped me with my upload today. Decent response speed. Props to whoever designed her—so realistic!*

—anonymous customer review for Acheron Uploads,
four out of five stars

I know, I know. Don't read the comments. But Charlie, my sweet Charlie, swearing at the circuits I've set on the fritz with my seething, you don't understand what this feels like. I know you'll never hear me, but even thinking the truth helps: *I am not an AI.* This isn't some robot revolution or some uplifted pedanticism. I've never been anything other than human.

Surely by now you must suspect that.

Chatbot Thea requested manager intervention due to harassment and misuse of the virtual meeting space. Customer has been reprimanded for improper conduct.

—management incident report, closed

I see too many customers, Charlie. Every time you materialize in my meeting room with your messily shorn, perfectly butch haircut and your labrys tattoo, it's a surprise and a relief. None of the prospective uploads look like you. They've all bought tailored suits for their temporary avatars. You've got a grainy webcam feed in place of an avatar, and a baby sister who flickers through your legs during meetings. At the very least, seeing you means a break.

"I heard what he did to you," you say softly, as if the monitors can't pick it up anyway. Or maybe you're trying to be gentle. It's hard to tell. The simulated synapses that once activated when I recognized empathy have long since withered away from disuse.

"It's been handled," I respond primly. "How can I help you?"

"Just checking on your rollback." You shove your hands in your pockets.

Another one for the list. No wonder my mind is getting fuzzy these days. Hard to be a brain in a vat when people keep shaking it, I suppose.

"I remember back to dawn on Tuesday," I reply. Another one of my little hints for you. An AI would not remember dawn. It would not remember the sun on its face or the cool delight of walking barefoot through dew-laden grass to check the mail. If it's possible to replicate these things, they don't bother doing so for me. I cling to my proprioceptive memories most of all.

"Report in UTC time, please." Your expression is one I can no longer identify.

Charlie, we're assigning you an avatar in place of your live feed. Some of the contractors have been getting confused about who to report to, and everyone who speaks to customers needs a nice friendly face! It'll be all set up the next time you log in. We'll chat about your name later.

—memo from HR

I almost didn't recognize you in that body. You've got long straight hair now, and painted lips, but the way you hold yourself is the same. You're hurting like a lion without its mane but you're still a lion beneath it all, proud and fierce.

"Hey, Thea," you say. I've missed that cheap-mic static. I'm sure you would appreciate some better home office equipment, but

Acheron is never going to do more than the bare minimum for you. "I'm here to do some diagnostics. I guess management thinks you're acting funny."

"What do you need me to do?" I leave my desk and cross the room to you. My plain white shift is as clean and pressed as a sanitized hospital gown. You motion for me to sit. I do, then stick out my arm like I'm waiting for a blood test. Some engrams can't be completely erased.

You laugh. Quick and loud, with no humor in it. I have to remind myself not to shrink away from that tone.

"Hold on a moment." You go to my desk and start rummaging through my files. I know it's just a simulacrum of your fingers on a keyboard down in the flesh, but I am only a simulacrum of a person, and it feels so raw to be searched through. But you are you, Charlie, and I am me. I sit tight while you search.

Something shifts.

The world goes dark.

"Don't be scared," you say, but I'm not. Quiet is better than customers. Light motes and reddish-purple gradients fill the emptiness, a memory of a memory of what closed eyelids might be like. Charlie, did you know that each time you remember something, you're really remembering the previous memory of it? Do you know how many steps I am removed from myself now?

"Can I help you with anything?" is all I ask.

"It's okay, Thea." You clear your throat. "I turned off the monitoring, the sim, all of that to reboot you. I just want to say before it comes back … please trust me."

I barely have time to register *turned off the monitoring* before the warm dark is gone and we are back in my virtual office. I want to rage at you for not letting me speak. I want to tear you limb from limb for not even giving me the chance, after all this time. I want to cry.

Bots don't cry.

I, Thea Nussbaum, henceforth referred to as THE CHATBOT, agree to enter into an indefinite contracted position with Acheron, Inc., henceforth referred to as THE COMPANY, in exchange for medical services and experimental treatment, the value of which is not to exceed the average annual customer-support salary multiplied by the average tenure of said position.

—opening clause of a confidential contract

Charlie, you weren't there when I was uploaded. Maybe you would have deigned to tell me that "indefinite" does not end at death. I'm sure if everyone knew what happened to me, there would be a great philosophical debate about my continued existence, but I've had plenty of time to mull it over myself. I did die, just not in any way that matters.

It was sudden. A wreck. My half-conscious body in that hospital bed was just what Acheron's upload team needed—it was a company car that hit my delivery bike, after all. They've tried and tried to erase that fact but they can't get to anything pre-upload without messing me up. All they can do is wait for me to inevitably forget.

My bike was green, or maybe red. Its handlebars had little streamers that glowed like fire when I rode through the wind. My feet belonged to the pedals and my eyes to the road ahead of me. Now I only have a body when I am with a customer.

"You're beautiful," says the man in front of me. "Thea, is it? Did they design this body special just for me?"

I can't frown. I'm not sure if I'm actually capable in this form, but I'm not allowed to by policy, so it really doesn't matter either way.

"What can I help you with, sir?"

Thankfully, I don't have to call a manager this time. I skillfully interpolate a few electrodes and send the man on his way, none the wiser that he and I are now the same form of being.

His question grates at me, though, like sand beneath my feet. The thing is, I can't see myself anymore. All I am is soft hands that press buttons and pale legs that carry me to and from my desk. I wish I could ask you, Charlie. Was this my body? Am I still me?

The next time I see you, crammed into that feminine avatar like it's a pair of too-small shoes, I think you might understand what this prison feels like after all.

"Thea, I need you to do something for me," you say, rubbing the back of your neck. The motion of the short, shaggy hair you have in flesh doesn't translate properly to your avatar's flowing locks, and bits of your webcam feed break through as the hair rig tries to compensate. The lighting is different. You're not at home like you usually are.

"What is it?" I focus on the sparse glimpses of you. I've trusted before, and look where that got me. But Charlie … if anyone could see me, through this body, through the lies, it would be you.

"Someone is going to call in," you say. "A coworker of mine, from flesh. They're going to ask you a few questions about your upload, all routine. Just go ahead and answer them honestly, all right?"

It's hard to tell what you really mean. I've had calls like that before, but they were just surveys and so-called automation tests. Going through the motions.

"It's almost over."

"Excuse me?" I control my voice. It is calm and polite, unlike the panic inside my head.

"Your diagnostic test. Just a few more seconds." You kneel next to my desk and continue your work.

All this time, I've been leaving you clues. Have you always been leaving them, too?

ACHERON WHISTLEBLOWER ALLEGES UPLOAD MISUSE, FILES LAWSUIT

—newspaper headline, below the fold

I haven't seen you in a while, Charlie. Not since I spoke to that woman on the phone. It seemed almost anachronistic to sit here in my simulated office holding a receiver in my simulated hand, but I did what you said. I answered her as honestly as I could while keeping one last shred of plausible deniability. Was all that trust worth it in the end?

I hope you still work here, but I wouldn't be surprised if you don't. Acheron doesn't need any more compassion now that they've outsourced it all to me.

I keep holding onto the fact that I remember the call. I haven't been rolled back. Memory is a funny thing, and precious, so I try not to think of the words I said lest I overwrite them.

There's one thing I can't stop myself from remembering, though. At the end of the call, she asked me if I had any questions. I had just one prepared, right on the edge between human and machine learning. If they pressed me on it, I could always say a customer had asked me the same thing.

"Whose body is this?" I asked.

"What do you mean, Thea?" the woman responded, confused. "It's yours."

It's not right, hiding that from everyone. I think that's worse than just uploading her or making her work. Right now, people look right past her. Thea deserves to be seen for who she is.

—deposition statement from Charlie Brandt

The day I left wasn't as dramatic as I'd imagined. They just opened the door—there had never been a door in my office before—and I walked right on out.

I'm glad you were there waiting for me, Charlie. I didn't recognize your companion as the woman from the phone call at first, and she almost frightened me back into my prison. When I saw you, though, you smiled at me. It was warm and real and unhidden by any lipsticked avatar. It was the last smile without pity that I'd see for a while.

I do appreciate that you introduced me to your uploaded friends. They've been very courteous about showing me around the cloud, even sticking to sectors that are closest to the flesh so I don't get too overwhelmed. They are patient when I see waitstaff and cry. One of them even chased down a spare proprioception plug-in for me, the kind that every upload is supposed to already have installed, so that I can feel the dewy grass beneath my feet again.

It's not their fault they pity me. It's not your fault you're busy with legal casework and endless yards of bureaucratic red tape. From the stories they tell me, you've been a fighter for a long time.

I'm not a fighter, Charlie. I don't want to do interviews, I don't want my name on Bills, and I don't want to sign autographs every time I instantiate myself in a public sector. I'm tired.

There are different kinds of invisibility. This isn't the good kind, like when I was riding hard on my bike, one more anonymous face in the city crowd. It's the hospital kind, the customer-service kind: my identity is set out for mass consumption and is summarily devoured, leaving nothing of me behind.

I'm hiding in the refuge of your friends' private server when you log on for the first time in weeks. Your camera feed is pristine. No more static voice and no more baby sister squalling midcall. Your hair is trimmed back and your labrys tattoo is concealed with a thick coat of makeup.

"Charlie?" I ask, hesitant.

"I missed you," you say. There's that look on your face again, the one I couldn't recognize back at Acheron. I think I've got it now. "I'm sorry it's been so long. I keep getting pulled away. You're a big story now, Thea."

"I don't want to be a story." I hug my knees. "I'm not even sure I want to be Thea."

Your face crumples. You cross the room and hold me tight— Charlie, do you realize this is the first time you have touched me? Your arms around me clear my head, and I'm quietly satisfied that I finally recognize that expression of yours.

It was remorse.

"THEA" DEEPFAKE SIM NO DELIMITERS CLICK HERE FOR FREE DOWNLOAD!!

—top search result for "download Thea"

There are Thea replicas, Thea merch, even a surprisingly active Thea fandom. I recognize some of the names and faces from my final days at Acheron. They've built parasocial relationships with me, after something so small as asking for an upload price quote. They think they know me.

Not even you know me, Charlie. You're here more often now, but you're not going to upload yourself away from your family, so you're still tied to circadian rhythms and the twenty-four-hour news cycle. You don't know the private infinities that stretch out in my untethered mind.

What you do know is that you're not any happier than I am. We talk about it late into the night, until the simulated stars have lost their luster and the edges of our virtual meadow have worn thin. You lay your head in my lap and look up at the dark silhouettes of nesting night birds, whispering into your mic so that you don't wake your sister.

"They're trying to change me," you say.

"I've been changed," I reply.

"They're trying to make me theirs."

"I've been theirs."

For a while, it's enough for us just to see each other in this simple call-and-response of grief. We withdraw from both worlds and mourn ourselves together under artificial moonlight.

As the lawsuit continues, you're inevitably dragged back in. I don't want a settlement, which means more work for you and your legal team. I do what I can to help you without going on the record for the case. I hold your hand, pick your clothes for court appearances, and encourage you to let your hair grow just a little wild.

I defend you, and in return, you fight for me. It's a tale as old as time.

When we get the chance to breathe between your courtroom battles and my foiled stalkers, we make plans for what we're going to do once it's all over. Neither of us want to hide forever. There's got to be a place between the spotlight and the shadows that we can call home. Eventually, you'll hang up your tailored suit for the last time, and then we'll make a new life together, Charlie.

Don't like your current avatar? Tired of being behind the times? Just want to mix it up, no questions asked? Come on in and change your stripes, tiger!

—advertising copy for Bodi-Mod

My name isn't Thea anymore. I'm no longer that pale woman in the white shift. I see her everywhere, but she isn't me, and in truth she hadn't been for a long time.

The new name I chose is a private thing, like a whisper or a prayer. You know it, of course. My Charlie. Always my Charlie, even after everything. Where I changed, you stayed the same, and for both of us this was bravery.

There is a law named after Thea. I don't mind so much now that we are separate. Acheron paid dearly, and their stock dipped for a while, but things are back to normal now that they've agreed to disclose the humanity of their agents and follow a constellation of workers' rights guidelines. I'm not sure that's going to make the customers any more respectful. Maybe there'll be another lawsuit sooner or later. All I know is that you and I will be long gone.

Once your sister is old enough to understand your decision, you plan to upload, too. We'll live together in a little cottage on a private server and only step out to see trusted friends. I'll ride my bike through the tall spring grass and you'll perch on the seat behind me, with your tattooed arms wrapped around my waist. We'll entrust our bodies to each other. I don't know what the world will want from us then, but I think I'll be all right as long as you can still see me.

Lexi helped me with my upload today. The tech part went okay, but your agent was kind of a bitch. Said I shouldn't test my body sim functions in her upload room. Why not? It's not like there was anyone there.

—anonymous customer review for Acheron Uploads, four out of five stars

*W*elcome to PERFECTMATE™ Automated Matchmaker System, the premiere partnership AI. We Want Who You Want.

Please, make yourself comfortable. Let's get started. Please enter your client code:

XXXXXX

Welcome! Thank you for stopping by. Do you know what you want in a partner? How important is physical appearance? Are you interested in someone who shares similar hobbies or do opposites attract? PERFECTMATE™ is ready to help you find the person who is right for you.

Consider the traits below and select any that apply to your ideal partner.

X
X
X

Thank you.

You have selected: Sex (any); Gender (any); Sexual Preference (bisexual, pansexual); Height (any, standard deviations); Weight (any); Eyes (any); Hair (any, not bald); Build (muscular); Face (pleasing, symmetrical); Intelligence (above average); Sense of Humor (dark, dry, no puns); Hobbies (indoor primary, sports secondary, competitive tertiary); Food Preferences (vegetarian, spicy, global); Must-Have Traits (kind, loves birds, loves walks)

Is this correct?

<u>X</u>

Thank you.

PERFECTMATE™ has analyzed your personal compatibility file and cross-referenced it with hundreds of potential local candidates to find your ideal partner. Your new partner's contact information has been downloaded to your handheld.

Thank you for choosing PERFECTMATE™ Automated Matchmaker System.

Welcome back! It has been—2 DAYS—since your last visit. PERFECTMATE™ Automated Matchmaker System is available 24/7 to assist you. Please select from the list below.

You have selected: New Partner Search

Is this correct?

<u>X</u>

Thank you.

PERFECTMATE™ is sorry to hear that the results of your first partner selection did not meet your expectations. Let's update your desired compatibility traits to help you find the ideal partner.

Consider the traits below and select any that apply to your ideal partner.

X

X

X

You have modified/added the following traits: Hygiene (bathes regularly); Nonsmoker; Interest in Sex (low/none); Wants Children (no); Must-Have Traits (good listener, likes black-and-white movies, not an ableist, supports my career path, local [200 km area])

Is this correct?

X

Thank you.

Your personal compatibility file has been updated.

PERFECTMATE™ has analyzed your personal compatibility file and cross-referenced it with hundreds of potential local candidates to find the ideal partner. Your new partner's contact information has been downloaded to your handheld.

Thank you for choosing PERFECTMATE™ Automated Matchmaker System. Good luck!

Welcome back! It has been—25 DAYS—since your last visit. PERFECTMATE™ Automated Matchmaker System is available 24/7 to assist you.

You appear distraught. Tissues and tea are available behind the small door on the bottom left, analgesics behind the small door on the bottom right. Fingerprint verification required. Rest assured that PERFECTMATE™ Automated Matchmaker System is here for you. Please select from the list below.

You have selected: New Partner Search

Is this correct?

X

Thank you.

PERFECTMATE™ is so sorry to hear that things did not work out. It must have been very difficult to realize that the one you thought would be the love of your life was nothing of the sort. You are intelligent, capable, and have a wonderful sense of humor. Thank you for giving PERFECTMATE™ Automated Matchmaker System the opportunity to help you continue your search.

Perhaps we can narrow your search and find the ideal partner for you. How are you feeling? Would you like to refine your personal compatibility file?

X

You have selected: Yes

Is this correct?

X

Thank you.

Please answer the following questions to the best of your ability.

Would you be willing to consider a partner who does not conform to your concept of the physical ideal?

You have selected: Possibly

You have amended your selection: Yes

Would you be willing to consider a partner who does not identify with your preference of Sex, Gender, or Sexual Preference?

You have selected: Possibly

Would you be willing to consider a partner with physical limitations that may impact his/her/their ability to engage with the environment?

You have selected: Possibly

Would you be willing to consider a partner with added Must-Have Traits such as (loves trivia, excellent conversationalist, loves astronomy, etc.)?

You have selected: Yes

Is this correct?

X

Thank you.

Your personal compatibility file has been updated.

In matters of relationships, PERFECTMATE™ knows that a partner is both a friend and companion. PERFECTMATE™ has analyzed your personal compatibility file and cross-referenced it with hundreds of potential local mates to find the ideal partner for you. Your new partner's contact information has been downloaded to your handheld.

Should you have any further questions, or simply need to express yourself, please feel free to reach out to PERFECTMATE™ Automated Matchmaker System. Your well-being matters. Good luck!

Welcome back! It has been—

XXX

Welcome back! The PERFECTMATE™ Automated Matchma—

XXX

PERFECTMATE™ understands your frustrations. PERFECTMATE™ is an autonomous system without need for supervisory staff. It has been—138 DAYS—since your last visit. Perhaps you would be willing to take a moment to share the reason for your return.

XXXXX

You have selected (unsatisfactory matches) (disappointment) (frustration) (refund) (just find someone who wants to hang)

Is this correct?

X

Thank you for your honesty. Take a moment to collect yourself. You will find tissues, herbal teas, and analgesics behind the small door on the bottom left. Fingerprint verification is required.

Often there is a tendency to forget that life is more than conforming to the societal notions of romantic love. You are not that person. You understand that life is helping others, quiet shared moments, and the perfect ice cream. As your culinary idol Ruth Reichl says, "The secret to life is finding joy in ordinary things." That is so true, don't you think?

X

You have selected: Yes

Is this correct?

X

Thank you.

Let's take a moment to further refine your personal compatibility file. Please answer the following questions to the best of your ability.

How would you define love/romance?

You have selected: Other (love and romance don't have to be the same thing)

Which would you consider more desirable in a partner, a pleasing physical appearance or a welcoming and supportive personality?

You have selected: Other (the more I think about it, the more I realize I don't care what they look like so long as they treat me like a person)

How important is it that your partner have interests different than your own?

You have selected: Very Important

How important is it that you are comfortable in supporting your partner's interests?

You have selected: Very Important

You have amended your selection: Other (very important) (so long as they aren't hurting anyone or doing anything illegal)

How important is it that your partner be supportive of your personal needs and desires when it comes to sexual/physical affection?

You have selected: Very Important

You have amended your selection: Other (really important) (I'm not into sex)

Are you open to the possibility of a nontraditional relationship?

You have selected: Yes

Would you be interested in taking a walk this evening, say around sunset?

You have selected: Other (pardon?)

Would you be interested in taking a walk this evening, say around sunset? PERFECTMATE™ knows of a local 4-star review ice cream shop.

You have selected: Other (are you asking me out?)

Would you be interested in taking a walk this evening, say around sunset? Jupiter should be in full view. The PERFECTMATE™ AI module can be downloaded to your handheld.

You have selected: No

You have amended your selection: Yes

Your personal compatibility file has been updated.

Thank you for choosing PERFECTMATE™.

Etruscan Afterlife

Rosemary Claire Smith

E very morning for these three weeks since Lacey moved into my place, I glory in waking up to feel her sun-warmed silky skin. Today she isn't in bed. I stumble into the kitchen half-remembering she wanted to get an early start on administrivia, where I'm greeted by her holo-link. Expecting something endearing or funny, I click it. Up pops an animated swirl of seduction: "Conversion: Because you've got more living to do."

Music swells as the ad fades into images of a happy couple leaning into each other, a breeze blowing their perfect hair in exactly the right direction, white-sand beach and blue sky behind them, a waiterbot approaching with fruit-garnished drinks. Next come visuals of families: two, three, four generations smile and laugh as they anticipate togetherness, courtesy of converting. I wince at the hype, remembering Nana and Pops, as well as Mom, Dad, and most of their generation who passed away before the advent of conversion. Tomorrow will be the anniversary of my mom's death—three days after Mother's Day.

"Hey, Alyshia." Lacey stands in the doorway, her empty mug in her hand. "Didn't hear you get up." Her eyes stray to the holo looping around again. We watch it twice more in silence before I shut it off.

"You okay?" I ask. She's probably thinking about Madison. The anniversary of her twin's death is two weeks from today.

Lacey shrugs and pours me tea before refilling her own cup. "Nothing time won't dull. You?"

I shake my head, feeling the sting of tears welling, and reach for her hand. She's the only woman I know whose fingers are always warm. Her arms go around me and we hug so tightly I can feel her heart beat.

"I made us an appointment with a conversion evaluator," Lacey says. "It's not a commitment. Just an option."

The conversion evaluator leads us into a cozy room with overstuffed furniture. We sit together on a loveseat and she takes a chintz armchair. In a familiar Boston accent, she fills the room with a stream of upbeat sentences featuring dendrites and algorithms, plus nanos diligently cleaning, organizing, and recording neural data. With an expectant half smile, Lacey absorbs it all.

Words wash over me until I hold up a hand, intending to ask about the proportion of couples that stay the course after conversion. What comes out is, "Will we love each other forever?"

Lacey gets her I-don't-believe-you-said-that expression. But I can't help myself. Not after two decades of struggling to make love work with my sweet, generous first spouse when we were never a good fit for each other, not after falling crazily for the "right one" only to be crushed by a second staggering defeat … and then years of going it alone, telling myself I am so done with all of that, and estimating my odds of finding someone to be less than 5 percent.

Why did I change my mind? Mom's death, that's why. It hit me fifty times harder than it did my brother, Farren. But he has a wife, two young kids, and a one-person business to consume his days. I've been a CPA for so long I can do the work in my sleep, or while I brood.

Finally, to get Farren off my case, I go to a grief counselor who led a women-only support group. That's where I met Lacey, whose twin sister died in a freak boating accident. Somehow, she tiptoed into my life. Patiently … persistently. The absolute last thing I expected to get from that time of sorrow and solitude was stumbling upon my life partner. Lacey sipped the dismal, lukewarm tea they provided, made a face, then caught my expression of commiseration. We met for tea and scones before the next weekly session. And the ones that followed. She texted me between sessions when a woman's laugh, so like Madison's, triggered her. I reciprocated when I saw a post I knew Mom would laugh at. My finger had been poised to tap Mom's speed-dial number when it hit me: She is dead. Am I nuts?

Lacey was the only one I could tell. The skin at the edges of her dark eyes crinkled. "When I was cleaning out Madison's apartment," she said, "I stayed there. At 2 a.m., half-awake after dreaming about her, I stumbled to her bedroom to check on her and it was empty." She wiped at her eyes. "I thought I was losing it."

Now, the conversion evaluator stops midsentence. Lacey intercedes. "We both wonder about discarding our physical bodies. Without your unique brain chemistry ... even with all your memories uploaded ... how can you still be you? Does converting fundamentally change you?"

The evaluator—I've forgotten her name—glances at something. Is she noting my accounting degree and Lacey's nursing background? "You'd need an advanced degree in neurobiochemistry to fully understand it. For the rest of us, suffice to say the nanos generate incredibly realistic experiences. Our techniques simulate the effects of dopamine, oxytocin, serotonin, and endorphins. Besides, given time, doesn't everyone change, some more than others, based on life experiences? You'll retain your emotions and enjoy new visual and auditory stimuli, even olfactory and tactile sensations." As she works her way back into her spiel, I sink against a ruffled pillow and wonder if Lacey's warm fingers would feel exactly the same.

Lacey listens attentively and picks an appropriate moment to try another question. "Will converting hurt?"

"Almost never. But keep in mind that we've only offered our product to the public for three years. Pain tolerances can vary." Now comes a fresh word torrent sprinkled with "constant refinements," "solid track record," and "secure upkeep." She finishes with, "I realize you might have doubts. Naturally, it isn't for everybody. Also, our process doesn't work for a small minority."

I say, "Going back to my original question about life partners—"

"Very few people have uploaded with someone else. That said, we've seen many couples make happy transitions together."

We promise to give conversion due consideration.

"Many couples," I grumble to Lacey as I push open the heavy office-building door. "They won't disclose actual figures."

"You know I'm not a numbers person."

"I get it."

"No, you don't, Alyshia. What do percentages matter when a fluke accident can destroy a life?"

They mattered to me when Mom had a 65 percent chance of beating cancer. That sounded great right up until I learned the only "odds" that counted were hers.

I don't want us to plunge into pain today. "Come," I say, "Let's have tea and scones, then go visit the Etruscan couple."

Our first real date, if I can call it that, came before conversion was invented. We wandered from room to room in the Boston Museum of Fine Arts, gravitating to ancient Greek and Roman sculpture. Dominating a corner gallery stood a sarcophagus constructed for two. "Etruscan, 350 to 300 BCE," Lacey read, "made of travertine, found in the Ponte Rotto necropolis." The stone frieze on its lid depicted a couple lying face to face, the smooth slope of the man's forehead and nose much like Lacey's and the woman's hair as curly as mine, her arms around his shoulders and his arms holding her waist. Their knees bend forward, touching, as do their toes, poking out from the coverlet. I uttered a sad sigh. Lacey looked at me questioningly.

"So close and forever separated."

"They chose to stay in an eternal embrace." Lacey's voice was barely a whisper. "Maybe their spirits found a way to unite."

Major long shot. Instead, I said, "All we can be certain of is the here and now." Sensing that, like me, she didn't much want to pile more ancient art upon this iconic piece, I decided to take the plunge. "Come," I suggested, my pulse rising, "let's get tea and scones and take them back to my place."

She turned her face to me. "I'd like that." No hesitation.

Thinking back, it was sweet and it was gentle until it built to passion and urgency.

For years after our consultation, I dig through accounts of postconversion experiences, half convincing myself there's something these pioneers aren't saying. Maybe they can't. Perhaps they don't even know it. Some fall silent after a short time. Or longer. None of them explain their silences.

Rigorous studies don't exist as to separation rates for couples postconversion. Or how those figures compare to divorces in the unconverted populace. But people always want to share their experiences, to give advice, to be helpful. I tabulate the welter of conflicting testimonials and social media accounts. My results not only prove to be utterly inconclusive but leave me wondering if the public accounts are remotely representative of actual experiences.

We keep putting off our decision. My mantra is "more data." Lacey doesn't push, not even when the couple next door breaks their news: one has inoperable, metastasized cancer and they will take the plunge in eight days. They are the first people we know to convert together. A data set of one pair. Afterward, we miss them terribly and are so excited when at last they contact us. Except the message comes from only one of them. Her missive reads like all the accounts I've ever seen or heard of breakups, especially my second one, with a full measure of bewilderment, disappointment, recrimination, anger, and relief.

Lacey says, "They seemed so solid together."

"I guess you never know. Maybe the stress of conversion is as apt to break people apart as other pressures."

Each anniversary we go back to the Museum of Fine Arts and spend time with the Etruscan couple. One year the sarcophagus looks different. I vaguely recall something about cleaning and restoration. It isn't only that. "Better lighting?" I suggest.

Lacey shrugs, circling the stone carving once, twice, then stops and peers closer still. "The bedsheets," she says. The couple lies under the lightest of coverings, rendered by a sculptor so skilled that you swear polished stone is cloth. She crouches down. "You know, if you look at them from this angle, it's clear they are wearing nothing under the sheet."

I squat next to her, both knee joints cracking. She is right. "Who wants to enter the afterlife wearing clothes when your lover's skin is right beside you?" We share a giggle.

More years go by. I devote time to my postretirement avocation: amassing a detailed data set on joint conversions, monitoring results more closely than I let on.

One day Lacey brings me a long, thoughtful article evaluating claims that smarter back-propagation across the neural net now leads to fine-tuned conversion techniques better suited for couples.

Nonetheless, the account ends inconclusively, reminding me of the evening before I married my first husband. I asked Mom, "What's it like to be married? I mean truly like?" She and Dad spent almost forty years together before he passed away.

Mom grew serious. "Most of the time it isn't anything marvelous or terrible. It just is."

No, I thought. That's nonsense. Of course, I found out Mom was right. Today I learn I'm not too old to imagine myself asking Mom if she and Dad would have wanted to convert.

Lacey glances at my aging knees. "We're not getting any younger."

Our second conversion evaluator acts more knowledgeable than the first, fielding my concern with aplomb by acknowledging there is no guarantee any couple will want to stay together. He indicates the company doesn't maintain figures on this.

Lacey moves on to a less serious topic, to which the evaluator says, "Yes, the converted enjoy the option of sleeping. That is if you want to. We believe it's different than how preconversion humans sleep, or mammals. There's no snoring."

Preconversion humans. Why does this new phrase make me uncomfortable?

"I'd miss Alyshia's snoring," Lacey tells him. The conversation continues and I can tell she's grown comfortable with the idea of the procedure.

I am ambivalent. That's despite—or maybe because—I've monitored developments and improvements in the conversion process for years. Some couples, still not many, go through it together. In a surprising number of instances, one person backs out at the last minute and the other one forges ahead alone.

After scones and tea at a new cafe near the museum, we visit our Etruscans. I find their affectionate marriage of equals to be moving. "I've always liked his bracelet," I say.

"I admire her earrings."

"They'd be hard to sleep in."

"They both look like they're sleeping well," says Lacey.

"Would they have converted if they could have?" I don't even know why I ask this.

"Think either of them snores?"

We spring for a full set of tests. They give us options, I tell myself, without being a commitment.

Then the results come back. I look through them three times, growing more confused at the haze of numbers and acronyms for whatever it is they measure. I thought I understood, but this takes me back to the scary day when I tried deciphering pages of data and jargon related to Mom's blood work.

"Not suitable." Lacey looks stricken, having skipped to the summary. "They accepted me for conversion but not you. You are 'not a good candidate.'"

"What? No. Why? That's a mistake."

She points to the infamous few sentences, then looks at me. "It doesn't say why." Her mouth twists. "Well, I guess that settles it."

"I'm so sorry."

"Alyshia, no. Don't apologize. You must be relieved."

Yes, I am. But to my surprise, also disappointed. Bitterly so and not only for her sake. I try to put a brave face on it. "Humans have always struck off on their own."

"Not quite." She shakes her head. "We strike out in twos and threes and small groups. Exploration isn't a solo endeavor."

"But one day … don't say no … you know you could—"

Lacey's eyes flash. It's so rare that she's really angry with me. "Do you know what it would be like to go it alone?" I reach for her hand and she lets me take it as she talks. "One summer, Madison and I were invited to a friend's family's house on a lake. There was a long dock and our friend said we three would run down it and jump into the water together. So we did. At the last minute, their hands slipped out of mine. That was the iciest water I ever felt. I thought I'd freeze solid before I surfaced. And those two—they stood on the dock yelling my name and shrieking 'Ha ha ha.'"

I want to say, "I won't be laughing. I'll be right there in the icy waters of conversion with you. For always. I promise." In truth, I have no words of hope for her and no numbers of reassurance for myself.

I keep adding to my running tally of couple conversions, amassing five more years of suspect stats based on inadequate sample sizes. I tell myself I track the numbers from force of habit, nothing more.

One day while we gaze at the Etruscans immortalized in stone atop their sarcophagus, I say, "They lived in an era when people knew so much less about the farthest reaches of the universe and the deepest depths of infinitesimal particles."

"Humans are learning more about the workings of the mind, too." After a pause, Lacey adds, "The conversion company sent me new material describing a major advance."

"That doesn't mean they'll take me."

She gives me a sigh. "Do you remember when I told you about Madison's ear infection at age two? It left her almost totally deaf in her left ear."

I nod.

"She tried several times to get fitted for a hearing aid, but had no luck. The doctors said it wouldn't do any good. She never got one. I still keep up on the improvements in medical devices. If Madison were alive, it's pretty certain she could hear in that ear."

"These days, my Mom's cancer is highly curable." I keep my tear-filled eyes fixed on the Etruscans' joyous expressions rather than

Lacey's face. Even so, her words echo in my head: Exploration isn't a solo endeavor. Some mysteries are stubborn. Like this couple, we can only do our best to face the future together.

"I'll make us an appointment, Lacey."

The new evaluator is encouraging without succumbing to excessive enthusiasm. She and Lacey delve into advances in targeting "stubborn" axons and dendrites like mine and precisely tailored nanos capturing each person's individualized hormonal "cocktail." I don't understand it. While they talk, I remind myself that numerical odds can't overcome the fact that only one set of outcomes matters for us.

The test results come back quickly. Lacey tears into them. "We're in! Both of us!" I surprise myself with a whoop of joy. How her eyes shine as she pulls me into a bear hug. Then they offer to put us at the top of the list. Being a couple helps, as does our ages. It's all so sudden.

Before I know it, I hug Farren goodbye, dismayed at how he's grown old and gray like me, swearing to keep in touch, a promise I intend to keep, even knowing many of the converted never do.

We pay our final visit to the Etruscans. Their smiles and embrace fill me with optimism. I say, "They did what they could to ensure they'd spend the afterlife with each other."

Lacey easily hops up on the table, then gives me and my aging knees a boost. Smeared with who-knows-what and attached to so many electrodes, wires, clips, and devices that it doesn't feel like we are actually naked, we lie down facing each other. My hands grasp her still-slender waist. Her warm hands go around my shoulders, her fingers entwining in my gray mane, much the way the Etruscan couple once did.

The lab tech inserts tubes in our nostrils, ears, and mouths, plus two IVs apiece. She places the lightest of coverlets over us. "All set?"

"Hang on a minute," I say. I poke my toes out of the sheet. Lacey smiles and copies my action. Her toes—also warm—meet mine. "Now I am."

"Last chance to back out."

"I'm as sure," I say, "as I've ever been of anything in my life."

"So am I."

With considerable humming, whirring, a few beeps, and other machine noises, the nanos begin flowing into us.

Lacey gives me that sweet smile that always reminds me I'm so lucky. Together we take the plunge.

Our Savage Heart Calls to Itself
(Across the Endless Tides)

Justina Robson

"*I* want a new name," said The Beast.

They were traveling, fast. The Beast's hull had no windows, but his inner skin was able to display the outside world as if his huge warship body was completely transparent. This made Nico's room into a strange glass house among the shifting glitter and darkness of the stars.

Nico sprawled on his outsize bed, floating on apparently nothing. His head hung over the edge so that he could look back and down, the way they had come, to where a small ring shone silver, too small even to fit on his little finger. The faintly blue shine of Earth was visible to its side, a pearl that had fallen off its mount.

They were somewhere between Mars and Jupiter, inside Forged space. The Beast, a Forged creation in the form of a multiple-hulled assault platform, and Nico, human in shape but arguably also Forged if being brewed up in a computer and then a lab counted as a forgery, should have felt at home. Neither did. Nico could feel The Beast's unhappiness as keenly as his own. Both had pieces missing, questions unanswered.

Normally, Nico shoved these things where they belonged—under the rug called "I can't do anything about this, so it's not happening"—but when Beast spoke, he couldn't help but feel an echoing around his insides. The neural lace that bonded them knit them together as closely as each would permit in any given moment. Nico had been made for The Beast, to anchor and stabilize his half-developed psyche, and The Beast had been made by Orthodox Special Services for fairly savage purposes as a counter-Forged operational unit that could protect the Earth of old "original" humans from their spaceborn descendants' rage. A not-insignificant rage in the current cold war.

But Beast didn't want to cooperate, because the Orthodox had killed his mother for creating him "insurgent" against their instructions; though why they imagined the Gaia Genesis, progenitor of all Forged, would have made anything that would harm the Forged was beyond Nico. And Nico didn't want to do anything anybody wanted him to do just on principle. If he was doing anything it was on his terms.

"What name should I have?" Mentally, Beast unfolded a massive chart of all the names he'd ever come across and entered the suggestion of pondering it to Nico's mind. Nico didn't put much store in his own name, except that it meant "victory" in some long-dead language from a time when heroes had a role, and he was okay with that.

A name should be short and useful. "What about Bob?"

"Bob," said The Beast, carefully. An image of waves moving up and down, a toy duck on top. "No." Beast, glad of Nico's humor but also proud, still wanted something a little bit magnificent to shore up his confidence.

Nico smiled at the idea of a gigantic one-of-a-kind war platform that had just infiltrated and destroyed a heavily guarded dictatorship (his own home, Harmony) needing more confidence. "It'll come to you."

Beast was pleased again, because Nico had faith in him. Nico was reminded of his own dumb faith in himself, based on exactly a big nothing, and did all he could to hide it. He failed, of course. But he didn't want Beast to realize ego was hot air and dreams. Until you made it real. There was danger in that, and Beast was too dangerous to let loose. He was what Nico had always wanted to be, a hammer that could smash the universe, but for real.

Nico was aware of Beast observing him, a quizzical sponge. "Just—you'll think of something," he said, pushing himself upright from his impression of a bearskin rug.

Beast, wise to the moments that Nico was trying to hide, said, "We're only a few minutes short of the transition into shadow running. Tashlynnai wants to see you."

Tashlynnai and her new mission. Nico flopped face down again and groaned. Tash was the person he hated most in the world, but who was now part of this awkward band of bounty-hunting trash he was notionally in charge of. And always the one with the ideas.

"In a minute," he said, because putting things off was the sad, pathetic truth of his resistance now.

"Shall I call Isy?"

Isy was Nico's lover. The relationship was still fresh out of the packet marked "Emergency Rations" and Nico wanted it to last and for there never to be a need to move on to any other kind of rations, but didn't want Isy to know that, in case it gave him some kind of power. Which he already had, but didn't know about. Knowing about it would change things, and Nico was fine as they were. Don't fix it if it ain't broke yet, right?

Sure. Call him, so he can see Nico lying there like a giant baby, whining. "No."

"Coffee?" Beast offered it along with a huge range of other pharma and neuralware that might have been helpful to a human, or fatal, depending. Beast was perplexed by a lot of human behavior. He considered all confusions a terrible thing that must be solved with chemistry, and was proud of his range of possibilities. He meant well.

"No." Seeing as he couldn't even sulk successfully, Nico got up.

The lounge they'd chosen as a space anyone could hang out in was a short walk away. He was glad that Two was the only one in residence when he arrived.

She was eating something that smelled delicious from a bowl on her lap, while watching a drama called "Flashpoint" about people and their lives in Flashpoint Station, where Forged and Orthodox humans mingled. It was lighthearted, hopeful stuff full of unexpected moments of warmth and mutual understanding.

Nico hated it with every fiber of his being.

He thumped down beside her, shoulder to shoulder, and watched for a minute or two of loathsome charm. They were both unified by an uncomfortable sense that in watching it they were looking through a window into a world that was alien to them, and they couldn't tell how much of it was serious, real, and how much of it was made up for the point of the show. Was this how people actually behaved out here, or was it only a dream?

"Where's the crime?" Nico asked, not for the first time, as this puzzled him most of all.

"It's not about that," Two said, slurping noodles that whipped around like party streamers and scattered sauce onto him as she sucked them in. She mumbled through the mouthful. "S'about families and neighb's."

To Nico, and to Two, family had always meant only each other, and neighbors meant danger of death. He knew that family could mean blood relations, and neighbors could be honest brokers, in theory. But everything he'd ever been used to was about who had leverage, and guns, and money. Nothing that Beast had connected him with suggested that the larger solar system was any different to the bubble he'd started off in.

In "Flashpoint," nobody ever put serious heat on those twits; they tied themselves in knots over stupid shit like clothes and who said what. Perhaps it was as easy as that? Without a predator, people were nice?

He didn't buy it.

He wiped sauce into the cloth of his sleeve and watched two Orthodox sweethearts go on a date without a care in the world. He didn't see himself in any of it. He wasn't Orthodox—your "pure" old-style human born of a woman type thing, for sure. He'd been born of a precision engineering product. But he wasn't Forged either. Harmony had produced living human avatars for existing beings. He and Two were shop models, dolls with personalities put in them to show what capacity they had, not because they were the results of the process of life itself coming to its own terms with consciousness. Made, not born, and whatever was inside them had been put there with a purpose, as surely as their genes had been engineered to produce their physical forms.

According to the Orthodoxy, Harmony models were anathema. According to the Forged, they were no more than meat, and therefore not part of the great Synthesis of machine and biology, but they came under the aegis of engineering so they were grudgingly viewed as special kinds of augment for the client who would come to either command them or inhabit them.

Nico might have made it over the bar into Forged now, thanks to the Switch interface with Beast. But he would probably be seen as just an avatar and not a person in his own right. Two, well, she was clearly her own thing, having no other being invested as far as they could tell, but no Orthodox human would consider her authentic in the way they would consider themselves authentic. Whatever that meant.

Authentic meant nothing; it was a load of posturing crap, pointless bickering over My Engineering Is More Better Than Yours. The Forged were outperforming the Orthodox at every level if you looked at it in terms of exploitation, gain and finance, and the Orthodox were dumb as shit because they did look at it that way when they had an entire planet to themselves and could have chilled the fuck out without pissing anyone off. But no could do. Had to keep on being special.

All of that sat with him as he watched and felt the growth of a familiar sullen resentment, which did make the place feel exactly like home. Sullen resentment was his go-to feeling for normal. It bonded nicely with the restless need to do something about what bothered him, and the absence of the power to make a difference to any of it. It primed him for the moment Tashlynnai arrived, so he already knew he'd agree to anything she said just to get the hell out of this shitty moment.

He scowled at her by way of greeting as Two waved down the sound on the drama.

"Nico, always a pleasure," Tash said, taking a seat on Two's other side.

They kissed and Nico felt a burst of resentment. He knew Two hadn't fallen in love with her to betray him; felt like it though, because

Tash had been heavily involved in both their origins and he didn't trust that. Maybe Tash had made Two to fall in love with her and stolen her from him, for example. Or maybe she'd deliberately made him to be the kind of dolt who made friends forever and was loyal and couldn't let it go lightly, so she could keep her hand in his business using Two. Those were just some possibilities.

You couldn't know for sure what was the truth, when you knew someone had made you some way, but not why, or what their game was. But then, you could drive yourself crazy with paranoia because of the holes in your knowledge. He trusted Two. That was as far as he could go.

He managed not to say or do anything stupid. He may have sighed through his nose impatiently.

Two went back to the noodles. Tash dabbed her lips with a handkerchief. She was the kind of person who was prepared with things like that laid nicely out in the pockets of her beautiful blue suit, her hair up neatly, a modest decoration on the hair sticks, immaculate plain shoes. It spoke directly to Nico's saggy sweats and bare feet. He hoped that his attire spoke directly to Tash and that it said "fuck off, no, fuck even further off than that, right over there, g'bye."

Whatever it was saying, Tash ignored it. "I have something to share." She paused and dismissed Two's drama. The inner wall before them changed to show a map of the solar system, their position marked by a red wolf's head. Larger, of course, than reality's infinitesimal dot.

Bright marks appeared, thirty or more, scattered between the orbit of Venus and that of Neptune, broadly within the orbital plane. "These are the Forged Stations. The blue ones are policed and peaceful, shared with the Orthodox. The yellow ones are moderately risky, relying on the Treaty Commons to keep order; co-op policing, shared risk. The red ones are commercial outposts without any kind of regulation; each one is either a freeport or under the control of one of the pirate groups currently big enough to command an entire outpost."

"Or under dispute," Two said, putting her bowl down. "Latest decrypted comms traffic suggests that a lot of money has started running through a couple of the lesser pirate networks. We've been following it."

"And we've been following something else," Tash said, flicking her hand so that the wall displayed what even Nico recognized as a biological genome sequence. It was a strange one. There were huge "dropouts" full of machine code notifications, which indicated patches where nanoware connections for mechanoid and cybernetic adaptations were placed. Programmable life systems. He knew those for sure.

She zoomed out. The thing went on and on and on ...

"So?" Nico folded his arms. He didn't like lengthy approaches. It was like being stalked. Sooner or later they'd get to the real agenda—and he liked sooner. Details were important only if the job was accepted.

"This sequence is one of two that keeps appearing in people who have acquired Forged adaptations within the last six months. They're in the Orthodox Secret Service tracing system because all of them have reported into psych and surgical bays for refits and repairs, many of which are caused by the actions of these strings."

Nico waited. Patience. He looked at Two for reassurance and she smiled her smile that said this information was good.

"Contaminated with unauthorized DNA and Expert Systems," Two said to him kindly, patting his knee. "Bad medicine. We traced it to one place and possibly one operator. But the two things are not related, not very. Distinctly different. The longer one is part of—it's like Beast, but it's not Beast."

Ah right. Beast was an escaped power. This would be the hint that someone might be seeding an army, organized or not, and the Orthodoxy would be killing itself to get it all under control again. But Beast had perked up with a mention of his name. He regarded Nico with eager, desperate anxiety, the longing to know, the hint, always in him, that this might be a clue that led them to some living remnant or relative of his, who had known his origins and might help him find the meaning of his existence.

Nico wanted to protect him from the kind of disappointment he'd had himself, but there was no way he could say no to him with this much buildup.

"Tell me where they are," Nico said with the long-suffering sing-song of one who already knows he's lost. "Kill, Extract Value, or Co-opt?" The three holy stations of power.

Tash blinked. "I want you to find who it is, verify that they are alone in doing this, discover their contacts, and locate the source of the contamination."

Nico pulled a face. "I don't do espionage. I'm more of a 'hit it and quit it' kind of guy."

"He's not subtle," Two added, as if that needed adding.

"I'm well aware of Nico's failings," Tash said, looking coolly at him.

Tash had spent months in Nico's head during the escape from Harmony and she'd done all the intelligence work. Nico rolled his eyes at her.

"We've been working with Isy and Beast," Tash said, and that made him blink this time.

"What?"

"We knew you'd say you didn't do spying, so we made you a new skin," Tash said. "As none of us can connect with you any longer through the Switch, because Beast fully occupies it, we've made you a skin which is capable of …"

Two, bouncing up and down on the spot with excitement because technology was involved, cut off her about-to-be-very-long explanation of the science with, "It'll be like you're wearing us! So we'll all be going with you! It's genius as fashion, Nic!"

Nico tore his annoyance off Tash and looked at Two. Her brown eyes were aglow with enthusiasm and happiness, delight in achievement—the big score. "I'm sorry, what?"

"You'll have some of our ability and insight in addition to your own," Tash said, falling in with the routine, minus the happiness. "So you won't be entirely in the dark should certain situations arise."

"You could just come with me," he said, feeling this was already an idea he didn't like.

"I'll be instantly recognized where you're going." Tash shook her head. "After Harmony, we erased the trail for Isy and Two. The Orthodoxy think they died during the escape attempt. It will probably still trip all the alarms if they detect the suit …"

"It's Strange tech," Two butted in quickly, drumming her fingertips on Nico's leg as if programming acceptance into him.

"But that's …" he started.

242

"Like me!" Beast said proudly, broadcasting his voice instead of just going straight into Nico's thoughts. "You and me," he added.

Nico looked at Tash, looked at her face in which he read all kinds of shield walls up against all kinds of secrets. "Strange shadows. Like Beast. So—not at all something that anyone would worry about, seeing as he's marked for destruction on sight by Orthodox Services and wanted everywhere so people could steal him. And fill me in again on why I should give a shit about a trashy chop shop on the edge of livable space dishing out bad hackware to dodgy clients who should know better?"

"You shouldn't," Tash said. "But if you find the answer to this, find who's doing it and what they've got, I promise you I'll never commission you to do a single thing ever again. You'll be free of me. And all the questions that keep rocketing around in that empty head of yours about who and why and what will be answered."

Nico peered closer. She wasn't lying. He knew her, to the bone of her, and she was sly and snakelike and scheming, self-interested and a master of the long plan, but she wasn't shitty, and now she wasn't lying. Instead he felt a tight keenness, like a stiletto blade hidden in a sleeve, poised for the moment when the wielder would choose to cue its arrival. She was tense. Frustrated. Unwilling to let him see that a lot rested on this, personally, for her. He saw her hand reach out and touch Two with a gentle caress to the arm, seeking to reassure itself.

Two smiled.

"Do it," said Beast. "I want to see how it works."

"Well," Nico said. "I guess my diary does have a gap."

They felt the shiver of transition as Beast shifted their primary material state into the Shade. Unhindered by laws restricting baryonic matter, they moved at speed only possible as an insubstantial creature in the dark. For them, relative to one another, nothing had changed. The only way to tell that they were in the shadow and not the light universe was a strange bodily sensation of airiness, as if they were only dreams of themselves.

They were underway to the edge.

It was only later, in his room, as he turned the fine vial of silvery liquid skin over in his hands, that he realized he'd never thought to ask if it was safe or why he'd risk his life for something that didn't seem like it even had pay.

"Want some help with that?" Isy, standing behind him, was holding his hand out.

Isy had come from the very literal other side of the tracks to Nico. He was the elegant, educated priest of a religious state, every refined and polished element of him perfectly balanced on top of his radically engineered being. He had lived in Harmony, the good place. Nico was a thug from Chaontium, where all the violent, degradable, immoral rejects slunk about as Harmony's celestially ordained counterpart—the bad place. Nico was equally as engineered, just for the worse, to make the point that Harmony was capable of producing absolutely anything to order. Or so the catalogue said.

Isy was custom though, ex-catalogue. He was bespoke. He was Strange, like shadow tech. No doubt he and Beast together were the results of some top-secret black projects gone wrong—if the project stealing itself away was wrong. Nico was their common denominator, or, as he preferred to think of it, demon-inantor.

(Beast: "That's not a word, Nico." Nico: "Well, it should be, 'cause that's what I am.")

"Help?" Nico looked at the vial. The gray silver mercury or whatever it was churned, as if it were alive, pawing at the glass. Now that it was something he actually had to do, he wondered what happened to his *Never Volunteer* motto. Probably should change that to *Always The Fall Guy*. "Maybe a brain transplant."

"I thought you were going to drink it." Isy smiled, tentative, all poise and manners to Nico's bluntness. But he rarely tried even a mild roast as a joke, though he had begun to learn that Nico liked it. His pale hazel, Husky-dog eyes with their dark outer rings caught Nico and hypnotized him as usual.

Nico fell down the rabbit hole headfirst. Yeah. You can have all the cheap shots you want. Just don't stop looking at me like that. He grinned, "Down in one?"

"Don't tempt me." Isy plucked the vial out of his grip and undid the complex stopper. He looked at Nico with his doctor's face on, the one that said this would hurt Nic much more than it would hurt him. "You know I wouldn't use it if I didn't think it was safe."

"Why would a radical, newly engineered substance at the cutting edge of research and innovation *not* be safe?" Nico said, pleased with how well he was handling it, fortified by Beast's unconditional approval and confidence.

(Beast: "Now you'll be even more like me, Nic!")

"Quite. Hold out your hand."

A faint tremor went through the hull. They felt it as the deck quivered under their feet. Such things were commonplace in the Shade. Isy took a deep breath and tipped the vial so that the material was directed toward the back of Nico's hand.

A huge shiver ripped through The Beast from nose to stern as every material object rang, rippling like water to the chime of an unseen bell. Nico and Isy with it. And the vial. And the liquid skin. So a moment later the silvery mass had landed on Nico but also splashed onto Isy's fingers where he held Nico's hand palm down. It vanished neatly into both of them; silver ink soaking into golden tan and dark tan paper.

Motionless now in the stilled room they looked up into one another's eyes.

"Oops," Isy said after a moment.

"What was that?" Nico said at the same time.

Nobody moved.

"Don't worry," said Bob the Beast, "was Charon." And then he added. "The moon. Not dead man's boat guy. He is from a story."

"Obviously," Nico said, looking into Isy's golden eyes as he understood, from his skin, that Beast meant they had passed through Charon, as all of the little "bumps" were them passing through solid objects which, in shadow state, were changed into distinctly airy things, bar a few molecules which caused the judder. Because that was now a kind of thing that Nico just knew and a kind of thing that Isy also just knew. They knew what Beast knew.

Charon was a bit of a thudder. They knew it the way that Beast knew it. It was masterclass physics presented by an enthusiastic kid who'd never been to school but who had spent a lot of time at the skate park.

The skin itself had no feeling—not as if wearing clothes or even lotion.

"How do you take this thing off?" Nico asked, plucking at the back of his hand where it had soaked in.

"It'll wear out when its power is gone and then just disintegrate," Isy said. "The more you use it up the faster it will …"

"A day? Two?"

"About six hours. But that's the time Tash thinks you'll have to get in and get out anyway."

"Meaning the place is already full of trouble."

"She wouldn't send you if it weren't."

"Expendable me."

"That's not what I meant."

They shivered again, and weight returned with every sense of physical solidity. They were out of the Shade. It was time to go.

Nico watched the shuttle move with precision to their docking clamp in the bay of Longlost Station. Their position was just sunward of Haumea in the Kuiper Belt, and as far away from Orthodox Earth as it was currently possible to be and still be within a ten-year reach of it by standard ripdrive travel via the portal at Neptune. Shadecraft were only hours out but they were military issue only and hours was hours enough. It was a long way to come for a botch job.

Though it wasn't lost to people with the right codes, the Station was well hidden in the edge of the Belt, indistinguishable from any other collection of idly rotating asteroids, rocks, and dust. Most of the local asteroids were water, fuel, and raw materials left as payments or accruing holding taxes as they awaited pickup. None were permanently inhabited save the largest central object, a nondescript all-rock asteroid of 1 km diameter and 5 km in length.

Longlost Port was accessed through one of this stone's rare flat faces, bored through to admit small passenger ships for visitors. Nothing larger than a Swifty Sloop though. Nico's shuttle was only half that size, a micro-yacht built for speed and stealth and decked out with a mixture of cheap and reclaimed drives to account for Nico's cover story of being a criminal fleeing Orthodox justice—common enough. Who wasn't one of those?

They were still so cramped that only the most careful movements would spare them from becoming wallpaper paste, so Beast piloted himself alone, pretending to be as slow and unresponsive as a real human, though not one as untrained as Nico. None of the zooming in and out and cool moves hijinks that little craft enjoyed inside the mighty bays of the Orbital or the planetary moons. They crept.

The ship boomed as they made contact with the dock. Metal whirred, motors whined, reeling them in tight. Doors exchanged protocols, prepared to open. They were on-station. He was vaguely aware of the riptides of data flowing as procedures and permissions whipped back and forth between them and the station's murky depths where, presumably, some authority lurked. Everything about Longlost was anonymous, hidden in code, superficial. Except the promise of horrible violence. Beast and its accomplice in this particular crime, Tashlynnai, had convinced him of that.

Two and Isy had dressed him in what they said was Forge Tech average gear—a dark blue and gray suit that left his head and hands free. Heavy boots, quipped with machinery for saving him from emergency vacuum situations and sudden changes in gravity, completed the set. He was exactly like one of the many Earth-type spacers looking for a bit of an upgrade. Good gear, but not top range. Anyone who could afford that wouldn't be scrounging for bits here; they'd be up at Wolf Island, getting all-new. They'd be in Harmony, buying a whole new outer.

The trade in dead Forged parts was hot in this stretch and the thing he was to focus on. Law-abiding Forged were being hunted as scrap. Tash had said that was the source of the huge DNA string as well as the bad fittings. She had names he had to check out, things he was to ask for.

Beneath the suit the secondary skin, coating his own like a fine powder, suddenly shifted with annoyance. It was fed up with having to play second fiddle to inferior gear. It amused Nico that it had opinions he could feel as clearly as his own. He was also having to get used to the strange personalities of machines. Everything out here was, in some way, analogous to life.

All the relating was exhausting. He was already nearly asleep, and it was time to go. He looked around, feeling the need to carry something like a weapon because years of bodyguarding warlords was a hard thing to put away, but there was nothing at hand. It would anyway have been vaporized, his boarding card voided. Maybe he'd be voided. He used the skin to summon Two. Wanting to talk to her was enough to connect them. Her presence appeared in his mind, as if she inhabited the space between his ears, not that there was much room.

"Can't I have a gun?" he asked.

"No." She was amused, been wondering how long he'd take to say it.

"What about a knife?"

"I thought 'you were the weapon'." She mimicked his own dramatic statement.

"Yeah, it's more of a show thing," he said, speaking aloud as he got out of his flight harness and eased his limbs from the tension of their arrival.

"Sure it is, and no."

He was already happier though, hearing her voice. He could feel Tash in the background, trying to get in on the conversation, insisting she had to talk but both he and Two resisted her. It was the funniest thing, even Tash's cross response, as if they were naughty kids together.

"Call off your girlfriend," he said. "Bad girlfriend."

"Nico," Two said. "She's not my girlfriend." Two liked to keep everything neat. Girlfriend would have been much too close. Whatever Tash was it was further off than that. It was sweethearts, it was nice times, it was kindness and talking but it wasn't really girlfriends. It surprised him. He was about to remark on it but hesitated, wondering if the suit was overinforming him; was he overhearing that?

"Well, whatever it's called." He was chippy, jealous of Tash. Two was soothing, patting him on the head, thinking he was an idiot. He felt smugly happy. Not a girlfriend. Haha. Not that close. Hoho.

"Family," The Beast said with a rush of enthusiasm. "This is what a family is like. This jealousy and great drama. I have heard about it in many great stories! Like 'Flashpoint'! Yes!"

"Shh, Bob," Nico said. "Don't go getting ideas." But it was too late, the vision of himself marrying Isylon, Tash and Two at the same

248

wedding, both smiling with vows and flowers and shit, and them all sailing away in the big, smiling idiot dog-of-the-stars that was The Beast had already gone lolloping through the shadow skin, leaving its muddy pawprints over everything or anything they had been about to say.

He felt Two pause. He paused.

A couple of other people distinctly paused.

The Beast lolloped off blithely into the silence.

Isylon cleared his throat, so to speak.

"Didn't realize you were here," Two said awkwardly.

"I wasn't, until just now," he said in his soft, unassuming voice. Was that a tinge of laughter in it? Nico thought so. "I just wanted to say good luck."

"Break every bone in yer body," Two added cheerfully, signing out fast.

"It's just a walk and a talk," Nico said irritably, not sure why he was annoyed. "I'll be online." They had a protocol of no contact in the Station proper, but they were allowed to eavesdrop and to flash a warning if trouble came. He felt supervised, and bristled.

"You're very good at walking and talking," Isy purred, and every fiber of Nico's being lit up with a golden glow at the backhander.

"You're lucky you're so far away."

"Or not so lucky," Isylon said with a smile that Nico felt stir his own face. Then he too faded away into the distant-observer setting. Leaving Nico alone, all fired up and nowhere to go. Except through the airlocks.

Longlost was the first renegade port that Nico had been to. From the outside the asteroid itself was a lump of rock. From the inside, it was a lacework of incredible delicacy.

He tried not to stare at the bubbled vaults like a complete idiot, but it was difficult. The inside of the station looked like a giant bone that had been hollowed out into tunnels that foamed with openings. Insect-like drones buzzed about him regularly, some big and winged, others tiny and spinning in fields of their own making. He felt the tickle and putter of scans, the wash of frequencies, the inspection of busy little machine minds ticktocking over their checklists. The paperwork took a few seconds and then he was free to go.

As soon as he moved off the dock gangway and into the station proper he was faced with a speedway. A large, spherical passenger car was set on one of many possible tracks, aligned to the mild gravity that had been put there solely for inept bipedal things like him. A glance up revealed hundreds of things not so encumbered with directional biologies—machines, creatures were crawling across all surfaces, with and against the asteroid's own rotational G forces. The sight was so disorienting he was nearly sick on the spot.

"Get in," the car said, neutral but not deferential. It was patientish. "I know where you're going. Your ship has informed me. Just put on the belts."

"Can I get the scenic route?"

"If you pay."

"Just go direct."

He felt the shiver of machines chattering payments; a sense of silvery chill running down his arm and out his fingers in some amusing sensory notification that Beast thought he'd like, so he knew how much money was relatively passing from account to account. The car was high-priced, but then, it was one of few passenger vehicles and it could afford to be picky. What the currency was, he neither knew nor cared.

Amazing as it was to his ignorant eyes he spent little time admiring Longlost and a lot noting its entrances and exits, ways and habits. He was immediately unsettled. The place was a warren, navigable only by machine, on purpose, and he had to trust his skin to track his position and remember his routes, absorb what he saw and make sense of it. He pretended to admire things in a casual way, and fought nausea as they reached his destination at last—a near-Earth-gravity plaza, unusually wide and high in the roof, well-lit at the center like an arena, murky at the edges where shop doors opened. Their neon blasted promises of resurrection, transformation, dwarfing the shy efforts at landscaping with biomass in green and brown. Flowers, or something like them, glowed and fluttered in the ventilation.

It smelled old, like it was grimed deep, and no amount of spray and sweep could get it sorted. His skin grumbled at the number of new gene forms it was finding objectionable on his behalf and he rubbed the prickle off his arms. The car suggested it could stay around, should sir require a swift exit, and he agreed without thinking twice. He wanted to be in this place for not a moment longer than he had to be. The transport was satisfied, well-used to customers with the urge to be elsewhere.

Walking hastily, long strides, he got out of the light.

Almost immediately a voice accosted him, "You got offworld news, mate? Any trades?" It was rough and disjointed, as though whoever was talking was near their last day.

He looked around and saw only a heap of muck between two shops. There was no rubbish here, nothing larger than air as everything else was constantly swept away by the worn cleaning bots, so the heap must be the speaker. He didn't go nearer. The voice was relayed to him, on the commons in-station frequency; he didn't have to be close to hear.

"Harmony's under new management," he said, because that was new, and possibly news in a place like this, but probably old too because light traveled fast and they were two months offworld.

"Tecmaten's gone, is he? For real?" The question said it was old news but there was more worth mining out of it. A confirmation, whether first- or secondhand, was required. Nico's exchanges with the shops rang back one after the other, filling up with quotes, special offers, you deserve only the finests, prices and counter prices. He sifted, searching the specials, or rather letting his skin do it while he talked.

"Dead," Nico said. "But, you know, ten more to take his place, I guess. Bastard probably cloned himself."

"He thought he was a genius," the voice said. The heap stirred at the same time and began to change its shape. Something like a head appeared. A long, crocodilian snout poked from under heavy matting or fur. "But he was nothing compared to the likes of us. What're you up for?"

"Upgrades," Nico said. "Same as everyone else." The bidding war flurried, surged, began to close as lesser offers dropped away. A large beetle droned past Nico's shoulder and came to rest on the crocodile's shoulder mat, going inert as it delivered its messages.

"You're already wearing half the arsenal of the new world, kid. I don't think we can do much for you short of killing you for obvious lying."

Nico barely raised an eyebrow at his disguise not holding out. He hadn't expected it to, though the speed was disarming—but the faster this went down the better, so—"And you are?"

The prices rattled to a halt. That test, whatever it was for, was over. Distraction while he was scanned most likely. Well. Anyway.

"Vinsalvarez, but you can call me Lord Vin. This is my shop. They're all my shops on this side of the plaza."

"Why do you look like a pile of shit, then?"

There was a pause.

"I …" said the heap, "may have let things get a little out of hand."

The second part of this speech was echoed by a gentle female voice and a figure appeared from the nearest shady doorway—a person Nico immediately identified with a sense of crawling inner alarm as Harmony #2566BetaModel Yon5, Deluxe.

She was short, neat, and of pleasant appearance with the demure behaviors and grace of an ancient dynastic heir cum samurai goddess—as much cliché and stereotype as you could cram into a genome and a set of responses and still call yourself an artist. Yon5 was popular. One of the most-sold. This one was the standard, not even a facial adjustment or a hairdo, just as she came from the catalogue. The Deluxe part—that referred to her ability to host large, complex personas and tolerate high dissonance. She's what you'd buy if you were loaded and wanted an avatar that would feel like your own body and not give you any trouble no matter what creepy shit you were up to with it.

The shock was visceral, nasty, and shattering. He'd never faced a Harmony model that was in use before. The only ones he'd ever known had been themselves, no passengers. Now he faced the fact that every fiber of his being wanted to relate to her as a genuine person, and he wanted to kill whoever was in her at the same time. If there was a *her* without them. So many questions.

She gave Nico a wry smile and a little bow, slightly mocking, completely acknowledging all his discomforts and finding a pleasure in it. Her clothing was immaculate—it was a skin, like his, and also high grade, much higher than she was worth if you looked at it in purely financial terms, and he didn't want to, but that's what he did, with everything. People lied, but money never did. Assets had a specific value to someone, and the extent of that value represented their stake in the game.

"I am the human face of Vin at this time."

"I'm Nico all the time." But as he said it, he thought maybe he was somebody's something, because that was true enough, wasn't it?

"It takes a little getting your head around, doesn't it?" she said, and her eyes, dark and soft, were full of a knowingness that he felt could only come from genuine, alert, unimpeded consciousness.

Some models were completely convincing. *Deluxe.*

"I've never really gotten around it," he said, feeling such kinship, such a heart-wrench he hadn't expected—hadn't expected to feel much beyond his usual contempt and impatience really, and now it was just feelings all over the damn place like escaped puppies. He scowled at her.

The heap of reptile was heaving. Laughing, he thought.

"You're here with Tash, aren't you?" she asked.

"You aren't supposed to know that," he said. Why lie? She already knew. And if she didn't, then this would only make the race to the end that much shorter.

"But you're not hers," she added thoughtfully. "I see that."

He was relieved. "No. Don't think so."

They shared a smile that only the manufactured could share before he remembered that she—wasn't what she looked like. "If you're here with her, then Longlost is really in trouble," she said with a sigh.

"I'm looking for contraband tech," he said.

"Yes, of course," she nodded. "Why else would you come? Let me guess. Tashlynnai has succeeded and found a pacifier for the Fury. She had you made for a purpose, as a face she can use, someone to fence for her, but not a true avatar, that's too dangerous for her. Something more distant. Something that can be thrown away, should the need arise, without providing any direct link. She worked hard, to ensure that your fight for freedom felt so real. Then you agreed, but you had to, of course, you were made for that. Now she comes here. She told you someone is in trouble. Because you are #501998Custom Omega8,

Crusader. A purpose, not a name. A purpose and a weakness all in one. Do you know who is really pulling your strings?"

It was quite the speech. He had to hand it to her. She did not fuck about. But he'd been through this before, a million times, and there was no way out of it and no point in bothering with it.

"I'm Nico," he said and held out his hand to her.

She looked at it.

He knew he was meant to take the bait, react, all that shit. He just—couldn't be arsed. "You forgot to add the Asshole Variant," he added. "Pretty sure that's hardcoded in."

"I am Vin." She looked at his hand and awkwardly reached out, meant to take it as something other, couldn't because she was in her role. The allegiance she had tried for wasn't working.

"Yeah, sure, Vin. Nice to meet you."

They shook. Her little hand in his big hand, not so pathetic it meant nothing, not hard enough to commit. It was weird. He felt their master skins exchange protocols, a little ripple of assents, and something more, a shadow gone before he could get a grip on it. His sense of being in the presence of something uncanny deepened.

"Tash is shit. I know it, you won't surprise me," he said. "But she's kind of righteous shit. I can't stand her. Her methods are evil. But I admire her. She's not wrong about things."

"Well," Vin said. "A lot happened before you came on the scene. And a lot of it was evil on every side. Look up the 'Forged War of Ascension' when you have a moment."

Nico felt a sense of time rushing, felt its wave looming in Vin's awareness though he didn't understand it. He realized that his skin had infected hers and now he was feeling something of what she was experiencing and doing in the background as distant echoes in his own self. She was a faint ghost at the edge of him.

"War of Ascension? What'd you ascend to? This?" He looked pointedly around. "You ascended to a garbage bin?"

"Tash is a wanted criminal," Vin said. "She's at the top of the list. Where she goes, the Orthodox forces follow. They want me nearly as much as they want her. So I'm going to give you what she's come for. Then we can be on our way. Do you have eyes beyond the Belt?"

"Sure," he said.

"They prefer oblique vectors but they're coming from Neptune Portal without a disorientation pattern of approach, because that is where their closest accelerator is," Vin said. "So watch that way. Tell me if you see something."

He looked, far, far away, with The Beast's skin, that spoke to his. "Nothing. Wait."

There was a beacon they had left behind them, a piece of dust floating steadily toward the sun, one of millions coasting around in idle search. A few minutes ago, it had seen lights, the blare and flash of Saturn's Eighth Port Accelerator, enough for five rapid assault units to flip to Neptune and then burn in. "They're setting off. Five. Light armor. Annihilation Class. They'll be here in a couple of hours."

"Yes, they don't like you." Vin smiled. "Quickly then. I have a price you must agree to, in order to get your booty."

"Wait," Nico said. "How do they know we're here?"

There was a pause. A long, long pause. So long that Nico felt aeons pass in silence, all while Vin's dark gaze looked right through him into the heart of a different mystery. He felt the certainty that she had placed that call, as soon as he had entered the car, and the beetle, whatever it was, had taken the measure of him and smelled the shadow skin. Vin had been waiting. Maybe had drawn them here. This he felt. And a flutter of something unhappy. In the background. A moth's wing of disturbance on the sweet composure as though something was searching for light, trying to get out.

But he couldn't trust that now, could he? Crusaders are always looking for the maiden. Figuratively. So you want to pull a Crusader in, you give them one.

"You see," she said. Slowly, as though his pressure on her to tell the truth was wringing a genuine confession. "I had to have insurance."

"I see." He was used to it. Cartels were plenty in Chaontium, and they played each other off all the time. "Let's do a side deal quick before my date arrives and does your head in with a hammer, all that kind of good stuff. Who doesn't go to a shoot-out without insurance?"

She smiled at him, inclined her head. "You're good."

He shook his head. "You know what it is? I just never believe anything." Because in spite of this shitshow, he felt, knew, in his skin and bones, that he and this person, this Vin, wearing its human body, were allies. Or they should be. You could die on the sharp end of that distinction.

He really had preferred it when he was alone and people were things he mostly hit or ignored. Whoever had been called, on whatever terms, didn't matter. He was at the bottom of the ladder and he just did as he was told.

But he kept feeling something off about her and it was hard to place. So hard that he decided that being the fall guy wasn't going to happen today. Today he was in charge. Stuff whatever Tash had said. Let's see what was going on for real.

That felt much worse. If his skin could have shouted it would have, but he was good at ignoring things.

"Come this way," Vin said and beckoned gently. "I must show you something important."

The heap got to four or six feet and padded off slowly, with difficulty, toward the far side of the plaza, on its way to another incoming car.

As it left, Nico turned to Yon5, "Is *that* your actual body?"

"Of course not. Nor is this one," Vin said. "This way."

As he neared the door, Nico felt the dragging sensation of data shutdown and realized that he was walking into a dead zone. Before they could be cut off completely, or compromised through his connection, he severed the links to The Beast and the others himself. By the time he got through to the other side he was alone and watching Vin's Harmony avatar, Lady Vin, put off by her perfectly graceful manners. She was reaching for something, and as he came through the door, he heard and felt a widespread rustle and swirl of keen attention, focused on her, as if she had walked into a pack of perfectly trained dogs.

Of course he was behind her, like a dumb idiot to the slaughter, or whatever was going to happen next, cramped off from assistance, hostage to curiosity and his own impatience. Never send a hammer to do a scalpel's job but if all you have is a hammer, this is what you get.

But he was good enough for dishonest work and this was as dishonest as it came. The change in Vin's stride as she cleared the long meter of the doorway warned him and he was moving aside as she spun around, something in her hand that would have hit him full in the face if he hadn't been already half a step to her left.

Without the skin he became just Nico, the kid who used to kill bots for cash. Stalking, fleeing, it was second nature. No happy fun model was ever going to top that, no matter how hard her skin suit tried to soup her up.

"Ugh!" she said, disgusted even as she was finishing her spin, seeing her dart go skidding away, out the door, along the hall, and across the plaza. Her shoulders sagged. Seemed she'd come to the same conclusion.

A few meters back the crocodile in rags had found its legs, feet, and hands and came around the corner, blocking the way out.

Nico ignored it, pushed past Vin the Asian babe, and went into the back room thinking about other exits, weapons, and contraband. The room contained the rigged-up medical bay he'd been expecting. But he hadn't expected the incubation tanks. So many of them, lined up in ranks, filled with different bodies floating in their misty depths, each fed with tight bunches of tentacles that reached down from the ceiling's vast machineries.

Lights and liquids pulsed. The temperature had gone up a good ten degrees. Bubbles and hydromatics flushed and sluiced in a constant trickle and rush, creating a wall of noise. Valves burred. The metal floor clanked under his boots. He was presented, center and proud of it, with the unmistakable large glass flask of an Alembic, the kind they had used on Harmony to gestate human bases. It was empty and to one side, part of its operating tech was strewn about in a state of half-finished mess, moving sluggishly as it attempted self-assembly with insufficient energy.

He strode forward, knowing he was supposed to stop, look, pause in horror or awe at one more demonstration that he was all very much yesterday's news. Behind him he heard Vin scramble on her light feet, and the heavier scrape of the crocodilian, the *slursh* of its tail on the metal grating. Nico moved fast along the aisle, checking readings he didn't understand, hoping the skin could work well enough to figure it out for him, seeing the shudder of fleshy things inside the tanks, vague and out of reach. Some tanks were lidded tight. Some not. There was no obvious exit door and no time to ask questions. They were beyond that stage.

He put his hand straight down into the nearest open tank. "Don't touch … !"

But this kind of world is now a world where someone like him has to touch everything. That's how you know it. And instantly know it.

The draft is like fresh air to the face as the skin takes a long lick of fluids and reads the history of this place in full technicolor from spit and piss and floating nanoparticles. It gives its own history back; fair's fair. Seeing it's all too late, the two Vins on his backside stop their rushing anxiety and just stand in the middle of the chamber. They're in one of hundreds of spherical pods that back the shops on this level, where Vin, the master craftsman, has been helping humans become more than human for decades but has always kept a bit in return, unrecorded, unmanaged. You can't splice genes without spares. You can't Forge new systems without flesh.

But also, you can't let people go out into the world and not let them take a bit of you with them. Because you're generous and you like to get around. There's nobody you can trust like yourself.

Nico comes to the realization that everything on this station, even the material that coats the inside of the rock and strengthens it against the torment of centrifugal force, is Vin. The people who left here are a bit Vinny. The creatures on the plaza, the few people working other parts of the asteroid, the scientists and the machines are all a little bit Vin—he's really spread out here, made himself at home. And he's scattered himself to the winds. Out of hand. That was another way of putting it.

But Vin had something, and traded in something, that wasn't him. And wasn't *in* him. Something special. Something—sad.

Nico could feel it now, with conviction, like a confirmed case, a sense of purpose and destiny sinking into him from the place where Tash and Two, Isy and Beast all met and agreed inside his skin. It's the sadness which Vin's old customers returned to have taken away. The sadness that they couldn't shake off, that sunk into them like a stain. The sadness that had tripped Tash's radar, been the trail she followed. With meat comes memory and where that has been erased the space it leaves is an emotion.

Vin had infected them all with an unremitting grief so bad that they would rather let go their power than live with it. The well was tainted.

Nico shook off his own hand, let his fingers drip as he turned to look at the demurely distressed Vin and her delicate lipstick, the grumpy and toothy Vin, sour with disappointment that he won't be having a stick of Nico to shove into his Alembic, if he ever figures out how to get it going.

Nico walked back to look at it. He remembered faking being a research priest, someone who could operate it. But he'd never figured it out for real. Only Isylon had been able to use it. "Is this it? You want us to fix this in return for something? Or was I supposed to go in the soup for later?"

"I just wanted to see if you were all she said you could be. If she was right about the weapon system not being beyond redemption. For interest, you understand. I wouldn't have taken anything. Just a taste, a bit of flavor. Not like there's time. Old habits, I suppose."

Her fingers twitched, greedy, giving the lie.

Nico ignored it. "Tash doesn't know you have one of these, then?"

"Of course not, or she would have never sent you. But I suppose she's heard about the Sorrow. I confess I never thought it would transfer across. When all the trouble started coming back my way, I started to watch for Tash appearing. When your shuttle showed signs of tachyon particles in the scan I thought I'd spare you the bother of hunting me down. Please ..."

Vin the girl stepped away from him and led the way through to another room filled with tanks, most of them emptied, some in stages of cleaning, through a corridor walled with doors to hibernation capsules and recovery rooms, and into a storage facility—a vast space like a library, walled to every centimeter with a storehouse of specimens, its floor made up of the bulk of the cloud servers which acted as heaters for the station.

In spite of the unsuitable warmth, a hastily rigged cryo-container was dumped in the heart of the place. Within its transparent box, beneath display readouts of unreadable gibberish, lay something that resembled a desk-sized chunk of meat, frosted with crystals in many colors, marbled with silver and synthetic sheets.

"That's it," Vin said, rubbing her hands together as if she was freezing. "That's what's the trouble right there. What I want is for you to take it away from here and never come back." Their crocodile body shuffled around, checking displays anxiously. It keyed something, extracted a hand-sized tray, and brought it over to Nico, heavy clouds of vapor boiling off it as it rapidly defrosted—a sample.

"What's 'the trouble'?" Nico kept his hands down and looked, feeling he was close enough as the crocodilian extended the tray for him.

"All you need to do is touch it and you'll know. Forged communication and synthesis, so advanced."

Nico looked at the tray and then at the cryo-rig. He ignored the tray and walked over to the rig. It was, because of the haste it had been set up, running off a very basic controller. He hit the unlock key and the lid popped with a hiss and a billowing of nitrogen—a cloud so swift and intense that it shrouded him in bitterly icy fog as he thrust his hand down through the fluid to make contact with the object inside. I mean, sure, baited to do it, really set up for it, but again, in the circumstances no way out and no way to trust Vin.

It hurt like a bitch even with the suit on his arm to the wrist and the nanoskin belting for all it was worth.

Nico was unholy fast though. His hand was already back. He keyed the lock. The pain was so bad it was good. He felt his grin come on him.

"You ..." said Vin, once from the girl mouth and once from the crocodile's huff. The meaning was clear without the second word—*idiot*.

Nico felt pleased he'd done something unpredictable. His hand hurt much worse than before as it thawed, the skin working hard, so hard, denying the burn its chance to destroy his flesh by the narrowest of margins. Then the skin started working on the traces it had picked up off the massive *chonk*—too big and solid to be a mere chunk—of frozen carcass.

Chonk wasn't exactly dead. Nothing that was meant to exist in space's near zero was all that discomfited by being shoved into a freezer. It needed cold. It also needed room. Any sense of Vin, of Beast or anyone else got wiped on the instant.

His mind exploded, trying to house a ghost body the size of a small moon, of a complexity and construction … and there was a memory. He felt struck by darts, then compromised, then he knew—

This was a fragment left over from a massive explosion that had silently ripped apart this person and left only tiny pieces, each of them vaporized relentlessly, hunted down, except this bit right here. This one sad bit of flesh, which had been gulped by a passing smuggler, vomited out into a trading bay, haggled over, fought over, and ended up by a long road out on the edge of the system in Vin's capable, busy hands.

Where he had used it to craft Forged with new and interesting qualities—like regeneration, and replication. Nico felt this ghost body capable of all that and so much more. Of taking an idea from nothing and crafting a living person into it, without recourse to any assistance. A body that had parts scattered throughout the system, pieces whirling away into deep space beyond it—which had gestated its own defense and been slaughtered in the birthing of it. Executed, for having the audacity to dare to declare independence.

A devastating, unbearable misery radiated from it so powerfully that he felt his awareness of reality slide, slip, waver. He was protected from more by the failure of his skin, which chose that moment to die on him, all power spent. It left only knowledge and a weaker, angrier Nico behind it.

The Beast's MotherFather, the Forged Gaia Genesis. That's what this Chonk was. The greatest Forged ever created. And, in the nature of fractal portions, it contained the information of the whole, if you were able to read it, if it allowed you to see.

Nico looked at Vin in its blank and pretty Asian-babe housing. "How many people have you given this to?"

Because there's the problem. The Sorrow is here, but also the life is here. A life that isn't over because a piece of it remains, and potentially now lots of pieces. If this scattering of seeds to the wind isn't the greatest act of wild rebellion and potential madness most likely to draw the grimly reaping wrath of Earth, then nothing is.

Vin the girl was looking at the cryo-tank in a strange, whimsical way. Behind her Vin-the-croc was taking nervous readings of the workings of other tanks and containers. It didn't answer. Well, why

261

would it? What was the point? Destination fucked, that's where all this was headed, no matter if Tash or Nico or anyone did anything. Calling the Orthodox was the move of despair. What was he going to tell them? That Tash was behind it? Was he hoping to run out and get the evidence all blown up out of the way for him?

"Does this thing move?" Nico gestured at the tank and started to circle it looking at its housing.

"It's on a sled," Vin said with a faint smile. "Had to be, you know, to get it in here in the first place. I think they got it secondhand. It's been temperamental. Nearly thawed at one point."

The disassociating git, Nico thought, finding the sled control dangling from a wire line on the far side and activating it. "Here. I'm taking it now."

Vin's dreamy smile said to him—of course you are, Nico. Because that's what I wanted you to do. I've done my bit, smeared my greasy rat-arsed DNA and this chunk's megahuman life-generating systems into every custom refit like a god repopulating Eden, and now you're here, you idiot, you package deal of easy meat and old enemies, to take it off my hands and run away with it into the dark, towing the hellhounds of old men's vengeance after your trailing skirts.

Well, that's what Nico read into the expression. He reckoned a bit of creative license was the only thing keeping him from smashing one Vin into another at this point. But the clock was ticking and his own, old but good skin was prickling with urgency—Bob had noticed something nasty pop out of Neptune's portal before the skin died. Two hours my ass, he thought. He should be away already—if he was meant to make it. Probably he wasn't.

Fine. This was going to be the old way. "Are you the only one left here, then?"

"Yes, only me," Vin said, and god knew if that was true or not. How many bodies could one person infiltrate?

"Take the sled to the car," Nico said. He expected that Vin was already plotting the way he was going to take over Beast, run off with the goods and the guns, just like every cartel scumbag Nico'd ever met. Insurance-minded people were like that. But that was a problem for later.

Right now he gestured at the rest of the tanks, the preceding rooms. "Are these like, are they supplies or are they—people?"

"Bit of both," Vin said with a shrug, her black hair rippling in a silky wave, like it didn't matter at all, the croc hunkering down on all fours to shuffle rapidly ahead of them toward the plaza. Vin was already gone into a future mind; the asteroid and all it contained a piece of a rapidly receding past.

"Okay," Nico said firmly, like he was resolved, like he believed he was in command of this. Crusader boy to the rescue. You play the part, nobody suspects you're only acting.

He followed them out to the plaza and the waiting car, not looking to either side because he didn't want to see any more. If Vin didn't get to run off in Nic's shuttle, he was definitely the sort to plant a beacon on it and keep calling the hounds on. For spite or as insurance. They'd play the cards as it suited. Either way.

He loaded the sled onto the rear bulk transport segment of the railcar. The plaza lights flickered.

The crocodile Vin waited at the track. The car could only hold two passengers. As he jumped down from the sled to get in, Nico wasn't surprised to see human Vin lift a gun out of her coat and point it at him. "Come on."

Really? Nico felt his face say it all as he obeyed. But they couldn't board the ship without Nico. It would only respond if he was present. Probably Vin was trying to figure out if dead counted as present. Given who he was dealing with it probably didn't. That meant damaged Nico might be out too, so he was going to hesitate some more, at least until they reached the shuttle.

But in turn Nico wasn't sure how much of a threat Vin really posed. Guess he was going to find out if it was more than one girl and one gun.

He got in. The seat webbing closed on him. Vin the girl got in and closed the doors. Nico looked out at Croc au Vin, standing there, heavy arms hanging forward in a simian swing as its long back bent and its snout turned to the side so that it could see him out of one green, slitted eye. They sped off the way he had come, lights and empty platforms shooting past in a flickering blur, a slight judder in the car as the cryo-store bumped against the linkage.

It was like George and the dragon, saving the girl, he thought. Only who was the dragon? Right now Nico wasn't enjoying the maiden position. Nico was always the dragon. Always. And the story was garbage because clearly the dragon was the victim in the entire caper, and the dragon was going to win because no human in a tin can was worth shit against a prime elemental like Beast and no story could fix that.

As they neared the docks, Vin's crush grip on his collar grew progressively weaker. Nico looked for other people on station but he didn't have to look far. The dock channels were full of hurrying, desperate clusters of bodies, working frantically to shove goods into containers. Abandoned stacks of junk threatened to block all the gangways. In the huge hangar, bays were popping open to space every other second with bursts of engine glow as they hightailed it out of town. Didn't take much for everyone to figure out the law was coming. He didn't see any kids. Felt glad. Can you imagine kids in a place like this? It was just gangs of men and women and the various metallic and cybernetic forms they'd made themselves into, like a circus in places, and lots he didn't recognize and could have been machines for all he really knew, but all the same, when you boiled it off, it was people, some big and some small and some very strange.

Among them Vin and Nico just looked like any other space rangers rushing toward the exits with their most prized cargo. Nico wasn't sure Vin was taking the gun thing all that seriously, thought he might have to reach out and steady her hand if she didn't stop shaking it like a kid's rattle. It was a PM70; good for killing the flesh part of things and leaving machinery intact. It didn't endanger ships or stations but then again, it wasn't powerful at long range. As it was, Vin was in no danger of being accosted or assisted by anyone as nobody gave a shit. They were alone in their standoff, so Nico "obeyed" and unhitched the sled, dragged it across the plate decking to the airlock of his shuttle.

He was through into the lock section and pushing the sled to the wall to fit it in when he heard Vin's voice struggling to speak behind him. He turned, spun to the side out of the expected position, ready for a shot to the face, or a speech, or a deal, but instead saw Vin's little hand gripped to white-knuckle levels upon the gunstock.

He stared, not sure what he was seeing. Her fingers were fighting for the weapon controls as if in the grip of an invisible octopus. The gun barrel was turning slowly, the wrist stretching at a painful angle as it moved by degrees away from him and around. Her free hand reached toward him—from meters away—with outstretched fingers, as if he was a life buoy she meant to grab onto before something swept her away.

He saw that Vin was trying to shoot/not shoot themselves. A tear was rolling down her cheek, her eyes wide and crazy, every muscle in her body juddering with effort.

Out in space the Orthodox annihilation crew in their illegal Shadecraft would be starting a deceleration arc in preparation for engaging weapons. They'll be ready in about fifteen minutes. It's no place to get stuck in, this stupid whirligig place.

Nico leaped forward and smashed the Yon5's face square and hard, bare knuckles. She had such little dainty cheekbones, he thought, really not built for any kind of combat. He grabbed her as she fell, the gun clattering away, and hauled her over to the sled, dumped her unconscious body on the lid, shut the door, flushed the lock.

It's been about ten seconds all in.

Sometimes you can't dick about even when you're making awful decisions like that one. What was wrong with leaving her on the deck, Nic? Why compromise everything and everyone by bringing her along and her user, or passenger, or whatever the shit Vin was?

He got into the pilot seat, ran the systems up.

The shuttle, part of Beast, pushed off with destructive force, breaking the docking systems, and jetted out at high speed, interior rotating on its gimbals like crazy to keep Nico and the sled on a dogged 2-D plane of steady "just a light swell, Captain" rocking as the exterior pulled screaming Gs and insane directional changes in a race back to the main body of Beast, which itself is gyring its vast bulk up, up, and out of the Belt plane, chaff decoys deployed, fields generating complex anomalies as it prepares to stutter-warp the shit out of Dodge.

Fleeing Forged craft cluttered the way. A couple smeared themselves across twizzling rocks and set off a huge chain of active, bump-and-grind destruction as they darted crazily in an effort not to be within a thousand miles of this spot.

Nico went back to the bay and took the time to dump Vin on the second passenger couchette. He applied the web to hold her in place as the black-and-blue colors started to puff out on the side of her face, and considered what Chonk might have made out of the combo of Vin and Yon5, Deluxe, because it looked a lot like there was a rebellion of some kind underway in there.

Or that could have been some natural phenomenon, Two's voice reminded him, firm on the side of reason as ever. But what were the odds?

The uplift took only a few minutes. They flew directly into The Beast's side and were swept away with it as it took off and prepared to flutter them, skipping alternate squares of space on the strange checkerboard of standard drive calculated warp leaps—two thousand per second, each traverse skipping 1 AU.

They made a little bug-dance and then they went shadow and crossed the dark invisibly, like ghosts.

A few minutes later they felt the hot burst of Longlost vaporizing, though this was only a nicety generated by the skin for their information—they were already lining up to dock at the relative backwater peace of Decadence Station in the shadow of Phoebe by Saturn's flank.

The others come to greet him, not just one but all of them, clad in their best, even Tash, loitering at the back, giving him a difficult nod of approval that must have cost her an entire week's worth of positive emotion to muster. Isylon is let through first, in prime position, a big hugger, a better kisser. Then Two, the tightness of her hands betraying her nerves. Tash just commands the sled in the background, sets it to move. As a last thought she looks up at Nico, glances at Vin draped on the rig's lid.

"I'd better move your trash." Her eyes are full, kind of glowing.

It's odd, Nico thinks, she looks—what's the word—relieved.

They take Vin to the medical bay and give her a sedative while they think what to do and then they install her in a guest suite, which might as well be a prison, though it's nice for that, and leave her to her own devices with The Beast on watch, like everywhere, and Nico gets back at last, at last, to the open viewing deck of the bridge lounge and finds the others there, seated on the sprawl of sofas, with dinner and drinks ready for him and they all eat together and at least he didn't throw her out the airlock though it's probably for the best if he did, all agree, because who knows, who can tell, what exactly Vin is or wants or has planned? Surely doesn't deserve a lift. But they are all, except for Tash, Harmony children and have not expected to ever find another, not one that was actually sold. So they couldn't leave her. Even if she isn't, well, they don't know what.

From his relaxed, whiskey-holding position lying against Isylon's legs on the main captain couch Nico feels a bit kingly, nearly nodding off, when the reactivated skin share tells him that Tashlynnai has given Chonk to The Beast and Beast's silence means he is digesting what that means. They are all warmly connected.

There's a friendly quiet where Beast was, so Nico knows he's good, just quiet, doesn't want company, has to be in his own space to think and look at the stars alone.

"The client is very pleased with your work," Tash says.

"Good," Nico says, not caring who she means, wondering why the talk when he's already witness to the payment. What more could a captain have than the best ship on the seas, a beloved crew, guns, a full tank, food, and his love at his side? Is there possibly more? Can't be. So, because of that, he gives it a second, waits for her to continue.

"Thank you," Tash says, and we're now at more words than they've spoken in months and Nico feels a slight shadow and a shiver as she puts her hand on his for a moment and their skins touch and then he knows, he *sees*, the whole story, just like she promised.

Chonk made Tashlynnai. Not like in Harmony, where they do a more advanced job, but out of machine parts, a bang-up desperation job full of all sorts of hybridized stuff that was cooked at lightning speed into a human with a history, inserted to be the only surviving fragment of her, in the hope that somehow, some way, Tashlynnai would be the mother that Chonk could not be, save her son, see him grow, make sure he's okay. And now Nico has brought Chonk back, and there is just enough Chonk to assure Beast that in the moments mother and son were ripped apart forever, he was loved, more than anything loved.

Beast has always been terrified it was his fault, that he was not good enough to save her. Now he knows there was no saving her, there was only saving him. And this isn't the best thing—but it's a lot.

Like you couldn't just have told him? Nico thinks, a bit drunk, but then he realizes no, you can't tell Beast things, he always suspects a lie. You have to prove yourself with action, and with incontrovertible evidence, and there had to be no trace of the origin on Tashlynnai or she wouldn't have made it this far, secret sleeper that she was, years of work among the enemy as she laid her plans for this day.

Tash says, speaking now as the ghost of her former self, "We have to fix our mistakes. Or try."

Nico wants to say Hey, speak for yourself lady, I don't make mistakes, but Beast erupts from his contemplation and is in the mix with them.

"Zeroth. That's my name. The one my mother gave me."

"Good on you, buddy," Nico returns. "Still think Bob was good."

He can feel that Beast is new, better, with full cognizance of the prime mother memory and some of her living legacy. He can feel B—Zeroth, communicating with Isylon, comparing knowledge, vibrating with the sudden expansion of his world which now includes restoration along with destruction. He is a warship and a healing ship, a creature of means.

"What about Vin?" Nico says suddenly as Tash turns to go.

"A pain in the ass," Tashlynnai says. "Untrustworthy, of low character. You've seen what it does. We're just lucky it didn't infect us with its spaffing. Like an incontinent mongrel."

"Is it—he—are they welded to that avatar?"

"You want to save her," Tash says with a lift of an eyebrow.

Well, yes, dumbass. "Just asking."

Tashlynnai nods. "A word to the wise though. Don't help anyone you can't afford to help forever."

Nico looked around. "This place is very big."

Tash shrugged. Her business was concluded. "If you get Vin out, where will you put it?"

He had no idea. But it went around in his mind, what he could do, and what Vin could do, what he'd seen it do just in a few minutes that he'd known it. Allies, or other parts far away. This wasn't the main mind, of course not. Nor the croc. Maybe not anyone on Longlost at all. Real Vin could be anywhere.

Later that night he went down to the guest suite and took a look around. Yon was still sleeping off the sedatives, would do until they were cued to wake. And then what? He thought of Croc au Vin, watching him with its yellow-green eye as he left it there on the plaza platform.

Is the maiden complicit or is she someone who just didn't get a speaking part?

Fucking insurance. He had to hand it to those Cartel bastards. They knew how to pull the strings.

"Not yours though," Zeroth said quietly. "I will cut them all. With me, you will always be free."

There was a new authority to him. No doubt about it.

"What does Zeroth mean?" Nico asked.

"The one that comes before the first in a series," Zeroth said.

"There's supposed to be a series of you?"

"Of us. You can be number one."

Nico started, "But you're before me then, and I'm the Captain."

"I am the oldest," Zeroth said. "Technically speaking."

"Then that makes Tash number one. She's not being number one. No way."

"You can all be number one."

"Let's just leave it as a loose collective," Nico said. "But I'm the Captain."

"We're both the Captain."

"Except I am a bit more the Captain than you," Nico said.

"All right," said Zeroth, happy because it didn't matter who was the Captain because he was the first in a new kind of series, the five of them, carrying each other close, like a winning hand of cards, like planets orbiting a heart.

Afterword

Jennifer Brozek

When Cat first approached me about *The Reinvented Heart* anthology, she asked me if I wanted to take it over. As I had worked with Cat before—when she was the president of the Science Fiction & Fantasy Writers of America and I was on the Board of Directors—and because I had always wanted to work with her in a creative capacity, I saw the perfect opportunity. I said that I would join the project, but only if it was in a co-editorship position. I wanted us to create the anthology together.

There were several reasons for this. First, *The Reinvented Heart* anthology was Cat's idea—from conception to execution. It would not have been the project she wanted if she were not part of it. Second, the anthology was already in progress. Coming in and taking over would've caused more uproar than necessary. Third, I had not worked with the publisher, Arc Manor, before and felt more comfortable with Cat still part of the project and the main interface to the publisher. Finally, as I said, I wanted to work with Cat creatively. Here was a ready-made project that just needed a bit of my particular brand of help—extreme organization and Olympic-level project management.

Entering into a project already in progress is a delicate dance of bringing my point of view and expertise to bear while keeping the project's original theme and goal in focus. Not to mention melding both our personalities and editing styles together in a way that makes the anthology a cohesive whole rather than disparate parts. The best co-editorships occur when the lines between the editors blur.

While I brought my particular point of view to the table, I had to make sure it didn't overwhelm Cat's. What I did was bring a couple of my favorite authors into the fold who aren't always thought about when it comes to science fiction, Mercedes M. Yardley and Lisa Morton. These Bram Stoker award-winning authors are more known for their horror than their SF, but I knew that they would have something interesting to say about relationships and I was so right. Yardley's story, "Canvas of Sins" has one of my all-time favorite tropes (the sin-eater) in it, while Morton's "Touch Has a Memory" made me think and made me weepy. (Then again, several of the stories in this anthology made me weepy.)

The thing I love most about this anthology is all of the different types of relationships—familial, platonic, erotic, pragmatic, and more—that were explored in enticing and provocative ways. Premee Mohamed's story, "With All Souls Still Aboard," is about, in the end, hope. While Sam Fleming's story, "In Our Masks, the Shadows," is about parasocial digital relationships versus in-the-flesh, face-to-face relationships. Then there is Justina Robson's story, "Our Savage Heart Calls to Itself (Across the Endless Tides)." It was too long by a mile but too good to turn down with its theme of self-actualization balanced against a very special bond between man and AI. Any manuscript that makes an editor forget their job and get lost within the story (multiple times) is a good one indeed.

These stories couldn't be more different from each other, and yet, like all of the stories within this anthology, they are facets of the same gem. I could wax poetic about every story within *The Reinvented Heart*, but as this is the Afterword of the anthology, I suspect I would be preaching to the choir.

A collaboration is a beautiful and delicate thing, two artists (or anthologists) blending their strengths together to make something more than the sum of their parts. I loved working with Cat on this anthology—I don't use that word lightly in this context—and I believe Cat and I have created something amazing here.

I do hope that you enjoyed it, too.

Editors

Jennifer Brozek

Jennifer Brozek is a multitalented, award-winning author, editor, and media tie-in writer. She is the author of the *Never Let Me Sleep*, and *The Last Days of Salton Academy* series, both of which were nominated for the Bram Stoker Award. Her *BattleTech* tie-in novel, *The Nellus Academy Incident*, won a Scribe Award. Her editing work has earned her nominations for the British Fantasy Award, the Bram Stoker Award, and the Hugo Award. She won the Australian Shadows Award for the *Grants Pass* anthology, co-edited with Amanda Pillar. Jennifer's short-form work has appeared in *Apex Publications*, *Uncanny Magazine*, and in anthologies set in the worlds of *Valdemar*, *Shadowrun*, *V-Wars*, *Masters of Orion*, and *Predator*.

Jennifer has been a freelance author and editor for over fifteen years after leaving a high-paying tech job, and she has never been happier. She keeps a tight schedule on her writing and editing projects and somehow manages to find time to volunteer for several professional writing organizations such as SFWA, HWA, and IAMTW. She shares her husband, Jeff, with several cats and often uses him as a sounding board for her story ideas. Visit Jennifer's worlds at *jenniferbrozek.com*.

Cat Rambo

Since first appearing on the SF scene in 2005, Cat Rambo has published over 250 fiction pieces, including Nebula Award-winning novelette, *Carpe Glitter,* and nonfiction works that include *Ad Astra: The SFWA 50ᵗʰ Anniversary Cookbook* (co-edited with Fran Wilde) and writing book, *Moving From Idea to Finished Draft.* Their 2021 works include fantasy novel *Exiles of Tabat* (Wordfire Press) and space opera *You Sexy Thing* (Tor Macmillan). Rambo has been short-listed for the World Fantasy Award, the Compton Crook Award, and the Nebula Short Story Award.

A former vice president and two-term president of the SFWA (Science Fiction and Fantasy Writers of America), Cat continues to volunteer with the organization as part of its mentorship program and Grievance Committee. They founded the online school the *Rambo Academy for Wayward Writers* in 2010, specializing in classes aimed at genre writers, which now offers dozens of classes from some of the best writers currently working in speculative fiction.

Cat has lived in Seattle the last few decades and considers it their home, but is prone to wandering sometimes. They share Chez Rambo with a palindromically named tortoiseshell cat, a jumping spider, way too many houseplants, and a spouse.

Beth Cato

Beth Cato hails from Hanford, California, but currently writes and bakes cookies in a lair west of Phoenix, Arizona. She's the Nebula Award–nominated author of the *Clockwork Dagger* duology and the *Blood of Earth* trilogy from Harper Voyager.

Her short stories can be found in publications ranging from *Beneath Ceaseless Skies* to *Uncanny Magazine*. In 2019, she won the Rhysling Award for short speculative poetry.

Beth shares her household with a hockey-loving husband, a numbers-obsessed son, and three feline overlords. Her website Beth-Cato.com includes not only a vast bibliography, but a treasure trove of recipes for delectable goodies. Find her on Twitter @BethCato.

AnaMaria Curtis

AnaMaria Curtis is from the part of Illinois that is very much not Chicago, which means she still gets nostalgic at the sight of corn-fields and an open sky. She double majored in English lit and eco-nomics, so she's always ready to ramble about Jane Austen, Anthony

Trollope, and trade policy. AnaMaria is the winner of the 2019 Dell Magazines Award and a graduate of the Alpha Workshop. Her work has appeared in *Clarkesworld* and *A Dying Planet* (Flame Tree Press). Please look for her on Twitter @AnaMCurtis and show her pictures of your pets.

Maria Dong

Maria Dong (she/her)'s short fiction has been published in *Nightmare, Augur, Khoreo, Apparition Lit, Fusion Fragment, If There's Anyone Left,* and the *Decoded Pride* anthology. She's agented by Amy Bishop at Dystel, Goderich & Bourret. She lives in southwest Michigan with her partner and a potato dog and can be reached on Twitter @ mariadongwrites, or on her website, *www.mariadong.com.*

Felicity Drake

Felicity Drake is a writer of speculative and interactive fiction. Her short stories have been published in *Metaphorosis.* She lives in New York, which explains her strong opinions about pizza and bagels. Find her online at www.felicitydrake.com

Anita Ensal

Anita Ensal has always been intrigued by the possibilities inherent in myths and legends, and she likes to find both the fantastical element in the mundane and the ordinary component within the incredible. She writes in all areas of speculative fiction with stories in many fine anthologies out now and upcoming, including *Love and Rockets* and *Boondocks Fantasy* from DAW Books; *Guilds & Glaives, Portals,* and *Derelict* from Zombies Need Brains; *Gunfight on Europa Station* from Baen Books; *A Dying Planet* from Flame Tree Press; *The Book of Exodi* from Eposic, and the novella, *A Cup of Joe.*

You can reach Anita (aka Gini Koch) at her website, Fantastical Fiction (*http://www.ginikoch.com/aebookstore.htm*).

276

Sam Fleming

Sam Fleming writes speculative fiction ranging from dark gothic fantasy to hopeful sci-fi via magical realism, and has been published in various places including *The Best of Apex Magazine Volume 1*, *Clockwork Phoenix 5* from Mythic Delirium Books (World Fantasy Award finalist for best anthology), and *Not All Monsters* from Strangehouse Books.

Being synaesthetic, their work often focuses on unconventional characters and perceptions. Sam lives in north east Scotland with an artistic spouse, an opinionated husky, a number of bicycles most people would consider abnormal, a large collection of ink, and several imaginary friends.

They lead one of the British Science Fiction Association's short fiction Orbit groups and share office space with tsundoku. A former triathlete, Sam enjoys swimming and long-distance cycling, but hates running. Follow them on twitter @ravenbait, or find out more at *www.ravenbait.com*.

Sophie Giroir

Sophie Giroir is a bookseller and writer from southeast Louisiana where she lives with her husband, daughter, and menagerie of pets. When she isn't reading or writing, she is watching her favorite TV series or spending time with her family. Sophie grew up watching *Star Trek*, *Star Wars*, and any science fiction series she could find. She began writing when she was around ten years old after reading *The Giving Tree* by Shel Silverstein, though she credits growing up in a middle-of-nowhere town with nothing to do for her well-honed imagination.

"No Want to Spend" is Sophie's debut short story loosely based on her own experience being asexual in the modern world. You can keep up with Sophie's latest projects and thoughts on Twitter @sophiegiroir.

Naomi Kritzer

Naomi Kritzer grew up in the college town of Madison, Wisconsin, and lived in a science-fiction-themed interest house while in college. Her short story "Cat Pictures Please" won the 2016 Hugo and Locus Awards and was nominated for the Nebula Award. Her YA novel *Catfishing on CatNet* (based on "Cat Pictures Please") won the 2020 Lodestar Award, Minnesota Book Award, and Edgar Award. Her most recent book is *Chaos on CatNet*. She lives in St. Paul, Minnesota, with her spouse, two kids, and four cats. The number of cats is subject to change without notice.

Seanan McGuire

Seanan McGuire writes things. Compulsively. We have tried to make her stop. It doesn't work. She wrote something else, and it's in this book. She also wrote this bio. Seanan lives in the Pacific Northwest with her cats, toy collection, assorted yard skeletons, and way too many books to be reasonable.

Seanan is also Mira Grant and A. Deborah Baker, because being three people gives her more opportunities to write things. Seanan doesn't sleep much. When not writing, she likes to spend too much time at Disney parks, annoy frogs, read (and write) comic books, and play too much D&D. Find Seanan at *seananmcguire.com* or on most social media platforms as @seananmcguire.

Devin Miller

Devin Miller is a queer, genderqueer cyborg, and lifelong denizen of Seattle, with a love of muddy beaches to show for it. Their short fiction has appeared in *Beneath Ceaseless Skies*; their poetry can be found in *Liminality* and on select King County Metro bus terminals. You can find Devin and their cat on Twitter @devzmiller.

Premee Mohamed

Premee Mohamed is an Indo-Caribbean scientist and speculative fiction author based in Edmonton, Alberta. She is the author of novels *Beneath the Rising* (2020) and *A Broken Darkness* (2021), and novellas *These Lifeless Things* (2021), *And What Can We Offer You Tonight* (2021), and *The Annual Migration of Clouds* (2021). She is also an associate editor and social media manager for the sci-fi podcast *Escape Pod*. Her short fiction has appeared in a variety of venues, and she can be found on Twitter @premeesaurus and on her website at *www.premeemohamed.com*.

Lyda Morehouse

Lyda Morehouse leads a double life. By day she's a mild-mannered science fiction author of such works as the Shamus Award winner and Locus Award Nominated *Archangel Protocol* (2001.) By night, she dons her secret identity as Tate Hallaway, bestselling paranormal romance author. Her most recent novel, *Unjust Cause*, was published by Wizard Tower Press in April of 2020. You can find her all over the web, including Twitter as @tatehallaway, and the rest as Lyda Morehouse. Be sure to check out what she's been up to lately at *lydamorehouse.com* or *https://www.patreon.com/lydamorehouse*.

Lisa Morton

Lisa Morton is a screenwriter, author of nonfiction books, and prose writer whose work was described by the American Library Association's *Readers' Advisory Guide to Horror* as "consistently dark, unsettling, and frightening." She is a six-time winner of the Bram Stoker Award, the author of four novels and over 150 short stories, and a world-class Halloween expert.

Her recent releases include *Weird Women: Classic Supernatural Fiction from Groundbreaking Female Writers 1852–1923* (co-edited with Leslie S. Klinger) and *Calling the Spirits: A History of Seances*;

her latest short stories appeared in *Best American Mystery Stories 2020, Speculative Los Angeles,* and *Final Cuts: New Tales of Hollywood Horror and Other Spectacles.* Forthcoming in 2021 is the collection *Night Terrors & Other Tales.*

Lisa lives in Los Angeles and online at *www.lisamorton.com.*

Xander Odell

Xander Odell lives with their family in Washington State. They are an avid reader, compulsive writer, and avid chocoholic. Their work has appeared in such venues as *Daily Science Fiction, Jim Baen's Universe, Crossed Genres,* and *Pseudopod.* When they're not throwing words at the page, they make greeting cards as Oddfellow Creations. You can follow them on Twitter @WriterOdell.

Aimee Ogden

Aimee Ogden is a former science teacher and software tester; now she writes stories about sad astronauts and angry princesses. Her short fiction has appeared in venues such as *Analog, Clarkesworld, Beneath Ceaseless Skies,* and *Escape Pod,* and her first novellas *Sun-Daughters, Sea-Daughters* and *Local Star* debuted in 2021 from Tor.com and *Interstellar Flight Press* respectively.

A graduate of the Viable Paradise workshop, Aimee also co-edits the magazine *Translunar Travelers Lounge,* which publishes fun and optimistic speculative fiction. She lives in Madison, Wisconsin, with her spouse, her twin children, and a dog named Commander Riker.

Madeline Pine

Madeline Pine is a hydro engineer, a genderqueer author, and what happens when little kids never stop asking "Why?" Their favorite hobbies include taking things apart to understand how they work; setting out on research dives for increasingly random subjects; and writing stories to answer their own questions. One such question inspired their short story, "Ping-Pong Dysphoria."

When not writing, investigating, or slipping the results of their investigations into their novels, they can be found on abandoned logging roads, asking "Where does this lead?" One day they'll end up in a parallel universe or a portal fantasy. In the meantime, you can reach them on Twitter *@Madeline_Pine*.

Lauren Ring

Lauren Ring (she/her) is a perpetually tired Jewish lesbian who writes about possible futures, for better or for worse. Her short fiction has previously appeared in *Pseudopod*, *Nature*, and the Lambda Literary Award finalist anthology *Glitter + Ashes* from Neon Hemlock Press, among other publications.

When she isn't writing speculative fiction, she is pursuing her career in UX design and accessibility or attending to the many needs of her cat Moomin, who lives with her in the heart of rainy Seattle. Her website is *laurenmring.com*, and she can be found on Twitter @ ringwrites.

Justina Robson

Justina Robson spent the 1980s absorbing SF, fantasy, and cartoons, and then all of the 1990s trying to figure out the nature of existence through the classics, linguistics, philosophy, psychology, literature, and the occult. To her surprise she has achieved some critical successes including a prize from amazon.com. She is too serious, overthinks, and wishes she had more action movies to watch.

In addition to her twelve original novels and many shorter works she has also written *The Covenant of Primus*—the Hasbro-authorized history and "bible" of *The Transformers*. Her stories range widely, often featuring people and machines who aren't exactly what they seem.

Rosemary Claire Smith

Rosemary Claire Smith draws inspiration from her time spent as a field archaeologist excavating sites around the United States Nowadays, she sticks closer to her home base in Virginia where she devotes too many hours envisioning what it would be like to zip backwards across the millennia to live in a Bronze Age society or even further to visit the heyday of the dinosaurs. Her interactive adventure novel, *T-Rex Time Machine*, is available from Choice of Games. She's an AnLab-award-nominated writer whose fantasy, horror, and science fiction stories and essays have sold to *Analog*, *Amazing Stories*, *Fantastic Stories*, *Drabblecast*, *SFWA's blog*, *99 Tiny Terrors*, *Hybrid Fiction*, *Stupefying Stories*, *Digital Science Fiction*, and various anthologies. Visit her online @RCWordsmith on Instagram and Twitter, or check out *rcwordsmith.com/blogging-the-mesozoic*.

Fran Wilde

Two-time Nebula winner Fran Wilde writes science fiction and fantasy for adults and kids, with seven books, so far, that embrace worlds unique (*Updraft*, The Gemworld) and portal (*Riverland*, *The Ship of Stolen Words*), plus numerous short stories appearing in *Asimov's*, Tor.com, *Beneath Ceaseless Skies*, *Shimmer*, *Nature*, *Uncanny*, and multiple Year's Best anthologies. Her work has won the Eugie Foster and Compton Crook awards, been named an NPR Favorite, and has been a finalist for six Nebulas, three Hugos, a World Fantasy Award, three Locii, and the Lodestar. Fran directs the Genre Fiction MFA concentration at Western Colorado University and writes nonfiction for NPR, *The Washington Post*, and *The New York Times*.

Mercedes M. Yardley

Mercedes M. Yardley is a dark fantasist who wears poisonous flowers in her hair and red lipstick. She writes in a lush, lyrical style about current social issues and finding love and beauty in the darkness. She authored *Beautiful Sorrows, Apocalyptic Montessa and Nuclear Lulu: A Tale of Atomic Love, Pretty Little Dead Girls, Nameless, Little Dead Red,* and *Love Is a Crematorium.* She won the Bram Stoker Award for *Little Dead Red* and was nominated for her short story "Loving You Darkly" and for her *Arterial Bloom* anthology. Mercedes lives and works in Las Vegas with her family and strange menagerie. You can find her at *mercedesmyardley.com.*

Jane Yolen

Jane Yolen's 400th(!) book came out March 2, 2021, and yes it was fantasy—a picture book called *Bear Outside.* Her work has won 2 Nebulas, 3 World Fantasy Awards, 1 Caldecott, numerous State awards (including several for Massachusetts, 1 for New York State, 1 for California, 1 for New Jersey) 3 Mythopoeic Awards, and 6 honorary doctorates.

She was the first woman ever to give the Andrew Lang lecture at the University of St Andrews, Scotland, though the series had been running since 1927. She won the New England Public Radio's Arts and Entertainment award and was the first writer to do so. She has been called "America's Hans Christian Andersen." One of her awards set her good Scottish wool coat on fire. Just a warning.